TRIAL OF THE SUN QUEEN

NISHA J. TULI

FOREVER

New York Boston

Copyright © 2022 by Nisha J. Tuli

Cover design by Miblart.com
Cover copyright © 2023 by Hachette Book Group, Inc.

Forever
Hachette Book Group
1290 Avenue of the Americas, New York, NY 10104
read-forever.com
twitter.com/readforeverpub

First Forever Trade Paperback Edition: September 2023

Forever is an imprint of Grand Central Publishing. The Forever name and logo are trademarks of Hachette Book Group, Inc.

The publisher is not responsible for websites (or their content) that are not owned by the publisher.

The Hachette Speakers Bureau provides a wide range of authors for speaking events. To find out more, go to hachettespeakersbureau.com or email HachetteSpeakers@hbgusa.com.

Forever books may be purchased in bulk for business, educational, or promotional use. For information, please contact your local bookseller or the Hachette Book Group Special Markets Department at special.markets@hbgusa.com.

Library of Congress Control Number: 2023943138

ISBNs: 978-1-5387-6748-1 (trade paperback); 978-1-5387-6764-1 (ebook)

Printed in the United States of America

LSC-C

Printing 2, 2025

For anyone who finds themselves driven
by both love and rage.

Author's Note

Thank you so much for choosing to read *Trial of the Sun Queen*. This will be the first book in what I currently think will be a four book series. I don't promise that won't change! I'm really excited about this one and encourage you to look for the many easter eggs scattered throughout the story. Some answers will reveal themselves here, but some won't until later books...and there's so much more coming! I hope you love it as much as I do.

This series is a bit of a slow burn, so the really steamy stuff comes in later books (I promise). Content warnings are listed below if you'd like to read them, otherwise you can skip ahead to Chapter 1.

Love,

Nisha

Content warnings: For those who'd like a heads up, this is an adult novel that involves some death and blood and people killing each other. There is mention of past sexual assault—nothing happens on the page. There are the usual F-bombs and a bit of smut.

CHAPTER ONE

LOR

That bitch took my soap. I rifle through the small wooden cupboard that holds my few worldly possessions. A threadbare tunic. A pair of socks. A few tattered novels I've read so many times they're practically dust. But no soap.

"I'll kill her," I mutter as I empty the contents of my locker onto my narrow cot. "I'll cut her face. I'll gut her from tip to ass. I'll—"

"It's just a bar of soap, Lor."

I stop in my tracks, whirling on Tristan. He leans against the wall, his arms crossed, one ankle over the other. A shock of black hair hangs in his eyes and a small smile curves on his lips.

The memory of what I did for the extravagant luxury of that single bar of soap slithers straight to my toes. When I run my tongue over the backs of my teeth, I can still taste the sour decay of the warden's sweat and...*not thinking about it.*

"It's not just soap," I hiss. "Do you know what I had to do for—" I break off as his smile vanishes. My brother narrows his eyes, dropping his arms and taking a step towards me. He's taller than me by nearly a foot, wiry and lean and, despite the dark circles under his eyes, impossibly handsome—a fact of which he is well aware.

"What did you do? Was it Kelava?" he asks.

My gaze catches Willow's. She sits on her cot, the one next to mine, as we share a moment of mutual understanding. My sister's big dark eyes are haunted with the same burden I know is mirrored in my own.

"Nothing," I say. The last thing I need right now is Tristan attempting to defend my honor with the warden.

What Kelava made me do is nothing new. It wasn't the first time I've had to earn my way through this place, and if it gets me what I need to survive another day inside Nostraza, I'll do it again and again. Tristan means well, but sometimes he forgets what it's taken to live within these oppressive stone walls.

"Lor," Tristan says, a warning in his tone.

"Just leave it alone, okay? It's better if you don't know the specifics."

A muscle in his jaw ticks, his dark eyes flashing. He's just being protective, but sometimes I need him to mind his own fucking business.

Willow rises from her cot, dusting off her thin grey tunic as if that would ever get it truly clean. Dozens more cots cram the space, lining up against each wall. The ceiling hangs so low,

Tristan has to bend his neck to avoid hitting it. Sheets that might have been white at some obscure point in their existence cover the beds along with anemic grey pillows that are so thin, it's hard to see the point. If you're lucky, you might have the luxury of a scratchy wool blanket, but like my bar of soap, that too is a rare indulgence. If you secure one not riddled with holes, one might call you Zerra's blessed.

"Let's get some breakfast. We'll get you new soap," Willow says, her voice soft as she links her elbow with mine. Her black hair hangs just past her ears, ragged and limp. That's as much as it's grown since the last outbreak of lice, when they shaved every one of our heads right to the scalp. For weeks, we resembled an army of potatoes encased in shapeless grey sacks. Running my hand through my own hair, I grimace. Like that of both of my siblings, it's midnight black and has grown just a little more than Willow's, almost brushing my chin.

The longest I've ever managed was almost to the middle of my back. But that was years ago and even then, it was so dry and brittle, I'd wake up with strands covering my pillow like a nest of desiccated worms. It does feel a little healthier now, but Nostraza has only become more and more crowded and rife with disease, and another outbreak is coming any day. It's a miracle it hasn't already happened.

I nod as I unhook my arm from Willow's and then stuff my things back into my cupboard, slamming the door so hard it shakes on its brackets. There's no lock—that's the problem. Nothing actually belongs to anyone here. Everything is on temporary loan, including our bodies and definitely our souls. The only thing they haven't claimed yet is my mind, though that seems less true with each passing year.

Tristan and Willow lead the way, and I follow down a dim, narrow hallway, flickering sconces lighting the way. The stone walls are slick and shiny with moisture. It's always wet inside Nostraza, and I'm pretty sure it's not all water. A long time ago, I struck a deal with myself not to think too hard about what else is oozing between those bricks. It's only through these countless bits of self-deception that I'm able to face another day.

We're going to be late for breakfast because of me and will probably get nothing to eat. They won't complain or blame me, but I'll make it up to my brother and sister somehow.

As we pass another dorm room, I peer inside, knowing this is where my nemesis, Jude, sleeps. Maybe I'll steal something from her to even the score. Maybe my soap is in her cupboard. She'd be stupid enough to hide it where anyone could find it. I make a move to dart inside when Tristan catches my hand.

"Don't. It's not worth it." My eyes meet his, fury nudging at the tight ball of anger that lives like a compressed rock in the middle of my chest. Only this one doesn't have a sparkling future as a diamond.

He doesn't get it. He's one of the favored in this shithole. For a prisoner, he's strong and able-bodied, not to mention charming, and has most of the guards wrapped around his finger. They call him the *Prince of Nostraza* and they mean it to be mocking, but since Tristan is in on the joke, he holds the upper hand.

"I'll get you some more." His expression softens. "I promise."

Even if the guards favor Tristan, that benevolence has never extended to me or Willow. Our family connection remains a secret from everyone else for our safety, and it's not his fault, but there are days when I resent how much easier he has it. That's not really fair, though. He's done everything he can to protect us both since the very beginning.

"Fine," I say, willing the unexpected tears in my eyes not to fall. I've learned the hard way how to hold them in and stuff them down. Tears are only useful when they're brandished as a weapon.

But some days are harder than others.

My stomach is perpetually hollow and my throat dry, like the deepest cave with no source of water. The healing wounds on my back, courtesy of a lashing I received two weeks ago, still ache whenever I move too quickly. They dealt out my punishment when I "accidentally" tipped a hot bowl of soup into the lap of a particularly vicious guard. He deserved it, and I regret nothing. I hope his balls shriveled up and fell off.

Today, I feel the suffocating heaviness of every one of the twelve years I've spent inside these prison walls. Twelve years for the crime of simply being born. For bearing the taint of a shattered legacy I never asked for or even truly understand.

Every second. Every minute I'm focused on the day I finally get free. I live it in my dreams and see it when I'm awake. I feel it in the shivering marrow of my bones. One day, I'll get out of here and pay back the Aurora King for everything he's taken. For everything he's done.

But I can't just run. Even if I could, I can't leave without Tristan and Willow. There is no freedom without them.

Someday, I will figure out a way to get us *all* out of here.

We continue down the hall, Willow taking my hand and casting worried glances in my direction. She's the gentle one in our ragged little trio. Despite the grinding harshness of Nostraza, she remains a soft-hearted butterfly who needs my protection. While we suffocate here, I'll do whatever it takes to ensure she's safe—insomuch as I can in a life where we have less than nothing.

But we all take care of each other, and sometimes, I need her too.

A moment later, I feel a hand squeeze my ass and I spin around, my fist cocked, prepared to deliver a crushing blow. When I see it's Aero, I snarl and swing my fist, anyway. He ducks, a grin stretching across his face, as I miss him by a hair.

"Come now, Lor, is that any way to treat your favorite inmate?"

"Favorite," I scoff before I turn away. But he wraps an arm around my waist and pulls my back against his chest, his chin resting in the curve of my neck. I can feel the grin he tosses to Tristan and Willow.

"She'll just be a minute."

Willow looks to me for confirmation, and I nod. "I'm coming. Save me some rocks." Willow snorts at my joke about the canteen's breakfast rolls, while Tristan glares at Aero with a warning.

"Just go," I tell him. "I'm fine."

"Hurt her and I'll kill you," Tristan says, and I roll my eyes while I free myself from Aero's embrace.

He holds up his hands in surrender, his grin growing even wider. "Got it, boss."

"Go on," I say, and Tristan turns with Willow before they walk down the hall and disappear around the corner. But not before Tristan shoots one more threatening glance at Aero.

The moment they're gone, Aero's hands circle my waist before he presses me against the wall, his mouth crashing into mine. Several inches taller than me, he's lean and rangy. Always just on the edge of starving, no one inside Nostraza has the comfort of extra meat on their bones.

His hands slide over my ass and down the backs of my thighs before he lifts me up, my legs cinching around his waist. My arms snake around his neck as we kiss, our tongues and teeth meeting in a wet, frantic clash. It's not gentle or sweet, but there is nothing gentle or sweet about life when it's spent contained by these walls. After so many years in this place, the memory of sweetness feels as distant and unreachable as the stars in the sky.

Our fevered breaths fill the narrow hall, and I'm thankful everyone has already left for breakfast. Aero grinds his hips into mine, his cock hard and ready against my stomach. My fingers tangle in his auburn hair as he thrusts against me, and I moan. When he arrived two years ago, he was the picture of a dashing young thief, but Nostraza has stolen that vital spark of life it takes from us all. His bright blue eyes, once clever with mischief, have dimmed with the understanding that, like all of us, he's going to die here eventually.

Still, he's one of the few beautiful things I can cling to in this hellhole.

"Meet me behind the forge tonight," he says, his mouth still against mine. His hands slide under and up the sides of my tunic, his fingers gently brushing my scars. "I need you."

The crush of his mouth muffles my reply, and I nod, groaning in satisfaction as his tongue sweeps against mine. In this bleak existence, this bit of pleasure is a feeble light shimmering through the narrow cracks of darkness.

"Slut," comes an acidic voice, and we break off from our kiss. Jude stands in the hallway, her dirty blonde hair hanging in limp waves to her chin. With her thin arms crossed, the curl on her lip is full of disdain. "Nostraza's number one tramp, aren't you, Lor? Rutting like an animal right out here in the open?"

Her piercing eyes dart to Aero, her frown deepening with dissatisfaction.

"Fuck off, Jude," I say, searching for signs of my soap, like she might be wearing it on a chain around her neck. As if she's read my mind, her mouth twists into a smirk before she casually trails her fingers down her throat and then up her arms like she's cleaning herself in the shower. But I return her smirk with one of my own. She might have my soap, but I know she's had her eyes on Aero since the moment he arrived after being apprehended on a charge of breaking and entering in the Emerald District, The Aurora's most wealthy neighborhood.

I'd be a liar if I claimed I hadn't wallowed in smug satisfaction when he'd shown an interest in me, instead. To worm under her freshly cleaned skin, I wrap one arm around his shoulders and drag the fingers of my other hand across his chest before I pull his head down for a deep, long kiss.

My feelings for Aero are complicated.

It's too hard to love anyone inside the walls of Nostraza, where, sooner or later, everyone is taken from you. The only people I've ever let in are Tristan and Willow, and I know it's a mistake. Every time they have a brush with death, every time one of them is beaten or locked in solitary, I try to carve them out of my soul, hoping it might hurt less when they die.

All I can hope is that one day, *someday*, I'll get us out of here. It's an impossible dream, but I cling to it like mist because it's all I have.

Jude lets out a snarl and brushes past us, her shoulder colliding with mine, before she storms in the direction of the mess hall.

"We should go eat, too," Aero says, "or there'll be nothing left. I'll meet you after your shift is done?" He takes my hand, and we also make our way down the corridor.

I nod. I've got laundry duty today. Hours upon hours spent in the sticky heat, straining my back and arms where I stir giant vats of soapy, waterlogged sheets that cling to a memory of the color they once were. I'll need cheering up later, and Aero is usually the temporary cure.

We turn the corner and enter the mess hall, already buzzing with hundreds of inmates. The noise, as usual, is near deafening as the cacophony of voices mingles. They clamor to fill every precious second of one of our few free moments each day—thirty minutes for breakfast, thirty minutes for dinner. We spend the remaining hours toiling—some in the jewel mines, some in the kitchens, some in the forge, some cleaning, some sewing, and the rest doing a hundred other soul-draining duties no free person would ever consent to.

Once you're done with your shift, you might chisel out an hour of respite, but that's only if you're not so exhausted you immediately collapse on your bed. Tonight I'll find the energy, because in a place where there's only misery, I have to find hope under every pebble I can.

Jude sits with her gang at a table near the end of the food line, each one more surly and rat-faced than the last. "Don't you just love the scent of my new soap? My skin smells positively like roses," she says, pulling up the sleeve of her tunic before thrusting her forearm into the faces of her minions.

I stop and stare at her, trying to burn holes into her skull. She looks up then, a slow smile spreading across her pinched face. *That bitch.*

I'm moving before I give a rational thought to what I'm doing. With a snarl, I leap, my hands wrapping around her neck. As I crash into her, the chair tips over, and we both strike the hard stone floor. Straddling her, I squeeze her neck, and she screams and claws at the skin on my forearms.

Jude swings a fist, catching me in the side of my head so hard my vision blurs. Disoriented now, my grip loosens, and she knocks me down, pinning me beneath her. Another punch to the jaw has me tasting blood. I'm going to fucking *kill* her.

This time, I grab her wrist and wrench it with all my might before I hear the sickening, but satisfying, snap of bone. Jude screams and I kick her off me, finding myself once again on top, raining blows to her stomach, ribs, and head with the fury of an unleashed demon.

"Lor!" I register the sound of my name and feel hands on my arms and waist, trying to pull me away.

"Let me go!" I scream, still thrashing Jude.

"Lor!" I recognize Tristan's voice, and I'm hauled off her, my chest heaving and my head throbbing. The guards have formed a circle around us, caging me in like the feral animal I am. Jude groans from where she lies on the ground, blood pooling underneath her. Warmth drips down my chin, staining the front of my tunic with crimson. I try to wipe it away, but Tristan has both of my arms pinned behind my back.

"Let me go," I hiss, wrenching my wrists in the vise of his grip.

"Not until you calm down."

The jeering, chattering mess hall slams into silence a moment later when heavy footsteps ring in the air. They've all been enjoying the show, glad it wasn't them who lost the tenuous grip on their sanity today. Catching shit from the warden is what passes for entertainment inside Nostraza, given the notable absence of any other options.

"What's going on here?" Kelava asks.

"Nothing, sir," Tristan replies in his most kiss-ass voice. Part of me wants to slap him, but this is how Tristan survives, and I can't begrudge him that. We all do what we must.

The circle of guards breaks, and Kelava strides through the opening, stopping in front of me, where I'm still struggling against Tristan's hold. Blood continues to dribble from my mouth, droplets splattering on the floor and the toe of my boot. My temple and lips give a painful pulse as the warden fixes his beady gaze on me.

"Didn't I tell you that if you caused any more trouble, there would be consequences?"

I say nothing, only glaring as I try again to liberate myself from Tristan's hold.

"Oh, Lor. Why must you be this way?"

Kelava's watery blue eyes fill with something akin to paternal concern for my tarnished soul. He really thinks he's the good guy. I want to spit at him. I want to punch him. I want to kick him in the balls so hard he still feels it when he's old and feeble, clinging to the shreds of his dignity.

Jude groans again from the floor where she lies, clutching a wrist that's definitely hanging at an awkward angle. *Fucking drama queen*. The warden looks down at her and then at me, his forehead furrowing.

"Did you start this?"

I open my mouth, planning to defend myself. No one is going to rat me out. There is a code of honor even amongst criminals and the fallen.

Well, except for Jude. She has no such compunctions where I'm concerned.

"Yes, she did," she spits, finally finding her voice, though it's muffled by her bloody, swollen lips. "She attacked me completely unprovoked!"

"She stole my soap!"

"I did not! You can't prove that!"

Kelava raises a hand, silencing us both. Jude's face is puffing up, and scarlet soaks the front of her shirt. She looks terrible. This doesn't bode well for me.

"Warden," I say, adopting a coy smile, grasping at anything I can to save myself. "If we go to your office, I'm sure we can work this out." The hint of suggestion in my words burns a sour line of bile up my throat.

I hate this, but it's the only currency I have to offer.

It's the wrong thing to say, because Kelava's calm, patient façade cracks, the pupils of his eyes blowing out into dark black holes. The guards may use us for their filthy urges, but apparently there is honor even among rapists when they all pretend nothing is amiss behind the closed doors of Nostraza. The warden points to two vicious guards whose fists I am intimately acquainted with.

"Take her to the Hollow," Kelava says as the guards wrench me from Tristan. To his credit, my brother doesn't give me up easily.

"No," I say, panic morphing into a fist clutching my throat. Not that. Anything but that. I almost died last time. A week in the Hollow left me nearly broken, my mind shattered, and my body in shredded ruins. "No, please. I'm sorry. It won't happen again."

The warden brings his face right up to mine as I continue to struggle against the hold of the guards. He's so close I can feel his moist breath on my lips, fetid with the remnants of whatever he gorged on at breakfast.

"Two weeks should teach you a lesson, since nothing else seems to work."

"No!" I scream, thrashing, trying to wrench my way free. "No! Please!" I'm sobbing now, a hot streak of tears coating my face, my screams echoing through the room. I've broken my rule about crying. These tears aren't a weapon. *These* will only be used against me.

Tristan is pleading with the warden, but Kelava's hard stare doesn't waver as he savors my distress, a thin smile on his bloodless lips.

My screams cut off when a guard punches me in the middle so hard I bend double, nearly hurling up the scant contents of my stomach. Gasping for air like a parched fish, I'm hauled upright by both of my arms with such force one of my shoulder joints pops and my scream ricochets off every corner in the room.

"Take her away," Kelava says again. "I'll see you in two weeks, *inmate*, assuming there's anything left of you."

At that, there's nothing but the roar of white noise in my ears as I'm dragged away.

Chapter Two

The guards lug me outside, over the dusty courtyard and through a massive set of iron gates open to the north side of the prison, where we enter the impenetrable forest that surrounds Nostraza, known simply as the Void. Once you go in, you never come out. In the rare case of a prison escape, the Void ensures one's freedom is a short-lived enterprise.

I continue to struggle, my shoulder screaming in pain, as the guards practically carry me between them, my legs windmilling in the air like a rabid marionette's. It's useless. They're both twice my size, and twelve years of prison life have left me weak and undernourished.

Which, I guess, is entirely the point.

As we pass through the gates, the guards touch the opalescent ovals pinned to their chests. They murmur a few words and the pins light up, encasing us in a shimmering, translucent bubble. While I can see beyond the surface, it obscures my vision like a pane of clouded glass. The guards are mortal, with no magical ability. They rely on these objects created by an Imperial or High Fae, in this case the Aurora King, to keep them safe, offering the only known protection against the Void.

The Hollow is nothing but a hole dug deep into the earth, located just beyond the walls of the prison. If they named the Void for its ability to suck people in, then the Hollow is named for the way it drains you out and leaves you empty and gasping for air.

It sits close enough to the prison that the guards needn't venture too deep into the trees, but far enough that when you're out here alone, it feels like they've abandoned you to the forest's monsters.

I've spent my fair share of time in the Hollow.

With a temper like mine, a girl is bound to get in trouble now and then...or often. The standard sentence is a night or two. That's usually enough of a deterrent, and most people never visit more than once. Whether it's because the life expectancy in Nostraza is so short or because it only takes one instance to breed eternal obedience, I'm not sure.

A little of column A, a little of column B, I suppose.

Only a handful of prisoners have ever survived more than a night in the Hollow without succumbing to madness. I'm one of them. Though perhaps I'm slightly mad. It's hard to tell anymore.

The last time, I'd broken into the pantry after the guards had cut our rations in retaliation for a minor riot. We were even hungrier than usual and needed something to eat before we all turned on each other. It was an act of self-preservation that landed me in the Hollow for seven agonizing nights. It was a minor infraction and my punishment didn't fit the crime, but that's what this place does to you. Brings you to the edge and when you're about to tip over, gives you a hearty shove onto the jagged rocks waiting below.

By the time they returned for me, I was a blubbering mess of bloody skin, matted hair, and jagged nails. It took weeks for Willow to coax a single word from my lips. Longer than that for my teeth to stop chattering and my dreams to be purged of an endless loop of nightmares. Those dark dreams happen only periodically, now. It's the best I can hope for.

As the guards drag me deeper into the forest, I recall how broken I'd been. How I'd ached in every way a person can ache, from the tips of my chapped fingers to the very depths of my fractured soul.

Two weeks.

My nerves break apart, panic hollowing out my limbs.

Comparatively, today's infraction was also minor, but I've always been the warden's "favorite." I'm not going to survive this. I'm going to die, all because of a fucking bar of soap.

The guards are as nervous as I am in the Void. I can sense the tension between them as they drag me along the rough ground. We stop in front of the deep rectangular hole dug into the forest floor. From here, I can see the tall spires and towers of the Aurora Keep that looms over the forest like a sentient toad. Black stone glitters as if infused with stars, the windows shifting from green to purple to red in undulating ripples of light.

One day, I will storm that eyesore and tear the head off the Aurora King for leaving me to rot here. For tossing me in here when I was only a child.

One day, I'll get free of this place and make him pay for *everything*.

My attention drags back to the Hollow, despair carving through my blood-soaked fantasies, knowing I'll probably never get the satisfaction of my revenge. If I survive this punishment, it will leave nothing left of me. I'll be a shell that once had a spirit and a dream.

Listening to the surrounding silence, I swallow a knot of tension. My mind is already playing tricks as I imagine the slither of monsters that are circling nearer like a noose fashioned from barbed scales and sharpened claws.

With a hand placed in the middle of my back, a guard shoves me forward. "In you go, sweetheart." My feet tangle and I stumble. The hole's edge slides beneath me, dirt giving way in a shower of soil and gravel as I plunge, collapsing into a heap. About ten feet deep, it's too high to climb out of, but shallow enough to offer zero protection.

I already know the walls are made of soft, crumbling earth, and if I try to scale up the sides, the only thing I'll accomplish is a miniature landslide that could very well bury and then suffocate me. No, the only thing I can do is alternate between sitting in the corner and pacing three steps in each direction, waiting for my sentence to end.

"Don't worry," one guard shouts down. "When you're out, we'll take good care of you. It's *so* lonely out here. You'll need some company." They both burst into laughter as one of them grabs his crotch and thrusts his hips.

"It'll be our little secret from the warden," he says, winking. I spit, willing it to grow wings and land in his eye. Of course, it doesn't, and they laugh even harder.

"No thank you," I shout back. "I've heard your cock is the size of a baby carrot. I need something much, *much* larger to satisfy me." The guard's face morphs from laughter into red-faced rage. I'm going to pay for that comment.

The second guard crouches down and grins.

"The mig'dran are especially restless lately, and I hear their favorite meal is sweet young girls." He winks, and I'm not sure if it's meant to be coy or seductive. It couldn't be further from either.

"Well, good thing there's nothing sweet about me, dick face," I snap, and they laugh again.

"Oh, I hope you survive this, darling. I can't believe I haven't had my fun with you yet. Fucking warden's pet." He glowers as if it's my fault. As if I'm the one that chose any of this.

I consider spitting again, but think better of it. Maybe if I shut up, they'll get bored and leave me alone. But even as I contemplate their departure, fear tethers itself to my muscles. Alone. Two weeks out here with nothing. It's a sign of my desperation that I'd take these two idiots over no one.

But they've clearly had their fun and turn to leave. I almost call out for them, but then I bite my tongue. Even if they stayed to torment me for a few more minutes, eventually they're leaving. I may as well get used to it.

Their moods are boisterous as they trade insults with each other until their voices fade, and I'm left alone in silence but for the sound of my breath and the thoughts screaming at terminal volume through my head.

Pressing my hand to my chest, I try to calm my breathing. There's no food or water provided in the Hollow—that would be too humane—so I have to hope it rains soon. As for food—I scan the empty dirt floor—well, there I'm shit out of luck.

Lucky for me, hunger and I are long-acquainted friends.

I sink to the ground, my back to the wall, and massage my sore shoulder. My face still throbs from where Jude hit me, though it seems I've stopped bleeding. I touch my temple where a lump has formed and wince. Just a few more scars to add to the chronicle of past transgressions already written on my skin.

The forest remains quiet, perhaps assessing how much of a threat I pose. I look up—there are no blue skies in The Aurora. There are only dark skies and slightly less dark skies. A monochrome rainbow that stirs from the color of cold ashes to inky black. The only way to tell the difference between night and day is by the presence of this realm's namesake, the aurora borealis.

At night, they cover the sky with ribbons of color, undulating like waves across the sea. Cobalt and emerald and violet and crimson. The colors are so vivid it's like someone melted a cauldron of jewels and poured them over the sky. Most nights, we don't get to see them locked down in our dorms, but on those rare nights I've witnessed them, their beauty has fused a tiny piece of my fraying soul back together.

This is the only advantage the Hollow affords. Here, I get an uninterrupted view of the show, even if it's through the lens of a tiny rectangle of dirt. As the sky darkens and the hours pass, I wait for my first glimpse of the aurora while keeping one ear trained for the sounds of the creatures that call the Void home.

I was a child when I was brought to Nostraza. The details of my life before that are hazy, lost to the erosion of hunger and time. It's only because of Tristan and Willow that I know anything about who we once were.

Though I spent my early days living in one, I barely remember what a normal forest feels like. I listen for the sounds of birds and insects. The wind rustling through leaves. Perhaps the sound of water from a flowing stream. But I hear none of those things.

The sky above dims slowly while night descends. If I strain, I imagine I can hear the noises of the prison in the distance: the whistle of the dinner bell and the steady drone of hundreds of voices after a day of work. I think of Aero and the meeting we had planned tonight.

"Sorry, Aero," I whisper to the deepening dark.

But mostly I worry about Willow and Tristan. They're probably beside themselves. Of the three of us, I'm the one who gets into the most trouble, and I know it breaks them every time the warden metes out my next punishment. I try to be compliant for their sake, but bowing to authority isn't high on my list of skills.

A chill comes with the darkening sky and I huddle into myself, wishing I had something other than this pair of thin leggings and the tunic that comprises standard prison issue. My stomach rumbles and my mouth is dry, my tongue thick and my lips cracked. I didn't even get breakfast this morning. Clouds roll overhead, obscuring any view of the aurora tonight, but perhaps this at least means rain.

The forest's troubling silence continues, but it does afford me the ability to hear the prison as it goes through the motions of the evening. Supper time. Shower time. Jude is probably using my soap and luxuriating in my penance. I imagine her humming a triumphant tune as she scrubs herself clean, and I grind my teeth.

I hope I broke her fucking wrist and it hurts for weeks.

If I close my eyes, I can still smell the soap's floral notes. Roses, the warden had told me. I don't remember if I've ever actually smelled one, but they must be beautiful.

It's not that they don't provide soap for showering, but it's harsh and acidic and the scent burns my nose and my eyes. That bar of soap had not only smelled like the heavens, it had been as soft and creamy as a velvety polished stone worn smooth by the mellow hand of time. My skin would have felt like silk. It's hard to imagine a world where people use soap like that every day.

Finally, the prison quiets as the inmates settle in for the night. I imagine Willow looking at my empty cot, crying herself to sleep on my behalf. Tristan is probably lying in bed, staring up at the ceiling, plotting a thousand ways to get me out of here, knowing the odds of that are impossible.

I think of Aero and wonder if he's alone or if he went in search of someone else to satisfy his needs. The thought makes my chest tight, but that's not fair. We've never promised each other anything. What would be the point?

My stomach growls so loudly the sound echoes through the hushed forest. I'm a dinner bell. A bright red signal leading every predator in the Void straight to my very visible hiding place. It doesn't matter, though. I'm sure they can smell me. Even if I were quiet as a ghost, they'd already know I'm here.

Rumors say the Aurora King creates these grotesque hybrids of the monsters he hunts throughout the continent of Ouranos and the worlds beyond. His magic has warped them into feral beasts that feast on the flesh of mortals should they enter the forest, while also protecting the Fae citizens of The Aurora and the Imperial family who dwells inside the Keep.

These monsters are master hunters. Nothing gets through these trees.

There's a snap of a twig and my heart trips inside my chest. Another snap and I press myself deeper into the corner, terrified of what might slither down into my hole. Until now, I've been uncommonly lucky. Though I've had many close calls, nothing has ever attacked me out here before. Other prisoners haven't been so fortunate.

Just a few days ago, I'd overheard the guards talking about a prisoner who'd been left here for one night, only to meet his end inside the snapping jaws of an ozziller.

"Nothing left but a puddle of blood and bones," one had said with a shudder. Even they'd been distraught over the idea. I imagine the ozziller now, slinking over the edge, licking its lips. Assuming it has lips. Though I don't know what they look like, my imagination conjures up visions of razor-sharp scales and dripping fangs and the very worst nightmares I can fathom.

At another snap of branches, the air grows thicker, black shadows swirling. They fill me, entering through my nose and my mouth, clogging my lungs with the heavy, curdled taste of death. My breath grows shorter, coming in tight gasps in a futile attempt to keep calm.

The darkness grows even more oppressive and is now accompanied by the sound of serrated breaths, like chains sliding through rusted bars. A shadow, blacker than the ones already consuming me, appears over the lip of the opening. There's the murky shape of a body, bent and broken, limbs longer than natural, attached at incongruent angles. A whimper escapes my throat as I ball myself tighter, trying to disappear into a puff of nothing.

I am nothing. I have nothing. Please go away, I scream inside my head, over and over.

My heart thrashes against my ribs, and I squeeze my eyes closed. I can't bear to look. At least if I die now, I won't have to spend the next two weeks suffering. I just hope this is painless and quick.

I wait for the strike, tension burning like acid through my thin veneer of courage. Unable to stand the suspense, I peel my eyes open and, at that moment, the thing lunges with unnatural speed in a blur of midnight shadow.

It's then I let out a blood-curdling scream.

CHAPTER THREE

A second later, a brilliant flash of light streaks across the sky, followed by a roll of thunder so loud it shakes the earth, debris and rocks shearing off the walls and tumbling over my head. Another bright flash, followed by an even louder crack of thunder, echoes across the firmament before it erupts and the rain starts to fall.

The creature seems to be gone, presumably spooked by the storm. I let out a sigh of relief, my heart still pounding so hard it feels like it's tripping over its beats. That was much too close for comfort. How am I going to survive two weeks of this?

But Zerra has answered one prayer tonight, and I tilt my face to the sky, opening my mouth to invite the cool rainwater to slip over my parched tongue and throat. At least I won't die of thirst. Not yet, anyway.

The temperature drops rapidly, and I shiver as the rain pounds a steady rhythm against my hair and skin and clothes.

After what feels like hours of relentless downpour, I realize I really should be more careful about what I fucking wish for. My hole is filling with water, the deluge too intense for the moisture to have enough time to sink into the earth. Right now it sits only a few inches deep, and I send up a stream of prayers to Zerra, begging for the rain to stop before this becomes a problem I can't handle. Or survive.

But my prayers go unheeded, because the rain doesn't stop. It continues to fall with the determination of an ocean trying to drown a whale.

A day must pass, the sky shifting from black to gray and back again like the most boring story ever told. The cloud cover is so thick, there's no hint of the aurora. As the rain keeps falling, my hole keeps filling until I can't sit on the ground anymore. When the water gains several feet, I'm forced to stand. I lean against the now-muddy wall, my tears falling with the rain. No one can see me cry here, and I allow myself this rare indulgence.

It keeps coming. Coming and coming in an endless flood. The water inches up my thighs, and then creeps to my waist like I'm a statue that's slowly being buried by tendrils of ivy. I'm so tired. So weak. I'd give anything to lie down. Even to sit. My feet and my legs ache, and I'm so cold. My fingers—they're completely numb. I keep checking my hands to make sure they're still there. I try to wiggle my toes in my boots, but they've been chilled to blunted nubs.

Propping my body against the wall, I try to sleep, but I might as well be trying to catch a few winks during a stampede of wildebeests. The rain falls and falls, soaking through my clothes and into my hair and right through my skin, raindrops stinging my eyes. I shiver so hard my jaw aches from the clack of my teeth. I wrap my arms around my torso, trying to find the relief of some warmth, but it's not there.

Spreading onto my back, I attempt to float, trying to relieve the pressure on my lower limbs. It helps, but now it becomes a choice between the ache of remaining upright or exposing more of my body to the frigid water and air.

Thank Zerra it's summer, at least, and the temperature is comparatively warm. The winters in The Aurora are brutal at best, deadly at their worst.

Finally. Finally, it stops.

I don't know how long it's been, but pain radiates through every limb and cell of my body. Numbness has spread through every pore, taking root and spreading out like cooling lava. As the sky clears and the clouds dissipate, I sob tears of relief. At least I didn't go thirsty. Ice coats my skin, a hard shell that rattles against my trembling limbs. Can you die from standing for too long?

It takes what feels like another lifetime for the water to seep into the earth. If I sleep at all, it's merely in batches of stolen seconds that offer no relief. I'm so tired. I'm so hungry. I'm a broken, hollow husk of nothing. Slowly, so slowly, my back drags down the side of the wall as I descend with the water level. My legs shake and my back spasms. My head throbs and my unsteady heart flutters.

After an eternity, I can finally sit, my body releasing like a puff of smoke with the luxurious relief of taking my weight off my feet and my legs. I'm so light, I'm floating on clouds, but my skin feels so waterlogged, I'd probably sink to the bottom of a lake like a stone tied to a boulder.

Pulling my knees up, I fold my arms over them and drop my head. A few hours later, when only a few inches of water remain, I collapse to the ground, no longer in danger of drowning. In that moment, nothing has ever felt so divine as the ability to just *lie down*. I'd cry if I could summon the energy.

My eyelids drift shut and then I sleep.

I don't know how long I've been lying at the bottom of this hole.

The days become one long smear as the sky oscillates from grey to black to grey again and again. When the aurora lights come out, I try to watch, but I can barely lift my head, catching only the joyless tease of red and blue and green and purple from the corner of my eye. If I hold my breath, I can *hear* the lights, though. They crackle as if imbued with energy like pent-up lightning that never strikes.

I try to count the days as they pass, but I quickly lose track, and my mind is playing tricks on me anyway. None of this feels real. I can't distinguish one second from the next one. I'm a broken clock, ticking forever into nothing.

It doesn't rain again and for that I'm thankful, except it's a minor consolation. I'm going to need water again soon. Hunger gnaws so deep, it chips away at the very marrow of my bones.

I *know* starvation. I understand its rhythm and heartbeat, the quality of its texture, but I'm not sure I've ever been this hungry.

There are moments when I sense the demon's presence, though it never ventures as close as before. I call out to it. Beg it to devour me. To take me apart, piece by piece, and end this. I don't even care if it hurts. I just want this to be over.

But it doesn't heed my anguished pleas. Something is holding it back. In the labyrinth of my turbid thoughts, I can sense its reluctance to approach.

I blink in and out of consciousness, dreams chasing nightmares into one endless loop that blurs into a haze of colors and darkness. Shadowed images of black feathered wings and leathery hides. A sky streaked with crimson forks of lightning and a river of stars. A bloody smile that spears through me with a sharp crackle. Screams that echo in some place I've almost forgotten. A place I know but I've never visited.

I dream of Tristan and Willow trying to move on without me. Of their bent heads and tear-stained cheeks. I see Willow rocking back and forth, a prayer on her lips, Tristan's arm wrapped around her shoulders.

I dream of Aero under an aurora-strewn sky. Of frantic kisses and needy hands. Of warm skin sliding against wet heat and feverish moans. I dream of his fingers and lips and tongue tasting, biting, and sucking. Of how something that should feel good can instead feel like agony when it's a fleeting moment of relief entombed inside a lifetime of pain.

I dream of the warden and his beady eyes and his putrid breath. Of his cruel words and sadistic intentions. I hear the rip of a zipper and feel the bruising on my knees as I will myself not to cry. Will myself not to hand over those last shreds of dignity I cling to like brittle straws.

It feels like I've been here for months and years. But that can't be right. My body aches, and the moisture has settled into my bones. I can't imagine ever being warm again.

With the absence of the rain, my throat is once again parched, my lips cracked and bleeding. I shiver against the cold, my clothes never properly drying, the air damp and thick. Mold is probably growing between my toes and under my arms.

Soon I'll become one with the forest floor, consumed and gifted back to the earth. With any luck, I'll be reborn into a better place.

When the forest returns to its normal volume of deathly silence, I can't distinguish between day or night, but then, somewhere in the clouds of conscious thought, it registers. A shift in the cadence of sounds. The crushing stillness is fringed with something echoing in the distance.

The sound of metal on metal. The sound of flesh hitting stone. The sound of screams. It's coming from the prison.

Once more, I try to lift my head but only manage an inch. It sounds like a riot. A big one. I've been through three of them at Nostraza and the result always means more left dead than alive. Tristan and Willow are in there. I hope they're hiding, but I know Tristan will be in the thick of it. At least, I hope he thought to get Willow to safety before he made his boneheaded way into the fray.

I whisper their names into the dark. *Willow. Tristan.* When we were brought here, I was just twelve years old. Willow is three years older than me and Tristan is two years her senior.

I remember flashes of my parents, many of my memories cobbled from my brother's and sister's stories. We've always been inseparable. Always there for each other. The early years were the hardest, and I'm not sure what's kept us alive all this time, but I thank Zerra every day all three of us wake up to see another turn on the calendar.

They charged Tristan with killing three of the king's men and they slapped Willow with her sentence for stealing a precious Artefact from the kingdom. When it came to me, they didn't even bother with an official ruling. They just tossed me in here and threw away the key.

I heave out a dry sob, brittle with regret. I wanted so badly to get us out of here.

The sounds from the prison grow louder. Thumps and shrieks ringing in the forest's silence. The clash of weapons and the cries of the wounded. The creatures seem to listen too—all paused on the edge of curiosity. The inmates outnumber the guards twenty to one, but they're tired and hungry and have no weapons or training. The guards have magic on their side, too, the king's wards preventing anyone from breaching the perimeter without being shredded into ribbons.

My eyelids droop. I'm so tired and hungry, but I can't go to sleep. I need to hear what's happening. Tristan and Willow. I hope they're okay, and I cling to the image of their faces as I continue to drift in and out of consciousness. I'm not sure how long it goes on, but hours must pass. Time has ceased to have any sway over my existence. Maybe I'm already dead.

But then I hear a thump right by my head, and I flinch at the sound, wondering what nasty beast has found its way to my tomb. As my eyelids shutter open and closed, I become dimly aware of a shadow moving above me. There's a soft rustle. The warmth of breath on my skin.

Someone is touching me. I'm rolled over onto my back and I groan. Everything hurts. My skin burns. My bones ache. I can feel every hair on my head like each one is a lit match, blazing across my scalp.

In my haze, I'm aware of hands shifting me where I lie. They're gentle but firm. And then I'm being lifted. Am I dreaming? Have I died? Am I being taken up to the heavens? Surely the list of my sins is far too long for me to be granted any kind of absolution. I've been in prison for twelve years. I've done so many things Zerra would frown upon to survive. There is no eternal peace waiting for me.

I've fought. I've thieved. I've whored. I've blasphemed so many times, my soul is as black as The Aurora sky in the depths of winter. Perhaps I'm being sent to live amongst the Fallen forever. It's where I belong.

But it doesn't matter if that's my fate. I've already lived on that desolate plane for so many years. How could the reality of hell be any worse than this? The arms holding me lift me up, and I tip my chin to the sky, prepared to fall at the feet of the lord of the underworld, where I will spend my wretched eternity.

If it's the ozziller finally coming to take me, then it will rip me limb from limb. I wanted to die, but some feeble shred of self-preservation clings to the tatters of what's left of my spirit and I flail. With the fleeting strength I have left, I claw and I scratch, but I'm no more dangerous than a newborn lamb. My teeth sink into flesh, a growl tearing from my throat. I hear a grunt and a sharp pain shoots across my shoulder.

And then I remember nothing but darkness.

CHAPTER FOUR

NADIR

Nadir cracked the joints in his knuckles and rolled his neck, doing his best to pay attention as he swallowed a yawn. He sat on the south side of the round council table in the center of his father's meeting room with eight others seated around the perimeter. They were High Fae of various stature, each one more in love with the sound of their voice than the last. The Aurora King sat directly to Nadir's left, occasionally tossing a disapproving glance his way in a not-so-subtle reminder of what a disappointment Nadir was to him. They'd all been debating for hours on taxation and what to do about the growing dissent in the mines of the Savahell Foothills.

Nadir knew these things were important, but these questions all had simple, decisive solutions. The problem was that each of these sycophants wanted to orchestrate an outcome that benefited them and them alone. It wasn't enough for them just to win; they had to ensure their rivals suffered at least a little bit, too.

And so in endless circles they went.

Each of these High Fae ruled one of The Aurora's eight districts, each one named for the primary colors of the borealis: Emerald, Crimson, Silver, Violet, Indigo, Teal, Amber, and Fuchsia. Their lives were an endless cycle of jostling for scraps of power and wealth, each one confident their own district's contributions were the most valuable and therefore deserved the most rewards. It was pathetic.

His father could put an end to this bickering. As king, his rule was nearly absolute. But Rion preferred to coddle the council, collecting their promised favors like jeweled treasures. After all, a favor owed was the most valuable currency to a king who had no need for more gold or riches.

When Nadir took the throne, he'd put an end to this nonsense. The only solution was one that would result in the least amount of unrest amongst the citizens and, more importantly, get him out of these meetings the quickest.

In fact, he relished the idea of impeding their plans if for no other reason than to see the looks on their faces when they were told, probably for the first time in their lives, the word "no." It wouldn't make him popular, but he didn't give a fuck what these windbags thought.

Nadir watched the king absorb every detail, savoring the words of the council like the finest wine to be sipped and swallowed and then pissed out when he was through. If Nadir wanted to change how things were done, he'd first have to get rid of his father, but that was a challenge he'd been considering for decades and had yet to come anywhere close to a solution.

A sharp knock sounded at the door, and ten heads lifted. Everyone knew the council wasn't to be disturbed for anything but the most dire of reasons.

"Enter," said Rion, and four of his guards filed into the room, their postures stiff and erect. Like Nadir, Rion stood well over six feet tall with a crown of raven hair and the penetrating gaze of The Aurora's night sky—black irises that sparked with flashes of vivid color. Unlike Nadir, Rion's hair was neatly trimmed around his delicately pointed ears, while Nadir's hung in waves past his shoulders, much to his father's eternal disdain.

"Your Majesty," the lead guard said with a quick bow. "I apologize for the disturbance, but there's been a riot in the prison."

Nadir observed his father carefully, looking for signs of a reaction, but the Aurora King was stone and marble, nothing ever cracking his shell.

"I see. What are they rioting about this time?" Rion leaned back in his chair, folding his hands over his stomach. Nadir's father was nearly eight hundred years old, but as High Fae, he had the hardened physique of a warrior and appeared little more than thirty in mortal years.

"We're not really sure," the guard said, his voice cracking, clearly nervous about his answer. "Things have been fairly quiet lately, so this took us by surprise."

"Where is the warden?"

"Still dealing with the aftermath, but we've subdued most of the prisoners."

"Body count?" Rion asked with cool detachment, as if asking for the number of emeralds they'd mined this summer.

"We aren't sure of the exact number yet, but the last I heard, it was nearly a hundred." The guard stood up straighter, perhaps attempting to create a shield against Rion's infamous wrath. But no amount of feigned confidence would save him from the king's retribution. "Kelava is on his way. He wanted to speak with you directly and asked that we alert you beforehand."

Rion gave a sharp nod, then turned to Nadir and the rest of the council. "We'll have to reconvene at a later time."

"But Your Majesty," Jessamine, a noble from the House of Violet, said, "we're not done with these statements." She ruffled the pile of papers in front of her as if to demonstrate just how much work they had left to do.

"I said 'out,'" Rion barked. "Now."

There was a shared huff around the circle, anger shading everyone's expressions. Eager for the excuse to leave, Nadir placed his palms on the table and prepared to stand.

"Nadir," said his father. "You will remain here."

Nadir sank back down into his chair with a nod.

The remaining eight members of the council stood, definitely insulted by the king's behavior but unable to do anything about it. Nadir didn't bother containing his smile, enjoying how they were all pretending they weren't being dismissed like a group of worthless underlings.

As the council was leaving, the warden appeared in the doorway. Sweat ran down his forehead, trailing his cheeks and down the line of his throat. Blood spattered the front of his grey uniform, crimson specks dotting his rumpled white collar. A streak of blood marred his cheek, and he wiped at it absently while he bowed to the exiting gentry.

"Enter," said the king, and the warden scurried inside. "Close the door." He did so, leaving only Rion, Nadir, and the warden in the massive room.

Bookshelves lined the walls, crammed with leather-bound titles. A large bank of windows opened to the north, where the lights of the sky rippled in their full glory. Though Nadir had been alive for nearly three hundred years, the sight of those ribbons of light would never cease to feel like home.

After pushing his chair back from the table, he leaned forward, elbows braced against his knees. Nadir held his hands a few inches apart, conjuring bands of colored light between them, like he was pulling strings of taffy dipped in paint.

"What happened, Kelava?" asked the king, and Nadir peered up to witness their exchange.

"It was a surprise," Kelava said, scratching his chin. "Things have been calm of late, and we noticed no signs of dissension."

"It's your job to keep incidents like this contained," the king said, and the warden nodded, looking as chastened as a schoolboy caught letting a frog loose in the middle of class.

"My apologies, Your Majesty. They have been subdued now, and the casualties were minimal. We lost two guards and one hundred and twenty-seven prisoners. It could have been much worse."

Kelava hesitated, and Nadir sensed there was more the warden wasn't revealing.

"Is there something else?" his father asked, clearly picking up on the same feeling.

The color from the warden's face drained to his feet.

"That's what I wanted to tell you myself, Your Majesty. Prisoner 3452 is...gone."

Rion shot a quick glance to Nadir as though he hadn't intended for the prince to hear this bit of news. Then Nadir watched several emotions cross Rion's face, but there was no mistaking how the tension in his shoulders eased, as though a great burden had just been lifted. Why would he feel relief about the disappearance of a prisoner? Nadir sat up. Who was prisoner 3452?

"Perished in the riot? You've seen the body?"

The warden's fist clenched before he opened his mouth and then closed it.

"Out with it!" Rion smashed his fist against the table so hard both Nadir and Kelava jumped.

"I believe so." He swallowed, clearly steeling himself.

"What do you mean you believe so?" The king leaned forward, menace in the shape of his large, imposing frame.

"The prisoner had been sentenced to time in the Hollow and was still there when the riot started."

"And?"

"And, when we went to retrieve them, they appeared to have met their fate with one of the ozziller."

"What do you mean, appeared?"

"There was nothing left but a puddle of blood. We have no reason to believe the prisoner escaped the Void. The wards would have stopped them even if the ozziller hadn't."

Nadir frowned. The warden was spinning circles, obviously trying to weave this into a convincing story.

"What was the prisoner doing in the Hollow?" the king asked. Nadir watched the conversation as it volleyed back and forth, a thousand questions forming. What was the fate of one lowly prisoner to his father? "You were under strict orders to keep 3452 in your sights at all times."

Kelava ducked his head, shame etched in the lines of his features.

"Yes, Your Majesty. The prisoner started a fight, and the punishment was two weeks in the Hollow."

"Two weeks." At that, the king stood, drawing up to his imposing height. He was more than a head taller than the mortal guard. "You let the prisoner out of your sight for two weeks?"

"No," the warden said, blanching at the violence in his king's expression. "No. Someone was always there watching, ensuring they didn't get away. I swear it. But when the riot started, the guards on duty abandoned their posts to help subdue the inmates. When things calmed down, they returned to find the Hollow empty."

"Except for a puddle of blood."

"Yes, Your Majesty." The warden's voice had dimmed almost to a whisper. "No one would survive the Void, even if they managed to climb out of the Hollow."

He said it with such weak hope, Nadir almost pitied the man. He flexed his hands, sparks of light playing between his fingers as he watched his father cycle through a myriad of emotions. Worry, fear, confusion, and then relief?

"Who is prisoner 3452?" Nadir finally asked, unable to stand the secrecy any longer. His father ignored him, the king's intent stare still focused on the warden.

"You've failed in your singular task," Rion said. "What further use are you?"

At that, Kelava paled even further, a knot bobbing in his throat.

"Your Majesty. It won't happen again."

Rion took a step forward, towering over the trembling man.

"How can it happen again when there is no longer a prisoner to watch?"

The warden was having trouble breathing now. He clutched his chest, sweat running down his temples and pooling around his collar. The king's hand clamped around his fleshy jowls before the warden went wide-eyed. Nadir said nothing, magic still dancing between his fingers, trying to puzzle out this strange sequence of events.

Rion squeezed the warden's neck, and Kelava let out a wheeze. The king's face morphed into a wicked grimace as he slowly, slowly cut off the man's air. He lifted the warden, whose feet dangled above the floor. Kelava continued to choke and sputter, clawing at the king's hand as though he were any match for Rion's Fae strength.

A moment later, the king crushed Kelava's windpipe, crumpling his entire neck like the bud of a dried rose. Blood drained from the warden's nose and mouth, spilling down the king's arm and onto the floor. Rion dropped the warden at his feet, weapons rattling as the final whispers of life drained from his ruined body.

Nadir looked up at his father, an inky eyebrow arched.

"Well, that was dramatic," he said. "You want to tell me what all that was about?" Rion's lip curled as he stared at the cooling corpse of the warden.

"I want you to search the forest and ensure no one is wandering around in there."

"Who am I looking for? Who is prisoner 3452?"

Rion turned his dark gaze to his son. "It's not important. Particularly if they are, in fact, dead."

"Then how do I know who I'm looking for? Is it a man? A woman?"

Rion placed his palms flat on the council table and leaned over. "You're looking for any lost prisoner wandering the woods, Nadir. Surely that should be easy enough? Even for you?"

Nadir ground his teeth at the condescension in his father's tone, but knew there was no point in arguing. The Aurora King always got what he wanted. Nadir stood and tugged on the hem of his tailored black jacket. "Yes, I suppose it is."

"Good. If you find anyone, bring them to me immediately." Rion cast another disdainful look at the mutilated guard. "And on your way out, send someone in to clean this up."

Chapter Five

Lor

Sunlight filters through my eyelids, turning the world into a blaze of orange and red. My body aching, I peel my eyes open, blinking as they water from the sudden brightness. The first thing I register is a window and a clear blue stretch of sky. So perplexed by the sight, I lie completely still, wondering if I'm still asleep and dreaming.

A blue sky is something I remember only in a shadowed memory. Like the images of wildflowers and the sound of my mother's cheerful laughter. Sometimes I think I've conjured these flashes of recollection from the ether, only to bring me comfort. To feel like there was some good in my life before I was reduced to nothing but a forgotten, tormented prisoner. That's when my memories changed, digging in their claws and refusing to let me go. Those are the ones I'll never forget, no matter how many years pass.

I shift, my muscles and joints protesting. The surface I'm lying on is a cloud. It's the softest thing I've ever felt.

No. It's a bed. I'm lying in a soft bed with soft sheets and a soft pillow under my head. Have I died? This *must* be the heavens. Nothing else could feel this wonderfully decadent. Moving again, I let out a groan of anguish, pain searing through my limbs.

Surely if I were dead, though, everything wouldn't hurt so fucking much?

"You're awake!" exclaims a voice I don't recognize, and now it registers that I'm not where I'm supposed to be. The last thing I recall is lying in the Hollow, barely conscious, listening to the distant sounds of the prison riot. Someone has kidnapped me. My bare legs slide against silky sheets, and I sigh in satisfaction.

I've been kidnapped and sentenced to lie in a luxurious bed?

That...doesn't seem right.

"How are you feeling?" comes the voice again, and this time I note its owner. A mortal woman—elderly with white skin, wearing a pale yellow dress, her silver hair knotted on top of her head. I scramble back, my skull knocking on a headboard. One that reaches so high I have to tip my head up to see to the top. It's then my surroundings sharpen into shocking focus.

"Who are you?" I ask, taking stock of where I am. A bedroom. Possibly the biggest room I've ever seen, other than the mess hall or the laundry in Nostraza. I'm in an enormous bed, surrounded by white wooden posts draped with golden fabric.

Blankets and pillows in various shades of cream and gold surround me like a fortress of embroidered clouds.

The floor is creamy marble striated with veins of gold, covered in thick golden rugs. A massive fireplace sits at the far end of the room, and an entire wall of windows looks out onto that same blue sky where a brilliant sun shines.

"Where am I?" I ask, drawing the blanket up to my chin when I realize I'm wearing nothing but a thin, white nightgown. The fabric is so soft, it must be silk. I've been kidnapped and locked in this room and made to wear the most beautiful piece of clothing I've ever seen while lying in a bed covered in pillows and sheets as soft as butter? This definitely doesn't feel right.

"They tell me you've had quite a time of it," the woman says, wheeling over a silver cart laden with food. "Have something to eat and you'll feel better."

"Who. Are. You," I repeat, every one of my senses firing with warning.

"I'm Magdalene," she says. "But most folk call me Mag."

"*Where* am I?" I ask again, trying to focus on Mag, but the smell of toast and butter and hail Zerra...*is that coffee*? My stomach rumbles loudly, and Mag's grey eyebrows draw together.

"You must be starving, you poor thing. Eat something first and then we'll get you ready for the Tribute Ceremony."

The what?

Mag holds up a strip of bacon, perfectly crisped, and I lunge for it like an animal, stuffing it into my mouth. This tastes nothing like the flaccid strips of greyish meat I'm used to. It's crispy and salty and fatty, and I groan as I chew, the richness coating my tongue.

Mag brings the cart closer, lifting off a silver cover to reveal fluffy pancakes and scrambled eggs, everything dripping in butter. I study Mag, wondering if this is all a trick and I'm about to wake up and find myself shivering at the bottom of the Hollow, but she continues smiling as she patiently waits for me to proceed. No matter, if this is a dream, at least I can go out on a note as high as a mountain.

I pick up the knife and fork with one hand and a glass pitcher of syrup with the other, dumping the entire thing over the plate. Mag's eyes widen a fraction, but she doesn't comment as I begin sawing away at the food.

"Tea or coffee?" Mag asks, holding up two silver pots.

"Both," I say, still sure none of this can be real. She huffs out a small laugh.

"Of course. How do you take them?"

"Take them?"

Her brow furrows.

"Yes. Milk? Cream? Sugar?"

"Yes," I reply before I stuff a massive bite of egg and pancake into my mouth and then another.

Mag does as I ask, filling two mugs—one with coffee and one with tea—followed by generous pours of cream and milk, along with heaping teaspoons of sugar. I watch in fascination. The only time we had coffee or tea in the prison, it was so pitch black and bitter it made your tongue curl like a snail searching for its shell.

Someone has kidnapped me, put me into a beautiful bed, dressed me in a silk nightgown, and now I'm being force-fed pancakes?

"Oh my dear, slow down," Mag says. "You'll make yourself sick."

I know she's right. It has to have been at least a week, probably longer, since I've eaten. But if this *is* the heavens and I'm dead, then surely it doesn't matter. If I'm dreaming, then I feel it's my sacred duty to inhale as much of this food as I can before I wake up.

A moment later, I'm reminded that I must actually be alive, because my stomach cramps and I drop my utensils. Mag, Zerra keep her, is no amateur though. She's already primed with a golden bucket under my chin, and I do her the courtesy of heaving the contents of my stomach directly into it.

As I retch, Mag rubs my back softly and makes cooing sounds like a doting nursemaid. Who is this woman? Is she one of Zerra's blessed? I can't figure out what's happening. When I've expelled everything, I wipe my mouth with the back of my hand, noting the clean, white bandages neatly wrapped around my arms. Thanks to my years in Nostraza, I've always been covered with cuts and bruises in various states of healing.

Mag notices where my attention goes, pity in her expression.

"Why aren't I dead?" I ask, and Mag sucks in a sharp breath, her lips pressing together. I should be comatose. I should be so weak I can't stand. I should be an empty shell. I was in the Hollow for so long, I should be so broken I can't be put back together.

Mag tucks the blanket around my hips with efficient movements.

"They fixed up most of your injuries. The rest should heal in a few days. I'm sorry they couldn't remove all the scarring. Some of your wounds were very old and...persistent."

Confusion flashes in the woman's eyes before she meets my gaze and folds her hands in front of her stomach.

Of course, I know which ones she means. The ones on my back. The one on my face. The charred brand on the front of my shoulder—three sinuous lines on top of a circle. The sigil of the Aurora King. The stamp they burned into my skin when I was only a child, marking me as the rightful property of Nostraza forever.

Now I feel even worse than before I ate, and I slump back on the bed, still marveling at how utterly soft it is. I want to lie here forever.

"I'll send down for something a little lighter," Mag says as she hands me a glass of water. "Drink this slowly."

I sit up, taking the glass and sipping the water with a frown.

"Is it not okay?" Mag asks, wringing her hands.

"No." I shake my head. "I mean, yes. It's fine." It's more than fine. It's cool and crisp and sweet, and I'd forgotten that water could taste like this. Whatever they gave us in The Aurora was borderline brackish and clouded with things I tried never to think too hard about. Rumors said they half-heartedly filtered whatever came through the latrines. The closest I ever got to fresh water was the rain I swallowed during my nights in the Hollow.

I take a large gulp, savoring the liquid as it slips down my aching throat. It tastes like sunshine and hope, and for some inexplicable reason, that makes my chest knot and tears burn the backs of my eyes. Why is this woman being so nice to me?

I take a few more sips, and my stomach allows them to settle. After placing the glass on the nightstand, I watch as Mag bustles around the room.

"Please," I say. "Where am I? Who are you?"

"Why, you're in the palace, of course, my dear. I know it's going to take some getting used to, but I'll help where I can."

I blink, willing something about those words to make sense. "What palace?"

I can't still be in The Aurora. The sky is blue. Everything is bright and gold. The Aurora is nothing but shades of black and grey and misery. The only beautiful thing I ever experienced was the precious, fleeting glimpse of the jewel-toned lights in the sky.

"Did you hit your head?" Mag asks, concern furrowing her forehead. "The Sun Palace, of course. I know it must be hard to fathom that a girl of your...upbringing would find herself here, but it's true! *You* are the Final Tribute!"

I squint at Mag, wondering if she's the one who's hit her head. What is she talking about?

"Final Tribute for what?"

Mag flattens her mouth and tosses me a stern look. She's getting annoyed now, but I'm not sure why.

"Stop this nonsense. What is your name, girl? They didn't tell me."

"Lor," I say. "My name is Lor."

"Hmm. Is that short for something? It's a little plain."

I shake my head. "No, it's just Lor."

Mag has her head buried in a wardrobe and, a moment later, emerges holding a stunning gold gown.

"Well, I suppose it'll have to do. It's not as though you won't stick out like a sore thumb anyway, is it? Though we'll do our best to make you presentable."

I look down at myself, starting to feel a little insulted at this line of commenting. It then occurs to me that my threadbare tunic from Nostraza is gone.

"My clothes," I say to Mag. "Where are my clothes?"

"You mean those filthy rags you were wearing?" She wrinkles her nose. "They're gone."

"I need them back. Please."

Mag pins me with another puzzled look, but whatever she sees in my face must convince her I'm serious.

She delivers a tip of her chin. "I'll have someone find them." Her tone suggests she can't fathom why, and I choose not to enlighten her.

"What happened to your hair?" she asks, brushing past my strange behavior, coming over and laying the dress at the foot of the bed. She lowers her voice to a whisper as she touches the jagged ends. "Did you do that yourself? I suppose there are no proper salons in The Umbra—you don't have much choice, do you?"

I run my hand through my shoulder-length locks, feeling self-conscious.

"The lice," I say, and instantly regret it when I see the horror on Mag's face. "It's okay. I didn't have it. They were just taking precautions."

Mag's shoulders relax. "Yes, that makes sense, I suppose."

"What's The Umbra?" I ask as she pulls back the blanket, leaving me exposed in the thin nightgown. She grabs my wrist and pulls me to my feet, peering into my face. I snatch my wrist away, clutching it to my chest.

"Are you quite all right? Perhaps we need to send the healer back in here." She turns to the food-laden cart again and picks up a piece of toast, handing it to me.

"You should try to get something into your stomach. Eat it slowly this time. I suppose we'll have to add table etiquette to the list of lessons you'll require." She grimaces at my abandoned plate of pancakes and eggs. It looks like a syrupy massacre.

"What lessons? What is going on?"

She ignores me again and shoves me towards a doorway where we enter a palatial bathroom. There's a giant tub in the center of the room, bubbles mounded so high they're spilling over the top. I've never been in a bathtub before. At least not one I can remember. The only time we bathed in Nostraza was the occasional icy cold shower, the water pressure so harsh it felt like being shot in the back with a million tiny needles.

They also didn't separate the men and women, so the only time Willow and I indulged was when Tristan guarded the door.

It's then I remember.

"Willow. Tristan," I say. "Where are they? What happened to them?"

Mag's answer is another confused look. "I don't know, my dear. Eat your toast and then we'll get you in the tub and see what we can do with this hair."

She's undoing the buttons at my back, and I leap away, making a sound of protest. Not because I'm modest. Life in Nostraza strips all that away when you live shoulder to shoulder with hundreds of prisoners. No, but because I still have no idea who this woman is, and I'm not used to being touched by strangers when it's not intended to hurt me.

I'm still sure I must've died, but this is a very strange afterlife.

She makes a tutting sound. "Nothing I haven't seen before, my dear." She spins me back around and then strips me of my shift before gesturing to the tub while I try to cover myself with my arms. "Get in."

The bath looks so inviting, but I hesitate, still waiting for a catch. I can feel the heat of the water from where I'm standing and the scent—Zerra, it's pure bliss. It makes that shitty sliver of soap I fought for smell like a trampled petal.

I smirk to myself. *Look at me now, Jude. Enjoy your crappy soap.*

While I figure out what in the gods' names is going on, I decide I might as well be clean doing it. I step towards the tub, and a ripple of pleasure pulls up gooseflesh across my skin when I dip in a toe. It's so hot it burns, but I inhale a breath and plunge in. It takes only a few seconds for my body to adjust to the sting, and I sigh in relief.

I'll never be able to go back to the brutal, ice-cold showers in Nostraza after this. Now I hope I *have* died because this would be worth it.

Mag moves about me, eventually washing my hair. Then, when she's satisfied, she holds up a thick white towel for me to wrap myself in. Before I'm covered up, I catch the sight of my naked body, covered in bruises and scars. My ribs stand out so much they cast shadows on my skin. My collarbones and shoulders are as sharp and lethal as weapons.

She directs me to a dressing table and tells me to sit before running her fingers through my shorn hair, that now feels like silk and smells like a garden. I hold a wet strand to my nose and inhale in appreciation. Mag slaps my fingers, making tutting sounds, and then brushes it, dries it, and pins it on top of my head. Somehow, she's made it look like I have three times the amount of hair than is actually there.

"That's better," she says, scrutinizing her dubious masterpiece from every angle. "Do try to refrain from taking the scissors to it again, hmm? If you need a trim, one of the palace stylists will be happy to do it for you. As it stands, I'll get one of them to come see you later to even this mess out."

I frown at her in the mirror. I think she's trying to be nice?

Next, she dips into the myriad of small glass jars and pots arranged on the table. As she dabs several things on my face, I sit as still as I can, worried I'll mess up her efforts. Makeup. I've never worn makeup before. The sheer scale of the riches surrounding me is staggering in its abundance. How much would that bath cost? And this room? These clothes?

What am I doing here?

When she's done, she turns me back to the mirror. "There," Mag says. "You might pass for a lady now."

I'm staring at my face, and I can't look away. There were no mirrors in Nostraza, and this is the first time I've seen myself in years. I touch my cheek and my bottom lip, marveling that these pieces are mine. I look terrible.

Compared to Mag, my cheeks are hollow and my dark eyes are sunken. She's done the best she can with the makeup, but whoever she is, she's not a magician. My black eyebrows angle up and my deep brown eyes are dull and haunted by memories, all of them forged in the ruthless fires of torment. My features are too big for my face, but my skin seems a shade healthier now that it's clean. A light brown, as opposed to its usual greyish hue. Maybe after a bit of sun, I won't look so anemic.

My fingers trace the scar that bisects my left eye, starting above my eyebrow and running to the middle of my cheek. I knew it was there even though I've never had the chance to inspect it. Whatever Mag has done with the makeup has covered most of it up. I'm not sure how I feel about that.

I don't have much more time to contemplate myself because Mag has returned to the bathroom—I didn't even notice her leave—and she swats my hand away from my face.

"Stop, you'll mess it up." She has the golden dress in her hand and is directing me to stand.

"Let's get you into this. You're due to meet the king any minute."

Those words send me crashing into reality with a thud. "The king? What king? Why am I meeting a king?"

Mag rolls her eyes. "They really didn't choose you for your brains, did they? It certainly wasn't for your looks, though I suppose you could be attractive if you worked at it and had a little meat on those bones."

I frown again, not sure if that comment is insulting. She's holding up the dress and gesturing impatiently for me to step into it. "Come on. We haven't got all day."

I do as she asks, still reluctant, but going along with this for now in the absence of any other options. She pulls the sleeves up my arms and moves behind me to lace up the back. I gasp when I catch sight in the mirror. The bright gold fabric drapes to the floor in layers. One sleeve is sheer, while the other is made of more of the same gold cloth. Sheer material cuts down the side of the bodice, where a sunburst of gold beading stretches across my ribs and my stomach. The dress is a little loose on my emaciated frame, but this is the most beautiful thing I've ever seen. I seem to be thinking that a lot right now.

I've been kidnapped and am being made to wear a dress fit for a queen?

"These next," Mag says, indicating a pair of gold slippers she's placed on the floor.

"I don't understand," I say, looking at them and then at her. "Please. What's going on?"

"Is she ready?" comes a deep male voice from the bedroom.

Mag turns to me with a flutter. "Put them on. It's time to go."

I lack the capacity to protest as she shoves the slippers onto my feet and then tugs me back into the bedroom.

Inside the room stands a ridiculously attractive male in uniform. He's young, and appears close to my age, with dark blond hair tied at the nape of his neck. Tall, he towers over me, all muscle and warrior breeding. I gape at the pair of snowy white wings that spread from his back. If those didn't already mark him as some type of High Fae, his delicately pointed ears and glowing skin would. A large sword hangs from his hip, and he looks like he knows how to use it.

I swallow a jagged string of nerves before Mag tugs on my hand again.

As I approach, the male bows and I pause, unsure of how I'm supposed to respond. Do I bow too? The women in the novels I read sometimes curtsied.

What I *do* know is I'm not supposed to stand here gaping at him like an idiot.

"I'm Gabriel," he says, straightening up and saving me from having to figure it out. A golden tattoo curves around the side of his neck, where the rays of the sun spread out like fingers over his tanned skin. "I've been assigned as your warder during the Sun Queen Trials."

"My what? The what?"

Gabriel looks at Mag. "You may leave." Mag does, in fact, curtsy, and I make a note to remember that for next time.

"I'll see you soon, my lady."

"No, wait." But Mag is already leaving and although she was a bit rude, she seemed to mean well. Now I'm left standing with this intimidating Fae who's studying me like I'm a bug he plans to squish with his boot.

When the door closes behind Mag, Gabriel turns to me, his sharp blue eyes burning.

"Lor. Welcome to the Sun Palace. You probably have some questions."

I take a step back. Gabriel's intensity is frightening me. I'm alone here. I have no idea why I'm in this room or what I'm doing in the Sun Palace. I don't know exactly where that is, but I do know it's a hell of a long way from where I was. I reason they probably didn't bathe me and dress me up just to kill me, but can I really be sure? Perhaps I'm the victim of some elaborate prank. But who would go to such lengths just for me?

"Yes, what in Zerra is happening? Why am I here? Who are you?"

Gabriel presses his lips together, his hand going to the sword at his side.

"You probably have questions," he repeats, "but they'll have to wait. Come with me."

He spins on his heel and makes his way to the door. When he sees I haven't moved, he turns and pins me with a stern look.

"I'm not going anywhere until you tell me why I'm here. Is this a dream? Am I dead?"

"It's not a dream and you're very much alive," he replies, his hand around the doorknob. "And you can come willingly, or I can make you. It's your choice."

There isn't one ounce of humor in his expression. I have no doubt he will do exactly as he says. "If you come with me, some of your questions will be answered."

I hesitate. What choice do I have, though? He's covered in weapons, and I can only assume a palace like this houses plenty of guards ready to do his bidding. And he's promised me answers. Though I note his use of the word *some*.

"Very well," I say, trying to make it seem like this was my idea all along.

"A wise choice, my lady." I'm sure I catch the hint of a smile on his dispassionate face.

"Why does everyone keep calling me that?" I ask, coming to a stop next to him. "I'm no lady."

Gabriel studies me closely, something flashing in his gaze.

"Perhaps you weren't, but that changes today."

"What is that supposed to mean?"

"As I said, if you'll come with me, your questions will be answered." He opens the door and gestures towards the hall. "After you, *my lady*."

I give him a suspicious look, wondering if he's mocking me, but there is only seriousness in his expression.

With a nod, I pick up the hem of my skirt and sweep out the door, ready to meet my fate.

Chapter Six

My mind can't fully absorb my surroundings as we make our way through the enormous hallways of the palace. There is gold in every direction I look. Layers and layers of it in hues from the softest yellow of freshly churned butter to the deepest, most intense shades of fiery orange.

There are mirrors and gilt and thick woven rugs worked with shimmering thread. We pass soaring vaulted rooms where the tinkling notes of festive music drifts into the halls. There is laughter and conversation and an ostensible sense of weightlessness in the air, like darkness could never find its roots here.

I hear the refrains of an instrument—is it a piano? And another one, somber yet beautiful. Perhaps a violin? They're things I've imagined, buried in my tangled memories.

"Come," Gabriel says, his voice low. I've stopped in front of a room filled with High Fae absorbed in the sight of a pale-skinned female in a golden dress, blonde curls piled on her head, strumming a towering golden harp. Tiny crystal goblets dangle from their fingers, filled with bubbling liquid. They whisper to each other and toss their heads back in careless fits of giggles. They seem so happy and light. So at ease and in tune with the world around them. What would that feel like? "You'll be able to listen to music later."

So entranced by the sight, I startle and turn to Gabriel, remembering he's there. With a reluctant nod, I go to follow his purposeful steps. We curve around several corners and through more wide hallways set with expansive arched windows revealing not just the bright sky, but a clear ocean, so blue it's nearly green. I've stopped in my tracks again, my hand drifting to my throat as I try to soak in this picture like I could dive straight into its depths.

"I never thought I'd see such a thing," I whisper, a knot cinching in my chest. "It's magnificent."

The ocean's waves roll over one another, white frothy caps tumbling in slow crests like playful clouds. Though I can't actually hear it, I imagine the sound it must make. Like the roar of lions and the resounding crash of thunder.

"My lady," Gabriel says, his voice softer this time, his expression less stern. "We are going to be late. Please. I promise to take you down there later if you'll come along."

"Okay." I nod, finally tearing my gaze away. I think I could sit there for a hundred years and never tire of this view.

Finally, we arrive at a tall set of double doors made of white painted wood and covered in a filigree of gold leaves and flowers. One door stands partially ajar, and Gabriel nudges it a few inches further, marching into the room and holding it open before he gestures me inside.

At my entry, the chatter cuts off abruptly, every eye in the room pointing my way, heads practically rotating behind them like owls. I swallow, and my hands ball in the fabric of my dress, probably ruining it with my sweaty palms.

This room is just as resplendent as every other one, with soaring ceilings and massive windows and the evidence of riches upon riches everywhere. What am I doing here? I don't belong here. There has been some grave mistake.

I count nine High Fae females, all of whom appear to be around my age, huddled in a group. Each one is more exquisite than the last, with pink lips and long lashes and big, vibrant eyes. With glossy hair and smooth skin and slender limbs. They each wear a golden dress that makes mine look like a dusty rag dug out from the back of a closet. How pathetic I was to think this dress was the most beautiful thing I'd ever seen just a few minutes ago.

The room also includes a line of nine more Fae guards in armor just like Gabriel's, each with a set of white feathered wings on their back and that same golden sun tattooed on their neck. Besides the females and warders, there are a handful of others, including a High Fae female with a severe expression who's currently peering at me over the glasses bridging her nose.

"Ah, it's about time. Our *Final Tribute* has arrived." Why does everyone keep calling me that? And why do their voices drop to an ominous level when they do?

The Fae sweeps forward, her critical gaze studying me from every angle. Her straight blonde hair is cut to her chin, and her eyes are a striking green. She wears a golden skirt with a billowing, buttery overcoat that hangs past her knees. Though she's about my size, her straight shoulders and the imperious way she tips up her chin make her seem at least a foot taller.

"You're a little thin, but you'll have to do." She grimaces, a hand pressing to her chest. "*What* is that on your face?"

Pushing her glasses up, she leans in so close I can smell her breath, and I wrinkle my nose. I'm fairly certain Fae don't require enhancements like glasses. Their vision is far superior to that of mortals, so the glasses must be for show. Maybe she thinks they make her look smart. Well, I have news for her.

"Is that a *scar*?" She says it like I've lifted up my dress and piddled on the floor. I touch my cheek, suddenly self-conscious. I've never been ashamed of my scars before. They are a living map of my physical pain, each one earned in the acrimony of my torture. They're badges of honor. Constant reminders of every moment I survived what so many couldn't. Of how I'll keep surviving if I just hold on tight enough.

How dare she judge me for them?

"Madame Odell, the healers did what they could, but some of them were too much, even for their gifts. They've promised to keep working on them over time," Gabriel says, appearing at my side.

Madame Odell sniffs and leans back, judging me from head to toe, definitely finding me wanting. "Well, she's here now. I suppose there's nothing else for it. What's your name, girl?"

I open my mouth to answer, but I'm so nervous it comes out as nothing but a pitiful squeak. I clear my throat and try again.

"I'm Lor," I say quietly, noticing the nine other females cover their mouths, their bright eyes dancing with glee. A few don't succeed at suppressing their giggles, and I hear a delicate snort, followed by a gentle ripple of malicious snickers.

"Lor who?" Madame Odell asks. "No family name?"

I shake my head. "I'm just...Lor."

I have no family name. My legacy is dead. They threw me into that prison as a child and stripped away everything.

"Hmm," she says. "Well, if you survive the Trials, perhaps you'll earn yourself one. I don't know why I'm surprised an Umbra rat is nameless. We really should just clear out the lot of them."

"I beg your pardon," I say, my neck flushing with heat in anger and humiliation. "What did you just say? What's an Umbra rat?"

The woman ignores me, turning to face the other nine females, and claps her hands. I look at Gabriel, sticking him with an angry glare.

"You promised me some answers," I hiss under my breath. "I didn't come here to be insulted. Don't they teach you any manners in this fancy palace? What the fuck is going on?"

"Patience," he says, his jaw tight. "And watch your mouth. You're a lady now." The look he gives me suggests he's not convinced of that, though.

"I will not be patient." I grit my teeth. "You've *stolen* me from—"

A hand clamps around my arm, and Gabriel yanks me against his broad chest. "Do *not* finish that thought, *my lady*," he hisses in my ear. "Or there will be consequences that will make your previous life seem like a sweet memory."

His blue eyes burn with an intensity bordering on dangerous, and for the first time since I've woken up in this strange reality, I'm truly afraid. It turns out I *have* been kidnapped and been made to wear a dress fit for a queen, wrapped in luxurious sheets, and fed buttered toast. But it's clear none of it was done out of kindness. I give a slow nod, somehow understanding it's best to keep my mouth shut for now—something I've never been very good at.

"Gabriel!" Madame Odell calls. "Bring her here. We're to enter the throne room *now*." She punctuates the last word like an arrow shot straight through my heart.

Gabriel nods and drags me over to where the other nine Fae wait with his large hand clamped around my biceps so tightly it's probably going to leave a bruise.

I'm going to kill this asshole.

As I'm unceremoniously dumped in front of the group, they all take a small step back, as if afraid to get too close. The crinkle of their elegant noses accompanies the curl of their perfectly painted lips. I get the sense that if I were to yell "boo" right now they'd all faint into a pile of golden-swathed matchsticks.

Madame Odell claps her hands. "Get in line. All of you." There's a flurry of gold fabric and silken curls tossed over shoulders as the Fae file into an orderly line. They smell like a rose garden, doused in rich perfume, the scent so cloying it coats the inside of my nose and thickens in my lungs. I'm shoved to the back of the line as I suck in deep breaths, panic swirling inside my stomach and tightening. What's about to happen?

The woman in front of me is so pale her skin glistens like snow. Her bright red curls are paired with striking emerald eyes, and she keeps peering over a slender bare shoulder as if I might leap up and help myself to a bite of her smooth, creamy skin. I won't lie—I'm tempted.

As I contemplate how she's probably never been touched by anything harsher than a feather, a door at the opposite end of the room swings open and the line in front of me starts to move.

I'm not sure why, but I search for Gabriel, seeking confirmation that this is where I'm supposed to be going. He hasn't exactly been friendly, but right now, his face is the only one that's familiar. He's watching me, his brows furrowed, his expression giving away nothing.

A hand stamps itself in the middle of my back, and Madame Odell shoves me. "Move," she hisses. "I knew digging you up from The Umbra would be a disaster. I'll never understand why the king entertains this ridiculous tradition."

Lurching forward, I process her words, following the procession into a room that's even more intimidating than every room I've already seen. It's so bright I have to squint against the glare of sunlight on gold. It's everywhere. On the floors and the walls and even the ceiling, except for a curved glass dome that arches overhead where more blue sky is visible. The sun's warmth beats down, and I wonder what that would feel like on my bare skin.

Giant windows are inset into every wall, revealing the sandy shores and tumbling waves of that crystal-clear ocean. Gleaming curtains stretch the height of the room, so many miles of fabric one could build an entire village of tents.

We file down the center of the room, where the bright red head of the woman in front of me appears to be floating as if she's gliding on air. We walk through parallel lines of more guards, these ones human without wings or tattoos, who stand with straight backs looking ahead as if we aren't even there. Hundreds of well-dressed High Fae and mortals stand beyond the guards, murmuring and whispering as they eye me and the other nine females with open judgment.

Up ahead, I catch my first glimpse of the dais, where two thrones sit backdropped by points of gold molded into the curving rays of the sun. They fan out like the palm of a hand held open, offering something that feels almost like salvation.

High Fae flank each side of the dais, garnished in jewels and silk and lace and the immutable security of their privilege. The wealth. The extravagance is almost painful to look at. I think of my rough grey prison uniform and my narrow cot and the meager scraps of food I was fed day after day when there are people living like *this*.

With a pang, I think of Tristan and Willow, wondering where they are and what they're doing. I pray to Zerra for the millionth time that they survived the riot, and that I'll see them soon.

The females ahead of me have arrived at the front of the room. They spread out into a line facing the dais, landing me directly in the middle, and it's then I come face to face with what feels inexplicably like a shift in the course of my entire destiny.

A High Fae male sits on one throne, dressed in more gold silks, including a fitted brocade jacket with a line of shiny buttons and a pair of breeches that look brown at first, but shimmer with gold thread when he moves. His soft brown boots come to his knees, and his hair gleams like polished copper, reflecting a shaded river of brown and orange and gold in the sunlight. Piercing aqua eyes, the same color as the ocean outside, regard me and the nine other females as his gaze sweeps over us all. He has high cheekbones, a defined jaw, and a pair of full, perfect lips. In a day where I've experienced the pinnacle of beautiful things, he shreds them all to dust. I go breathless just being in his presence.

This could only be the Sun King.

When his eyes land on me, they pause, a curious spark accompanying the barest curve of his mouth. But I must have imagined it. There's no possibility he'd ever notice me next to the rest of these other nine perfect specimens of feminine beauty.

"Welcome," says the king with a smile that reveals a set of flawless white teeth. His eyes are bright with warmth. "It's been over five centuries since Aphelion has had the good fortune of crowning a new queen." His thoughtful gaze floats to the empty throne at his side before he regards us again.

"As you know, it is the greatest of honors to be chosen as one of the ten Tributes to compete in the Trials. You've beaten out hundreds of other hopefuls to find yourself here, and I am counting on you all to give your very best. Only the bravest, most loyal, and most clever female can hope to ascend and rule by my side."

I blink rapidly, shaking my head, sure I've just misheard him. I'm in Aphelion? I harbor only a vague notion of the details that define the continent of Ouranos, but I *do* know this southern kingdom is about as far as one can get from The Aurora.

Forgetting that puzzling fact, what's even more pressing is the notion that I'm here to compete for the title of the Sun Queen?

Again, I'm convinced I've died, and this is all an elaborate dream. My mind must have truly shattered when I was in the Hollow. I didn't know my imagination was capable of weaving such impressive tales.

A Fae male in a golden robe has stepped forward, his hair so light it's nearly white. He stands with his hands behind his back and clears his throat.

"The Sun Queen Trials are a tradition dating back through Aphelion's history." His head held high, his voice booms through the large chamber. "For thousands of years, the Trials have chosen the line of queens to rule over the kingdom. Ten of the most beautiful and most skilled females from the finest families in Aphelion are selected to compete in the areas of etiquette, grace, stamina, logic, wit, and seduction."

At that, I frown, vertigo pulling the golden rug out from under me. There are so many questions perched on my tongue they threaten to drown the entire room. Gabriel catches my eye and, as if sensing my thoughts, silences them with an admonishing glare. He mouths the word *don't* from across the room, and I push back with a glare of my own, my nostrils flaring.

"Save one," continues the Fae male, and his eyes fall to me with the heaviness of an anchor sinking to the bottom of the sea. "One human Tribute is selected from The Umbra, whereby they, too, will have the chance to win this most coveted of prizes. It is a reminder to all mortals that anyone with the acuity and desire can change their lot in life if they choose. A reminder that we are the ones in charge of our own destinies."

A murmur runs through the room while I contemplate his words, a polluted laugh threatening to burst from my chest. They dragged me here to compete as some kind of evidence that the dregs of society can alter their fate if only they work hard enough?

Again, someone is claiming I'm from The Umbra. Mag. Madame Odell and now this Fae. I can only surmise from everyone's reaction this must be some kind of Aphelion slum, or perhaps another prison? But I didn't come from The Umbra. Nor am I even from Aphelion. A tingle fractures at the back of my neck and a burn twists in my stomach.

None of this seems good.

The Fae male is speaking again. "The ten Tributes will compete in four challenges over the next eight weeks. Each challenge is designed to test a variety of skills and attributes. If you fail to complete the task in a manner we deem satisfactory, you will be disqualified. These challenges are not for the meek and many Tributes have succumbed to death over the centuries. In between challenges, you'll receive lessons and training designed to help you survive."

The crowd meets that declaration with a swell of excited chatter.

Death? My already queasy stomach tightens into more knots.

"The Tributes who pass all four challenges will then stand before the Sun Mirror, the arbiter and judge of who is worthy of ascension to Imperial Fae and to rule as Sun Queen. Only the Mirror sees the truth and future destiny of who is meant to be queen." The man stops and takes a dramatic pause, his gaze skating over us as though he's looking at some of us for the very last time. "Good luck to you all, and may Zerra bless you and keep you."

A round of polite clapping fills the room, smiles on everyone's faces. Well, not everyone. The perfect complexions of the other nine Tributes are now tinged with green, and they look as ill as I feel. Being a Tribute may be an honor, but it's clear it comes at a great cost. The reality of what we're being asked to do has dimmed their earlier smugness.

Why am I doing this? *What* am I doing here?

While the chatter continues, I look up to find the king watching me. He's breathtaking, and I return his open stare, somehow understanding this is what he expects of me. His brown hair sparkles in the sun and his blue-green eyes seem to find a place buried deep in my spirit I hadn't known I'd lost. I make out the lines of his muscled body through his clothing—broad shoulders and narrow hips and strong thighs. When he leans an elbow on the armrest, I note the beauty and strength of his large hand.

I'm caught in a spell, unable to move or speak. But then a hand circles my arm, distracting me. Gabriel towers over me with all the warmth of an iceberg. He looks over at the king, and they exchange a look I can't interpret.

"I'm going to compete to marry *him*?" The words slip out in a breath that floats into the air and then coalesces into the whisper of a promise I once made when I was barely old enough to understand it.

Gabriel's lip curls. "You're going to try, I suppose."

"I have to win the trials first," I say.

He snorts out a laugh, and my gaze snaps to him. "That's not exactly what I mean."

"What are you talking about?"

"It means you're the Final Tribute." Gabriel takes in a deep inhale, his gaze sliding once again to the king, who is now conversing with another Fae. "And in nearly eight thousand years of the Sun Queen Trials, the Final Tribute has never once survived."

CHAPTER SEVEN

"What?" I ask, the spell the king just had me under splitting into hairline cracks.

"Come on," Gabriel says, pulling on my elbow.

I dig in my heels and yank my arm back. "What do you mean the Final Tribute has never survived?"

Gabriel blows out a breath, his eyes once again meeting the king's. He's watching us again, and I bristle as they exchange a significant look.

"What's that? Why do you keep looking at each other that way? You said I would get some answers if I came with you, but I'm more confused than ever! Tell me what's going on!"

"Keep your voice down," Gabriel hisses, his teeth gritted.

"No! No, I will not keep my voice down. I demand to know what I'm doing here!"

I'm causing a scene, a few curious heads swinging in my direction. Gabriel exchanges another quick look with the king and then turns to me, bending over and hauling me over his shoulder. I let out a screech and pound his back before I aim my foot at his crotch. My toe connects with a rock-hard bulge and I cry out. Fucking armor.

Dark laughter accompanies a face full of white feathers, and I sputter, trying to bat them away. Gabriel spins around so he's facing the crowd. "Sorry about that, ladies and gentlemen. You know how these Umbra rats can be sometimes." He smacks my ass pointed straight at the room, and there's a twitter of laughter solely at my expense. As soon as I figure what the fuck is going on, Gabriel is first on the list of people I'll murder with a blunt object.

He spins around again, and I close my eyes as my stomach lurches. I'm still suffering from the effects of my earlier meal, and my body is still exhausted from my days in the Hollow. Gabriel opens a door, and we enter a room before he slams it behind us.

A moment later, I'm hauled off his shoulder and dumped onto a soft settee. We seem to be in some kind of windowless antechamber, the walls covered in patterned gold silk.

"How dare you!" I jump up, my fists balled. "I demand an explanation this instant!"

"Keep your voice down," Gabriel says, his blue eyes flashing.

I stand up straight, take in a deep breath, and prepare to let out an ear-piercing shriek mined from the depths of my frustration.

"Do that and I'll send you back to Nostraza so fast your head will spin."

I pause mid-inhale and then drop my shoulders, the air wheezing out of me.

"That got your attention, did it, Lor?"

I narrow my eyes. "Tell. Me. What. Is. Going. On."

Gabriel runs a hand down his face and paces to the other side of the room. "Atlas secured your release from Nostraza to compete in the Trials."

I shake my head. "Who?"

"Atlas. The king."

That brings me up short. "Why?"

Gabriel studies me from the top of my head to the tips of my toes, but there's nothing suggestive about it. He's a scholar trying to solve a complex riddle and missing a vital clue.

"I don't know," he says finally. "I was told to retrieve you from The Aurora and bring you back here to stand in as the Final Tribute during the Sun Queen Trials."

I spread my hands out. "That doesn't make any sense. Why me? Why not get someone from this place you call The Umbra?"

Gabriel rubs his chin and shakes his head. "I don't know that either."

"Well, then I'm going to ask the king." I hike up the front of my ridiculous dress and march to the door, but Gabriel blocks my exit.

"You will do no such thing, my lady."

"Get out of my way right now!"

Gabriel takes a step forward, hands circling my shoulders. "You have been brought here to compete in the Trials. You will pretend you are from The Umbra and you will tell no one of where you came from. You may die, but you may also see your every dream come true. What mortal wouldn't dream of marrying the Sun King? You'll ascend to Imperial Fae and have all the power and riches you could dream of. You would have magic, Lor."

"What kind of magic?" I ask, because that does sound pretty good.

"I don't know. The Sun Mirror decides that."

I arch a skeptical eyebrow.

"Lor, you have no choice in this. You will compete in the Trials to the best of your ability, and if you do not win, you will probably die. If by some miracle you manage to survive, you will be sent back to Nostraza to rot for the rest of your miserable life. Do I make myself clear? I don't know why Atlas wanted you here, but this is his desire, and it is my duty to see you follow through on it."

I'm so taken aback by his words, I don't speak for a moment.

"Can you get Tristan and Willow out too? I won't stay here without them. If you can get me out, you can get them out." The pitch of my voice rises at the end. Maybe I can finally secure their freedom. "There was a riot happening when you took me. I don't know if they're okay. I need them."

"There was no riot," he says.

"There was. I heard it," I insist.

"You must have been hallucinating."

I cant my head, studying him. Is he telling me the truth? But why would he lie about that?

"Can you get them out? Please?"

"I can't do that," Gabriel says, his expression resolute, his wings giving a soft shudder.

"Why not? You got me out. Why can't you get them out?"

"It doesn't work like that."

I ball my hands into fists. "I'll scream this time. I will."

Gabriel takes another step closer, wrapping a large hand around my throat, and when I try to wrench away, he grips it harder, my breath stuttering. A moment later, he shoves me against the wall, looming over me like an angel of death.

"Don't make this difficult, Lor. If you don't do as you're told, your friends will be in danger, too." I try to free myself again, snarling in fury. He grips my throat hard enough that I'm starting to feel genuinely afraid.

"Did you just threaten them?" I choke on the words, tugging on his strong arm, to no avail. He's steel and I'm an insignificant flea.

"I did. Keep acting like a spoiled brat and not only will your friends' lives be forfeit, I'll ensure you spend the rest of your days in that hole where I found you. Once again, I ask: do I make myself clear?"

He stares at me with such ferocity, my defenses begin to crumble. The sting of tears burn the backs of my eyes.

"Why is this happening? I don't understand."

Gabriel lets go of my neck and takes a step back, smoothing his hands down his front like he's trying to remove a wrinkle from his golden leather armor. "That isn't important. What matters is that you do everything you can to survive this."

"You just told me the Final Tribute has never survived. How am I supposed to do that?"

Gabriel answers with a slow smile. "You were on the edge of death when I found you in that hole, and somehow you still managed to fight me. Do you remember biting me, Lor? Use some of that grit."

I'm too confused and surprised to respond. This must all be some kind of mistake.

What does the king know about me?

Gabriel says nothing else before he opens the door and gestures for me to follow. The throne room is now empty and our steps echo against the marble. I walk over to the pair of large golden chairs, taking in their magnificence and feeling the weight of everything they represent.

"Don't tell me you don't want it," Gabriel says softly, directly in my ear. It's a deadly caress designed to lull witless girls into places from which they can never return. "A girl like you."

I give him a sharp look. "A girl like me with nothing, you mean?"

"Yes, that's exactly what I mean."

I snort and fold my arms, picturing myself next to the king. I'd be lying if I said the idea wasn't tempting. I was sure I'd spend the rest of my life in Nostraza. Eventually, disease or violence would kill me. That I got out of there at all is a miracle.

"I don't even know him," I say, gesturing to where the king was sitting. "What if he's a vile monster? What if he's as boring as drying mortar? What if he has bad breath?"

Gabriel rolls his eyes. "You'll get to know him. All the Tributes will have the opportunity to spend time with him."

I swallow at that. Me in a room alone with an Imperial Fae so beautiful he makes my eyes hurt? What would I even say to him? I'd be completely lost, because I'm pretty damn sure there is nothing about the king that's vile, boring, or smelly. I *am* a rat compared to the nine other butterflies I'll be competing with. He'll just laugh me out of the room.

"You could get your friends out if you win," he continues, and that right there is all the incentive I need. If I'm the Sun Queen, I'd finally have some iota of power. If I ascend to Imperial Fae, I'd have magic and resources. Money. A crown. A fucking *army*.

Yes, I'd get Willow and Tristan out and then I'd pay the Aurora King back for everything I owe him. For every lash of the whip that tore open my back. For those endless nights in the Keep when I screamed so loud my voice gave out. For allowing the warden to use me for his sick pleasure. For every night I went to sleep hungry and cold and aching. For tossing a group of children into the worst prison in Ouranos and leaving us there to die.

For *everything* he took.

Gabriel is studying me carefully, but I keep the vengeance of my thoughts to myself.

Still staring at the Sun King's throne, I nod slowly.

None of this makes any sense, but I'd be a fool to turn away from this chance. They've just handed me the opportunity of a lifetime. Living in Nostraza, my days were always numbered, anyway. I have nothing to lose by competing in the Trials, and now I might have a chance at a future I've only dreamed.

Chapter Eight

Nadir

N adir burst through the heavy wooden doors of Nostraza, slamming them so hard they bounced off the walls. He wore his black leather armor with a sword strapped to his back, the top half of his wavy midnight hair tied up in a knot.

Dozens of wary eyes found him where he stormed into the stone foyer. The guards exchanged confused glances and stood straighter as he strode like an arrow down the wide hall. The anguished screams of the prison's residents echoed through the walls. There was nowhere to escape the symphony of Nostraza.

Nadir stopped, looking around.

"Your Highness." A guard rushed forward and bowed so low his nose nearly brushed his knees. "What brings you here?" The man straightened, wringing his hands, his eyes darting around the room as though expecting an attack from every corner.

"You're the new warden," Nadir said, noting the crest on the man's uniform.

"I am, Your Highness. I'm Davor." He bowed again. "What can I do for you?"

"I need to see the prisoner records," Nadir said. "Where are they kept?"

The warden's lower lip quivered, his skin bleaching to ash. Who had assigned this mortal fool to guard the most notorious prison in all of Ouranos? He'd crack like an egg at the first sign of pressure.

"Is there something I can help you find, Your Highness? I can assign someone to assist you with whatever you need."

"No," Nadir replied. "I'll do it myself."

Clearly unhappy with that response, the warden pressed his thin lips together. "Very well. Please follow me." Davor turned and proceeded down the hall. Nadir followed in his wake, his steps loud and firm, punishing the stones beneath him. The king was hiding something, and he was determined to find out what.

Davor took Nadir through several dank corridors, finally arriving at a narrow wooden door, where he fished a keyring out of his pocket. "This is where the prisoner records are kept." He inserted one of the keys into the lock and turned.

"All of them?" Nadir asked as the door swung open, revealing a large room lined with shelves and cabinets. Glass orbs filled with ribbons of pale yellow light ran in a line across the ceiling, created either by his father or one of his ancestors to provide illumination.

"Every prisoner that has ever spent a night inside Nostraza is listed somewhere in these files. They're arranged by year of arrival and then by number."

Nadir stepped inside the room, scanning the labels, some of them so old the writing was barely legible. Though he had no notion of when prisoner 3452 had arrived, he assumed they'd been inside Nostraza for at least a few years, given his father's interest. Nadir had learned Kelava had been the head warden for a little over twenty years, which gave him a timeframe at least.

"Leave me," Nadir said, holding out his hand. "And give me the keys. I'm not to be disturbed."

The warden swallowed, but did as the prince asked, placing the keyring in the center of his large palm. Nadir spun around, his black eyes flashing with bursts of violet.

"And tell no one I was here."

"Yes, Your Highness," Davor said, his wavering voice barely a whisper.

As soon as the warden closed the door, Nadir sprang into action. The folders were labelled by year, but thankfully, the numbers were still ascending. It didn't take him long to find the prisoners numbered in the three thousands. Twelve years ago. Someone who had arrived and lived in Nostraza for over a decade. How had they endured that long? That was too much time for any mortal to survive here and still be mentally sound.

He flipped through the files, finding prisoners 3449, 3450, 3451, 3453. He stopped, flipping back. The file was missing. Of course it was.

He kept digging, flipping through the rest of the three thousands, coming up with nothing. Had it been misplaced? He circled the room. No, this had to be deliberate. The king was no fool, and there was a reason he was keeping this a secret. He flipped through the next few drawers just in case, but they revealed nothing further. Frustrated, he ran his hand through his hair, dislodging a few strands from their tie.

He whipped open the door and shouted for the warden.

"Yes, Your Highness," the man said, breathing heavily when he arrived a few seconds later. "You called for me."

"Come inside and close the door."

Davor did as he was asked, standing in the center of the room still wringing his hands, a bead of sweat sliding down the fleshy skin of his cheek. Nadir smirked. This was too easy. The man was about to dissolve into a puddle.

"Do you know who prisoner 3452 is?"

The warden blinked. "I'm sorry, Your Highness, but there are hundreds of prisoners in here and I don't know all of their numbers. What is their name?"

"I don't have a name, and they're no longer here. They...perished in the riot." Nadir hesitated, unsure of how much to reveal. He didn't want his sleuthing getting back to his father. This wasn't part of his marching orders.

"I'm terribly sorry, Your Highness, then I don't know. Perhaps their file will reveal something. What number did you say? 3452, was it?"

Fuck. Now the warden knew too much.

"They were in the Hollow when the riot happened. Does that ring a bell?" Might as well lay it all out now. Nadir would have no choice but to take care of the warden, though.

Davor looked up from the drawer he was rifling through, his eyebrows drawing together. "I do remember Kelava had just sent someone down. A girl, I think. I don't remember who. They all look the same, you understand. Filthy things."

A girl.

Why did a girl have the king so worried?

Well, at least that was something.

"You're sure you have no idea who it was? Their file appears to be missing. You know nothing about this?"

"Sorry, Your Highness. Missing?"

Nadir believed the man was sorry. The worry on his face was clear, and the desire to please was obvious. Nadir believed Davor would have revealed what he knew if he could have.

"This is very peculiar," the warden said. "I'll have to open an investigation to look into this. This shouldn't be missing. Nostraza maintains impeccable records."

Nadir stepped forward. He towered over Davor, and the man cowered at the stormy look on his face. "I apologize, Your Highness. I've only just taken this job, but I assure you, we'll sort this out and ensure it doesn't happen again." Davor trembled, entirely mistaking the reason for Nadir's ire. He didn't give a fuck about Nostraza's record keeping.

"Where is the Hollow?" Nadir asked.

"The Hollow?"

"Where the prisoner was kept. Where is it?"

"In the forest, just past the northern gate. I can show you." The warden was speaking quickly now, perhaps sensing things were about to go very poorly for him.

"I apologize for this," Nadir said, though he didn't really sound that sorry.

A moment later, the warden's eyes widened as ribbons of colorful light peeled off Nadir and circled the man. A crimson thread, the width of a finger, slid past his lips and down his throat. Davor whimpered as Nadir pulled the light down through his esophagus, wrapping it around the guard's heart before he squeezed. The warden gaped, his mouth opening, only a gurgle coming out.

"Your Highness," he choked. "Please."

Nadir squeezed harder while the warden's face turned blue and then his heart burst inside his chest with a mushy throb. He collapsed to the ground, skin already turning grey as Nadir's threads of magic dissolved in the air. He toed the man's foot with his boot. It was a shame. Two wardens in two days. This prison really had a problem.

Rolling his shoulders, Nadir opened the door and retraced his path. When he passed a pair of guards waiting at the end of the hall, he called to them. "Your warden had a heart attack. Better go check on him." He thumbed in the direction over his shoulder, not even pausing his steps. He heard the guards take off running as he stalked through the prison. He was the crown prince and The Aurora's Primary. No one would question him. As for his presence here—well, his father had ordered him to search the forest. Nadir had just made a little detour beforehand.

"Where is the north gate?" Nadir asked another guard, his voice hard and his expression harder. The trembling man rattled off a set of directions. Continuing his quest, Nadir marched through the damp stone halls, the ever-present sounds of the prisoners moaning and screaming evident through the thick walls. He curled his lip. This place was an abomination. Someone ought to raze it to the ground. Perhaps once he was king, he'd do just that. But then, where would all these human degenerates go?

A girl.

A girl who had been here for twelve years. Unless she'd been a toddler when she'd arrived, Nadir reasoned, she must at least be a young woman if Davor had referred to her as a girl. How had she survived this long in Nostraza? The usual life expectancy was no more than a few years at best. And more importantly, *why* had his father been interested enough to have Kelava keep an eye on her?

Nadir burst through the northern doors, making his way across the courtyard, his boots crunching on the gravel. Guards watched him from the walls, their expressions cautious. It was understandable. Nadir and the king rarely ventured behind the walls of Nostraza.

When he found the north gate, he asked again for the way to the Hollow and a few minutes later found himself standing over it, looking down into the small, dark space. He dropped into it, light on his feet. A mortal would be trapped here, especially given the soft crumbling texture of the walls, but for a High Fae, it was an easy jump.

Nadir crouched on his haunches and searched for clues. Whatever blood had been here had already soaked into the earth. He took a deep inhale, noting the smell of what must've been the girl. It was sweet and fresh, and something nudged at the edges of a memory he couldn't place. Nadir closed his eyes, taking another long deep breath, and frowned.

There was the distinct smell of the girl, no doubt, but there was something else. Another smell he almost recognized. A scent that someone had tried to cover up? The twist of something familiar combined with something designed to obscure it. But they hadn't quite succeeded.

What he didn't smell was any trace of the ozziller Kelava had been so sure about. No, something else had taken the girl. Nadir stood, running his hands along the walls, as if to read them for hints with his fingers.

Someone *else* had been here. Someone from another court.

Another High Fae.

CHAPTER NINE

LOR

The next morning I'm awoken by the cheerful trill of Mag, who bears a tray full of food suspended between her hands. After Gabriel returned me to my room last night, I'd changed into a silken nightgown and promptly fallen into a deep sleep, exhausted from literally everything.

"Let's see if this goes down a little better," Mag says, placing the tray on a table near the long bank of windows on the far wall. Over her arm is a familiar piece of grey clothing. She holds it up between two fingers, like it might poison her if she lets it touch too much of her skin. "I had them clean this for you. Though I still can't imagine why you want it back."

I scramble from the bed and snatch it, stuffing it under my pillow for safekeeping. Mag eyes the bed and then me, clearly mystified by my entire existence.

She gestures me over and sets down a bowl of porridge and a few thick slices of bread. I eat slowly, allowing my stomach to adjust to the food.

"You're so thin," she tuts. "We need to fill you out a little. A few weeks of proper rest and nourishment, and we'll have you looking much healthier."

Sure, but there's probably not much point, since I'll be dead after the first challenge. I don't bother to correct her, but I take a nibble of the sweet, creamy porridge and decide I might as well enjoy these comforts as I await my future demise.

"The captain said to get in a proper breakfast before he comes to collect you," Mag says. "You'll need your strength."

"Who?" I ask.

"The captain. Your warder for the Trials."

I frown. I don't know much about military rankings, but a captain sounds important.

"Gabriel's a captain?"

"Of the king's personal guard, yes."

I take another bite of cereal and put my spoon on the table. "Doesn't the king's captain have better things to do than babysit me?"

Mag raises an eyebrow as she hangs up my dress from last night and moves about the room, tidying the space. "It's his duty. All the warders are a part of the king's principal guard. Ten warders and ten Tributes. It's how it's always been done. However, the captain is usually assigned to the favored contender. I admit, I was a bit surprised to see him assigned to you."

She waves an idle hand, obviously trying not to say what she's thinking. That there's no way *I'm* the lead contestant. "But the king must have his reasons," she continues. "They go way back, those two, despite the circumstances of their relationship."

I contemplate that cryptic statement as I butter a slice of bread and pop a small piece into my mouth before moaning in appreciation. It's still warm—soft and yeasty—the butter melting and rich.

The pity in Mag's expression makes me sit up straight, humiliation coloring my cheeks.

"You poor thing," she whispers, looking away and shaking her head, but I catch the shine in her eyes. I don't want this woman's pity. All it does is serve as a reminder of how pathetic my life has been. I feel guilty enjoying this food and this room and sleeping in that luxurious bed when Willow and Tristan are still rotting away inside Nostraza. I hope. I'm still worried something happened to them during the riot. No matter what Gabriel said, I know what I heard.

"What does the captain want with me this morning?"

Mag folds a blanket and drapes it over the armchair next to the bed. "He'll be escorting you to your first lesson with the other Tributes."

I wrinkle my nose. The other Tributes. I'll have to spend who knows how much time with them, listening to their snickers. They were all so smooth and beautiful and none of them were so wasted away you could see their ribs. None of them have hideous scars on their faces. They were plump in all the right places and slender where they're supposed to be, with unblemished complexions and creamy skin. They're a garden of flawless roses in a golden palace by the sea, and I'm the weed growing between them, clamoring for a sliver of sunlight.

I don't belong here for so many reasons.

Mag sends me another pitying look before she reaches over and pats my hand with a sort of motherly affection. I resist the urge to flinch away from her touch, my hands fisting against my nightgown. She's not here to hurt me, I remind myself.

"Don't let them get to you. They're from all the finest families in Aphelion and have spent their lives preparing for this. You can't expect to keep up with them, my dear."

My brows draw together. Did she just mean that to be encouraging?

"You'll do your best," she continues, squeezing my shoulder now, and this time I shrink from the contact, twisting out of her grip. "No one would blame you if you're the first one out."

After issuing a muttered curse under my breath, I rise to look out the window. My room doesn't overlook the sea, but rather the city. The entirety of Aphelion spreads before me. Golden domes and spires and walls all glow softly in the morning light as the sun rises. It's disorienting to witness the shift of day to night after the perpetual eventide of The Aurora. Why would anyone live there when they could have sunshine and brightness like this every day? The lights of the aurora were beautiful, but they were like a single drop of ointment used to tend a gaping wound, and I'm not sure they can compare with the shimmering landscape spreading below me now.

I study the streets and buildings, the city arranged in orderly lines. A shadowed corner at the far edge catches my eye, and I assume this must be the notorious Umbra from which I was supposedly taken. What kind of place must it be and why, with all the wealth apparent in this place, does it even need to exist? Surely the king could stand to have one less gilded mirror to ensure everyone in his kingdom had enough to live in comfort?

I replay Mag's earlier words, and something crumples in my chest. She's not even pretending she might believe in me. But why should she? She's absolutely right. What chance do I have against a group of Fae who've waited their entire lives for this?

But then again, these are a bunch of pampered princesses, and I've spent the last twelve years in the most unforgiving prison in Ouranos. Surely that must give me some kind of edge.

"Come now," Mag calls from the other end of the room. "You need to be ready when the captain arrives." She helps me into a suit of supple leather armor, all in a chestnut hue, the fitted leggings allowing for freedom of movement. I'm wearing a thin white shirt covered with a leather bodice that cinches up the front with laces. Mag attaches a pair of black vambraces to my forearms, and I pull on a pair of brown leather boots that rise past my knees. It's a far cry from yesterday's golden dress.

"What is all this for?"

"Your first weapons training," Mag says as she ties off the bodice and then spins me around for an inspection. She touches the shorn edges of my hair and then the scar on my cheek as if I'm a grain of sand that failed to materialize into a pearl. I bat her hand away.

"Stop that."

A moment later, there's a knock at the door and Mag opens it to find Gabriel, also wearing leather armor the same color as mine. It's less formal than what he wore to the Tribute Ceremony and, if it's possible, makes him even more handsome. He looks me up and down with disdain and the pointed suggestion that he considers my presence to be an obligation.

"My lady."

"Gabriel, please call me Lor. I beg you."

His mouth flattens into a line. "If that's what you'd prefer."

"It is."

He bows again. "Then we should be going. *Lor*."

I nod and brush past him through the antechamber of my room and out into the hallway. I follow Gabriel as we, once again, make our way through the winding, resplendent halls of the Sun Palace.

"How big is this place?" I ask as we pass room after room.

"Big," Gabriel says.

"Oh, very helpful."

He glares down at me, not breaking his stride. His legs are so long, I'm practically running to keep up.

We pass a pair of mortal serving girls about my age, wearing the same golden livery as Mag. They stop when they see us, dropping into deferential curtsies before rising. They both smile at Gabriel with hearts in their eyes, and he grins and winks.

"Ladies," he says, catching the hand of the closer woman. She's lovely, with golden blonde hair, a trim waist, and ample breasts that spill above the neckline of her uniform.

Gabriel presses his mouth to the back of her hand. "You look luscious today, Annabelle." The woman gasps, her hand fluttering to her throat as she drops the pile of towels she's holding. I let out an audible snort that everyone ignores. Gabriel then turns his generous bow to the second woman, saying, "You as well, Seraphina," before focusing his attention back on me, the smile dropping from his face.

"Let's go." Not waiting, he turns on his heel and starts walking. I glance at the two women who eye me with suspicion, their fists planted on their hips.

"Don't worry." I throw up my hands and grimace. "He's *all* yours."

"Lor!" Gabriel shouts from halfway down the hall, and I scurry after. When I catch up, I study him out of the corner of my eye.

"What?" he barks.

"Nothing." I roll my lips together to keep from smiling. Gabriel's a flirt? Not with me, that's for sure.

Finally, we enter a large room with a high ceiling and racks of weapons lining every wall. The floor is lined with gold and cream marble, and the walls are painted in the hue of buttercups. Large windows surround the space where dozens of people, including most of the other Tributes, wait. One Tribute stands off to the side with her warder, talking to a group of Fae who scribble on notepads while she speaks.

"What's going on there?" I ask Gabriel as he directs me towards a rack full of gleaming swords.

"The royal note-takers," he replies. "They're documenting the entirety of the Trials for posterity. They also distribute it to the public daily so they can hear about how it's going."

"Why?"

"People are interested, Lor. Whoever wins will become their queen. They take these trials very seriously."

I listen as one of the note-takers asks the Tribute a question. She's beautiful, with honey-blonde hair woven into a thick braid that hangs to her waist. Her golden skin looks as soft as silk, and her armor fits her like a glove, smoothing over generous curves and full breasts.

"I've been training with a sword since I could walk," she says, flipping the braid over her shoulder, a smile curving on her perfect pink lips. Her lashes are so long they must produce a breeze when she blinks.

"Am I going to have to do that?" I ask Gabriel, my stomach dropping out as I clutch his forearm. He gives me a disapproving look.

"Yes. But *you're* going to say as little as possible. Let them think you're a bit dim. Shouldn't be hard."

I nod slowly, too worried about the prospect of having my words judged and documented forever to comment on Gabriel's insult. I can say as little as possible. That seems like a very good plan.

"Choose a blade," Gabriel says next, and I turn to study the rack of weapons. They're incredibly intimidating. Polished hilts and gleaming blades are all stamped with a sun with eight curved rays—the Sun King's insignia. It's emblazoned on everything, including his personal guard, I note, casting a glance at the gold tattoo on Gabriel's neck. I guess there's no mistaking who the warders belong to.

"You're giving us swords?" They never let us near anything that might resemble a weapon in Nostraza. All of our food was to be eaten with fingers or a spoon, and they made even those from the flimsiest of tin. They searched us regularly to ensure we hadn't gotten our hands on anything that could be commissioned for self-defense.

"Yes, the Trials might include fighting off an opponent. And I'm guessing you're way behind."

"But why?"

"Because you're training to be a queen, and these are dulled for practicing. Don't worry."

I frown at that. "Why do I need to know how to fight to be a queen?"

"Because a queen needs to lead armies and establish her strength," he says, starting to lose his patience. He sweeps a hand down the rack. "Pick one."

"I imagined being a queen was more about sipping tea in frilly dresses and looking down my nose at everyone," I quip as I meander down the length of the rack. Gabriel's quiet chuckle follows me, and I look over at him, delighted to see his smile. Maybe he'll warm up to me. I need a friend in this place.

"Well, I suppose there's a bit of that too," he says when I stop.

"That one," I say, pointing to an especially shiny one with a polished silver hilt.

Gabriel reaches out and pulls it off the rack. "Excellent choice." He hands it to me with the hilt pointed in my direction.

A whistle blows, and Gabriel directs me to the center of the room, where I line up in a row with the other Tributes. The beautiful girl who was speaking with the note-taker stands next to me.

"Hi, I'm Lor," I say, because honestly, what have I got to lose? She eyes me up and down, an awkward silence dragging between us.

"I'm Griane," she says finally, before turning to the girl on her left and whispering something in her ear that makes them both giggle. I grind my teeth. Is this what the next eight weeks are going to be like? Me against them?

Griane is talking to a Tribute with sleek black hair and light brown skin. Her dark, angled eyes highlight the perfection of her sharp cheekbones.

"I'm Elanor," she says, looking at me with that arrogant expression I'm becoming intimately acquainted with. It's then her eyes widen as she looks past me and the entire room erupts into furious whispers.

The king has arrived.

He glides into the room, as graceful as a lion. Gleaming brown hair slashed with copper frames his face, hanging to his shoulders in untamed waves. His aquamarine eyes sparkle like a pair of jewels. He wears a pair of leather pants like the rest of us, along with a fitted white shirt that highlights every honed line of his body, every rounded curve and ripple of muscle. Not a single person in the room can take their gaze off him as he makes his way towards us. He stops next to the Fae male with the whistle, folding his muscular arms over his chest.

"Please proceed, Master Borthius," he says, his deep voice resonating like the plucked string of a cello. "I'm only here to observe."

The warders line up in front of us, and Master Borthius calls out instructions to run through a series of drills. It becomes instantly clear how woefully far behind I am.

"Thrust!"

"Parry!"

"Dodge!"

I don't even know what these words mean. The extent of my sword training is confined to snippets from books and the occasional prison brawl. Though the guards had blades as part of their arsenal, they seemed to prefer using their fists.

Gabriel swings his sword, missing my cheek by a hair.

"Watch it," I hiss. "You almost hit me."

He stops and rubs a hand down his face. "This is much worse than I feared."

"What is that supposed to mean?"

"It means you're even further behind than I'd guessed."

I press my mouth together.

"Well, I'm *so* sorry I'm not living up to your standards, considering you dragged me here and—"

Gabriel slashes his blade again. This time he nicks the tip of my chin, a bright spot of pain blooming before I touch it, my fingers coming away stained with blood. I glare at him. "What the fuck? You said the blades were dulled!"

"I said *your* blade is dulled. Mine is perfectly lethal." His blue eyes flash. "And I told you to keep your mouth shut." His voice has dropped so low, no one else in the room can hear. His gaze flicks to the king, who is watching us both intently. "We're going to have to start from the beginning. And you're going to need extra lessons. You have less than two weeks before the first trial."

I open my mouth to do something. Argue? Protest? I'm not really sure, but Gabriel is behaving like such a monumental ass, I feel the need to resist in some way, just to make his life difficult.

But then I remember Tristan and Willow. I remember the Aurora King.

Looking over my shoulder, my gaze meets a pair of clear aqua eyes, and I consider everything that's at stake. The king tilts his head, the corner of his perfect mouth tipping up as if we're both in on some kind of private joke. My stomach bursts into a cloud of butterflies, and I tear my gaze away, focusing back on Gabriel.

"I see you're getting more comfortable with Atlas?" he asks, his voice dripping with rivers of sarcasm. "That didn't take long."

"Shut up," I reply and hold up my sword. "Teach me."

Gabriel's answer is a slow, lazy smile that I'm sure must have every maid in this castle ready to toss up their skirts and spread their legs.

"Glad you're able to see reason, my lady."

Over the next few hours, I train alongside the other Tributes. Gabriel teaches me the basics, barking at me when I get it wrong. Making me repeat the drills over and over until I'm a little less like a duck tripping over its own feet. By the time we're done, I've dissolved into a pool of perspiration, my muscles twitching so erratically I fear they'll leap from my frame and run for cover.

Griane, the beautiful woman who was speaking with the note-takers, looks like she's barely broken a sweat. She's still perfect, and I'm panting like a dog left too long in the sun.

Master Borthius claps his hands together. "That's enough of that," he declares. "Tributes, now you'll face off against one another."

Shit. Panicked, I look over at Gabriel. He might take pleasure in torturing me, but at least he wasn't trying to kill me. I think.

I can feel the stares of the other Tributes, not only assessing me, but each other. What better way to eliminate the competition than accidentally running a sword through her gut? Our blades are dulled, I remind myself. They're still blades, though, and could do some permanent damage if one put their mind to it.

"You'll be fine," Gabriel says, his large hand wrapped around my biceps.

"Aren't Fae much stronger than mortals? And don't they have magic?"

"Yes, and some do." He studies me. "But they don't come into their full strength until about their twenty-fifth year. Everyone here is younger than that, and any magic they might have is restricted during the trials. You'll be fine," he repeats. But I can detect the uncertainty in his voice.

"Will I?"

He pauses. "Sure. Of course. And if not, you lasted a day. That's longer than anyone expected, especially me."

"Well, thank you for that resounding endorsement." At that, his mouth compresses as if he's trying to hold in a smile.

"I'm thrilled you think this is so funny," I snap as I'm called to stand in front of a female Fae. She's taller than me by several inches and is willowy and elegant. Her skin is pale and her long black hair cascades like a midnight waterfall down her back. A pair of cobalt blue eyes burn as bright as the lights of the aurora.

As I approach, she scans me from top to bottom, her nose wrinkling before she snorts and brandishes her sword. "Did they drag you from somewhere even worse than the sewers?" she asks. "I can still smell the stench of whatever hovel you used to call home."

Oh, isn't this lovely?

"Did you miss the lesson on how not to be a raging bitch at that fancy finishing school?" I ask with a sneer. Her self-righteous smile slips for a fraction of a second before she flips her hair back and squares her shoulders.

"At least I'm not here as just a scapegoat," she says.

"A moment," a voice calls through the room, the king's rich baritone turning us all into chess pieces standing at attention. "I said I was only here to observe, but I've decided that after today's session, one of you will dine with me tomorrow evening."

A giggle of excitement races through the Tributes. My opponent tosses her hair again, batting her eyelashes at the king with such force I'm surprised they don't shatter right off her face. The king gives her an admiring smile with those perfect white teeth, and something green twists in my stomach.

When the king has returned to the sidelines, I face off against my opponent.

"Lor, is it?" she asks, saying my name like she's just stepped in horse shit. "I'm Apricia."

"It's so nice to meet you," I reply, slicing her with my sarcasm.

"I'm going to wipe the floor with you, Umbra rat."

"I'd like to see you try."

There's no warning as she launches herself at me, and I lift my blade at the last second, clumsily deflecting her blow. She doesn't wait for me to recover, attacking again, and it's all I can do to dive out of the way. It's obvious she's far more skilled, a fact she underlines by baring her teeth with glee.

"Umbra scum," she hisses. "You don't belong here and I will ensure you don't become the Sun Queen if it's the last thing I do."

She leaps for me again, and I'm so focused on the blade aimed at my head, I don't notice when she spins and swipes a leg behind me, kicking up my feet and sending me crashing to the floor. I land on the marble with a grunt, the air whooshing out of my chest. I'm still too tired and weak from my time in the Hollow. The Fae healers did a remarkable job tending to me, but I need more time to recover.

Apricia looms over me, flipping her stupid hair again, and smirks.

"Do us all a favor and throw yourself into the sea."

She spins her sword in some fancy maneuver that might be impressive if I didn't want to rip every strand of hair from her head. Catching my breath, I watch as she preens and basks in the admiration of the other Tributes. Without stopping to think about it, I launch myself up and leap onto her back. I may not understand how to use a sword, but I've been in hundreds of fights throughout my life, and I know how to make a man twice my size weep. This twig of a bitch is no match for me. Even if she is Fae. I hope.

She goes down like a pile of straw, collapsing beneath me. Her shrill scream is a soothing caress, and my satisfaction knows no bounds. Apricia bucks under me wildly, my arm banding around her neck. I won't kill her. Maybe. I'm very tempted. No, I can't do that. She just needs to understand this is one rat who won't put up with her shit.

My ears ring because she's screeching so loud, but it's a beautiful sort of music. She twists beneath me, dislodging my hold before she sinks her teeth into my arm, and she must be part tiger because I feel it even through my leather vambraces. It's my turn to scream when she flips me over and we trade blows. I get in a punch to the side of her head and one across her cheekbone before she cracks me across the face with the back of her hand.

There are snarls and teeth and hair and tangled limbs of fury.

A moment later, she's hauled off me and someone drags me to my feet, an arm banding around my waist as I try to launch myself back at her again.

"Enough!" the king's voice rings through the room, and that's enough to shut us both up. Apricia's luxurious hair is now in snarls, blood smeared across her cheek. Part of me is humiliated I behaved like an animal in front of the king, while the other is satisfied I wiped that smirk off Apricia's pinched face.

"I think that's enough for the day," the king continues, tossing both me and Apricia a look I can't interpret. The rest of the Tributes also watch us, trying to contain their smiles, knowing there's no chance either of us are going to be chosen to dine with the king. The expression on Apricia's face could melt all the gold in this palace into a misshapen heap. *Good.* At least I took her down with me.

The king takes a few steps, stopping in the center of the room, and I roll my eyes as the Tributes all smooth back their hair and straighten their clothes. One Fae even pinches her cheeks and licks her lips, casting a coy look over her shoulder and winking.

Gabriel still has me caged in his grip, clearly worried I'm going to attack Apricia again if he lets me go. I might, actually. Especially when she also simpers for the king like an overcompensating peacock.

"I'm looking forward to getting to know all of you," the king says. "I can already tell this is the most remarkable crop of Tributes the Sun Queen Trials has ever hosted. I'd love to get to know the Tribute who showed so much *spirit* today." It's then his gaze finds me. Gabriel's grip on me loosens a fraction, mirroring my own disbelief. "Our Final Tribute, Lor."

Chapter Ten

Gabriel clears his throat and snarls in my ear. "If I let go, can you behave?"

I'm too stunned to respond. The king is watching me with a smile more brilliant than the sun itself.

He walks over and somehow becomes even more magnificent the closer he gets. Like his unfiltered magnetism is being concentrated and distilled into a potent tonic, designed to make everyone fall hopelessly at his feet. He passes through the lines the other Tributes have formed while they continue smoothing their hair and batting their eyes, but the king appears focused solely on me. Probably because I just made a complete fool of myself. He just wants to get a good look at the crazy girl they dragged from the gutter and stuffed into a pretty dress with the misplaced notion they could transform me into someone presentable.

"Lor?" Gabriel asks again. "Are you ready to act like a *lady*?"

I scowl at him over my shoulder. They're really all delusional if they think they're ever going to make a *lady* out of me. Whatever the hell that means.

The king is standing in front of me now in all his unrelenting luminosity. High Fae are always beautiful to behold, but the king is an Imperial Fae—a member of royalty—and his beauty eclipses his surroundings. I've only been in the presence of one other Imperial Fae before, but that was a very long time ago. And whether he was beautiful was the last thing on my mind.

What would I look like if I were to ascend to become the Sun Queen?

"I think you can let her go, Gabe." The king's voice is like sun-warmed wood and light filtering through honey. I feel its cadence snake its way down through my bones where it hums. Like a moth to a flame, I am completely and utterly dazzled.

"Are you sure about this, Atlas?" Gabriel asks, and the king nods.

"I'm sure."

Gabriel complies with reluctance, staying in arm's reach and giving me a stern *I'm watching you* look. Good, he should be watching. For a split second, my attention darts to Apricia, who's staring at me with shards of ice chipped from the heart of a demon.

The king takes my hand and my breath catches. Zerra, what do I do? He's so tall I have to tip my head to look at his face. This close, I can see the flecks of yellow and violet that dot the endless aquamarine of his eyes. I also catch the breath of his scent and it's heady and delicious. Something spicy and something fresh, like a twilight breeze after a thunderstorm.

"My lady, would you do me the honor of joining me for dinner in my private chambers tomorrow evening?"

He asks it as though I have a choice, and when I feel Gabriel shift in warning behind me, I know there is only one answer. I could pretend I don't want to, but every part of me yearns to agree. Of course I want to have dinner with him, even if I'm already so nervous my knees feel like melted butter.

"Yes...Your..." I stop, looking around, the tips of my ears growing hot. I lean in and the king cants his head so our cheeks are nearly brushing. I repress a delicious shiver. "What do I call you?"

I attempt to say it low enough for his hearing only, but we're surrounded by Fae and are currently the center of attention. Laughter bubbles from the other Tributes and their warders. It's snide and mocking. I am not in on this joke. I am the butt of all of them.

The king smiles then, but his feels genuine. It's kind, not cruel, and I unearth a tiny kernel of hope. Even if the citizens of his court are monsters, maybe the king's soul reflects the golden warmth of this palace.

"You may call me Atlas," he says smoothly, and there's a gasp in the room.

I scrunch my nose, considering his response.

"Not like an important title or something? Your Majesty? Your most exalted and benevolent one?"

Atlas lets out another chuckle, this one, too, threaded with kindness, not disdain. It's deep and rich and settles over my shoulders like a protective mantle. Who cares what the rest of them think if the king...if Atlas...finds me charming? Perhaps I'm getting ahead of myself, though.

"Not at all. I'm here to find a partner. I'd hardly expect my most treasured companion to refer to me by a title. My bonded will refer to me by my name." He winks, and every rational thought flies out of my head. I'm supposed to have dinner with this Fae? I'll make a complete fool of myself. I have no idea how to behave or to act around someone like him.

"Please say yes," he urges in that same way that makes it sound like it's my choice. The look he gives me makes me feel like I'm the only girl in this room. In this palace. In this entire kingdom. Maybe in all of Ouranos. I've never been treated like anyone important or special in my life. I could get used to this.

"Yes..." I whisper, and he tilts his head in an expectant gesture, waiting for more. "Yes...Atlas," I try, and at that, he breaks into a radiant smile. My hand still held in his, he presses his mouth to the back of it and I stop breathing. His lips are warm and soft but firm, and I wonder what they would feel like against mine. As if reading my mind, he looks up with a gleam in his eye that makes my heart nearly fly from my chest.

"Wonderful," he says. "I look forward to it."

At that, Atlas drops my hand and sketches me a quick bow before turning to the other nine Tributes. "Ladies," he says, "I also look forward to learning more about each of you. Please wait for an invitation to visit me soon." He then bows again with a fist pressed over his heart before departing the room. When the door closes behind him, everyone bursts into conversation.

Gabriel wraps his hand around my arm and hauls me towards the door.

"Let's go," he says, obviously furious with me. At a look over my shoulder, I find Apricia watching me like she's contemplating the best way to slice me up and have me for dinner, probably served in a stew laced with bitter spices.

Gabriel tugs me into the hall, his grip so tight I wince.

"You're hurting me!"

He shoves me against the wall, pressing his forearm across my throat. "Is this a game to you, Lor?" His eyes flicker with anger. "Do you think I won't send you back to Nostraza in a flash if you fail here?"

I cling to his arm, trying to relieve the pressure on my windpipe. I open my mouth, my answer caught in my throat. When he sees what he's doing, Gabriel eases up. But only enough so I don't pass out in the middle of the hall.

"What is wrong with you?" I hiss. "Didn't I win dinner with the king?"

Gabriel shakes his head. "You did. And I'm not sure why. Why is Atlas so interested in you, Lor? Who are you?"

He narrows his eyes as if he's sure I'm keeping something from him.

"I'm no one. I don't know why he chose me. Frankly, no one is more surprised than I am. He probably just feels sorry for me." The words tear out of me, but I can feel them for how pathetic they sound. That's all this is. He's humoring the poor Final Tribute before I inevitably meet my death at the end of one of these insane challenges. That way, he can tell everyone an amusing tale about how he dined with The Umbra rat who really believed she had a chance at becoming Aphelion's next queen.

"Let's go," Gabriel says. "Next time, keep your temper. No one wants a queen who would be more comfortable in a tavern brawl than a ballroom."

"She provoked me!" I shout, indignant. Gabriel stops, turns, and looms over me. *Zerra, he's really intimidating.*

"So be the bigger person, Lor. That's what *queens* do."

Again he turns his back to me and stalks away and I have to admit, as his words sink in, I feel more than a little ashamed.

After Gabriel delivers me back to my room, I head straight for where I stuffed the old grey tunic Mag retrieved for me earlier. Pulling it out, I run my fingers along the hem and rip it open where I feel the hard bit I'm searching for.

A small red jewel tumbles into my hand, and I stare at the precious family heirloom, grateful to have it back. Having it with me makes me feel a little bit closer to Willow and Tristan. I hold it up to the light, the facets winking, except for one smoothed side that looks like it was sliced from an apple.

On the dressing table sits a jewelry box and I rummage through the contents, picking out a golden locket large enough to fit the stone inside.

Snapping it shut, I hang the chain around my neck and secure the clasp. Staring into the mirror, I take a deep and grounding breath, gripping the locket tightly in my hand.

Chapter Eleven

The sun is sinking over the horizon when a knock comes at my door the next evening. Mag has already helped me dress in a floor-length gown of golden silk draped to hide the angles of my still-gaunt frame. I almost look voluptuous thanks to the way she's stuffed me into this thing.

Once again, she's covered my scar with makeup, so it's nearly invisible. I'm still not sure how I feel about that. I haven't been sleeping well, and there are dark circles under my eyes that she's also hidden away. It's so quiet here at night compared to the prison, where I was used to being surrounded by the sounds and smells of the other inmates. I miss Tristan and Willow so much it makes my heart cramp, and without them I toss and turn, the nightmares of the past twelve years poisoning my dreams.

A Fae male enters the room, pushing a cart laden with bottles, scissors, combs, and pins. His white-blond hair is styled into an artful coif that doesn't budge an inch as he stomps towards where Mag is dabbing streaks of golden dust onto my cheeks at the dressing table.

"Callias," she breathes, clearly relieved by his entrance. "Finally. I sent for you days ago."

The male sidelines her with a glare, his eyes a brilliant shade of violet. "I am Aphelion's most coveted stylist. You think you can just snap your fingers and I'll come? I have a list of clients as long as my cock." He holds his hand up against his mouth and says to me in a conspiratorial whisper, "And believe me, that is *very* long, sweetheart."

Mag lets out a sound of indignation and slaps him on the back of his head while I smother my snort.

"This is a Tribute," Mag says, gesturing to me. "Who desperately needs you. Surely you understood what it meant when I said this was an emergency? Don't make me go to your mother. I've known you since you were in diapers, young man."

Callias's nostrils flare as he rubs his head and bestows Mag with a dark glare. "Well, I'm here now." He flicks his head, but nothing moves on his perfectly gelled hairdo. Mag doesn't seem to have dislodged a single hair with her slap, either. "Tell me what we're working with."

His attention turns to me and his face falls before his lip curls. I'm getting so used to curled lips and wrinkled noses and prolonged once-overs, I see them when I close my eyes. I throw up a hand before he can speak. "I know. I'm vile. I'm disgusting.

I'm an Umbra rat. I'm beyond hope. I've heard it all. Can we save the insults and get on with it?"

At that, Callias blinks his bright purple eyes, a slow smile stretching across his face. "Well, well, you're going to make things interesting around here, aren't you?" He moves behind me, where he catches my gaze in the mirror. "I think you're already my favorite Tribute."

I can't help the smile that surfaces at his approval. Something tells me Callias, Aphelion's-most-coveted-stylist-with-a-very-long-cock, doesn't impress easily.

"But this hair," he says, picking up my ragged ends and running them through his fingers. "We must do something about this immediately."

"Can you fix it?" Mag asks in a whisper, as if they're discussing cutting off my leg.

"Of course I can fix it," he snaps. "But it won't be easy. My cart."

To my surprise, Mag dashes across the room and wheels over Callias's cart, stopping it next to me. He rummages around in the contents, procuring a golden comb and a pair of shiny scissors. Without another word, he sets to work, chattering away as he gossips about a hundred people I've never heard of and will probably never meet. From the way he's talking, I presume they must all live in the Sun Palace or be part of the nobility.

"...and Gemma claims the captain doffed her in the pantry, but I've heard a rumor it was actually Gemma *and* Irving." He snorts. "Amateur. When you've juggled two females and one male all at once, *then* come and talk to me."

"You mean *Gabriel*?" I ask, incredulous, as his scissors snip away.

Callias pauses. "On a first-name basis with the captain, are we?" I see his eyebrow go up.

"And the king," I add, and that makes Callias's smile widen.

"Well done, Umbra rat." He winks, and I smile again, not minding the way he says it.

Mag makes a sound of impatience and rolls her eyes. "If you two would stop flirting? Someone from the king's retinue will be here any minute." She wrings her hands, looking at the door.

"Yes, yes, I'm done," Callias says. He smooths my hair back and I have no idea what kind of magic he possesses, but I look like a completely different woman. He's cleaned up my ends and made my hair shine like starlight reflecting off a dark surface. Somehow, he's made it look longer and less blunted. I touch it and turn my head left and right.

"You're amazing," I say in wonder.

"I know," Callias says with a nonchalant air. "There's a reason I am the most coveted stylist in Aphelion." He picks up a small glass jar full of tiny capsules and hands it to me. "Take one of these a day. It'll help your hair grow faster. I can't bring it all back at once, but within a few weeks, it should be a respectable length."

"Really?" I ask, taking the pills and opening the bottle. They're transparent, with tiny flecks of gold suspended inside. "That's incredible." I swallow one down.

"Just a bit of beauty magic." He shrugs, though I can tell he's pleased by my reaction. When I stand, he snags my chin between his thumb and forefinger, tilting my face so it catches the light.

"I'll see what I can do about this. Those healers have no finesse. Slap a bandage on and call it done. It's barbaric."

I shake my head, pulling my face away and covering my cheek with one hand while the other clutches the golden locket hanging around my neck. "No. I don't want you to do that."

This scar is a reminder of the two most important people in my life. I received it trying to protect Willow from the warden's anger. I'd stepped in front of her to shield her just as he was about to strike, and he caught me instead. He was so angry he beat me bloody until Tristan intervened and then Kelava turned his wrath on him instead.

It took three other guards to get him off Tristan and we were both in the infirmary for weeks. When I got out, this scar, several broken ribs, and countless bruises remained. It probably seems silly to anyone else, but this scar is a reminder of what I'm here to do and what I'll lose if I don't win a place at the Sun King's side.

Tristan and Willow are the only things that matter.

Callias must see something in my expression, because he gives me a grim nod and doesn't argue. "Let me know if you change your mind."

"Thank you," I reply.

His answering smile is crooked. "Good luck with the king. Something tells me he's going to have his hands full with you."

Mag shoos him out of the room just before a pair of guards arrive, dressed head to toe in golden armor. Next strides in Gabriel, who gives me an assessing sweep, his wings rustling.

"Looking a little more presentable, are we?" he says, and I narrow my eyes. "Let's hope you can pretend you're the lady you're trying to impersonate."

"You're such an ass," I say, stepping into my slippers.

"I've been called worse, Tribute." He jerks his chin towards the door. "Let's go. You're going to be late."

"Zerra, you're so bossy," I snap, following him out of the room. We make our way through more winding halls. The sun has almost set, and the palace seems even more lively than it does during the day. We pass numerous rooms where people are drinking and laughing while music floats through the corridors.

In another room, couples dance, their feet as light as air as they spin about the room. Past another door, I glimpse some of the other Tributes and I come to a stop, watching them. They're gathered in the corner of a salon as they observe a trio of performers. A juggler, a fire breather, and a Fae who's bending herself into curves that don't seem possible or natural.

Apricia catches me looking, her glare hard as she whispers to a Tribute with pale skin, white-blonde hair, and icy blue eyes. The second Tribute gives me a shy look and then smiles. It's not especially big or welcoming, but at least it isn't a scowl. Perhaps I can find at least one ally in this group. When Apricia notices, she bats the Fae on the arm and she turns away.

"What are they doing?" I ask Gabriel. Even though they've all been terrible, a part of me wishes I was in there too. This environment seems far less intimidating than where I'm currently headed. Nerves bunch in my throat as I think of the Sun King and his radiant smile. What am I going to say to him?

"They're enjoying their evening and would gladly give their left eye to trade places with you." Gabriel's words are pointed.

I look over at him. "Right. Of course. Let's go." He nods and continues leading me through the palace until we arrive before a set of the tallest, widest doors I've ever seen. They could fit several carts through and accommodate a giant with ease. They gleam in polished gold, the emblem of the Sun King emblazoned across them.

A pair of guards wave us through and if I thought the palace was grand, it nearly pales compared to the opulence of the king's apartments. Gold and gemstones and silver and pearls cover every surface. As we walk through the space, the thick golden carpet muffles my footsteps. Gabriel leads me into an enormous semicircular room with a window that stretches the entire length of the wall and looks over the sea.

The setting sun paints the water in hues of pink and orange, and every time I think I've witnessed the most beautiful thing I've ever seen, I find yet another to surpass it. I wonder if I'll ever get over this sensation of seeing everything as if for the very first time. I've barely lived. My entire life has been experienced on the edge of nothing.

"Lor," comes a smooth voice as I enter. The Sun King is resplendent, if casual, in brown pants and a white shirt open at the collar. He's beautiful. He could be wearing the drab grey uniform of Nostraza and still be dazzling. "I'm so glad you're here."

He approaches and kisses the back of my hand while my thumping heart tries to kill me. "Your Majesty," I croak, and he raises a chastising brow. "Atlas," I correct. "Thank you for inviting me. It's an honor." I think. The king is so extraordinary, I'm sure this is *supposed* to be an honor, but I still have so many questions about why I'm really here.

"The pleasure is all mine. Please have a seat." He walks to the table and pulls out a chair before addressing Gabriel. "Thank you for bringing her. I'll call for you when we're done."

Gabriel hesitates, looking between me and the king as if he can't decide which one of us to scold. "Behave," he says to neither of us in particular. Atlas lets out a low chuckle as I settle into my seat, and he pushes in the chair. While he takes a seat at the corner from me, Gabriel's footsteps fade out of the room.

It's then several servants emerge from a doorway, bearing large tureens and platters of food. They place everything before us, someone filling my glass with sparkling wine. The array of food is dizzying. I don't know what most of it is—all I know is that it's fresh and colorful and smells incredible.

A servant places several heaping portions of food on my plate. Roasted chicken and potatoes and some concoction of leaves and nuts and dried fruit smothered in a creamy dressing. Before me sits a basket of fluffy white bread with soft butter and a dozen other things for which I have no name.

"Please eat," Atlas says, and I hesitate for only a fraction of a second before digging in. The moment a bite of chicken touches my tongue, I groan. It tastes so good, this feels like magic. How is it possible for anything to taste like this? "Do you like it?"

"Like it?" I say. "This is beyond anything I've ever eaten."

Atlas looks around the room at the servants stationed along the perimeter. "Leave us," he commands, and a moment later, we find ourselves alone.

"What was it like in Nostraza?" he asks, catching me off guard. This wasn't the topic of conversation I was expecting this evening. "I take it by the way you're devouring that bread, they didn't feed you very well."

My face heats at his comment. I'm such an animal. I'm sure the other Tributes only nibble at their food and pretend they're stuffed after just a few bites.

"I'm sorry," I say through a mouthful. Now that I've been getting sustainable amounts of food, it feels like my body is trying to make up for lost time, a constant ache of hunger gnawing inside my stomach.

"Don't be sorry," Atlas says, his smile gentle. "Please. I'm happy I can provide this for you. And that you're out of that place."

"But you're going to send me back if I lose," I say. "That's what Gabriel told me."

Atlas furrows his brows, his expression turning serious. "Unfortunately, that is the agreement we have with The Aurora."

"Agreement?"

Atlas sighs and sits back, taking a languid sip from his wine. "It's complicated."

"Well, I think I have a right to know, since this concerns me and my welfare." I've stopped eating, my hands sitting in my lap, gripping the soft silk of my gown.

Atlas leans forward, resting on his elbows, getting so close I can smell his warm cinnamon scent. I want to bury my nose in his throat and inhale every drop like this food.

"You *do* deserve to know, Lor, but this is a secret that can never leave this room. The only people in all of Aphelion who know the real truth about the Final Tribute are myself and the kings who came before me. And soon, you."

I can't help but feel like he's trying to dance around a secret he doesn't want to reveal. I wait, doing my best not to be dazzled by his very existence and focus on what's important. Mostly answers about what, in Zerra's name, I'm doing here.

"How much do you know about the Sun Queen Trials?" Atlas asks, studying me.

"Nothing. Until a few days ago, I'd never heard of such a thing. I've spent half my life behind the walls of that prison. I know very little about Ouranos at all. I know we're south of The Aurora, but that's mostly it."

Atlas looks me up and down and then opens his mouth to speak. "A long time ago, a very long time ago, Aphelion and The Aurora came to an agreement. I won't bore you with the details of how it came about, but essentially, The Aurora was granted one mortal Tribute in the Sun Queen Trials. And vice versa."

"Why?"

"A balance of power," Atlas says. "The Aurora and Aphelion are the two strongest realms in Ouranos. As a check, both realms agreed that whenever the Trials took place, there would be the opportunity for one of their own to become queen."

I frown, trying to follow the chain of what he's laying out for me.

"That seems very complicated," I say. "Why would they do that?"

Atlas shrugs. "I can't claim to know what the kings and queens of thousands of years ago were thinking. But the agreement is binding and the Final Tribute has secretly come from each other's home for as long as memory."

"Why secretly?"

Atlas smiles as though my string of questions amuses him.

"First off, it's a secret because the people of Aphelion would not be happy if their new queen came from the north. Even though it's never actually happened, the fallout would be unpleasant."

"By never happened, you mean the Final Tribute has died every time."

Atlas presses his lips together and nods. "Yes."

"And I suppose those were all 'accidents'? Is the Final Tribute *conveniently* disposed of? Surely you don't want someone from The Aurora ruling as your queen, either?"

Atlas regards me carefully. "In theory, I don't, but I'm forbidden from interfering with the Trials. There are emissaries from The Aurora keeping a close eye on the proceedings. You asked why my ancestors did this, and while I can't be certain, I suspect their reasons have to do with ego and pride. If the Final Tribute were to ascend, it would be enough to know one of their own sat on their rival's throne. It was never meant as a way to infiltrate the other's court, but rather to serve as a symbol that no one's power in Ouranos is absolute."

"Why are you rivals with The Aurora?"

"Aphelion and The Aurora are two opposing sides, Lor. The warm light of day and the cold lights of the night. Our power works against one another, and we've always battled for dominance. It's just how things have always been."

Atlas picks up his fork and pulls off a piece of chicken from the roasted thigh on his plate. I watch as he puts it into his mouth, mesmerized by the way his throat bobs on his swallow. His eyes never stray from me, his clear blue gaze intense as a wild storm.

"The Sun Mirror will ultimately decide our next queen," he continues, gravity in his tone. "She will then ascend and become Imperial Fae. And I will gain full and unlimited access to my magic." He pops a piece of bread in his mouth.

"What do you mean?"

"That's the point of the Trials. My power depends on forming two halves into a whole. While I am currently in possession of considerable magic as High Fae, this union serves to complete the maturing of that power, multiplying it and bestowing it on both rulers to wield. Every court is in possession of an Artefact that determines the ascension of their respective rulers." He pauses. "In The Aurora, it is a torch," he says before I have the chance to ask the question already perched on my tongue.

The heaviness of that information falls between us like a stone. *Magic.* Gabriel had said if I won, the magic of an Imperial Fae would be mine. High Fae magic would be one thing, but Imperial magic would give me more power than I've ever thought possible.

"What kind of magic do you have?"

Atlas smiles and takes a sip of wine. "I can control light. Illusions are my specialty."

"What does that mean?" I ask, intensely curious.

He sits back and waves a hand. Suddenly, we're sitting on the ocean floor, surrounded by blue water, tendrils of seaweed, and schools of colorful fish. I gasp. "This is incredible. It looks so real."

Atlas shrugs. "It can be surprisingly useful."

I stand up, noting how there's even sand at my feet, swirling as I step through it. I reach out, and my hand goes through the mirage, the illusion sparkling with points of light where I've touched it. If I look carefully, I can see more of them shimmering around us. They're the only hint the image isn't real.

Atlas laughs at my wonderment before he waves a hand and the sea melts away, leaving me once again in his dining room. I hold my hand to my chest and look at him.

"It doesn't scare you that The Aurora might have a claim on your crown?" I ask, returning to the thread of our previous conversation. "Despite what you say about it being only a symbol?"

Atlas takes another sip of his wine and gives me a skeptical look as I return to my seat. "I trust that if the Sun Mirror chooses you, it will be because your intentions towards me and my court are pure. That you will fight for what will become your new home."

"I have no loyalty to The Aurora," I say with resentment, not sure why I'm telling him this. But I owe The Aurora nothing. It isn't my home, and it took everything from me. If given the chance, I'd crush the entire kingdom to dust.

Atlas's mouth tips up into a satisfied smile. "Then all the more reason I don't need to worry."

He studies me over the rim of his glass, his bright aqua eyes boring into me. There's a look so raw and open, I feel stripped down to my skin. "I also maintain the possibly foolish hope that I will fall in love with my queen and that she, too, will fall in love with me. A Fae's life can be very long, and longer still if they're bound to someone they don't love."

If I'd thought the idea of magic took the wind out of me, this one bats me clear across the sky. I swallow and stab a piece of potato with my fork just for something else to focus on. Stuffing it in my mouth, I chew slowly as I wait for my heart to settle.

When I've regained my composure, I ask, "Why me?"

He shakes his head, resting an elbow on the table and his chin on his fist. "Because the Final Tribute has always come from Nostraza, and you were the right age, I suppose. Rion didn't share his reasons with me."

"Rion?"

"The Aurora King," Atlas answers, his expression going soft as he reaches out and pushes a lock of hair behind my ear. The brief touch of his fingers brushing my cheek draws goosebumps over my skin. "They really kept you in the dark about every-thing, didn't they?"

The kindness in his words, the sympathy in his voice, makes tears flame behind my eyes. Even if they brought me here to die, no one has ever spoken to me this way. It breaks some-thing loose inside, shaking me from the stranglehold of a life I thought I'd be trapped in forever. I was sure Nostraza would be the only existence I'd ever know.

But why did the Aurora King let me go after all this time? Why offer me this slim chance at freedom now? And why not send Willow instead? That seems like it would have been the safer choice for him. Nevertheless, I'm grateful she's not the one here with her life and her dignity hanging in the balance.

"Please," I whisper. "Can you get my friends out? Tristan and Willow? They're all I have. Gabriel said it doesn't work that way, but you're a king."

Instead of answering, Atlas pushes back from the table and stands. He holds out his hand, and I glance at it before I slide mine in. He draws me to stand and then leads me through a set of doors to a balcony that looks over the ocean. The sun has set and the stars bloom brightly in the sky. Everything about this place is so wondrous and surreal, I can't believe I've had the opportunity to spend even a moment as part of it.

I inhale the sea air as it cleanses my lungs.

Atlas draws me to the railing, letting go of my hand and leaning on his elbows.

"I'm sorry," he says. "But I can't do that. Our agreement is for the Final Tribute only. If you fail, then you have to go back to Nostraza, or I risk a war."

"And you can't do that for a lowly prisoner," I say, my voice wooden.

"Lor—"

I raise a hand. "It's fine. Of course, I don't expect you to go to war for me. I'm just one mortal who means nothing to you. I'd never want that blood on my hands."

He stands up straight, tipping my chin up with his finger so his gaze meets mine. "I'm sorry. I wish I could change this."

"If I win...could we get them out?"

Atlas smiles then, his thumb sweeping over my jaw, the comforting gesture thawing the heavy block of emotion that always sits frozen in my chest. "We could definitely negotiate with Rion then."

Before I let that tenuous hope dig in its claws, I remember the enormity of what I'm facing. I pull away and face the water, gripping the railing. "But the Final Tribute has never won. So this is all entirely hypothetical."

"Lor, there's a first time for everything. I'll do everything I can to protect you."

"Why?" I ask. "So you can continue your feud with the Aurora King?"

He lets out a soft laugh. "Not at all. I said that's how my ancestors felt, but it isn't how I feel. I'm not interested in the ancient politics of Ouranos and petty grudges that have existed so long no one can even remember what they're about. I want to find someone who is worthy of that crown. I want to build a life with her and experience all the love and passion of a symbiotic union. I will protect all the Tributes. You're here because of me, and if you get hurt, then it's my shame to bear. I couldn't live with that."

I marvel at the male before me. "How can you be real?" The question slips out without my meaning to, and Atlas laughs. It comes from deep within his chest, a mellifluous sound that's as warm as the tendrils wafting off melted chocolate. He's radiant when he smiles, but like this, he's incandescent.

His gaze meets mine, swirling pools of blue searing into me with a heat that curls deep in my stomach. Moonlight glints off the planes of his cheekbones and the line of his jaw. His brown hair shimmers like it's spun from copper. He touches my cheek, a finger tracing my scar with a careful touch. I brace myself, waiting for the inevitable comment about covering it up, but instead, his expression turns thoughtful.

"The Final Tribute has never survived, but that doesn't mean it's a rule of the game. Perhaps the right one just hasn't come along yet."

He's standing so close I can feel the whisper of his body against mine. I fail to resist the overwhelming urge to lean into him as I press myself against the hard planes of his chest and the strong curves of his thighs. He dips his head and my breath goes ragged when he presses the gentlest kiss to the corner of my mouth.

I'm a helpless minnow as he reels me in closer, an arm circling my waist and tightening against me. He's all muscle and hard lines encased in warm skin. He shines so bright, it's hard to believe Zerra didn't build him from individual droplets of sunlight she was holding on to for safekeeping.

He tips my chin up again, his mouth now so close to mine, I feel the nips of his breath against my lips. He tastes like berries and lemon and a hint of the smoky wine he just drank.

"Lor—"

"Your Majesty," a guard interrupts, cutting off Atlas's next words. His white wings establish him as one of the other nine warders. Atlas arches an eyebrow that suggests he's not happy about being disturbed, but he doesn't drop his arm from my waist. If anything, he pulls me tighter.

"What is it, Jareth?" he asks in a clipped tone.

"You're needed in the council room. The messenger you've been waiting for has arrived." Jareth's eyes flick to me for a fraction of a second before returning to the king. Atlas dips his head before Jareth retreats inside the palace.

Atlas looks back at me, his fingers tracing the curve of my jaw. "I'm so sorry to cut our evening short. Lor, I would like to know you better. I hope we can do this again. It's important to me you're comfortable in my presence. I meant every word I said tonight."

The air in my chest twists into a snarl thanks to his overwhelming presence and the countless surprising revelations he's shared. "Of course," I say, trying to sound in control of myself. "Thank you for dinner. It was something I'll never forget."

Atlas smiles and finally drops his hold, stepping away. I feel his absence, like it's a physical thing sheared from my body. "I'll send for Gabriel to walk you to your room."

I lay a hand on Atlas's arm, feeling the flex of muscle beneath his shirt.

"If it's okay with you, I think I can make my own way back. Is it all right if I explore the palace? I'd love to go out to the beach. I've never seen the ocean before."

"I suppose that means you've never gone for a swim in the sea?" he asks, his smile patient, and I shake my head.

"You must think I'm such a fool. I have done so little and experienced almost nothing in this life. Compared to the other Tributes, I'm so ignorant and...uncultivated. You can put me in this beautiful gown, but you can't hide what I am." My words drop off at the end. The last thing I need is to draw attention to my differences, but something about Atlas makes me feel welcome and safe, and that he won't judge me for anything I tell him.

He lowers his head and peers at me, meeting my eyes. "No. I can see the life you've lived in the depths of your eyes. You are no fool, and you are not ignorant. Perhaps you didn't learn how to waltz or play the piano, but those are things the rich do merely to fill their time. They aren't important and they mean nothing. You've *lived*, Lor. You must have experienced so many terrible things in that prison."

I suck in a breath, feeling my eyes burn again. It's getting harder and harder to hold back the tears I've kept leashed for so long. Here in this place with the sun on my face and the roar of the sea in my ears, I feel like I can let go of the reins that have bound my spirit for so long.

Now that my days are more than just cruel words and empty stomachs and sharp fists, my tears beg for the release I've never allowed. A key has been turned on every door of my life and nothing will ever be the same again. *I* will never be the same again. If I'm returned to Nostraza, I fear for my ability to survive. In just a few days, Aphelion has scratched at the surface of the shell I've worn like a coffin.

"I'm so sorry again," Atlas says. "I don't want to cut you off, and I want to finish this conversation. Will you dine with me tomorrow?"

I blink, wiping the tear from the corner of my eye. "What about the other Tributes? They already hate me enough without me spending two nights in a row with you."

Atlas frowns. "Right. I wasn't thinking. I'll find another way to devote some time to you then, so it doesn't look like I'm playing favorites. Give me a few days to figure something out."

"Okay," I whisper. "Thank you."

I push away my questions about why Atlas is being so kind and why he wants to spend more time with me. I suppose he must harbor some measure of guilt for bringing me here, and there's definitely pity. No matter what he says, he can use me to make a statement to his enemies, and I'd do well to remember it. But the way he spoke to me and looked at me tonight doesn't make me feel like I'm any of that.

"And of course, feel free to explore wherever you like," he adds. "You'll be safe anywhere within the palace walls."

Jareth appears at the door again. "Your Majesty," he says, impatience threading his tone. "You're needed now."

"I'm coming," Atlas says. "Good night, Lor."

"Good night," I say, and then the Sun King is gone.

Chapter Twelve

Nadir

N adir held the invitation in his hands, the golden paper scrawled with shiny gold ink invoking an ostentatious contrast to the somber blacks and greys of his study.

"What's that?" Mael asked, dropping onto the black velvet couch in the center of the room, his feet kicking up on the low table in front of him.

Nadir scoffed, rereading the missive. "It's from Atlas. Aphelion is holding their ridiculous Sun Queen Trials again, and I'm invited to a ball in the Tributes' honor before the final challenge to *celebrate* whatever wretched females are still alive after Atlas has done his best to torture them. Barbaric tradition."

Mael cocked his head, a dark eyebrow arching. "And he invited *you*?"

Nadir responded with a low chuckle. "Probably one of his lackeys who didn't know any better. I'm sure he's not actually expecting me to show." He tossed the card on his desk and then kicked Mael's feet.

"Get your filthy boots off my table."

Nadir walked to the bar situated under the long bank of windows, pouring himself a shot of brandy. He tossed the contents back in one gulp, the smooth liquid burning down his throat and warming his chest, but it did nothing to soothe his agitation.

He glanced over at his beloved pair of ice hounds, Morana and Khione, lounging in front of the fire. They bore the stature of small wolves and could tear out a man's throat on command. Their faces rested on their paws, the tips of their thick, white fur glowing from the light of the flames.

"So you have no idea who took this girl?" Mael asked, getting back to the previous subject of their conversation.

"They were Fae," he replied. "That's all I could tell. The scent was faint."

"And there's no hint of which court might have taken this mysterious prisoner?"

"If I knew that, don't you think I'd already be there?"

Mael leaned back, folding his hands behind his head. He wore black leather armor polished to a shine, and his black curls were cropped short. His deep brown eyes and skin gleamed with tinted reflections of the violet and crimson aurora rippling in the sky, offering the only source of illumination in Nadir's study.

"What did you tell your father?"

"That I found no trace, other than evidence the ozziller did, in fact, get her."

"And you're sure it didn't."

Nadir poured himself another glass, the first one going down a little too easily. "I tracked the one that was lurking around the area and found its nest. There were no signs any mortal was ever there. She was taken. Flown out if the lack of a scent beyond the Hollow is any indication."

"So it could be Tor or The Woodlands or Aphelion," Mael answered. "Likely not Alluvion." He paused, and Nadir turned to look at his lifelong friend and captain of his personal guard.

"When's the last time we did surveillance inside Heart?" Nadir asked, peering out the window. The sky was black and cloudless, ribbons of purple and pink and teal running in blazing streaks of color.

Mael leaned forward, resting his elbows on his knees and clasping his hands. "Heart? Why? You think Heart is involved in this?"

Nadir shrugged. "Stranger things have happened."

"It's been a few months," Mael answered. "But I can send some scouts. Ensure things have remained...quiet."

Nadir nodded. "Yes, do that. And set up a regular schedule. Something about all this feels off."

He looked back at Mael. "Where the fuck is Amya?"

Mael rolled his eyes. "She'll be here. Zerra's blessed, you're in a shitty mood."

Nadir smirked into his glass. "Can you tell the difference?"

"I really can't. Give me a glass of that."

Nadir turned back to the bar and poured a second drink. He walked over and handed it to Mael when both their attentions were drawn to a thud at the window. Nadir turned to find Amya hovering outside, whips of colored light forming wings on her back, keeping her aloft.

Casting out a thin tendril of cobalt light, she flicked the latch on the window before it opened. She shot through and landed on the carpet in a crouch, as light as a feather. Like Nadir, her eyes reflected the colors of the aurora backdropped against midnight irises.

She wore black leather leggings and a fitted corset, her brown shoulders bare. Streaks of crimson, violet, and emerald ran through the twin braids that hung down her back. Another flick of light slammed the window shut with such force it rattled every pane along the wall.

"Will you be careful?" Nadir snapped. "If I have to replace those windows again..."

Amya grinned and Nadir rolled his eyes as she took the glass from his hand, polishing off the remaining brandy before she handed it back. Addressing Mael, she planted a hand on her hip, cocked her head in Nadir's direction, and asked, "Why is he so pissy?"

Nadir let out a low growl from his throat.

"He's mad your dear old dad is keeping something from him," Mael stage-whispered across the room, and they both burst into laughter.

"If you two are quite done," Nadir said, folding his arms over his broad chest. Mael and Amya exchanged conspiratorial smiles right before she dropped onto the sofa next to him. She propped her boots up on the low table in front of her and leaned back.

It was then Morana and Khione both roused from their places in front of the fire and padded over, resting their heads on Amya's lap, both of them begging for her attention.

"What's up, big brother?" she asked, scratching Morana behind the ear, while Khione let out a plaintive whine.

Nadir's eyes dropped to her feet, but he said nothing, wanting to get on with things. He filled Amya in on what he'd already told Mael about what he'd learned regarding prisoner 3452.

"And you don't know who she is? Or who took her?" Amya asked, leaning forward with her elbows braced on her knees.

"Is there a fucking echo in here?" Nadir asked, and Amya narrowed her eyes.

"Why are you so sure this is important?" she asked. "Has Father said anything else about this prisoner? Ever?"

Nadir shook his head. "When I told him there was no sign she'd survived, he seemed relieved, though I got the sense he was trying to downplay her existence. It makes no sense that he'd care about the fate of a single girl. Why does she matter, and why did he have Kelava watching over her?"

"Those are all good questions, but it could mean anything," Amya said. "What makes you so sure this is worth pursuing? This girl could be anyone. Maybe she's an illegitimate sister he disposed of in Nostraza and is just relieved she's gone."

Nadir scoffed. "Don't be ridiculous. Father wouldn't care that much about any of his children, bastard-born or not." He gritted his teeth, squeezing the empty glass in his hand.

"You have a point," Amya said, and their gazes met, a lifetime of pain filling the hollow between them.

Mael rolled his eyes. "Zerra, you two are so *damaged*."

Nadir and Amya pinned him with their unsettling twin gazes. "Shut up," they chorused, and Mael snorted out a laugh.

"You know, therapy would be a lot more beneficial, and decidedly less dangerous, than these revenge schemes you two are always hatching."

Amya looked back at Nadir, ignoring Mael. "What do you want me to do?"

"Sniff around the other courts. See if you can uncover anything about a mysterious girl who's appeared. She might be hidden or out in plain sight."

Amya nodded. "I've got reliable spies in Tor, Alluvion, and The Woodlands. My Celestria contact was just captured, so I'll need to find a replacement. Shame. She was good." She bit her bottom lip. "And of course, I still haven't managed to sneak anyone into Aphelion."

Nadir nodded. "Start with the rest. With any luck, Aphelion has nothing to do with this. I'm sure Atlas is far too busy fucking a stable of eager young females under the guise of finding a bonding partner. He'll have his hands quite full."

Amya wrinkled her nose. "Not the Trials again. You'd think after what happened last time, they'd put an end to this."

"We need to find that file," Nadir replied, dismissing Amya's comment, not giving a shit about Aphelion, Atlas, or the future Sun Queen. "It went missing for a reason. I just hope it hasn't been destroyed."

"Where are you going to look?" Mael asked.

"My father's study, to start."

Mael and Amya exchanged a wary glance. "That's a little risky," she said.

Nadir made a noncommittal sound as he turned back to the window. "With risk comes reward. I hope."

"Nadir?" Amya asked, and he looked over to where she sat. "You really think this could take Father down? Is that what this is about?"

He shrugged, running a hand through his loose dark waves as he let out a deep sigh weighed down with centuries of grief.

"I don't know, Am, but there's only one way to be sure, and every option we have is worth exploring."

CHAPTER THIRTEEN

LOR

O ver the next week, I spend my mornings training with Gabriel for hours as he works to build my strength, stamina, and dexterity. The healers have returned a few more times, reversing the damage done during my time in the Hollow. I'll never be a master with a sword, but at least I know how to cope without seriously hurting myself. He's loosened up around me a little and glares at me only sometimes instead of all the time now, so I check that off as an improvement. I hear nothing from Atlas, despite what he said about wanting to see me again soon.

I try not to let it sting. He's a king—he has an entire realm to rule, and he has nine other Tributes to spend time with, too. I have to remind myself not to be dazzled by his charm and beauty, no matter how much I'm drawn to him. I'm the Final Tribute. I am here as nothing more than a sacrifice, and despite what Atlas claims, he doesn't want an alleged criminal as his queen. That night, he'd let me think I was special, but I remind myself that I am nothing and it will always be that way.

My afternoons are spent with Madame Odell and the other Tributes while I'm schooled on the fine arts of etiquette and decorum. There are music lessons and dance lessons and art lessons. All of it is lost on me. The other Tributes have training in piano and the violin and play like angels. They already know all the steps to the lilting waltzes of Aphelion. Their brush-strokes are perfect, conjuring painted golden roses that look real enough to pick and sniff. I fumble my way through as the others scrutinize me. Some are wary, some are cruel, and some pretend to ignore me completely.

I've been in Aphelion for nearly two weeks when Gabriel arrives to walk me to the dining room for lunch. I'm in another golden dress, the array never-ending. Around my neck hangs the golden locket I've claimed as my own. No one will miss one trinket in this sea of decadence. I clutch it in my hand to ground myself as I prepare to face yet another uncomfortable meal. Gabriel eyes me as we walk, something clearly on the tip of his tongue.

"What?"

"You're looking better. Healthier."

I shrug. "Thanks. A lot of good it's going to do me in the first challenge."

"You hate it here." It's not a question. "You'd rather be in Nostraza? Starving and beaten and locked away?"

Still clutching the locket, I look at him. "It's hard to explain." Of course, I don't miss the damp and the cold cruelty of Nostraza, but I miss Willow and Tristan with such ferocity it leaves me dizzy. Nostraza may have been miserable, but there I was with two people who loved me. Who cared if I lived or died.

"They all hate me," I say, referring to the other Tributes. Gabriel cocks his head, raising an eyebrow.

"So what?"

"So—" I frown at him. "So I don't want them to."

Gabriel shakes his head. "If you're going to be a queen, Lor, you have to get over worrying about what people think about you. Rulers have to make hard decisions that don't always make them popular."

I huff out a laugh. "And behave like a bastard, like you?"

Gabriel stops, placing a hand on the door handle, and winks. "Something like that." He pushes open the door and directs me inside.

When I enter the cozy dining room, the conversation comes to an abrupt halt. I suppress a sigh, trying to take Gabriel's words to heart. Inside Nostraza, I held a certain kind of notoriety as the prison troublemaker. While the other inmates may not have all liked me, most of them respected me. In Nostraza, I understood the hierarchy. I knew how to manipulate the system to my advantage. After all the years I spent there, I was comfortable in my somewhat elevated role as one of its longest-standing prisoners. Here, surrounded by the wealth of Aphelion, I'm a fumbling amateur trying to navigate a new set of rules that soar way over my head.

The other nine Tributes are already seated on either side of a table running down the center of the room, Madame Odell perched at the head like a snooty gargoyle. An empty seat waits at the far end, presumably for me. Everyone stares as I sink into it and do my best to appear somewhat elegant. Next to me sits Halo, a woman with a head of curly black hair and deep brown skin. She gives me a tentative smile.

"Hi," she says, nudging my shoulder with hers. I try not to flinch at the movement, still uncomfortable with casual contact from others and desperately trying not to look weird because of it. None of the other Tributes have addressed me directly before without my initiating it.

"Hi," I say, returning her smile with a careful one of my own. Across from me sits Marici, the icy blonde-haired woman I noticed in the salon the night I had dinner with Atlas.

She too smiles, her pale blue eyes like frozen lakes. "It's nice to see you." She lowers her chin and curves her shoulders inward. "How was your dinner with the king? I've been dying to ask."

Halo giggles, covering her mouth with her hands. "Marici, it's not nice to pry," she says, her smile revealing a set of perfect white teeth. In spite of everything, I find myself grinning back.

"He's very..." I wave a hand at my face as if to indicate I've grown warm, and both Fae burst into appreciative laughter. Apricia sits at the far end of the table, glowering at us as if she wants to put a stop to any fun we might dare have in her presence.

"Ahem," Madame Odell says, silencing the general chatter around the room. Halo sends another smile my way, and the tight band that's taken residence around my heart loosens a fraction. Perhaps things can improve if I keep trying.

"I know you've all been busy with your training and lessons, but I thought it prudent for us to get to know one another better. Though most of you are already acquainted thanks to your place in society, not everyone here travels in the same...circles."

She levels a thin-lipped smile my way as nine more sets of eyes study me. My hand clenches around the fork next to my plate. It's hardly my fault I've never been to any of their stupid parties.

"Why don't we all introduce ourselves properly?" Apricia asks, tossing her long black hair over her shoulder. "I'll go first."

Madame Odell eyes her, clearly not a fan of being interrupted, but gives Apricia a slow nod. "Very well. Proceed."

Apricia wiggles in her chair, her smile smug. "I'm Apricia Heulfryn, first daughter of Cornelius Heulfryn, warden of the 24th district, leader of the Sun Stars and veteran and hero of the First and Second Sercen Wars. I am skilled in the fine arts, interpretive dance, and have won the Golden Bell at the Aurelius Festival three years in a row."

When she finishes, the room is so quiet I hear a mouse roll its eyes in the corner. Everyone in the room regards her with wariness, not sure what to make of her monologue. Madame Odell clears her throat, giving Apricia a bemused look.

"That's very...nice, Apricia," she says and gestures to the woman sitting next to her. It's the pale red-haired Tribute I walked behind during the first meeting with the king. She introduces herself as Hesperia, keeping her introduction a little less grand than Apricia, though still full of self-righteous ass-patting. I'm glad I wasn't born into their society—not if it makes me an unbearable snob.

They proceed around the table, everyone listing some accomplishment or family tie that must be important and, I guess, is supposed to be impressive, but it mostly sounds like posturing. Maybe Gabriel is right, and I don't need their approval.

Nevertheless, a cold sweat breaks out at the back of my neck as the introductions move around the table. Madame Odell appears to be saving me for the end. I wrap a hand around my locket, feeling the edge of the hinge dig into my palm.

I'm not shy. I've spoken in front of hundreds of people in the mess hall in Nostraza, usually when I was out to stir up some trouble. But they were the lowest scum of the earth. Murderers and rapists and thieves. Many of them didn't deserve even the indignity of Nostraza. Here in this beautiful room and this beautiful palace, faced with ten of the most elegant females I've ever seen, I feel like a worm curling over the toe of their delicate silk shoes.

Madame Odell drops her piercing gaze on me. "And you, my dear?" The way she says the last two words suggests I'm anything but.

I try to speak, but my throat is starched dry. I clear it and try again. "I'm Lor. I'm from...The Umbra," I say, remembering no one can know the truth about Nostraza.

I think about Atlas and how I'm being used like a pair of dice on a gameboard. My life is worth nothing to these people. I think of the Aurora King, still wondering why he chose me for this. If I somehow manage to win this game, he'll face me as the queen of his rival. After everything he's done, why would he risk it? What does he have to gain?

My fingernails dig into my palms. I don't care what agreement brought me here. I'll win this contest, and then I'll storm Nostraza and tear it down brick by fucking brick with my bare hands. I'll get Tristan and Willow out, and then *Rion* is next.

He probably still thinks I'm harmless, broken, and beaten, but I'll prove to him otherwise.

"Lor?" Halo has laid a gentle hand on my arm, and I realize everyone in the room is staring at me. Again. "Are you okay?"

I blink, surfacing from the well of my thoughts and returning to this golden room and this golden palace with its spread of luscious food, most of which I don't even have a name for. Before me sits a bowl of soup, thick and yellow, dotted with a dollop of cream and a sprig of green.

"I'm fine," I say, pushing a piece of my hair out of my face. It keeps coming loose from the pins Mag uses to make it more presentable. It's grown a bit longer thanks to Callias's pills, brushing past my shoulders now.

Madame Odell tosses me a pinched look, and I wonder if she's ever had a genuine smile for anyone in her life.

"As I was trying to tell you," she says, folding her hands on the table, casting one more irritated look in my direction, "I brought you here today to prepare you for your first task. It will occur in two days' time, and you'll need to be ready." Whispers erupt from the Tributes while we all exchange fearful glances. Madame Odell raises a hand, calling for silence yet again. "Ladies, please. I'm not at liberty to disclose the details of the challenge, but I *can* tell you that you might want to brush up on your history lessons."

It's then she finally cracks into a slow, delicious grin, her vicious gaze finding me. Though the corners of her mouth are turned up in the imitation of a smile, there is nothing warm or welcoming about it. "You've all had the finest tutors gold can buy in Aphelion, and I hope you've all paid attention."

Even if I were from The Umbra, I wouldn't have had tutors or lessons. Half the people from The Umbra probably can't even read. Not only that, I've spent my life behind thick stone walls, ignorant of the ways of Ouranos.

I know the continent comprises six realms, including Aphelion, bordered on the east by The Woodlands and the west by Alluvion. In the north, The Aurora is bordered by Tor and Celestria. There was once a seventh realm in the center of the continent, but it has been gone for a very long time. These are simple questions even a child with a map could answer.

I pick up my wineglass and take a large gulp, hoping it will steady my fluttering pulse. The only consolation is that a trivia contest doesn't sound especially dangerous, so I cling to that speck of hope. When I invariably lose, the worst that can happen is I'll be sent back to Nostraza. I'll be no worse off than I was, and at least I can see Willow and Tristan.

But then we'll all be trapped there and our one chance at freedom will be gone forever. I'll never get an opportunity like this again. I have to win this somehow. For them.

The Tributes converse amongst themselves while the next course is served, and I turn over the options in my head. Maybe

Gabriel will help me, though he was clear that warders could only assist with weapons training.

I'm sure no one in this room is going to be eager to offer their guidance. I'm the competition—even if I'm not much of one. There must be a library somewhere. If nothing, I learned how to be resourceful in Nostraza. I need to use that to my advantage.

A servant sets a plate before me. Bone china is edged in a glossy rim of gold and topped with what appears to be a tiny chicken. I poke at it with my fork, assessing it from every side.

"Game pheasant," Halo says, leaning over with a whisper. "Very tasty."

Sure she's mocking me, I look up at her with my forehead furrowed, but there is only kindness in her expression. "And those are fiddleheads," she says, pointing to the strange curled vegetables nestled next to the bird. "Toxic if cooked improperly, but delicious when eaten with salt and sauteed with butter."

"Toxic?" I ask, poking the deadly greens with my fork. Halo covers her mouth, holding in her laughter.

"They'd only give you a tummy ache. Don't worry. The king's chefs know what they're doing."

"Oh," I say. "Okay. Thank you."

Halo nods and, as if to put me at ease, spears a fiddlehead and pops it into her mouth, chewing with a flourish. I grin and follow her lead. It crunches between my teeth with just the right amount of give, the flavor earthy and fresh.

I'm so used to bland and more bland, I'd forgotten this is what food could taste like. Once again, the tears I've spent my life clutching threaten to fall. I've never pitied my position in life, instead choosing to accept the lot I'd been given. It was a price that had to be paid until I found a way to my freedom. But for the first time ever, I despair at how the hand I was dealt had been played with a stacked deck.

While I was wasting away, getting beaten, worked to death and worse, these soft and beautiful Fae were living in silks, drinking wine, and sleeping on pillows made of feathers. It's difficult not to harbor some bitterness about that.

Madame Odell raises her hand, asking for silence yet again.

"I also brought you here to discuss a rather delicate subject." She dabs her napkin at the corners of her mouth as the servers sweep into the room to retrieve our plates.

Despite my nerves about the challenge and supposedly toxic food, I managed to eat half of my pheasant and most of my vegetables. Thanks to a steady diet of decadent cooking, I'm filling out, my dresses no longer hanging off me like a sheet draped over a skeleton. I've never looked or felt physically better in my life. A few sore muscles from Gabriel's training, but that's a minor inconvenience.

"Throughout the Sun Queen Trials, it's imperative you are on your best behavior," Madame Odell continues. "You are here not just representing the court, but seeking the king's hand in a bonding. I don't have to tell you that to portray yourself as anything but the most chaste of future queens would be to your detriment."

Some of the girls turn red as they cover their mouths in embarrassment.

"I bring this up because during every Sun Queen Trial, there is at least one Tribute who finds herself in a compromising position with someone. Be it their warder..." A chorus of gasps whips around the table and I resist the urge to roll my eyes. "...a member of the king's staff, or even the king himself."

That stops us all dead.

"The king?" Ostara asks. She has chestnut hair woven into a braid that wraps around the crown of her head and dark grey eyes that complement the olive tone of her skin. "Could that happen?" The tone in her voice suggests the thought doesn't scandalize her, but rather that she is very, very hopeful about it. As I think about Atlas and the feel of his fingers on my cheek, the way he smelled, the way his chiseled body felt against mine, I can't really blame her.

"It has happened," Madame Odell says, pursing her lips together. "And it never ends well for the Tribute. So you'd do well to remember that if you want to warm the king's bed for the long term, you'll forgo doing so now, no matter how charming and handsome he is. He's just a male and can't be held responsible for his actions. It's up to you to ensure your relationship remains appropriate."

Again, her gaze flicks to me as if I'm a dark stain, blotting out the purity of a blanket of snow. If they were hoping for a virgin queen in me, that ship is sitting at the bottom of the ocean.

"Well, you don't need to worry about me," Apricia says, once again tossing her black hair over her shoulder. Someone should really get her some pins if it's so very bothersome all the time. "I am still a maiden and plan to remain so until the day I'm bonded to my beloved."

The way she says it suggests she's very confident that her beloved is, in fact, the Sun King. Unable to help it, I let out a snort and then try to bury it in the rim of my glass. It fools no one, and ten pairs of eyes swing to me.

"And you?" Apricia asks with the arch of one of her dark eyebrows. "I suppose a gutter rat from The Umbra has been used more times than a dishrag. Spread your legs for a bit of coin, maybe?" She snickers and Griane, the honey-blonde woman sitting across from her, snickers back. I guess Apricia found an ally and fellow contender for the role of head bitch.

"Apricia," Marici scolds. "That is so unbearably rude. Surely your *tutors* taught you better manners than that." Something warms inside my chest at her words. That she'd actually defend me, given she probably feels the same about my presence here.

If I thought Apricia could be shamed, I thought wrong, because she sniffs and lifts her pointed chin even higher. "We all know she's here as a sacrifice. As a 'message.' Don't pretend she's one of us." At that, she looks at me and wrinkles her nose, sniffing again.

"That's enough," Madame Odell finally interjects, but I can tell she's relishing my humiliation. When she looks over at me again, I shrink into my seat, wishing I could melt into the floor. I hate it here. I hate this. How can I be longing for the enclosed walls of Nostraza right now? Gabriel might not understand it, but in its own strange way, it was home.

"I want to hear the answer," Madame Odell says, and I blink.

"Answer to what?"

"Whether you've been *used*"—she makes a circular motion with her hand—"like a dishrag, as Miss Heulfryn so eloquently put it. It's part of my job to report back to the king on what happens when he's absent and inform him of the Tributes' less desirable qualities."

The room goes so silent I swear I can hear the blink of Halo's long lashes as she stares at me, open-mouthed. I catch her glance, finding sympathy in her expression. Whatever she must see on my face snaps her back to the moment. "Madame Odell, that hardly seems fair to single out Lor."

"I'm not interested in your thoughts," Madame Odell says. "Need I remind you failing a trial isn't the only way you can be eliminated from the competition? Mind yourself."

Halo's mouth snaps shut, and I send her a look that I hope conveys my gratitude that she tried to stick up for me. Everyone else is watching expectantly. I could just lie. I *should* lie. This is no one's business, and no one can prove anything.

"I'm waiting," Madame Odell says, leaning forward, her elbows on the table and her hands folded under her chin. I open my mouth, but no sound comes out.

I'm not pure. I *have* been used and broken. But how do I tell them that most of it wasn't my choice? That I was at the mercy of depraved prison guards who saw me as nothing but a tool to be taken for their pleasure? That I had no recourse and no way to defend myself? That I've spent every day trying to shut out those memories and forget what happened? That I sought comfort in men like Aero to dull the shame of it never being my choice? With Aero, it *was* my choice. It was mine to take when and how I wanted it.

There was so little to cling to in Nostraza. So little comfort to be found within those damp stone walls.

A few snickers circle around the room as I twist my napkin in my hands, my cheeks burning and my eyes filling with tears. I can't hold them in anymore. Halo reaches over and wraps a comforting hand around my wrist. This isn't her fault, but I appreciate the sentiment.

It's with horror that I feel a warm droplet splash against the back of my hand. I can't let them see me cry here any more than I could in Nostraza. These Fae are no different from the guards. They're also searching for my weaknesses. A way to poke holes into the tissue-thin armor I wear.

How dare they treat me this way? They brought me here against my will as a fucking joke. An example to be made. And they think they're all so superior. I take a deep breath. It shudders with the intensity of my fury. My tears dry up and I stuff them back down. Down, down, down where they belong. Where they have always belonged and where I will keep them forever.

I look up, pinning Madame Odell with my most withering glare. She raises an eyebrow, the corner of her mouth lifting into a sneer. Instead of answering, I stand, shoving my chair back with such force it echoes with a loud screech that causes everyone to wince. Without another word, I slap my napkin on the table, turn, and storm from the room.

CHAPTER FOURTEEN

I walk as quickly as I can, trying to put as much distance as possible between me, Madame Odell, and the other Tributes. Right now, I'm about one inch tall. I wipe at my cheeks, clearing away the single line of moisture that marks the moment I nearly cracked.

But I can't crack yet. I have the entire Sun Queen Trials to endure, and I intend to survive.

Don't cry. Don't cry. I repeat it over and over. Even if they can't see it, they'll know. Females like Apricia can smell it. She's just like Jude was in Nostraza, always digging into every shallow innocuous scrape, forcing them to fester into raw, gaping wounds.

Not paying attention to where I'm going, I find myself in an unfamiliar part of the palace. But this place is so huge, it's all unfamiliar. The halls are empty, devoid of the servants usually bustling about their duties.

I have work to do. I need to find a library. Madame Odell said I needed to know Aphelion's history, and I have a lifetime of learning to cram into my head, with less than forty-eight hours to do so. I have no time to waste.

I open doors at random, finding them either locked or leading to empty bedrooms, sitting rooms, and salons. Music floats down a hall, and I follow the sound, hoping to find someone I can ask for help.

After I turn a corner, I find myself in a populated part of the palace, golden marble and gilt gleaming in every direction. A set of double doors sits open at the end of the hall, servants scurrying in and out of a room packed with Fae and humans.

I raise an eyebrow at the sight. It seems the Sun Palace is the venue of endless parties happening at all hours of the day. I know little about entertaining, but I always assumed this kind of celebrating occurred in the evening.

As I approach the fete, I attempt to stop a harried servant to ask where I can find a library, but they brush past me in their haste, ignoring my question. But they also don't stop me as I enter the room. This is definitely a party and these people are definitely having a very good time.

Someone plays a piano in the corner while others lounge on settees, laughing continuously as though they're telling a joke that never ends. A table laden with colorful treats sits in the center, Fae and mortals feeding each other morsels with their fingers.

A male Fae has a female pressed up against the wall where I enter, her leg wrapped around his waist and her skirt pushed up to expose her smooth bare thigh. I can't tear my eyes away as he devours her mouth, his hand sliding under the fabric of her dress as she arches her back and gasps.

They're not the only ones enjoying themselves. More couples, trios, and one quartet are in various states of undress and various throes of passion. Thinking of the incident with Madame Odell makes me even angrier. How dare she demand chastity from me when this sort of debauchery is going on right in the king's palace?

It's then I notice the Fae I was just watching is familiar.

"Gabriel?" I ask and he looks over, nonplussed for a heartbeat, before his confusion morphs into a cocky grin.

"Lor, what are you doing here?" The female he has pressed against the wall eyes me with disdain, her nostrils flaring delicately.

"Relax," I tell her. "He's just my annoying babysitter."

Gabriel barks out a wicked laugh and steps back from the female, unwrapping himself from her leg and returning her skirt to its normal position. "I apologize," he says to her. "It seems duty calls. I'll come find you later."

She pouts and then leans over to whisper something in his ear that makes his eyes sparkle with anticipation, a grin cracking his face. Tossing one more glare my way, she saunters off, her hips swinging generously. Gabriel watches her ass, his smile never leaving, until she disappears through the crowd.

"This is what you do when you're not busy with me?" I ask, folding my arms over my chest.

"That's hardly any of your business, Final Tribute."

I drop my arms and resist the childish urge to stomp my foot. "Don't call me that."

"What do you want, Lor? Why aren't you doing ladylike things with the others?" He peers at me more closely then, analyzing my face. "Have you been crying?"

"No," I snap, but it's obvious I'm lying.

"What happened? Who did that?" he asks, his tone suddenly fierce. If I didn't know better, I'd think he was being protective. That almost sets off a fresh wave of tears, but I close the tap on their flow.

"I don't want to talk about it," I say, grabbing his arm and tugging him out of the room. "I need your help. Madame Odell said the first test is in forty-eight hours and that I'll need to know my Aphelion history to have a chance."

Gabriel snorts. "And you don't know any Aphelion history."

I roll my eyes. "Is this a talent of yours? Stating the obvious as though it's some profound revelation?"

He laughs as though I haven't just insulted him. Must be nice not to care what anyone thinks about you. "So what's your plan, Tribute?"

"I need a library. With books."

"As opposed to a library full of squirrels?"

I suck in a deep breath, mining the depths of my patience. "Will you just help me?"

Gabriel ponders for a moment, scratching his chin, his stubble making a rough sound. His blond hair is loose today, brushing just past his chin, and the laces on his shirt expose an expanse of smooth bronzed chest. He's not as dazzling as Atlas, but he has a certain appeal. No wonder that Fae was reluctant to let him go.

"I'm not supposed to help you," he says, narrowing his eyes. "That would be cheating."

"You won't. You're just giving me a tour of the palace." His expression turns skeptical. "This contest isn't fair, anyway. All of those Tributes have been studying for their entire lives. You showing me a library isn't going to offer me any real advantage." I pause and inhale deeply. "But I have to try."

He considers me thoughtfully. "Okay, Tribute. Let's go."

I let out a sigh of relief as he strides past, not looking back as I scurry to catch up. He directs me through several halls and corridors until we reach yet another set of wide doors, these carved from pale yellow wood. One stands partly ajar and we slip inside the room.

What I see makes my heart stop. More of that pale yellow wood has been assembled into hundreds and hundreds of shelves that arch up to a soaring ceiling. A library. A real library.

The only "library" at Nostraza was a single rickety shelf at the back of the mess hall where the occasional new book might have appeared when a guard brought one from home. Since most of the inmates couldn't read, I always claimed them. I had to make do with reading the same books so many times they nearly fell apart, and I could recite them line for line.

Tristan and Willow could read too, but Willow had little interest in books and Tristan enjoyed reading, but only when he had nothing else to do. Books were my obsession, but I'd never been able to get my hands on enough.

This library exceeded every whimsical fantasy of what I thought a library could be. I run my hands along the shelf closest to me, seeing the titles blur together before my eyes. Romances and adventure books. Medical books and atlases. Books on religion and ones filled with pictures meant for children. I could spend the rest of my life reading and never get through them all.

Gabriel is watching me with a curious expression. "I'm sorry," he says, and I furrow my brow at the uncharacteristic softness in his tone. "Had I known you'd like this so much, I would have brought you here sooner. You're free to borrow anything you want."

Scanning the walls of shelves, I feel something twist in my chest. I'll never get the chance to read them all. I'll be sent back to Nostraza or to the afterlife before I get anywhere close.

"I need the history books." First, there's the trivia challenge to overcome, and then I can dream about books. "I'll start there."

Gabriel tips his head. "Let's ask the librarian for help." A few minutes later, we're directed to a small alcove lined with books bound in golden leather. It seems even Aphelion's history echoes the grandeur of this palace and its king.

Gabriel helps me carry a stack of thick volumes to a small table, and I put another pile down next to them.

Dropping into a chair, I puff a lock of hair out of my eyes. These books are huge. It would take someone months to get through them all, even if they read all day.

The despair on my face must be apparent because even Gabriel is moved to ask, "Is there something I can do to help?"

I shake my head. "You're not supposed to help me." I look up at him. "I have to win fairly. They're going to be looking for reasons to get rid of me." His answering nod is grim.

"You're perceptive, Lor. You may not have grown up at court, but you already understand its ways."

I'm surprised at the compliment, and an involuntary smile tugs on the corner of my mouth.

I don't know why I care what he thinks, except something about Gabriel reminds me of Tristan. His irreverence. The way he talks and swaggers like he doesn't give a shit what anyone thinks. In Nostraza, I was terrified that attitude would get Tristan killed, but instead, he always managed to charm everyone into falling in love with him.

I pull a book off the pile, running my hands over the cover embossed with scrolls and vines of gold. "The Complete and Unabridged History of Aphelion," I read, then look up at Gabriel. "I guess this is as good a place as any to start."

His face is contemplative. "Good luck. I'll come and check on you later."

"Gabriel," I call, before he leaves. "Thank you."

He gives me a wry grin. "Don't thank me, Tribute. If you win, you make me look good. Imagine how it felt when I drew the short straw. The other warders are still ridiculing me for it."

Then he winks and walks away, laughing as I glare at his wide back and mutter "asshole" under my breath.

Hours later, my eyeballs ache like someone plucked them out, ground them into the sand, and then stuffed them back into my skull. I've lost track of the time I've been here, skimming through reams of pages.

Thankfully, there's a lot of overlapping information, but the history of Aphelion stretches through millennia and there are literally a million things the test could include. Will they expect me to recite the endless legacy of Aphelion's kings and queens? Perhaps it will be questions about the area's primary source of commerce and trade. Maybe they'll ask about the very Trials we're competing in, which have a long and sordid history unto themselves. When I'd reached that section, I'd read carefully for a hint of the pact with The Aurora that Atlas had mentioned, but there was nothing. He hadn't been exaggerating when he'd said it was a closely guarded secret.

Gabriel stops to visit every few hours, bringing me food and water and tea, which I accept gratefully. Eventually, Halo and Marici find me where I'm spread out over a mountain of books.

"Can we help?" Halo asks, sitting down across from me and pulling an open book towards her.

I give her a suspicious look, mistrusting everyone's intentions. They were nice to me earlier, but they've both been pretending I didn't exist until now. "Why?"

Halo blows out a breath and leans back in her chair. "I'm sorry about what happened earlier today. That was really unfair."

I say nothing, waiting for her to continue.

"And I'm sorry we've been ignoring you. Apricia—" She looks over at Marici, who is now sitting on the chair next to me, her hands clasped in her lap. "Apricia forbade any of us from speaking with you. Her family is powerful, and she could make life difficult for us if she chose to."

I look between them. "And?"

"And Apricia is a bitch and I'm sorry we ever listened to her," Marici says. "We're sorry, and we hope you'll accept our offer of friendship. No one should have to face this contest alone."

My shoulders collapse. I'm tentatively optimistic about her words and even more furious with Apricia. I could stay mad at Halo and Marici, but I recognize an olive branch when I see one. Right now, I need allies more than I need to hold on to a grudge.

"Okay," I say. "I would like that."

Marici beams, her icy blue eyes sparkling.

"Let us help you," Halo says, flipping through the book in front of her. "I'll show you some techniques my tutors taught me to help remember all these boring facts."

Marici giggles, covering her mouth. "Me too. I happen to be an expert on the royal family."

Finally, I've found some support, even if it took them a while to get there. But I can't say no to their help. I need every advantage I can get. "Thank you," I say, reminding myself to keep up my guard. This could all be a ruse to trick me somehow.

But Halo and Marici exchange a sincere glance and then turn to me, rolling up their sleeves with determination.

"Okay, tell us where you've left off," Marici says, her voice brooking no nonsense. I point to the page I was reading and set to work, deciding to push aside my reservations for now. For the next few hours, they share their tips, helping me remember the heads of each of Aphelion's twenty-four districts and the names of the most powerful Fae families.

As my brain expands with more and more facts and figures and dates, they start to jumble like they've been dropped into a barrel and rolled down a mountain. Still, I keep reading. Keep making notes. Halo and Marici quiz me until I can recite facts and figures by rote. When they've had enough, swaying in their seats from exhaustion, I send them away. But I remain in the library, still studying, refusing to stop.

After all, one more page could mean the difference between my life and my death.

It's late at night, the first challenge only hours away, when I awake with a jolt. My face is pressed to a book, and the lantern on the table flickers with dim light. I know I should go to my bed for a few hours.

It's then I realize I'm not in the library alone. The king sits across from me, and that causes me to sit up straight. His hand is clasped around my forearm from where he must have nudged me awake.

"Are you okay?" he asks, concern in his clear blue eyes. "It's late. You should get some sleep."

"I can't," I say, shaking my head and gesturing to the scattered books. "I have to keep studying."

The king squeezes my arm and my heart squeezes in response. "Gabriel told me you've been reading for two days straight." I nod, wondering if I've broken some rule and am about to be scolded. "I'm impressed, Lor. Anyone who shows this much dedication to the Trials would make a worthy queen."

His encouraging words threaten to uncork the tears I don't have the freedom to shed. In this vast palace full of cruel mortals and crueler Fae, why is the one person who doesn't need to be kind making this effort? Atlas must truly be a worthy ruler, and the type of king every citizen of Aphelion deserves.

"I have something for you," he says, reaching behind his back, his leg pressing against mine under the narrow table. The touch rouses my heartbeat, and Atlas's gaze shoots to mine before he licks his perfect, luscious lips. I imagine what it might be like to sink my teeth into the bottom one, still feeling the ghost of the gentle kiss he placed at the corner of my mouth a few nights ago.

Subconsciously, I touch my face in the same spot and his gaze follows my fingers, his eyes darkening as if he understands exactly what I'm thinking. There's a brief pause before he places a slim book on the table and pushes it towards me.

"What's this?" I ask, dragging it closer. Bound in dark green leather, only flecks of the gold embossing remain. I note the absence of a title as I turn it over in my hands.

"A little something to help you out," Atlas says. "I may have a clue about the first challenge."

I flip open the book, realizing it's about Atlas.

"This is your book?" I ask, scanning the pages, wishing there was a way for me to absorb this knowledge simply by the sheer force of my will.

He shrugs his wide shoulders. "There are many biographies of me floating around Aphelion, but very few tell the complete truth."

I look up at him. "Why is that?"

His smile grows, the corners of his eyes crinkling in a way that leaves me strangely breathless. In the low light of the library, he's like a lighthouse standing on a foggy shore, calling ships home.

"It's not safe for anyone to know too much about me, so I tell different versions of the truth when it suits my purposes. No point in giving anyone information they can use against me." His hand still rests on my arm and he drags his fingers along my bare skin, past my elbow and along my shoulder as he watches his hand carefully. My body erupts into shivers, and I hold completely still, wanting to remain frozen in this spell.

His fingers make their slow journey back down the length of my arm. "Someone I've known and trusted for a very long time wrote this particular edition." When he reaches my wrist, he circles it with his fingers and flips over my hand before he starts to trace loops in the center of my palm. I try to focus on his words as he speaks, but my thoughts have burst apart like soap bubbles. "So it holds the real answers of who I am."

His gaze flicks up to meet mine, those aqua eyes full of something I don't quite understand. The look is so intense, my insides squirm and snap like ribbons whipping against a strong breeze. But the sensation is far from unpleasant. Rather, it brims with anticipation and the promise of something that tastes like freedom. It's how I imagine a bird feels soaring over the clouds.

But I need to stop this. I'm being ridiculous and naïve. We barely know each other and I'm no one special. I have to survive so I can get Willow and Tristan out of Nostraza. Nothing else matters.

"Well, it doesn't seem to be very long," I joke, trying to dispel the tension. "Should be pretty easy to get deep into your head."

I wince, realizing what I've just said, but he responds with a low rumbling chuckle and shakes his head, his radiant copper hair glinting in the lamplight.

"Lor, the Sun Queen Trials have never met the likes of you." He pauses and then leans in close, dropping his voice to a conspiratorial whisper. "I suggest you wear something...practical."

Before I can react to that statement, he winks and stands. With one last lingering look I feel to the tips of my toes, he turns and leaves.

Chapter Fifteen

We stand on the edge of a vast ocean cove, the water so blue it's hard to tell the difference between the surface and the sky, but for the thin line of green rolling hills separating them. A cool morning breeze blows off the water, pulling up gooseflesh across my skin.

After Atlas's hint last night, I opted for my thin leather armor this morning, despite Mag's admonishments. She thought a dress would be more appropriate for the first trial, not understanding why I'd need pants to stand around and answer a few questions. But I couldn't tell her why I knew I had to wear something more protective. I was sure Atlas wasn't supposed to be giving me hints. Besides, after a decade of wearing tunics and leggings every day, I feel more comfortable like this. While I adore the beautiful gowns, I don't feel worthy of them. They're meant for some other version of a Tribute who looks nothing like me.

When we arrived at the shore this morning, I knew I'd made the right choice by listening to him. This promises to be far from a simple game of trivia.

Our head trainer, Master Borthius, faces us, his hands linked behind his back, his dark brown hair blowing in the breeze. He's also wearing leather armor, and now I'm even more sure I made the right decision. Griane stands next to me, shivering in her dazzling gown. Even though her pale skin is turning red from the cold, her golden blonde hair reflects in the rising sun like the perfect Aphelion queen.

We're just outside the city and have a small audience who arrived in the carriages behind ours. Gabriel told me at least one trial would take place in Aphelion's heart, where the citizens could watch, but the rest would be more private affairs. Balling up the strings of my nervous energy, I decide to worry about *that* event later. There's little chance I'll make it that far, anyway.

All ten warders are present, along with Madame Odell and a few others I don't recognize. And, of course, Atlas stands in front of them like a shining beacon where they wait on a nearby hilltop that hangs several feet above the water.

"Welcome to the first trial," Master Borthius says, pacing with his hands laced behind his back, kicking up sand where he walks. "Today we will test you on your knowledge of Aphelion and its history. I hope you've all been studying."

The back of my neck prickles, and I find Apricia smirking in my direction. She also skipped the dress today and is wearing a practical tunic and thick leggings. I wonder if Atlas gave her the same clue. All eight of the other Tributes are wearing the shimmery gold fabrics favored by the king's court. Their faces fell when they were ushered onto the beach and realized their error.

Borthius waves his hand and conjures a giant apparatus from the air. We all gasp at the unexpected sight.

Made of wood, A-framed bracers prop up a long beam suspended over the calm water. Attached to the beam are ten thick ropes woven from rough hemp. They stretch over the water, their ends tied with a giant knot where they land at our feet. More thick knots have been placed at intervals along their lengths. I catch Halo's worried dark eyes across the beach. Everything about this spells trouble as clearly as if someone had written it in giant letters in the sky.

"Please take a hold of your rope," Master Borthius says. "When I give the word, you'll be transported over the water, where this rope will be the only thing keeping you from falling in." A wicked grin spreads over his face. "You'll then be asked a series of questions about Aphelion. For every answer you get right, nothing happens. For every answer you get wrong, the rope will lower. If you answer incorrectly five times, the rope will release." He stops his pacing and sweeps his gaze over us. "And I assure you that no one wants to find out what's waiting in the water. Once you've answered five questions correctly, you've passed the challenge and will continue to the next round."

A million questions singe the tip of my tongue, but he doesn't give me a chance to ask them. He snaps his fingers and suddenly we find ourselves clinging to our respective ropes over the sea. As we lurch into place, the rough rope scrapes my hands and I clench tight as the fibers bite into my skin.

Grateful for my leather armor, I wrap my legs around the rope, bracing my boots against the knot, thankful I'm not wearing those useless golden slippers Mag is always forcing on me.

The rope sways, and I cling even tighter when I hear a scream followed by a splash. A golden bird has already fallen off her perch. I scan the line, trying to figure out which Tribute fell when a dark head emerges from the water, her arms frantically slapping against the surface. "Help!" Elanor screams. "Help me!" A moment later, she sinks suddenly, her scream cut off.

A series of horrified squeaks come from both the Tributes and the spectators, the sound carrying over the water. When I look down, I spy a series of murky shapes streaking beneath me. Dark and lithe, they slither like serpents borne of the sea.

The surface bubbles where Elanor went under and we all hold a collective breath. Nothing happens as the silence stretches so thin it nearly snaps. Terrified, I cling to my rope with all of my strength, my limbs trembling. Why aren't they helping her?

"Get her," Borthius finally says, flicking a lazy hand towards the water. It's then that two High Fae I hadn't noticed earlier march across the beach and dive into the ocean, disappearing beneath the waves.

I hold my breath, counting the seconds and then the minutes as they fail to resurface. What's down there? Did it attack her? From the corner of my eye, I see another dark shape streak through the water, deep below the surface. My hands are already burning from the rope as I cling tighter. But no matter what happens, I won't let go.

Finally, the surface of the water parts and the rescue Fae emerge with Elanor's limp body. Her eyes are closed and her pale skin is blue. I can't tell if she's breathing. A large gash runs across her forehead, blood covering the entire side of her face.

The Fae drag her on to the beach where another Fae wearing a white cloak with a golden cross on his chest waits. A Sun Palace healer. He leans over Elanor, touching her gently.

"Name the thirty-seventh king of Aphelion," Borthius barks, pulling my attention from the fallen Tribute.

"King Diell," a crisp voice replies. I blink, unable to believe we're just moving on with the trial when Elanor might be lying dead on the beach.

"Correct!" Borthius says with a nod to Tesni, a Tribute with deep brown skin and shining silver hair that hangs almost to her waist. He then points to Ostara, who waits next in the line. "And his queen?"

She hesitates and her eyes flicker before her gaze drops to the water where she, too, must have seen those dark shapes waiting.

"Did I mention this is a timed exercise?" Borthius asks, his tone conversational. "When the bell rings, your turn is up and the rope will drop."

Ostara looks up with wide-eyed fear. "Queen Akino," she chokes out, then watches Borthius with bated breath.

"Correct!" He then points to the next Tribute in line, which, unfortunately, is me.

"What were their children's names?" he asks. "As a hint, I'll remind you there were two."

Trying to steady my shaking limbs, I inhale a deep breath as I scan through the reams of information I've crammed into my head over the past two days. A litany of possibilities surface, all jumbling together into an alphabet sludge, but none of them seem right. I toss each one aside and drill into the depths of my brain tissue for another. Colena. Sevannah. Relius. Litsa. Greta. Nope. Nope. Nope.

"You have five more seconds," Borthius says. I grip the rope, the rough weave chafing my hands so they feel like they've been dipped in liquid fire. A bead of sweat slides down the side of my face despite the chilled air.

"Hathor and Osbert," I throw out, desperately grabbing on to the next two names that pop into my head, already knowing they aren't right.

"Wrong!" Borthius cries, and before I can think, the rope drops several feet, my stomach flipping. A scream tears from my throat as I grow weightless for a split second. When I stop, it's with such force my feet pop off the knot that I've been using as an anchor, and my hands slide several inches down the rope, my skin tearing in white hot sheets of agony. I scream again as blood oozes between my fingers, pain lashing up my arms in fiery bursts.

Forcing myself to breathe, I curl my body and find the knot which is now skimming the surface of the water. With measured movements, I carefully reach for the higher knot, hoisting myself up. My hands shriek in protest, but I hold on tight, trying to shut out the pain.

When I've securely recovered my position, I feel the release of a mutual breath from everyone standing in the cove. At least now I know what to expect next time.

Borthius smirks, says nothing, and then points to Hesperia, the next girl in the line. He fires another question at her I don't hear as I try to calm my heartbeat and focus on my surroundings. Whatever she says must be correct because he moves on to the next Tribute. Question after question is lobbed over the water as I try to pay attention, hoping someone else's answer might help me later. But I've barely slept and my head is swimming.

The next girl up is Solana, whose olive brown skin glistens with a sheen of sweat. "What are the names of the primary trade guilds?" Borthius asks. My rope swings around and I watch as the answers cross her face in quick succession.

"Carpenters, Blacksmiths, Goldsmiths, Tailors, and Money Lenders," she answers hastily. But then her eyes widen instantly as she realizes her error. At the same moment, Borthius shouts, "Wrong! You missed the Shipbuilders!"

Solana's rope drops in a sharp descent, and I suck in a sympathetic breath, knowing how jarring the experience is. Wearing those pretty slippers, her feet slide from the knot and her head snaps back as she bounces off the rope and plummets into the water. The only sound is the splash and the echo of her scream as we all crumple into deathly silence.

Again, Borthius waits, staring at the water. He waits and waits. Too long. I want to shout at him to send someone to help her. He checks the golden pocket watch in his hand and then finally looks over at the rescue Fae, jerking his chin towards the water. "See if you can fish her out." Once again, the rescuers trudge into the sea, though they don't seem to be going very fast.

They plunge through the surface and we wait. A few seconds pass. Everyone on the clifftop is leaning forward, peering over the edge like wheat stalks in a windstorm. Atlas runs a hand down his face and then along the back of his neck. He looks worried.

He scans the rest of us as if reassuring himself we're all there. The rescuers are gone only a few more seconds when the head of the first one emerges, and I blow out a relieved breath. But when the second one comes to the surface, I realize they're both empty-handed. Solana isn't with them.

My mouth expands into a silent scream as the two Fae look to Borthius and give him a noncommittal shrug. Bile climbs up the back of my throat, stinging my tongue. Just like that, she's gone. My eyes catch Halo's again while we both turn in slow circles like death's cold hand is spinning us for his pleasure.

Not breaking his stride, Borthius launches back into the challenge, firing question after question down the line. I don't know how long I cling to the rope as he cycles through us. Apricia is predictably the first to answer all five of her questions correctly and is relieved from the test, but not before she bestows us with a smug smile and another toss of her fucking hair. She's then followed closely by her friend Griane, the two embracing before they turn their calculating gazes on the rest of us.

Halo is the next to complete the challenge, and I say a prayer to Zerra when she's delivered safely back to shore. As I continue to languish over the water, I get a few questions right, but mostly, I get them wrong. I didn't have enough time to study. How was I supposed to cram years of learning into two days?

Every time I drop, my hands tear, blood slicking the rope as I cling to it with every shred of my waning strength. My arms are tired and weak and my legs feel like rubber. My feet ache from clamping on to the knot. My vision blurs from exhaustion. I'm not sure what's worse—this agony or those hellish days in the Hollow when I nearly drowned in the rain and was almost ripped apart by a monster into a thousand pieces.

I can't help the tears that stream down my face as my eyes water from the pain. They aren't a sign of my defeat, and I take consolation in that. They're only a physical reaction.

The rope spins me around, and I catch Gabriel's gaze. He's standing at the very edge of the cliff, watching me with intensity. He tips his head—a small nod that seems to say *you can do this*. I stitch up that tiny shred of belief and tuck it into my heart. I *can* do this.

Finally, the only two people left are me and Marici. The skirt of her golden dress is in shreds, and I wince at the reddened welts blooming on the insides of her thighs. They stand in stark, bloody contrast to her snow-white skin. That must be agony. Her icy blonde hair has escaped its braid, the snowy strands blowing in the wind.

It's my turn again, and Borthius clears his throat. "What is the Sun King's favorite color?"

I blink. It seems like such a stupidly simple question with an obvious answer. Gold. Of course, the Sun King favors gold. Right? But which book did I read that in? Again, I flip through the inventory of knowledge I've gathered during the past two days. *I know this.* The answer is so close I imagine I can reach out and jiggle it free from wherever it's been locked away in my mind.

Then I think of the secret slim volume he passed to me. The one he claimed shared his truth. I close my eyes, trying to dredge up the memory. There had been an entire chapter on his likes and dislikes. He prefers strawberries to plums, the violin to the harp, and tea to coffee. But what the fuck is his favorite color?

I cast my gaze up to the hill where both Gabriel and Atlas watch me intently. Gabriel takes a small step forward and crouches on his heels, as if trying to get just that much closer. *You can do this, Lor.* I read the words in his expression again.

My hands slip and I cry out in agony, pain tearing through every limb and pore. The rope is crimson with my blood, slicking the surface. Two dark shapes circle in the water beneath me, monsters waiting for their prey. Can I survive another drop? Can I hold on? Fuck, is this my last question? I've lost count and panic scrapes sharp talons down my spine.

"Red," I whisper, dredging up the word from the bottom of an endless pit. "Atlas's favorite color is red." But my throat is raw and I barely make a sound. Borthius is watching me, and I know my time is running out. I try again, willing the answer from my lungs, gathering the letters, one by one, so I can shout them out across the water.

Then several things happen at once.

A bell rings.

"Red!" bellows from my throat, followed by an audible gasp from everyone gathered on the shore.

Borthius fixes his eyes on me. "Correct," he says, but before I can take a breath of relief, he raises a hand. "But you were too slow."

He lifts his arm in a gesture of finality, and I brace myself, waiting for the inevitable jolt. But it doesn't come, because I've miscounted. I glance up, watching the twisted end of the rope break free from the beam.

Then I'm in free fall. My stomach does a somersault, and I plunge into the icy water with an ear-splitting scream.

Chapter Sixteen

T he water is colder than I expect. It shocks me through to my bones as I sink deep under the surface. The open wounds on my hands and the welts on the insides of my thighs burn like I've been dipped in acid when they make contact with the salty sea. I want to scream. Instead, I screw up my face, wincing and willing myself not to pass out from the pain.

The rope is tangled around my arms and legs, and I frantically try to kick myself free, knowing I only have a matter of moments before those swirling dark shapes come for me.

I force my eyes open, feeling the sting of the seawater. Two murky shapes swim towards me, sinuous and lithe, making a circuitous route and taking their time. Soon, they're close enough I can finally see what they are. Half Fae, half fish. Mermaids? But these are no long-haired beauties from a fairy tale.

Their hair *is* long, but it's tangled and gnarled, floating around their heads in nests of black and blue and green. Their bare torsos and arms are covered in mottled blue skin that shimmers softly. Their eyes are nothing but bright blue orbs with no whites, and their teeth are so sharp they look like they could grind me down to raw beef.

A scream rises in my throat as one of them lunges and then swims back without touching me, its thin black lips spreading into a vicious smile. They do it again, together this time. Swimming for me, they come so close, I feel a current pulse against my skin as they pass.

They're taunting me. Playing with their supper before they sink their teeth in for a juicy bite. With the rope still gripped in my hands, I attempt to fend them off, but I'm quickly running out of air. When one of them lunges again, I dive for it, catching the creature off guard. Its hiss vibrates through the water.

The monsters lunge for me again, but then something distracts the one to my left, and it shoots away, disappearing into the depths of the sea. I don't have time to wonder what's happening. I'm just grateful I only have to face down one of these things for a moment.

Air. I need air. I kick to the surface, bursting into the atmosphere and inhaling a ragged breath. It's barely a sip before I'm yanked back down into the water, coming face to face with the creature, its sharp teeth bared in the imitation of a smile. Digging into my endurance, I cock my arm and punch the creature in the nose so hard its head snaps back.

I hear its howl shudder through the water as it grips its face and writhes, a small puff of crimson dissipating around its head. Taking advantage of the distraction, I pounce, wrapping the rope around its throat and squeezing its neck. I maneuver so I'm floating behind it, and the creature thrashes its gangly arms, attempting to scratch me with its claws while also trying to slice through the noose cutting off its air. I squeeze tighter and tighter. Can you suffocate something that can breathe underwater?

Its chest moves in and out and I take that as a sign it breathes something. Emboldened, I pull on the rope with every ounce of strength. Eventually, the creature's movements begin to slow until its body finally goes limp and it starts to sink. I let go of the rope, hoping it's enough to keep this thing down while I swim for safety.

I kick for the surface, exploding up for a gulp of cleansing air. For a few seconds, I pant, my chest tight and my limbs quivering. I'm exhausted, my body worn and broken. I turn to head back to shore when I notice Marici is no longer hanging on her rope. After a quick scan of the beach, I realize I can't make out her bright white head of hair. *Fuck*. That's what distracted the other creature.

Did she lose her grip, or did they move on to the next question without even bothering to see if I survived? Something tells me it was the latter. I dive under the water, desperately searching for her, but I can't see anything. Swearing under my breath, I plunge into the water again, hoping the creature I choked doesn't return. I swim further, but I'm so weak and tired.

What am I doing? I should just save myself. I've already lost the challenge, and if I make it out of the water, I can at least go back to Tristan and Willow. I don't owe my life to anyone in

Aphelion. But Marici is one of the few people to show me any kindness in this place. I can't just leave her here. Despite my initial mistrust, her help was genuine last night.

Finally, I spot a dark blur in the distance and, after another gasp of air, I swim for it like my feet are on fire. I don't have any rope this time. What do I think I'm going to do? I slip through the water, hoping a brilliant plan somehow materializes.

The creature has its hands wrapped around Marici's neck, its face close to hers like it's offering a lover's kiss. Marici's legs kick feebly and it becomes obvious that her strength is dwindling. It feels like it's been an hour since she fell, though I know it has to have been only minutes. Her movements continue to slow, her limbs going slack. Panic spirals in my gut and I jet forward.

Thankfully, the creature doesn't notice me coming. With what little strength I have left, I ram into it, elbowing the back of its neck and pulling on its hair hard enough to rip out a clump the size of my fist.

The creature lets out a high-pitched screech. I feel the sound ripple around me as it reaches for its head and, thankfully, releases Marici. She's fainted and is sinking fast, so I aim a pointed punch at the creature's windpipe, silently giving thanks to Zerra that my years in Nostraza taught me to fight. I might not know who the thirty-seventh king of Aphelion was, but at least I know how to throw a fucking punch.

The creature crumples, bending in half, its hands circling its throat as its mouth gapes open and closed. I snag Marici around the waist and begin to kick frantically for the surface. My muscles ache and my bones creak from the effort. My toes and fingers are completely numb. There's a movement in the corner of my vision and it's with horror that I see the first creature has recovered and is now streaking through the water. We're finished. This is it. Kicking harder, I know there's no chance I can outrun it this time.

My heart skips as I swim with every bit of my flagging strength anyway, praying for a miracle from Zerra.

Suddenly, the monster stops in its tracks, like a fishhook has embedded itself in its torso. It snaps back, its limbs and head jerking with the movement like a rag doll. I don't pause to wonder what just happened. Instead, I kick even harder.

Once again, we break the surface, and I gulp a deep breath before I start paddling across the cove, focused on the shore. My lungs burn and my legs feel like they're made of clay.

Marici remains prostrate, and I pray she isn't dead. Black spots form before my eyes as I kick and kick, my head spinning. I need healing and rest and someone to save me. I lost and I'm out of the contest, but the last thing I'll do before I'm thrown back behind the wet stone walls of Nostraza is get Marici home alive. Leaving her out there would have meant lowering myself to the same level as the Fae who've done this to us.

Finally, I feel the sandy bottom of the ocean and press my legs against it while I choke on a cry of relief. With a heave, I drag Marici along the sand and then turn around to hook her under her arms. With my back to the spectators, I lug her inch by inch until we finally reach the safety of the beach.

I collapse, falling onto the wet sand, my cheek pressed to the ground as I hack on seawater and the adrenaline screeching through my veins. Marici is so pale it's as though colors have forgotten her existence.

"Someone help her," I whisper, my voice thick and raw. "Someone. Help her."

As the healers descend on Marici, I feel a swarm of bodies around me, calling out instructions to one another. I lie on the beach, my head spinning, while I pray to Zerra for a miracle. I'm too weak and tired to move, pain echoing across my body. My eyelids are so heavy they feel like iron curtains. I groan, my cheek pressing harder into the sand. It's rough and scrapes against my skin, reminding me I'm still alive.

Then my eyes drift shut, and the world disappears.

CHAPTER SEVENTEEN

NADIR

N adir hovered outside the window of his father's study, the swirling lights of his magic forming a pair of multi-hued luminescent wings on his back. He'd already flown past a few times, ensuring his father wasn't still in the Keep. After another pass, he decided the study was as empty as it was ever going to be. Rion had flown to Tor that morning to meet with their tentative ally, the Mountain Queen. But it was best to always be extra sure when it came to the king of The Aurora.

Softly, Nadir landed on the balcony that ran the length of the study. With a flick of his wrist, the lights surrounding him burst open like a flower welcoming the sun before shrinking back into his frame. With a vine of cobalt light, he unlocked the door before he slipped inside.

The thick, dark rugs muffled his steps as he paced slowly through the room. Guards were stationed outside for show, but the king was arrogant enough to believe no one would dare enter this space without his permission. Anyone caught snooping through his things would find themselves at the end of Rion's legendary temper. On any other day, Rion was probably right, but Nadir was too mired in the mystery of prisoner 3452 to keep himself in check.

Nadir cast a ward to muffle any sounds from the room as a precaution. He scanned the many shelves and the spotless desk, wondering where he should start. Perhaps it was foolish to think the king would keep the file from prisoner 3452 in his study, but Nadir had to start somewhere. He was sure the king had it. Something deep in his gut told him uncovering what his father was hiding was important.

Beyond the fact that Rion had been interested in this girl, no one else could have removed a file from Nostraza without setting off an alarm. Only the king could walk in, take what he wanted, and keep it under wraps. Therefore, Rion's study and his desk seemed like the most logical place to start.

Nadir's gaze flicked to the window when he heard a sound, his eyebrow arching as Amya dropped onto the balcony, her own lights dissipating in a fission of color. She swung open the door and stepped inside, rubbing her arms. She wore a short black skirt made of ragged pieces of tulle, her legs covered in thin translucent silk patterned with diamonds. Her black corseted top laced up the front, leaving her arms and shoulders bare. She refused to dress appropriately for the weather, claiming it restricted her movements too much.

"I hate this room," she said, smoothing down the two braids that ran over her shoulders, strands of the bright colors of the aurora running down their length. "Why is it always so fucking cold in here?"

"The temperature is just fine. Perhaps if you put on a sweater, you'd be more comfortable," Nadir replied, resuming his examination of his father's desk.

She wrinkled her nose. "You know that's not what I meant." Amya stomped over in her heavy black boots and hoisted herself onto the desk, crossing her legs. "So. What are you doing in here?"

Nadir glared before he waved his hand over the top drawer of the desk, a burst of colorful mist erupting as he tested for any signs of magic. Maybe a trap or a trigger that might sound an alarm.

His mouth pressed together when he felt it. A snag in the air that surrounded the desk. With careful precision, he pulled apart the threads of magic one fiber at a time, using braided colors of his own light.

"Nadir, I—" Amya started, and he held up a finger to his sister.

"Shut up for a minute."

This work required all of his concentration. One false slip and his father would undoubtedly know of his presence. Amya huffed, but said nothing else as she folded her arms and waited in silence.

Nadir worked quickly but efficiently, circling the desk and dismantling all the bits of warding magic surrounding it. He mentally catalogued how the threads had woven together, knowing he'd have to reconstruct them exactly before he left the room.

After several minutes, he finished and stepped back, letting out a deep sigh. A lock of hair had freed itself from its tie, and he tucked it behind his ear as he looked up at Amya.

"May I speak now?" she asked.

"You may," he replied, and she rolled her eyes.

"Why are you so obsessed with this? If he catches you here, Father will lose his mind."

"If he catches *us* here," Nadir said as he opened the top drawer and started rifling through the papers, taking care to disturb the contents as little as possible. Nadir had never been privy to Rion's secrets and as his eyes skimmed over the documents, he knew there were things that, at any other time, might be valuable.

"Nadir," Amya said, a warning in her tone. "Talk to me."

He stopped and looked up at her. "I can't explain it, but something tells me this girl is important." He resumed his search in the next drawer.

"What is that supposed to mean? Important how? If Father was really keeping this from you, why would he have let you hear his conversation with the warden? Why ask you to go look for her? Aren't you worried you're playing right into some kind of trap?"

Nadir didn't answer as he continued rifling through letters and papers, dismissing them all and moving to the next drawer.

"Of course I'm worried," he said a moment later. "But I don't think he intended for me to hear it, and now he seems to be pretending it doesn't matter, which makes me even more suspicious." He paused and then said quietly, "I don't know." He gritted his teeth, knowing he sounded absurd. "I just have a feeling."

Amya jumped off the desk and walked around to stand next to him. Sensing her gaze, he looked up. "What?"

"I'm worried about you, big brother."

Nadir let out a breath and dropped his head, his hands braced against the drawer he'd been searching.

"You haven't been the same since—"

He shot her a dark glance. "I *don't* want to talk about it."

She raised her hands in surrender, the lights of her magic rippling around her in agitation. "Okay, okay. So you've made clear many times before."

"You think you'd take the fucking hint then," Nadir said, standing straight, planning to move to the other side of the desk. Amya stood in the way, her arms folded and her feet planted wide. She was much smaller than him, coming barely past his chest. But what she lacked in size, she made up for in determination.

"Move," Nadir said, and she spread her feet, squaring her stance.

"You need to talk about this."

"I said, move." Nadir glared down at his sister, his swirling gaze meeting hers. The sky was cloudy tonight, the lights obscured and invisible, but he could feel them as they rippled across the sky. They were as much a part of him as the blood that ran in his veins and the heart that beat in his chest.

Her expression softened. "I just want to be there for you. Like you've always been there for me. It's not your fault. It has *never* been your fault."

Nadir closed his eyes slowly, counted to three, and opened them again, trying to calm the churn of emotions that always felt on the edge of drowning him in a sea of guilt.

"I'm fine," he said. "And it's my job to take care of you, not the other way around."

Amya's nostrils flared at that. He knew his answer would make her angry, but it was the truth. "You know that's not how it is."

"Can you please move? We shouldn't linger here much longer." As if on cue, voices sounded on the other side of the door, and his eyes flicked their way. Amya gave her brother one last lingering look and then stepped aside.

Nadir nodded and recommenced his search. Amya paced in front of the window while he continued rummaging, still coming up empty-handed. When he'd searched the last drawer, he let out a sound of frustration.

His gaze cast about the room. There were shelves and cabinets he could look through next, but a quick check told him none were as heavily warded. It seemed unlikely his father was keeping anything of value there. Nadir wove the warding on his father's desk back together as he considered his options.

Amya stood by the fireplace watching him, but he avoided her gaze, knowing she'd probably start in on him again.

More voices sounded outside the door, and Nadir scowled. It seemed his time was up for today.

Amya moved towards the balcony. "Come on." When Nadir heard his father's voice, his shoulders tensed. As much as he hated to admit it, there was only one thing in the world that frightened him, and it was the king who stood on the other side of that door. Nadir flexed his jaw. He'd risked too much coming here, and it had amounted to nothing.

"Nadir!" Amya hissed. "Come. On."

He hesitated, watching the door. He knew what would happen if his father caught him here, but part of him wanted the confrontation. Maybe he could force the truth about what the king was hiding, but it wasn't worth the fallout. He'd caused enough harm already.

A moment later, the handle on the door turned down, and Nadir lost his nerve. On silent feet, he glided to the balcony door, where Amya was holding it open. As he stepped outside, he heard it click shut, and then he leaped onto the railing.

Multi-hued ribbons of his light erupted around him with a swoosh a moment before he dropped off the edge and let himself fall.

CHAPTER EIGHTEEN

LOR

A soft hand rests on my forehead. With my eyes closed, I lie still as the hand travels down to my cheek, fingers ghosting across my bottom lip before skimming over my chin and then leaving. I frown at the loss of the soothing sensation when I hear a low, deep chuckle and the hand resumes its voyage across my skin.

When I feel the mattress dip, my eyes flutter open.

Atlas sits next to me, a gentle smile on his face. "Hello there," he says, his warm, honeyed voice as soothing as a balm. "Welcome back, Lor."

I close my eyes and suck in a long breath before I open them again.

"Am I alive?" It's hard to be sure. I shift in the bed, testing for a sharp sting of pain, but the movement is surprisingly easy. There's an ache, but it's not the lashing pain I felt lying on the beach before I passed out.

"You're alive and you were amazing out there," he says, awe in his voice as he runs the back of his hand down my cheek. I shake my head, squeezing my fists in frustration.

"No, I answered too late. I failed the test." I push down the tears, pleading to be released. Of course, they were going to send me back to Nostraza at the first opportunity. I'm shocked I'm not already there. My ridiculous dream to become the Sun Queen is over. What was I thinking? Of course, this wasn't my future. My future has always been far more uncertain. At least I'll get to see Willow and Tristan. At that, I nearly start crying again.

"You didn't fail," Atlas says, and I peer up at him, my brow furrowed. "You passed the test, Lor."

"What do you mean? I fell into the water."

"But you got out," he replied. "The trial wasn't only about answering the questions—anyone could read a book and do that. The challenge was also a test of your determination if you failed. That's why the rescuers didn't go in right away when the Tributes fell in. They were giving them a chance to get out on their own. If you made it back to shore alive, then you passed the test."

Tears burn my eyes for an entirely different reason now. "I passed." It's not a question, but a statement. I passed. They're not sending me back to Nostraza. At least not today.

Atlas smiles and winks. "You did. And I'm happy I could help with my little book."

"Right, thank you." Except I'm not sure how much it helped, since I still had to swim back to shore after fending off two deadly monsters, but I guess it's the sentiment that counts.

"What about Elanor?" I ask. "She fell in and had to be rescued."

Atlas shifts where he sits next to me on the bed, his hip pressing against my thigh. "I'm afraid her role in the Trials is over, but eliminated Tributes are given a place of honor in my court. She'll be fine."

"And Solana…" Her name comes out as a breath. The Tribute that never resurfaced.

"That was unfortunate," Atlas says, his expression grim. "It's always a tragedy when we lose a Tribute during the Trials."

"But her family," I whisper.

"They'll be taken care of." Atlas squeezes my hand, lifting it up and holding it in his lap. Bandages are wrapped around it, and I flex my fingers, wincing at the dull pain that shoots up my arm. My heart clenches at his words, as though gold or treasure could ever make up for losing a daughter. A sister. I knew nothing about Solana, but surely someone will miss her. Even this rat from Nostraza had two people who loved her.

"The healers are allowed to give you something for the pain," he says gently, brushing the bandages. "But they're not to heal you, except to prevent your death."

That's when I remember. I shoot up, my body protesting at the sudden movement.

"Marici," I ask, panicked. "Is she okay?"

Atlas presses down on my shoulder, settling me back on the soft pillows. "She's fine. They revived her on the beach, and she's going to make a full recovery. What you did was very brave, Lor."

"Is she out of the Trials?" I ask, knowing how much this must mean to her, too. She told me how much her family was counting on her to win.

"She is, but she's alive, thanks to you." Atlas traces a delicate pattern up the inside of my arm, sending tingles to my fingertips. "Why did you do that, Lor? You risked your life going back to save her."

I shake my head, my hair rustling against the pillow. "I couldn't just leave her there," I say, angry that he would doubt me. "What kind of place is this, where anyone would question that?"

The look on Atlas's face turns inscrutable, his eyes darkening. "You're right. I've grown so used to Fae who exist only to serve themselves and their own ambitions that it's hard to comprehend when someone acts out of selflessness." He peers at me, his gaze intense. "Was it not that way in Nostraza?"

"Of course it was. That doesn't mean I had to give into it completely." I bite the corner of my lip. "Though you should know I did plenty of things I'm not proud of to survive."

He nods as if he understands. And maybe he does. I remember what Gabriel said about the difficult choices kings and queens must make.

"Then you are even more remarkable than I originally thought," he says, rubbing the back of my hand.

I scoff, sure he's mocking me, and look away. He grabs my chin between his thumb and forefinger, turning my face towards him. "I mean it, Lor. When you walked into that throne room the first day, I thought you were the most beautiful woman I'd ever seen."

"I was an hour from death," I say, wanting to dispel this strange sensation in my chest at his words, but he only shakes his head.

"No, you shone like a star. The determination on your face, the fierceness in your eyes. I knew right then you were no ordinary Tribute. You already carried yourself like a queen."

My breath puffs out from my lips as I absorb the absurdity of what he's saying. But what does he have to gain by flattering me? I am nothing to him. And with Elanor, Marici, and Solana out of the contest, he has six far more beautiful and far more cultured Tributes to choose from.

Atlas leans down, his face so close to mine, I inhale his scent. Without meaning to, I take a deep breath as the aroma of cinnamon and honey fills my lungs. The corner of his mouth ticks up, his bright blue eyes playful. He can probably hear my heart pounding. Being this close to him is overwhelming.

"How are the others?" I stammer out, trying to focus on something other than the line of his throat and the way his shirt allows me to glimpse the exquisite curve of his collarbone. His hip presses against mine harder, and I wonder at the appropriateness of him being this casual in my bedroom, recalling the humiliating conversation with Madame Odell.

"I think they're fine," he says, his mouth still inches from mine, his bright eyes lighting up like the sun is awake in them.

"When you're feeling better, will you join me for dinner again? I promise there will be no interruptions this time."

"You've spent time with the others?" I ask, not sure why I'm trying to push him away, but I'm acutely aware of the sensations he's inciting. This is nothing like what I'd felt for Aero back in Nostraza or any of the boys who'd come before him. This is all-consuming. This is like drowning in fire. I could perish in those eyes. Lose myself in his scent. Wrap myself in those strong, muscled limbs and never resurface, content to die and never draw another breath, all with a smile on my face.

His soft chuckle rushes through me like a handful of sparkles dropped from above. It's indulgent but kind. "Don't worry, Lor. I am giving due attention to all the Tributes, as is my duty. But I am only a male and I am searching for my queen. I'm allowed to have my favorites."

I swallow a string of fiery nerves. *His favorites?* Am I happy to be counted among that group or should I be worried he said favorites, plural? Who else is on the list?

"What if the Mirror chooses someone who isn't your favorite?" I ask, sure the hallowed Artefact of this court can't possibly think I'm fit to be its queen.

The look on Atlas's face grows thoughtful. "It has happened in the past," he says, "but it's understood the Mirror knows and takes into consideration the feelings of all parties. It's never been wrong about who would make the ideal queen."

I let out a deep breath. "Well, that's good."

He chuckles again and shifts closer, his big body leaning over mine. Our hips are still pressed together, our chests nearly touching, and my breath flees from my lungs.

He picks up a lock of my hair, twisting it between his fingers gently. It's grown a bit more since Callias's visit and is looking far more respectable. He tucks it behind my ear and then presses his hand into the pillow next to my head.

"I'd very much like to kiss you, my lady," Atlas says, fire burning in his expression. "Would you allow me to do so?"

Unable to speak, I let out a ragged gasp and then nod. His smile grows wide as he lowers his head and, like the softest brush of wings, presses his mouth to mine.

The kiss starts out warm and tender, a delicate touch of silky lips. But then his tongue sweeps against the seam and I part them, wanting more. Wanting to feel him in my mouth. He makes a low sound in his throat before he deepens the kiss. He tastes like cedar and wind mixed with something smokier, like an ancient tree standing in an enchanted forest.

It's then the mood in the room shifts as our kiss grows hungry and frantic. He leans closer, his chest brushing against mine until he's poised above me on the bed, the barest space separating us. I don't have time to wonder why this beautiful Fae is kissing me before he lowers his body, and I moan at the sensation of his weight crushing me.

"Lor," he says, my name filling his mouth in a strangled breath as we writhe against each other. There's the sensation of his hardness between my legs and I lift my hips, pressing harder into his stiffening cock. I marvel that I've been able to incite this kind of reaction in such an ethereal male. He's lived a long time. Surely he's been with many other women and females. I'm just another in a long line of conquests, I remind myself, but right now I don't care, because this feels amazing.

He groans as he swivels his hips. I can feel everything through the thin material of my nightgown, the insides of my thighs growing damp as his tongue plunders my mouth, a hand gripping my hip with possession. He sucks on my bottom lip and then drags his mouth down the line of my throat, where he leaves a scorched path on my skin, like someone has painted me with a brush made of flames.

"Atlas," I say, my hands sliding into his shiny hair, gripping it as I pull him closer. Whatever this means, whoever he is, I want more. I've spent my life surrounded by darkness and the cold, relentless echo of stone. Atlas is the very embodiment of lightness and warmth. The opposing force of ardent fire against unrelenting ice.

The Sun King. Glowing and golden and glorious. I touch his cheek, running my fingers along his smooth skin. I've been peeled out of a nightmare and anchored on top of a golden mountain. Arms thrown wide, I stand at the peak, screaming a tattered song that sounds *almost* like freedom.

He moves against me, making my back arch and my hips lift. His hand slides down the side of my thigh, dragging my nightgown up with it. When his palm stamps into my bare skin, it burns straight to my core. Fingers dance along my ribs, his thumb coming so close, but not quite brushing the bottom of my breast. His mouth continues exploring, his lips questing over my throat and down the angle of my collarbone. I moan, drinking in every sensation. Every moment.

This is *nothing* like I've ever experienced. Atlas isn't a boy, he's a man grown. I can tell from the way he touches and kisses me that a night in his arms would be like being undone and put back together in the best possible way.

"Lor," he begs, his voice cracking on the rhythm of my name.

"Ahem," comes a polite voice from the door. We snap apart to find Mag, a tray laden with food and a silver pot suspended between her hands. "I see you're awake, my lady. The kitchen sent supper."

To her credit, she pretends she sees nothing. Shuffling closer, her eyes on the floor, she sets the tray next to me as though she hasn't just caught the Sun King practically devouring me. Atlas pushes himself up, sitting on the edge of the bed and squeezing my hand with a tipped smile before he stands up, smoothing down the front of his now rumpled shirt. My cheeks heat when he throws me a roguish grin.

Mag keeps her eyes on the tray of food for another moment and then looks up.

"Your Majesty," she finally concedes. "It's kind of you to check on my lady during her recovery."

Atlas sketches a bow, the picture of a proper gentleman. "Of course. It is my sworn duty to ensure the safety of every one of my Tributes."

Mag nods, her lips pressing together as if holding back a clump of words fighting for space on the tip of her tongue. Atlas looks at me where I'm now seated on the bed, my nightgown arranged back in place.

"Mag," he says, not taking his eyes off me. "Once Lor is feeling better, I've requested her presence for dinner. You'll send word?"

Mag drops into a curtsy. "Of course, Your Majesty, but perhaps this should be cleared with Madame Odell? I was told all Tribute activity was to be approved through her first."

Her expression is uncertain as Atlas's smile drops off his face.

"I wasn't aware Madame Odell was the king of Aphelion?"

Mag shakes her head, her eyes falling to her feet, her hands clasped. "Of course not, Your Majesty. I just thought—"

"When I want the opinion of the Trial Mistress, I'll be sure to ask for it," Atlas interrupts, cutting off whatever Mag was about to say next. I frown, watching the exchange with a curious eye.

"Of course, Your Majesty," Mag says, her voice small and quiet.

Atlas looks at me again, his smile returning. "Excellent. I look forward to seeing you again soon, Lor." Before departing, Atlas takes my hand, pressing his lips to the back of it before he spins on his heel and tosses me a wink over his shoulder.

CHAPTER NINETEEN

"Ready?" Gabriel asks, regal in his golden armor, his dark blond hair tied at the nape of his neck. This morning, he dragged me out of bed to train with him, stating I'd had more than enough time to recover from the first trial.

It's been about a week, and Atlas visits me each day. Sometimes he stays for a while and sometimes only a few minutes. He sits by my side and talks to me, asking me questions about my life in Nostraza. He tells me about Aphelion, and I ask all the things I've always wanted to know about Ouranos.

He tells me about the rulers in each realm. Cyan, the king of Alluvion to the west, and Cedar, the king of The Woodlands to the east. He tells me The Aurora is in league with Tor and the Mountain Queen Bronte, as well as D'Arcy, the Queen of Celestria. He shares his knowledge of each court's Artefacts.

The Stone of Tor, the Celestrian Diadem, the Alluvion Coral, and The Woodlands Staff.

I soak up these bits of knowledge like water over dry sand. I've spent so many years in the dark. He tells me of the forgotten realm of Heart and its fallen queen. Its lost Artefact—a crown with a blood-red stone. Her tainted realm is a black stain on the history of Ouranos.

What happened to her? I'd asked, and Atlas shook his head and told me not all magic in this world is meant to be touched by the Fae. That she'd almost destroyed everything on which we stood with her thirst for power. After that, he touches my cheek, telling me I should get more rest. He doesn't kiss me again, a fact that leaves me bitterly disappointed. Perhaps he's found one of the other Tributes more appealing.

Now Gabriel stands at my door, waiting to escort me to lunch with Madame Odell and the other Tributes. I wince as I tuck an errant curl behind my ear. If I thought Gabriel would take it easy on me because I was still healing, I was sorely mistaken. He worked me so hard this morning that I can already feel an ache settling in my muscles.

My hair has grown, though, reaching past my shoulders now. Mag took the opportunity to fuss with it as much as possible. While I preferred its natural wave, she'd twisted it into thick, glossy curls that I had to admit were rather lovely.

I catch Gabriel's smirk through the mirror.

"What?" I ask, turning around to meet his gaze with narrowed eyes.

"Nothing," he says. "It's nice to see some meat on your bones. You don't look like a walking corpse or like someone took a butcher knife to that hair."

I roll my eyes. "You really know how to flatter a girl." I toss my hair again, fluffing it in the mirror, amazed at how smooth and shiny it is. "Callias is helping me grow it out," I say. "It's going to be down to my waist soon." I glance at the mirror and then back at Gabriel. "Does Atlas like long hair?"

It's Gabriel's turn to roll his eyes. "Don't tell me you'd change your appearance just to please him. That doesn't seem like your style."

"I wouldn't," I say. "But I might as well play to my strengths."

Gabriel doesn't respond, and I look back at him.

"Well?" I ask.

He shakes his head, his expression inscrutable. "Who are you, Lor?"

I frown and meet his questioning gaze. "I'm a prisoner from Nostraza. You know that. You're the one who retrieved me."

"Yes, but *who* are you? There is something more I haven't quite figured out yet."

I snort and shrug my shoulders, not meeting his eyes. "I think your imagination is running away with you, Captain."

"Atlas is very interested in you," he says, still studying me as though trying to peel back the layers of my skin.

I arch an eyebrow. "Why shouldn't he be? What you mean is, how could he find me interesting when I'm surrounded by far more beautiful, educated, and cultured females? Why would a king be interested in prison scum like me?"

If I think Gabriel might feel bad that he's insulted me, I'm entirely wrong. "Yes, exactly," he replies, nothing wavering in his expression. "No offense, but there doesn't really seem to be anything that special about you. You're pretty enough, but not compared to the others, and you've got a serious attitude problem. Atlas's type is usually a little...less abrasive."

I'm so startled by his complete honesty that I bark out a laugh.

"You're a real asshole, you know that?" I say, stepping into my shoes and cinching my belt tight.

Gabriel shrugs his wide shoulders. "I just call it as I see it."

"Can we go now?" I ask, after checking the mirror one last time and scrutinizing the scar on my cheek. Mag had insisted the healers try working on it again, despite my protests, and called them in. I had sat perfectly still as they attempted to work their gifts, but the scar was resistant to their magic. I didn't even try to keep my smile contained when they failed, and Mag looked so crestfallen you'd think someone had stolen her puppy. It was then I'd firmly told her I wouldn't be doing that again.

We leave my room and stalk through the palace. I sigh as we near the dining room, wondering what humiliation Madame Odell has in store for me today.

I'm the last to arrive, as usual, and I shoot Gabriel a dark look to remind him this is his fault. He lifts a casual shoulder that suggests he really doesn't care, and I wonder if I can put in a request for a new warder who isn't such a dick.

As usual, Apricia sits next to Madame Odell, her nose already so far up her ass it's a wonder she hasn't run out of air. Halo sits at the end and gives me a small smile as I slide into the seat next to her.

Across from me sits Tesni. Her deep brown skin is contrasted with a sheet of shiny silver hair that hangs down either side of her face. I nod, having never spoken directly with her before.

After I sit down, food arrives, ushered out by servants on large golden platters. Today, everything is bite sized. There are creamy spreads and small black beads I learn are fish eggs piled on top of tiny round pieces of fried bread. Everything is delicious. I shudder at the notion of returning to the mess hall in Nostraza, where everything tastes like sweat-soaked socks.

"Have you seen Marici?" I ask Halo, who gives me a grim nod.

"She's been sent to purgatory," she replies, popping a tiny cracker topped with red jelly and creamy cheese into her mouth.

"Where?" I ask, remembering that Atlas said the eliminated Tributes would be given a place of honor in Aphelion's court. I pick up a small round toast topped with a curl of bright pink fish I'm told is called salmon. It has a dollop of white cream and a small sprig of green on top. I pop it into my mouth and can't suppress my groan of appreciation.

Tesni giggles across the table from me, covering her mouth. When she notices me watching, she stops, straightening her shoulders, color darkening her cheeks.

"It's okay," I say. "I know I'm a source of amusement. I don't mind if you laugh, as long as you aren't cruel about it."

I'm not sure if it's guilt in her eyes, but it clears away when she smiles, showing off her row of straight white teeth.

"Not at all. I think it's delightful watching you experience all these new things. What a wonder to behold all this through fresh eyes." She gestures to the table. "Sometimes I think we're all far too jaded and definitely much too privileged to understand the wonders that surround us. You remind me that not everyone has it as good."

I'm taken aback by her speech, surprised to hear such sentiments.

"Right," I say, not entirely sure how to reply. "Exactly." Tesni smiles again and takes a bite of her food.

I return my attention to Halo, remembering what she'd just told me. "What is purgatory?"

"Don't you know?" she asks, her brows knitting together. "It's a silly nickname given to the state of fallen Tributes as they wait out the end of the Trials."

"And then what?"

"And then when the Sun Queen is chosen, they all become her handmaidens, destined to serve her forever."

"Oh," I say, not understanding the grim look on Halo's face. "That doesn't sound so bad?"

I think about my own fate if I lose. How I'll return to my own personal pit of hell. They'll probably make me finish out my sentence in the Hollow. Becoming a lady's maid hardly sounds like a punishment in comparison.

"No, I suppose not, except that most lady's maids are eventually free to marry and have families of their own," Halo says. "However, a failed Tribute will never have that. Once she enters the Trials, she becomes the property of the king, whether she wins or loses. The only escape from that bond is death."

Halo takes a long sip of her wine as if searching for strength at the bottom of her glass. Then she turns her dark, shining gaze on me. "Surely you know all this?"

I shake my head. "No. They didn't tell me that."

They didn't tell me because that isn't *my* fate if I lose. I'll be tossed back to the wolves while the rest of the Tributes continue living in luxury. An eternal bond to the king may be a different kind of prison, but I'm having a hard time feeling much sympathy.

"I've heard," Tesni says from across the table, eavesdropping on our conversation, "that past kings have been known to take from the failed Tributes whenever they please. That they're required to warm his bed."

Halo and I both grimace while Tesni's eyes shine. I can't tell if she just enjoys the idea of shocking us with this information or if she relishes the idea of sleeping with the king, even if she loses. I can't imagine a future queen supporting this.

My heart sinks when I think of the way Atlas kissed me. Gabriel is right. What could a male as glorious and beautiful as Atlas possibly see in me beyond these other stunning Fae who surround me? He's probably kissed them all that way.

"Has he kissed you?" I ask Tesni, leaning forward and lowering my voice. Her eyes spread wide.

"No, he hasn't. Has he kissed you?" I can feel the curious looks from a few more Fae at the end of our table as they catch wind of our conversation. Halo also studies me, wariness carving into the lines of her face.

"He's not supposed to kiss anyone before the end of the Trials," Tesni says, her tone accusing.

"Of course he hasn't," I lie. "I was just wondering. That's all."

Tesni sits back, visibly relieved, and everyone else returns to the circles of their own discussions with that matter settled. I look around the table and catch the eye of Apricia. The corner of her mouth crooks up and the shift in her gaze suggests she's trying to send me a message. One that's coated in filth and doused in acid.

Atlas told me to keep our kiss quiet, and I wonder if he told the others the same. Apricia flips a lock of her hair over her shoulder, as usual, and I really hope she doesn't strain her neck. I feel like she's trying to tell me she's kissed him and is attempting to get under my skin. These court politics and games—I'm in way over my head, and I don't know who to trust or believe.

After lunch, we're offered a rare afternoon of respite from lessons or training.

Halo and I wander in the direction of the palace gardens. It turns out purgatory is less restrictive than it sounds, because Marici finds us a little while later. While I'm not entirely convinced that being bound to the king forever is really such an honor, I still think these fallen Tributes could have it a lot worse.

"We've been friends since we were girls," Halo says as we lounge in a circle on a patch of green grass. I lie on my back, my hands on my stomach and my face to the sky, soaking in the warm rays of the sun. "Our families wanted us to enter the Trials, but we never dreamed we both would make it." Halo and Marici exchange a cautious look I don't understand.

Marici turns back to me. "Our families vacationed every summer together. We've become very close over the years."

I wonder what it would have been like to grow up that way. To have memories of family dinners and childhood friends and sprawling beach houses to idle away the days.

"What about you?" Halo asks. "What's your family like? I mean...do you have family in The Umbra?" The question is careful, as though she's not sure if she should ask. Momentary irritation flares at the idea of it being incomprehensible for someone like me to have a family. But maybe it's not Halo's fault. These Fae have clearly been coddled and sheltered from the realities of how the rest of the world lives.

"My parents are gone. The only people I have left in my life are my brother and sister," I say, deciding not to answer the question directly. They both give me a sad smile.

"I'm sorry," Marici says. "That must be very hard."

I shake my head and shrug. "You get used to it. It was a long time ago."

We all fall silent for a moment, and Halo gives me a sly look. "Why did you really ask Tesni if the king had kissed her earlier?"

"What?" Marici asks, her icy blue eyes widening into orbs of interest.

"I think the Final Tribute might be keeping something from us," Halo says, grinning and bumping her shoulder against Marici's.

I lean up on my elbow, plucking a blade of grass and twisting it between my fingers, avoiding their stares. "No reason," I say, but even I can hear the false protest in it.

"Fess up," Marici says, crossing her legs and leaning in. I look up at their faces, wary of their reactions, but there's no jealousy or anger, only fascination. "Did he kiss you?"

I bite my bottom lip. "Maybe, a little." They both squeal and clap their hands together.

"What was it like?" Halo asks.

"It was..." I blow out a breath. "It was like being filled with the sun."

There's a snort of laughter from beyond the small clearing, followed by a chorus of snide laughter. Apricia, Hesperia, and Griane all emerge from behind a hedge from where they were clearly eavesdropping.

I sit up straight, my hackles rising at the cruel sneer Apricia tosses my way.

"As if the king would deign to kiss you," Apricia says, her hands on her hips, looking down her nose.

"Jealous?" I ask, trying to maintain an outward show of calm. "He's probably not fond of kissing cold, dead fish." I ease slowly to stand, clutching my locket in my fist.

"Please," Apricia says, flipping her hair. "You're a liar. Everyone knows that had he kissed you, it would only be out of pity." She wrinkles her nose.

"Has he kissed you?" Halo asks innocently, her big eyes wide. I want to kiss *her* when Apricia's cheeks flush.

"Of course he has." I notice Hesperia and Griane exchange a glance. "Not only that, he's told me repeatedly I'm favored to win, both by himself and the Sun Mirror. It's basically a lock." She checks her nails, and I wonder what her friends think about that. She's just dismissed them as much as she has me.

"So what does he have tattooed on his ribs, then?" I ask, plucking the question out of thin air. I have no idea if Atlas has a tattoo anywhere, but let her think I've seen enough of him to know.

Apricia blinks, her mouth flopping open and her eyes narrowing. I let out a derisive laugh and turn to address Halo and Marici, who stand behind me, trying to contain their grins. "I thought so. Pathetic." To twist the knife a little deeper, I look over my shoulder and say, "Losing to an Umbra rat. How *embarrassing*."

With a smirk, I face Halo and Marici and widen my eyes to tell them we should probably get the fuck out of here immediately.

"You tramp!" Apricia yells, and pain bursts at the back of my head. She's got a handful of my hair and yanks it so hard, I swear I feel the follicles pop. Twisting myself under her arm, I wrench from her grip, panting heavily.

"You bitch!" I scream and crash into her, shoving her so she stumbles back and lands on the soft grass.

"Lor! Stop!" Halo cries. "Help! Someone help!"

Glaring at Apricia, I stalk towards her, and she scrambles back on her hands and feet.

"If you touch me, you'll know the wrath of my father! He's very powerful!"

"What's he going to do, Apricia? Take all my gold and riches? Make me live in a hovel where I won't have enough to eat? Force me to work all day in some thankless job where I'm paid in scraps?" I take another step closer, baring my teeth. "You forget, *Tribute*, I have absolutely fucking nothing to lose."

Priming myself, I leap, but something snags me around the waist, jerking me back and hauling me away. I'm lifted off the ground by what I realize now is an arm, my legs flailing under me.

"Lor!" It's Gabriel, and he sounds pissed. "Calm down!" He hisses it with such viciousness that I go limp in his hold. With his arm still cinched around my waist, he spins and carries me at his side like I'm a naughty rag doll.

After marching across the garden, he stops and drops me on the ground.

"Ow!" I say as my hip makes bruising contact with the hard earth.

"What is the matter with you?" He leans over me, his teeth gritted and his blue eyes flashing like tidal waves in the middle of a hurricane.

"She started it!" I point in the general direction of where we've just come from.

"That's always your excuse. Do you know how to deal with anything without resorting to biting and scratching like a wild animal?"

I scramble up to stand, my anger now directed at him. "No, I don't! I've lived through hell and this is all I know, okay? If there's a better way, no one has ever taught me!"

Gabriel takes a step towards me and every instinct tells me to move back, but I stand my ground while he towers over me. "Oh poor little, Lor. So hard done by. Every time I think there might be a chance you'd make a decent queen for Atlas, you behave like a spoiled little child. *You* don't deserve any of this."

My chest is so tight that my breath is snipped into staccato notes. I glare at him, his words taking out a bite out of my pride.

Gabriel gives me one more look, hard enough to cut steel, and then turns and walks away.

"Asshole!" I scream at his back, but he completely ignores me.

CHAPTER TWENTY

The thundering crash of the ocean is audible even before the doors swing open. Made of glass, they reveal the horizon stretching across my view. It's nearly evening, and the sun is setting, casting the water in watercolor hues of orange and pink while the sand sparkles in the waning light like a carpet made of crushed diamonds.

I take a steadying breath, remembering the last time they brought us to the sea, where they dangled us like worms on hooks as we fought for our lives. I think of poor Solana, gone forever, and the ferocious burn of my wounds when I fell into the water.

But tonight, there is no trial.

As promised, Atlas has invited me for dinner post-recovery, and I'm eager to see him. Despite my worries and misgivings, I also can't stop thinking about the way he kissed me. I've turned

Apricia's words over and over, trying to uncover how I feel about him kissing her, too, but this is a competition. He has every right to see who he's compatible with, and he's promised me nothing.

Tonight could be my opportunity to stand out from the crowd, though. I'm good at this. I know how to use my body to get what I want. I've certainly whored myself out countless times for much more insignificant prizes than a crown. This is a completely different situation, anyway. The two aren't comparable. Atlas is a glorious king who makes my heart race, not a sleazy prison warden with an inferiority complex.

My hands ball into fists when the doors swing open, and I resolve to do whatever it takes to win. I *need* to stand before the Sun Mirror. It may be the only chance I'll ever get to reclaim everything that was taken from me and Willow and Tristan. Though nothing will ever give us back our mother and father, maybe I can still find a way to honor their memory and make them proud.

A wide boardwalk traverses the sand, the planks sun-warmed beneath my bare feet. Mag dressed me in a stretchy two-piece suit made of soft, silky material that exposes the skin on my legs, stomach, and arms. Over it, I wear a sheer golden robe embroidered with hundreds of tiny beads. It floats behind me on the breeze, exposing my bared legs.

On my ankles are delicate gold chains that tinkle like miniature wind chimes as I walk. My hair has been left loose, and it tosses in the breeze. I shake my head, reveling in the sensation of free-flowing locks. I'm living in a dream, and I keep pretending the rooster won't crow at any moment.

Gabriel marches ahead of me, down the length of the board-walk, to a white tent erected at the end. He's still furious with me after what happened with Apricia in the garden and has resorted to speaking to me only in monosyllables. That's fine—I'm pissed at him, too. What a self-righteous prick.

Gabriel stops, pulling back one of the tent flaps, and gestures me inside. The boardwalk widens into a large round platform, sanded down so the planks are as soft as velvet. The far end has been left open, offering a dazzling view of the water.

In the center of the tent sits a small table laden with a sparkling gold tablecloth and golden plates. Glittering goblets and silverware nestle next to a centerpiece made of creamy white and shiny gold roses.

And while the setting itself is beyond coherent words, it's the Fae male standing next to the table that truly sucks every shred of breath from my lungs.

Atlas waits with a casual tilt to his stance and smiles, his bright aqua eyes glowing like tide pools lit by fallen stars. His coppery brown hair hangs loose around his shoulders, and it's all I can do to resist walking over to grab a fistful for myself.

He, too, wears a scant costume, the same silky material covering only his bottom half. A loosened robe hangs off his shoulders, exposing everything he *isn't* wearing.

My gaze drifts over the curve of his thighs, the arch of his hips, and the prominent bulge between his legs I can't help but notice. Gabriel clears his throat and I jump, realizing he's just caught me staring.

Still, I can't seem to look away. My cheeks heat as my gaze wanders over defined arms and a carved stomach, soaking in the smooth planes of his chest. Turns out he doesn't have a tattoo on his ribs after all. There's only a tanned canvas of warm skin just waiting to be touched by my itching fingers.

I admire the swoop of that collarbone I've glimpsed through the opening of his shirt and note the bob of his throat when he swallows before our eyes finally meet. His gaze darkens and now I wish I'd left my robe untied. Would it be too obvious if I did it now?

Something crosses his face—there for a moment and then gone, to be replaced by an expression that hooks into my center. No one has ever looked at me like that. This entire experience is like a fantasy I conjured every night I spent curled up on a rock-hard cot, barely covered by a thin grey sheet.

"Lor," he says, stepping forward and holding out a hand. "I'm so happy you're feeling better." He looks over at Gabriel and tips his chin. "You can let them know we're ready for dinner."

Gabriel says nothing as he turns and departs from the tent. Before he leaves, I cast a glance over my shoulder, noting the shrewd look in his eyes. He's still wondering why Atlas is bothering with me, and quite frankly, I'm wondering the same. But then I remember what Apricia said and wonder if he's already invited her here, too. I'm just another Tribute here to give him access to his full power. We are all a means to an end, and I can't lose sight of my true purpose.

"Please sit," Atlas says, directing me to one of the plush chairs at the table. The velvety seat is soft against my skin. "You look beautiful tonight." He smiles and tips his head. "Well, you always look beautiful, Lor."

I can't help the flush that his words cause, a blush feathering up my neck. Either his expressions of interest are genuine or he's an excellent actor. When I'm seated, he pours me a glass of wine and then one for himself. The tent flap opens and a stream of servants pours in before they set out large steaming platters on the table.

After these weeks in Aphelion, I'm learning to recognize the cuisine. Platters of saffron rice dotted with peas. Tureens of chicken floating in creamy, spiced sauces. Fish poached in rose water and flat mounds of fluffy white bread to soak up the sauces. I could never tire of any of it.

When the food has been laid out, Atlas dismisses the help with a wave. "You may leave us. We can take it from here." They bow their heads and scurry off, leaving me and Atlas alone again.

"What would you like to try first?" he asks as I survey the bounty.

"Everything," I say, breathless, and he chuckles indulgently as he scoops heaping piles onto my plate.

"It's such a wonder to behold your joy," he says. "I forget how special this all is."

Though my mouth is stuffed full of rice, I say, "It's hard to believe this all exists in the same world as Nostraza. How can anyone be okay with this kind of disparity? Why does anyone deserve this any more than anyone else does?"

His elbows on the table, Atlas frowns. "The people in Nostraza are criminals. Murderers and thieves. They deserve their punishments."

My throat twists tight. "Most of the people in Nostraza were born with less than nothing," I say, trying to regulate the anger in my voice. "They steal and kill because it's the only way for them to survive. They have nothing. And no one—least of all the Aurora King, or any of the other rulers of Ouranos—does anything to help them."

Atlas's expression is thoughtful as he leans closer, a line pinching between his brows. Have I said too much? Crossed a line that shouldn't be crossed? Does one speak this way to a king? Not in my experience.

"Is it any different from the people who live in The Umbra? Based on the fact that everyone thinks it's where I came from, I can only assume the people there aren't that different from the prisoners of Nostraza."

His eyebrows climb up his forehead. "Is that what happened to you? Did you grow so desperate?" His voice is so tender in support of my defense that it shutters my mounting anger. I shake my head, looking down at my hands in my lap, pushing away the sting of my tears.

"No. I don't know why I was in Nostraza," I say, and though that's not the entire truth, I'm ever wary of revealing too much without understanding all of his intentions. "I was a child, and I remember little of my life before that time."

"They locked up a child." He says it with dark condemnation.

"Are there children living in The Umbra?" I ask. The idea of that shadowy dark place plagues my thoughts, though I try to block them out. I want to forget the darkness exists until I'm forced to face it again.

"Of course there are," Atlas says, taking a sip of his wine. "But The Umbra isn't a prison. Anyone is free to leave and make a better life for themselves. I can't control how people behave."

He says the words with such certainty, I resist the urge to slap him.

"Just because there are no walls and no guards doesn't mean it isn't a prison," I say, sure I'm going too far now. He's going to get angry and send me away. No one questions a king.

But he doesn't do any of that. Instead, he stops what he's doing, dropping the piece of bread in his hand on his plate. "What do you mean?"

"I mean, it's the same situation. When you have nothing, you can't build anything. When your days are spent wondering where your next meal is coming from or how you're going to survive the night without having your throat slit, you don't have the time or the energy or the motivation to make your life better. You're too busy simply surviving."

Atlas picks up the bread again and pops it in his mouth, chewing slowly. "I've never thought about it that way," he says, the words coated in carelessness.

"I suppose not, as you sit here in your golden palace, never venturing anywhere near the poor." The words slip out like serpents lashing out their tongues. When Atlas cuts a sharp glance my way, I worry I really have gone too far this time.

When he reaches for me, pushing down the shoulder of my robe and his fingers gently brushing the blackened brand of Nostraza charred into my skin, I hold completely still. Am I about to suffer for my insubordination? But then his face softens. "Thank you, Lor." He takes my hand in his. It's large and warm and the touch shoots tingles down my arms. "I already had a suspicion you would make a good queen, but hearing you speak this way, I understand how lucky the people of Aphelion would be to have you leading them."

"Really?"

"Yes." He shakes his head. "You're right, I've rarely visited The Umbra, and even when I have, I've spoken to no one, nor tried to understand their plight."

I can hardly believe he's saying this. "So, you'll do something about it?"

Atlas squeezes my hand before tucking an errant lock of hair behind my ear. His fingertips linger against my cheek, his thumb sweeping the scar along my cheekbone, sending another shiver down the back of my neck.

"I'm going to gather my advisors first thing tomorrow to see what we can do." His smile is warm and genuine and if he wasn't already the Sun King, he'd be the brightest thing to rise on any horizon. "Thank you, Lor. One thing I've always hoped for in a bonded partner is someone who can make me become a better version of the Fae I am."

"Thank you," I say, hoping I've made a difference and wondering where his truth lies. He doesn't seem to delight in cruelty like the Aurora King, and it's a relief to realize not every ruler in Ouranos possesses a completely withered heart, shrunk down to nothing but a dry mote of dust. While there's no mistaking my physical reactions to Atlas, I sense there are layers to uncover, and I want to get to know him better. Maybe this is someone I *could* build a life with.

It's at that moment my resolve to win the crown fossilizes into amber.

Not just for Tristan and Willow. Not only for my revenge on the Aurora King and everything he took.

But because for the first time in my life, I deserve some happiness too.

CHAPTER TWENTY-ONE

"Do you want to go for a swim?" Atlas asks after we've eaten our fill, but not before I've devoured no less than four different pastries, each one more delicate, creamy, and decadent than the last. I hold my stomach, more full than a turkey stuffed inside a chicken. I might regret this later.

"A swim?" I look out to the ocean, remembering the first challenge and those mermaid-like creatures that tried their best to gut me and shred me up for dinner.

Atlas must sense the train of my thought, because he takes my hands and pulls me up to stand. His hands find my hips before he directs me onto his lap, my heart kicking in my chest.

"A swim," he repeats, his large palm sliding up my bare leg where my robe has left it exposed. It comes to rest high on my leg, the tips of his fingers brushing the crease of my thigh. My heartbeat is desperately trying to keep up as his other hand slides up my back and cups the nape of my neck. "I promise there's nothing that can hurt you."

I huff out a derisive snort, eyeing the water. Against the setting sun, it sparkles like a treasure chest, spilling out a horde of jewels. It *does* seem impossible that anything that lovely could be dangerous, but the cove was pretty, too. I turn back to look at Atlas, who's watching me, intensity smoldering in his aquamarine eyes. They drop to my mouth and then up again, making my stomach tighten in response.

"Have you kissed the others?" I ask and then immediately regret the question. It's none of my business, and I don't really want to hear the answer. His expression turns thoughtful before he peers at me with a look I can't interpret.

"I have," he says simply, and a sharp knot twists in my chest. Of course he has. I shouldn't expect anything else. Apricia wasn't lying. "I want to be honest with you, Lor. But I have to give everyone a chance. Obviously, I am naturally more drawn to some Tributes than I am to others."

I press a finger to his lips, clipping off his words. "It's fine," I say. "I understand. Of course, you have to 'test the waters,' so to speak." He arches a dark brow and then opens his mouth, nipping the tip of my finger with his perfect white teeth.

I let out a yelp and snatch it away, clutching my hand to my chest and giggling. He's laughing, too, his eyes bright and his smile glorious. A moment later, his expression turns heated, and he draws me to him, his arm wrapping around my back. I place my hands on his shoulders, feeling the flex of warm, hard muscle beneath my palms.

My face is so close to his, the soft exhale of his breath dusts my lips.

"Would you believe me if I said the kiss with you was my favorite?" he asks. I snort and then bite my bottom lip, wishing it were true.

"No. I wouldn't. I'd be sure you were saying it to get me to agree to kiss you again."

His answer is a smile and a low chuckle. "Would it work?" He tips his head, watching me from beneath dark lashes.

"Possibly. After all, the only way we can get better is to practice. Wouldn't you agree?"

His smile grows wide. "I'd definitely agree, my lady."

He presses his forehead to mine, sliding his hand higher under the fabric of my robe. After tugging on the tie, it falls the rest of the way open, exposing him to all my bared skin. A delicious shiver rolls through me, as sweet as honeyed berries. His gaze traces a map over my body, his hand sliding over my stomach and up my ribs, where I erupt into gooseflesh.

When his gaze meets mine, it's so fiery it makes the tendons in my thighs flex. His mouth gently brushes mine, but the kiss is tentative, lasting only for a second before his large hand presses against the back of my head and his mouth consumes mine. I moan as his tongue sweeps into my mouth, and then he sucks on my bottom lip. He's shoving the robe off my shoulders and I help him, shirking it off and letting it tumble to the floor. I'm not exactly naked, but our clothing is scant and our skin is touching in so many places we may as well be.

With a low growl, his hands grip my hips and he lifts me up, maneuvering me so I'm straddling his lap, the unmistakable and generous length of his cock pressing into my aching center. "Lor," he moans into my mouth, deepening the kiss. My hands run down his shoulders and over his thick biceps, running along his corded forearms. His hands roam over my body, up my thighs, skating up my back and then down, where he grips my ass and pulls me harder against him.

I scratch my nails down his chest, fingering the grooves and ridges that define his torso. A moment later, he grips the backs of my thighs and lifts me up, my legs wrapped around his waist. He carries me over to a round settee placed in the corner of the tent. Covered in pillows, it's as soft as a cloud when he drops me onto the golden velvet.

"Tell me to stop if you want me to stop," he says, his voice rough and low as his mouth drags down the curve of my neck and over my collarbone before he places hot wet kisses down the center of my body, stopping at my navel and then working his way back up again.

"I don't want you to stop," I say, breathless, my hands snaking into his hair, pulling his face to mine. I never want him to stop.

I'm not inexperienced when it comes to sex, but I've never been given the luxury of this sort of privacy or time. All of my amorous encounters have amounted to hurried, stolen fucks in a darkened prison courtyard beneath the shadow of whatever building might hide us best, hoping we wouldn't get caught. Rough and frantic. Desperate and raw. Never tender or careful. There was never time for that. No one has ever kissed me this way or touched me like this. I've never even been fully naked with a man before.

"You're sure?" he asks, touching his forehead to mine where we lie sprawled next to each other, our legs tangled. "I'm not supposed to be doing this...but I can't seem to help myself around you."

"I'm sure," I say, his words firing an ardent optimism in my chest when he kisses me again, his fingertips sliding under the edge of the tight bottoms I'm wearing.

"I want more of you." His finger now skates the front edge of the fabric along the sensitive skin of my stomach, stopping below my navel. His gaze meets mine, intense and shadowed with a question. I think of Madame Odell's admonishments that even if the king wasn't required to control himself, we were to "do better." But I study Atlas's face. Those intense eyes and those full lips. That chiseled chest and his taut stomach. The way he smells like sunshine and joy and how hot his skin is against mine.

And seriously, fuck Madame Odell.

Maybe it's a mistake. Maybe the king wants to use me and then discard me like a tissue. The gutter rat from The Umbra. Or Nostraza, depending on which story you're telling. But his kindness is addictive. The soft way he touches me and makes me feel like the only person who matters in the world has cracked the shield I wear like an eroding shell. No one has ever shown me this is how it can be.

It's been so long since I've mattered to anyone but two ragged prisoners who I love with all my heart, but who can never be *enough* on their own.

His hand skates up my side as my ribs expand with my deep breaths.

"I want more too," I whisper, throwing caution to the wind. What chance do I really have to win? When I told Apricia I had nothing to lose, it was the truth. I have nowhere to go but up.

At least I can enjoy this ephemeral pleasure before I'm sent back home or to my death. I want him. Not just because he's intoxicating, but because this is my choice. Like Aero. Like the men before him, it was one of the few choices I've ever been allowed to make for myself, and that makes all the difference.

Atlas dips his head, capturing my mouth with his, the kiss spiraling straight through to my toes. It grows hungrier, our chests and stomachs colliding, the thin fabric of our swimming costumes almost like skin on skin. His hands knead my flesh as he hooks my leg over his hip and then pushes me back, rising above me, his strong arms braced on either side of my head.

He kisses me again and then slides down my body, his mouth taking in tastes of me along the way. His large palm cups my breast, and I let out a gasp as he wedges his hips between my legs. As he teases my nipple through the material, my back arches into him.

"Lor," he murmurs into my skin. "You're so beautiful."

He tugs down the stretchy material of my top, exposing my breast and closing his mouth around my nipple, his tongue flicking against the tip. I bury my hands in his hair, my knees coming up as my hips writhe against him.

After tugging up my top to cover me again, he continues his journey, kissing my stomach and my navel and then swirling his tongue in the tender space below. I'm so achy in my core, I let out a whimper. The warmth of his breath slides across my skin as he lets out a low chuckle.

"What do you want, Lor?" he asks, smoke in his voice, his eyes deep with longing.

I look down at him, completely taken in by his beautiful face and sculpted shoulders, when he drops to the floor and pushes my knees apart. His lips trail up the sensitive skin of my inner thigh, making my legs tremble.

"Tell me," he orders. "What do you want?"

I've never been shy about these things. I've never had a problem asking for what I want, but it's so hard not to be overwhelmed by his beauty and his presence. He's more than anyone I've ever known. Is this what all Fae are like? Or is it just him? He's kissing the inside of my thigh again, his hand propped under my knee as his other hand rests on my hip, his thumb sweeping the edge of the thin scrap of material between my legs.

Finally finding my voice where it's disappeared somewhere around my hips, I gasp out, "Touch me. I want you to touch me." His grin turns feral, a wicked gleam sparking in his eyes.

"I knew you wouldn't be shy." And then he does as I ask, his thumb slipping under the fabric to find my hot, aching core. I gasp as he rubs my clit, sending tendrils of heat through my blood. His touch is featherlight and I squirm against the settee, trying to find the relief of friction. But he holds me down, not letting me move as he drives me to the edge with his light teasing.

He lets out a low sound, almost like a growl, and pulls his hand away, leaving me empty. The next thing I realize, he's tugging on my hips, dragging me to the edge of the settee. Wasting no time, he hooks his fingers into my waistband and slides off my bottoms, tossing them to the side. His hands spread me wide, and this isn't something I'm used to. A part of me nearly collapses into self-consciousness, but another part, a part that never wants this to stop, revels in the way he's staring at me like a hungry golden tiger preparing to swallow me whole.

He looks up at me with an arched brow and a tipped smile and that same wicked gleam in his eye and then, without warning, dips his head and, with the flat of his tongue, laps my core with a luxurious sweep. I moan, my hips coming off the furniture as he does it again, his tongue exploring the wet folds, pressing against that spot where it feels amazing.

"Oh, Zerra," I breathe, burying my fingers in his hair as he continues to make delicious circles, winding me tighter and tighter. I want more. I want to feel this in the marrow of my bones. I lift my hips, driving them forward, craving more friction. Atlas makes a deep sound of satisfaction and complies, his attention growing rougher as he slides a finger inside me and I groan.

Still feasting on me, he adds a second finger, pumping in and out as he curls his fingers, sending flutters vibrating through my body. I'm so close to the edge, my head tips back and I let out an extravagant moan. I feel the first signs of my edges fraying and then, in a sudden flash, I tear apart and cry out over and over as release twists through me in rolling waves.

Atlas doesn't move from his position between my thighs, placing soft kisses as he waits for me to stop shaking. When I finally catch my breath, my muscles limp, he pulls away and stretches over top of me, pressing his mouth to mine. I can taste myself on his lips, and it feels strangely erotic.

"Fuck, that was amazing," he says, his mouth in the curve of my neck. I look down and take in his cock, swollen and pressing against the stretching fabric of his swim costume. I want to touch it. To taste him like he did me. I reach for him, closing my hand around it through the fabric. For a moment, he closes his eyes, his head tipped back as I grip him, moving my hand up and down.

But then he gently grabs my wrist and shakes his head. "No, that's not necessary."

"But I—" He silences me with another kiss, his hands cupping my face.

"There will be time for that after the Trials. Today, I'm content to just enjoy you."

I blink, not understanding. I've never been with a man who didn't also want to seek his own pleasure, even if he delivered mine first. He smiles, the corners of his eyes crinkling. "I told you we'd go for a swim." He reaches down, picks up my swim bottoms, fits my feet through the holes, and then pulls them up my legs.

"Come on," he says, taking off his robe and tossing it on a chair, baring his glorious wide back rippling with muscle. I'm so confused by his refusal of my attention I haven't moved. He turns and looks over his shoulder. "Are you okay, Lor? Was that all right?"

Worry furrows his brow as he comes towards me, and I shake my head. "Yes, no. I mean, yes, I'm okay and, of course, that was okay. It was...incredible." He grins and holds out his hand, pulling me up to stand and kissing the back of my hand.

Then he winks. "Race you to the water."

Without another word, he drops my hand and goes bounding out of the tent, casting a smile over his shoulder.

"Hey!" I shout and then break into a run, chasing after him.

CHAPTER TWENTY-TWO

The stadium rumbles with the beat of drums, chatter, and ambient noise as I enter with the other six Tributes through a massive gate, our warders at our sides. Gabriel wears his thin leather armor, his blond hair tied back from his face and his strong jaw set as we march to the center like we're facing a firing line of poison-tipped arrows.

The sky is its usual bright blue, and the ground is comprised of pebble-strewn dirt. The stadium is massive, thousands of people crammed into stands that sweep high around us, forming a chanting curtain of bodies. Gabriel had promised one trial would take place in the city and today is the big day. I've been told the citizens of Aphelion have been waiting for this. They're taking bets and will have parties that run well into the night. It's a holiday and everyone has been given the day off from their usual work and duties.

I watch as ale sloshes from tankards before carelessly dribbling down chins, everyone already enjoying themselves to their fullest. The mood is jovial and exuberant, although one of us might die today. No skin off their noses, I guess. That notion is further driven home as I eye the ominous contraption squatting in the center of the stadium.

It's made of large wooden beams and is adorned with a series of knives and swords, along with heavy round sacks covered in stitched leather like cheerless Yuletide decorations. The entire monstrosity sits suspended over what appears to be a deep black hole.

"What is it?" I ask Gabriel, my gaze fixed on its glinting edges and clearly sinister intentions.

"A gauntlet," he says, his voice grim.

"A what?"

He lets out a deep breath and looks down at me. "It's an obstacle course. When they turn it on, those bags will swing and the swords will spin. It's all designed to throw you off as you try to pass through."

"And fall in that hole." I stare at the black void, the pit in my stomach sinking to my feet.

"And fall in that hole," Gabriel repeats.

"I suppose they don't mean for anyone to come back out of the hole."

Gabriel opens his mouth and then closes it, and that's when a ferocious snarl rips through the stadium. Every chattering voice clips off, thousands of wary glances exchanged before they all turn to the shadowy pit. I swallow the bile rising in my throat and catch Halo's gaze as we share a moment of mutual terror.

"I'm going to die," I whisper.

"Probably," Gabriel says, and I shoot him a dirty look.

"You could at least pretend you have some faith in me."

Gabriel smirks. He's deigned to speak to me in more than single syllables again, but it's clear he isn't campaigning for a spot in the Lor fan club. "Come now, Tribute. We both know you're too smart to fall for that." I narrow my eyes, not entirely sure if I've just been insulted or complimented.

"You're such a dick," I mutter, turning my attention back to the gauntlet as Gabriel chuckles.

"So you've said."

The chatter has resumed, though the overall volume is more subdued, as if the gravity of this event has finally penetrated their indifferent walls. It cuts off completely when a horn trumpets and the gate at the end of the stadium opens. This time it's Atlas with his entire retinue, who enter to a round of clapping and cheers. He offers a curt bow to the crowd, that beautiful smile on his face before he makes his way to the dais on the opposite side of the stadium.

It's been a few days since our dinner on the beach and I can't stop thinking about how good it felt to be admired by him. We spent the rest of the evening in the ocean, swimming until the stars came out. While we kissed many more times, that's as far as Atlas allowed it to go again. I haven't seen him since he said goodbye to me in the tent and Gabriel escorted me to my room, throwing me scathing looks and generally being an ass.

Atlas sent me an enormous bouquet of golden roses the next morning with a handwritten note that read, *Thank you for a wonderful evening. I can't wait to do it again soon.* The gesture warmed me straight through, like I'd swallowed a ball of sunlight. No one this important, this powerful, this beautiful, has ever made an effort for me. It was like he genuinely cared what I felt and thought.

As Atlas and his people make their way through the stadium, I look over to Apricia, who, as usual, is flipping her hair and primping for the king. He looks over at us, smiling, his gaze lingering on her for a moment longer than the rest. As much as it hurts, I remind myself not to get carried away with his attention. This is a contest and I'm just one of many contestants. The one least likely to win, at that.

Apricia tosses a smug look to the rest of us and I wonder what's between them. Did he also taste the place between her thighs? Did he refuse her touches, too? I shake my head, trying to rally my focus. I have a challenge to master and not dying is my priority right now.

Master Borthius is speaking, his voice amplified for the massive crowd, who dangle on the edge of every word. We are to make our way through the gauntlet, attempting to do so without being knocked off. If we land on the floor of the stadium, we're disqualified. The good news, though, is we live to see another day.

However, if we fall into the pit, we become dinner for the thogrul that lurks below. As if to punctuate Master Borthius's statement, the monster roars again, shaking the entire stadium.

I've faced down so many foes in my lifetime, but these challenges are testing every resolve I have. Nothing in my past has prepared me for this. My limbs trembling, I take a deep breath, trying to calm my pounding heart.

A moment later, the six other Tributes and I are ushered to the far end of the arena. Today, everyone wore their thin leather armor, leggings and jerkins, and boots. No one would make that mistake again.

There are some more announcements I don't hear as I study the contraption before me. It stands like a great, feral spider made of timber. The first obstacle includes a long beam with a series of swinging arms above it. On the end of each arm is a giant tear-shaped pillow made of stitched leather. Clearly, they're meant to knock us off as they swing back and forth in opposite directions with the rhythm of a metronome.

Apricia moves to the front of the line. Her long hair is now cinched into a high ponytail, and I guess she does own a hair tie after all. That doesn't stop her from flicking the end over her shoulder and casting a disdainful glance my way.

We have one hour. If we make it through the gauntlet in time, we'll move on to the third challenge. If we don't, we're out.

Rolling my shoulders, I dig into the reserves of my resilience. I can do this. None of these Tributes deserve this prize more than I do.

The signal sounds for the game to begin and Apricia wastes no time scrambling to the top of the high platform. We can only go one at a time, so I understand why she's bullied her way to the front. However, I hang back, deciding it might be best to watch the others and learn from their mistakes.

Apricia stands on the end of the narrow beam, one foot placed in front of the other. She holds her arms out like an acrobat and then steels herself, running past the first pendulum and coming to a stop, waiting for her next opening. She continues in the same vein, clearing the next two pendulums with ease. On the fourth and last, she stumbles, her foot slipping off the beam, and a collective gasp races through the stadium. But she's clearly well-trained, and she recovers easily, lightly stepping off the end onto the far platform.

I let out a breath of relief. Not because I'm worried about Apricia, but because I'm heartened that making it across is actually possible.

Apricia's friend Hesperia is next. She too clears the obstacle, moving on to the next one. I wait my turn as Tesni and Halo both make it across. Then it's my turn. I stand at the end of the beam in a crouch, my arms out, and then run through the first pendulum, but I don't stop. From watching the others, it's obvious that if I find the right rhythm, I can keep going without the stops and starts that might cause me to lose my balance. It's a risk, but I'm already falling behind.

Tempering my pace, I calculate the swing of the next pendulum and continue, clearing the second and then the third. I'm not sure if it's Gabriel's training or the years in Nostraza that have taught me to focus, but I lose myself in the machine's cadence and before I know it, I'm at the end.

As I alight on the platform, I nearly collapse in relief, my limbs as limp as flowers in a winter garden. Panting, I close my eyes, my hands on my knees as I try to settle my breathing. A shriek pierces the air, and I spin around to find Griane clinging to one of the pendulums, her legs and arms wrapped around it as she screams. Her blonde hair floats as if weightless at the peak of each swing.

I study the next obstacle, which is a spinning column of swords and knives. Apricia has already cleared it and Hesperia is currently maneuvering her way to the other side. I should keep going. This is a contest. The other Tributes aren't my responsibility, and Griane is a bitch.

Griane screams again, and the thogrul in the pit below roars louder. I can practically hear it licking its lips in excitement as it scents its delicious meal. I drop to my knees on the platform and lean out to Griane.

"You need to jump off when it's at the highest point," I yell. There's no chance she can get off the end of the pendulum without falling into the pit, but there's a chance she could clear the hole and land on the stadium floor if she lets go at the right moment.

I scream at her again. "Griane, you have to jump before you fall off!" She meets me with a terrified gaze as she registers what I'm saying. Tears stream down her lovely face and she shakes her head. I see her mouth the words, *I can't*.

"You have to! If you don't, you're going to fall in." I watch the pendulum, gauging its path. "I'm going to count to three and then you jump as far as you can! Do you understand me?" Griane says nothing, scrambling against the leather bolster as her grip slips. She won't be able to hold on much longer. "Griane!" She nods then, her eyes wide and her white skin ashen.

"Okay. I'll count you through it. Ready? One... Two..." I wait for the pendulum to reach its zenith and then scream, "Three!"

Griane must dig into the very depths of her courage as she heeds my order, letting go and hurling her body into the air. There's a collective gasp as she arcs into the sky, time standing still as she traces the curving line to her safety. It's so close, I fear she won't make it. I squeeze my fists, my body mimicking her path as I will her over the chasm.

She lands with a crash, just her feet hanging over the edge. She screams as she lands, clutching her arm. The crowd is screaming at her, too. To get up. To clear the rest of the hole before the thogrul reaches up and snatches her. She drags herself forward and then collapses in a heap. The crowd chants their support, cheers filling the air.

I press my hand to my chest and blow out a breath. But I have to keep moving, so I steel myself for the next obstacle.

A dozen long swords revolve on a slowly spinning cylinder. Tesni is currently clearing it, her body folding and bending over the blades. After she's done, her face is gleaming with a sheen of sweat and she's covered in small slices, tiny trickles of blood dripping down her arms and legs.

As I prepare for my turn, a scream from above draws my attention.

A body is plummeting through the center of the gauntlet. It looks like one of Apricia's sidekicks, Hesperia. The flash of her bright red hair seems to signal a warning as her body crashes into another wooden platform before she bounces off, her arms and legs flailing.

She continues dropping with a wild shriek before tumbling down, down, down into the pit below.

Chapter Twenty-three

Silence resonates through the stadium, the crowd looking on in shock as Hesperia's last scream slices off with an echo. A moment later, the unmistakable sounds of bones crunching and flesh slapping and teeth shredding fill the air. I don't move, suspended in horror. In time. In the remnants of Hesperia's last cries. Another Tribute is dead.

I scan the layers of the gauntlet, finding Halo and Tesni on the platforms above. Our gazes meet as the grim understanding of everything that's at stake filters in through the cracks of my resolve.

There are moments when we're surrounded by the decadence of Aphelion when it's easy to forget why we're really here. When I recall my dinner with Atlas, I was so distanced from the bitter reality of my true purpose. I was a fool in a dream, and I need to remember they brought me here against my will to die in a contest I never entered.

A bell dings, reminding me there will be time to mourn Hesperia later. One quarter of our time has passed. Time to get moving.

Squaring my shoulders, I face down the spinning blades, mapping out a path. When I was in Nostraza, I had to fight weaponless against the guards' swords countless times. Years ago, there was an incident when four of those assholes surrounded me, taunting me, while they swiped their blades and laughed. They nicked my skin while I dodged and leaped, forced to posture for their entertainment. I survived then, and I *will* survive now.

The crowd is already cheering again, the crescendo swelling as the gruesome sounds of the monster feasting on Hesperia's body continue to fill the air. I let out a dry sob, clutching my stomach and willing myself not to vomit.

Murmuring a desperate prayer to Zerra, I clench my fists and run. *Duck. Spin. Jump. Spin again. Leap. Duck.* Over and over, I focus on the flash of each blade as they come at me with the precision of an assassin's knife.

Pain. Distantly, it registers in my left thigh. My teeth grind together as I push it away. *Focus*, I remind myself, and then I'm nearly through. *Jump. Step. Duck. Spin.* My foot catches a blade just before I make the final leap and I collapse on the far side, groaning.

For several heartbeats, all I can do is lie on the sun-warmed planks, trying to bottle the threadbare sips of my breath. But then pain lances through my leg like I'm being whipped by fire.

I'm bleeding. A lot. A blade has sliced clean through my pants, carving a deep gash into the meaty part of my thigh.

Fuck. Fuck. Fuck.

My movements stilted, I tear off the sleeve of the thin white shirt under my jerkin and wrap the fabric around my leg, tying a snug knot. It won't hold long, but it'll have to do.

Thankfully, my foot appears to be fine where a sword caught my exit. There's a slice in the leather of my boot, but it stopped just short of breaking my skin. A small mercy, at least.

The bell dings, its metallic chime cheerfully counting down to the moment of my expiration. Half my time is up. I have to keep moving.

Gingerly, I rise, testing my injured leg. Pain sears up my thigh, blooming into my ribs and my shoulder when I take a step. Wincing, I press my lips together, sweat beading on my forehead. The figures of other Tributes move above me like ants, racing back and forth. Pushing on, I limp forward, climbing a wobbly rope ladder and coming face to face with the narrow beam that sent Hesperia to her death. Going slowly feels like a smart strategy this time.

Carefully, I place one foot on the beam, bouncing to test its strength and ignoring the lash of pain in my leg. It's solid and doesn't shift under my weight. Focusing on the beam that's about the width of my foot, I ease myself forward, my arms out to steady my balance. I try to shut out every sound. Every distraction.

The crowd is getting drunker now, the noise bloating like an inflating bubble pressing in on me from all sides. Zerra, I wish everyone would shut the fuck up. I try not to think of Atlas watching me below, nor of Gabriel with that smug smile I want to slap off his face.

Another step and then another as I shuffle towards the center of the beam. Gabriel had me do balance drills for hours this week. Did he know something? Or is this standard training for soldiers? Either way, I owe him my gratitude, even if he is the world's biggest asshole.

High above the stadium floor, the wind challenges my stability, cooling my warm cheeks. My leg throbs with each step and my leggings are soaked with my blood.

Focus, Lor.

After another few steps, I'm almost two-thirds of the way across.

"Lor!" someone shouts my name and I blink, willing myself to steadiness. Ignore it. Keep going. "Lor! Help!" the voice shouts again, and it sounds just like Willow. A memory surfaces of Willow being beaten by a guard while she screamed for me, and I make a fatal error, searching for the sound. It's not her. Of course it isn't, but it's enough to break my concentration, causing my foot to slip. The second one also slides out from under me and I drop, the beam slamming between my thighs with a shudder that ricochets up my spine.

I cry out in agony as pain radiates out through my torso and down my legs, spreading like a fungus. It takes me a moment to register that the world is tilting at the wrong angle. I'm sliding off. I hurl my body forward, wrapping my arms around the beam just as I spin beneath it. Now I'm hanging off it like a sloth in a tree, my legs and arms clenched around the wood.

Below me, the monster roars with such ferocity that its hot, fetid breath envelops me in a cocoon of its bloodthirsty longing. Its appetite is whetted, and it's anticipating another snack.

The wound on my leg drums like it has its own heartbeat. I'm losing blood, my limbs weak and trembling. I have to get myself turned around. Squeezing my eyes shut, I suck in deep, measured breaths. I want to cry and scream out my terror, but there will be time for that later.

I hope.

Steeling my quivering limbs, I hoist myself closer to the beam, my arms and legs screeching their vocal protest. I have no idea how to do this other than through sheer grit. So I shut out the pain and do just that. With every ounce of strength I can rally, I use my arms to crane my upper body to the side of the beam. Grating my teeth, I use my legs to do the same, attempting to twist myself around. My vision goes dark for a moment when I move my injured leg, but I force myself to stay awake. If I faint, then I'm done. Goodbye, Lor.

But I don't have enough power. I'm not sure this is even within the realm of physical possibility. My leg slips and I scream before I fling it back up and then with the mightiest lunge I can muster, hoist myself again. I'm not sure how I do it and if anyone were to ask, I could only tell them I felt Zerra's divine hand find its way to my back and offer me a gentle shove.

But there I am, back on top, about to weep with relief.

After I get myself righted, I cling to the beam with my legs and arms like a crab. My chest is so tight I can hardly breathe and my leg is so drenched in blood I can hear the slick sound it makes as I slide myself along the wood. Like an inchworm, I shuffle my upper body and then my lower body forward. I don't dare stand, worried I'll lose my balance if I try. The laughter from the stands confirms that I look ridiculous. I glare at no one and everyone, angry I'm here.

Fuck these people. Fuck this entire demeaning experience.

Finally, I make it to the far platform. Cringing in pain, I push myself up and face the next obstacle. It's another cylinder that rises from the next platform, fitted with small protruding handholds intended for climbing.

Halo stands at the base, studying the surface. She watches me limp over, her gaze dropping to the scarlet makeshift bandage on my leg and then to my face, her lips set in a determined line. She seems to be in better shape than I am, with only a few cuts and bruises on her cheeks and arms.

"Are you okay?" I ask, my voice ragged as I grimace through the ache in my leg.

"Better than you, I think," she replies softly.

"Why are you just standing here?"

Indecision flickers in her expression, and she opens her mouth to speak when the bell dings again. Three quarters of our time is up.

"Come on," I say. "We need to keep going."

I latch on to the highest handhold I can reach and pull myself up. When I've climbed a few feet, I look down at Halo, who's watching me with a guarded expression.

"Coming?" I ask, not sure what she's waiting for. She wrings her hands and then looks behind her as if searching for some-thing. She then turns back and I frown. Something clears in her eyes and she shakes her head before she grabs a handhold and hoists herself onto the wall.

"Right behind you," she says, and I nod. We continue ascending, following the path of the footholds as they circle around the pillar. As we get closer to the top, they get further and further apart, testing the limits of our abilities. Halo stays next to me the whole time. It feels good to be doing this with someone. The entire experience of the Trials has me surrounded by people every minute of the day, but I've never felt more alone in my entire life.

We speak little, too busy concentrating on our movements, but there's something about Halo's quiet, steady presence that grounds me. When I get to the top, I scramble over the ledge in relief. Spinning around, I lie flat on the platform and reach down to help Halo up the rest of the way. My fingers are raw and red, and my limbs are shaking. I think the wound on my leg has slowed its bleeding, at least for now.

"Lor," she whispers as she approaches from below, an unreadable expression on her face. "I need you to help me out of this competition."

"What?" I ask, sure I've misheard her. "Why?"

She shakes her head, her dark eyes filling with tears. "I don't want to do this anymore."

"I don't understand."

"I can't explain right now. Lor, I'm going to pretend to slip. You try to catch me, okay?" She looks down at the ground below us.

This is crazy. What is she talking about?

But before I can question what she's thinking, she does as she says and slips. She slides a few inches down the wall, catching a lower foothold. I don't know if she's changed her mind or if she's just acting, but she keeps sliding down and screams. I don't *try* to catch her. Instead, I *do* catch her, my hand snagging her wrist just as she's about to drop.

"Halo!" I scream as she dangles from my hand, my other one gripping the platform for purchase. I inch out over the edge to get a better hold, using my other hand to ground me against the motion of her swinging body inching me forward.

"Let go!" she yells. "Pretend I slipped. I'm going to jump to the floor." We're high enough that she'd likely break a leg, but at least she'd survive. But the monster's black pit sits directly beneath us, and the distance is too great. Maybe if she took a running leap, she might clear it. But if I drop her, she's going to fall into that hole.

"No," I grit out, her skin sliding against mine, both our palms coated in sweat. "Are you crazy? You're never going to make it."

"Lor," she begs. "Please."

I firm my grasp on her and look her straight in the eyes. "I don't know what this is about or why you want to stop, but you cannot do this. If I let go, you're going to die. It's too far for you to jump. Halo. Please. Help me haul you up." Her weight drags me forward, threatening to send us both over the edge. The ground spins and I grunt. "Halo!"

Her dark eyes become worried as she finally looks down and then around her. I see the moment she seems to understand what I'm saying. Her eyes close as though she's resigning herself to some unwelcome fate I don't comprehend. She says nothing as she uses a foot to grip the wall and boosts herself up. I pull with all my waning strength and tow her onto the platform.

As we both pause to catch our breath, she doesn't meet my eyes. I don't admonish her for this stupid move that nearly just got us both killed. Something tells me she feels bad enough already. When I feel like I can stand, I say to her, "Let's go."

Time must be running out and sure enough, the bell dings, signalling our final minutes. Thankfully, there is only one ob-stacle left, and that's a fox run. A long rope stretches out over the stadium floor, ending at the far end, where I can make out several figures watching us. A group of pulleys waits tethered to a post.

I grab Halo by the arm and shove her towards one. "Get on." I'm not leaving her up here alone where she can make another reckless decision. The bell dings again, marking one minute remaining. "Hurry!" I snap at her, no longer in the mood for her dithering. If she gets me thrown out so close to the end, I'll never forgive her. What was she thinking?

She does as I ask, casting me an anxious look. As soon as she's holding the device, I give her a hearty shove off the platform and she zips away, accompanied by the drone of the pulley sliding along the rope.

I waste no time readying my own. Clinging to the handles, I take a deep breath. My arms are so tired, I hope I can hang on until the end. The bell dings. Thirty seconds left. I heave back on the pulley and then take a running leap, hurling myself into the air with a battle cry that rips from the center of my chest.

My hands are throbbing and slip against the wooden handles. I grip them so tight my fingers ache. The pulley picks up speed, my heart racing as my legs flail. This is terrifying. I'm going so fast my heart leaps into my throat. Wind fills my mouth, making it hard to breathe.

The crowd is chanting the final seconds now.

Ten! Nine! Eight!

I'm so close. So close. The ground races towards me.

Seven! Six! Five!

I'm not going to make it. I'm too far away. I will myself to keep my eyes open. I want to bear witness to my end.

Four!

Three!

Two!

My feet slam into the ground over the finish line and I go stumbling forward, crashing to my knees and landing face-first into the dirt just as the crowd shrieks so loud it shakes the very earth beneath me.

OOOOOONE!

Chapter Twenty-four

Nadir

Nadir adjusted the lapel of his black suit as he strode down the wide hallway in his wing of the Aurora Keep. His long hair hung loose around his shoulders, and he ran a hand through it.

"Mael!" he called. Where the hell was he? He was supposed to brief Nadir twenty minutes ago. Nadir was already late, and his father would have his ass. A servant in dark livery approached with a stack of towels balanced in her arms.

"Have you seen the captain?" Nadir growled and the servant, wide-eyed and trembling, used the towels to gesture to a small room down the hall.

"I saw him go in there," she said, then bent her head and scurried away. Nadir's nostrils flared. He approached the room the maid had pointed out, slammed the door open, and stormed inside. It was mostly empty and used only when he needed extra space for entertaining. Like most of the Keep, the floor was made of black marble striated with crimson, emerald, violet, turquoise, and fuchsia. The walls were covered in brocaded silk except for the far one, which boasted a long bank of windows open to the night sky.

Nadir stopped in the center of the room and let out a low snarl. A large muscular body pinned Mael to the wall, and the fact that Nadir had just walked in was obviously the furthest thing from either of their minds. He folded his arms and cleared his throat in an exaggerated manner.

Mael's companion whirled around, his eyes widening as he fumbled with his pants, tucking in his cock with all the discretion of a marching band in a library.

"Nadir," Mael drawled. "What brings you here?" Mael straightened the hem of his tunic and ran a hand along the tight curls on his head, grinning like a cat with a mouthful of feathers.

"You were supposed to meet with me twenty minutes ago."

Nadir arched a dark brow as Mael wrinkled his nose. "Sorry about that. I completely lost track of the time when I ran into Emmett here." Mael gave the third male in the room a licentious wink, smacked him on his ass, and clucked his tongue. "Run along, Emmett. I'll come find you later."

Emmett said nothing to Mael, only looked at Nadir and bowed, his tanned cheeks as bright as rubies. "Your Highness," he said in a deep, rumbling voice, and then marched out of the room.

Nadir watched him leave and then turned back to his friend. "Is it really appropriate to be fucking your own soldiers?"

Mael beamed and shrugged. "Probably not, but what can a Fae do in the face of such brute strength and raw animal magnetism?"

Nadir pinched the bridge of his nose. "I ought to have you thrown into Nostraza for a week."

"Probably," Mael replied, striding over to where Nadir stood. "Until then, shall I update you?"

Nadir sighed and spun on his heel. "Walk with me. I'm late for this ridiculous party." The two Fae exited the room and continued on Nadir's previous path.

"Amya's sources have turned up nothing of note in Alluvion, Tor, or The Woodlands," Mael said, his voice low and guarded.

"And the others?" Nadir asked, keeping his eyes forward.

"She's still waiting on Celestria. She has a new woman in there, but information has been slow to trickle out."

"No hint of a mysterious girl?"

"None whatsoever."

Nadir growled low. This riddle was getting more and more confusing. He'd returned to his father's study several more times in the past weeks, still turning up no information on prisoner 3452.

"Anything in Heart?" Nadir asked now as they neared the hall where the tinkling sounds of a party in full swing could be heard.

"The usual," Mael replied. "Much of the same. Everything is dead, gone, barren. We even ventured through the castle, but it's as much a tomb as it ever was."

He hesitated, and Nadir's keen senses fired.

"What? Tell me."

"I'm sure it's nothing, but we found this." Mael reached into his pocket and pulled out the head of a single red rose, its petals slightly bruised from being stuffed into his pants. Nadir furrowed his brow.

"What's this?"

"It was growing on a bush in front of the castle."

"I thought you said everything was dead," Nadir said.

They now stood just past the entry to the party. A couple arrived, arms linked, and Nadir and Mael exchanged nods with the pair as they entered the room. Nadir pulled Mael further away.

"Everything but this." They both stared at it for a moment.

"What does it mean?" Nadir asked.

"I don't know." Mael looked up. "Probably nothing."

Nadir rubbed his chin as he regarded the flower, thoughts churning through his mind like freshly tilled soil.

"There's something else," Mael added, and then paused.

"Well?" Nadir asked. "Do I have to drag it out of you?"

Mael's dark eyebrows drew together. "There's been word that your father's army visited the settlements recently."

Nadir frowned. The small towns and villages that existed on the edges of the fallen realm were some of the most destitute in Ouranos. Attempts had been made to relocate the orphaned citizens, but they remained stolid in their faith that the Queen of Heart would return and restore them to their former glory someday. They were nothing but fanatics and fools. Dangerous and unhinged at worst, delusional at best.

"For what?"

Mael shrugged. "Apparently, they've been searching through homes. Quite...thoroughly, if the reports are to be believed."

The gazes of the two Fae met. "So he's looking for something," Nadir ventured.

"Or someone."

A swell of music and laughter burst from the party's direction and Nadir let out a deep breath steeped in ideas he wasn't ready to name yet. "I need to go."

Mael tipped a quick bow as Nadir stuffed the rose into his pocket.

"Have fun," Mael said with a smirk, knowing how much Nadir hated these things. Nadir scoffed and brushed past his friend, entering the room. He scanned the space, finding his father seated at a large round table.

Knowing this was his duty, he fortified himself against an evening of groveling and small talk and went over to sit next to the king.

"Nadir," his father intoned. "How nice of you to join us. *Finally*." At the table sat some of the council, with their partners in tow. Dressed for an elegant evening, jewels dripped from their necks, their clothing sewn from luxurious fabrics in the colors of the districts they each called home.

"Apologies, Father," Nadir said as someone placed a glass of dark red wine in front of him. "I was held up."

Rion said nothing as he took a sip of his own wine. The surrounding chatter continued while Nadir sat back and surveyed the room. The guests were a mix of Fae family members, some of very distant relation, other Fae nobles, and a sprinkle of high-ranking mortals who held positions of importance within The Aurora. Though humans generally existed below High Fae, there were those, usually of dubious morals, who managed to claw their way into the aristocratic ranks.

Rion thought it prudent to gather the realm's most powerful people on occasion to ply them with food and wine and favors to remind them he was always watching what they were up to.

Father and son sat in silence for several minutes, when Rion asked in a soft voice, "Did you find what you were looking for?" Rion sipped from his glass, his eyes focused on the room.

Nadir looked at his father. "What?"

"In my study," Rion said, still not looking at Nadir. "You've been in there, four? Five times? What is it you're seeking?"

"I don't know what you're talking about," Nadir said, an icy finger wandering down his spine.

"Come now," Rion said, finally looking at Nadir. "You don't really think you went rooting through my study without my knowledge. Surely you know better than that by now?"

Nadir swallowed, trying to tamp down his nervousness. How did his father manage to always make him feel like he was still a small boy and not a three-hundred-year-old High Fae who'd fought on the front lines of the Second Sercen War?

"You lied to me," Rion continued.

"About what?" Nadir asked, needles of tension pricking under his skin.

"About prisoner 3452. The ozziller did not kill her." There was something cold in Rion's eyes that Nadir couldn't interpret. "I don't like it when you lie to me, Nadir."

Nadir flexed his jaw. "Oh, I'm so sorry. It'll never happen again," he replied, his words as dry as the overpriced wine he was drinking.

Rion's expression sharpened. "Why did you lie to me, and why are you trying to find the file?" Nadir cut a glance to his father. "You didn't think I'd put it all together? Suddenly, my second warden in a few days dies, found in the filing room, no less. And then my son breaks into my study repeatedly, clearly searching for something."

"Who is she?" Nadir asked.

Rion rolled his shoulders as if this conversation was beneath him. "I want you to find her," he said, dodging the question.

"I'm already looking."

"I know," Rion said. "Don't think you can do anything without my knowing, Nadir. You should have learned that by now."

Nadir glared at Rion over the rim of his glass, silent loathing bursting in every locked chamber of his heart. "Who is she?" he asked again. "Why does she matter?"

Nadir caught a flash of something in Rion's eyes. It was inscrutable. There for a moment and then gone.

"She is no one. A loose end I should have dealt with years ago," he said, and Nadir pushed down the flare of his temper that threatened to throttle his father. The king was lying about her significance. Nadir was sure of it. Was it to throw him off?

"What is that supposed to mean?" Nadir attempted to keep his voice even, pretending the answer was of little interest. They were both playing this game, it seemed. But if Rion already knew how hard he'd been searching for evidence of her background, he was already aware of how much Nadir cared.

"It means that as much as you might rail against it, I still rule this kingdom. The next time you lie to me, Nadir, I will take something, or *someone*, of importance to you. That captain of yours has been especially bothersome lately."

Rion's expression was as cold as the windswept peaks of The Aurora, not a flicker of feeling or emotion on his face. Nadir had spent centuries trying to perfect that same façade, but there was always something untamed and wild that ran through his veins, refusing to be caged. Nadir was too emotional. Too tied to the feelings that ruled him to construct the same stone fortress made of skin and bone.

It's what had made Rion such a shitty father. To be that indifferent to everything and everyone required a level of self-absorption that could turn a Fae inside out.

"What should I do if I find her?" Nadir asked, pretending to ignore his father's threat, but if Rion hurt Mael, he'd tear the king limb from fucking limb while whistling a cheerful tune. He wouldn't care what the consequences were.

"Eliminate her," Rion said. "As much as I once hoped otherwise, she is of no use to me or to anyone."

Nadir waited, hoping his father might reveal something more, but Rion had gone silent. Sipping on his wine, Rion surveyed the room with his cold eyes.

"I need you to go to Aphelion in my stead for this ridiculous Sun Queen Trials ball," Rion said, and Nadir let out a derisive snort.

"No fucking way."

Rion slowly swiveled his head and pinned Nadir with an arctic expression. "It wasn't a question."

Nadir blinked, knowing he'd have no choice. He'd go prance around with the other court rulers, maintaining this farce as Atlas and his Mirror condemned some unsuspecting female to his eternal servitude. The only way Aphelion's king could get anyone to bond with him was to trick her into thinking it was some great honor. It was pathetic.

Once again, father and son fell into silence as Nadir plotted how best to make his exit from the room early.

The timing of the invite might be auspicious though, as he recalled that Amya still hadn't gotten a spy into the Sun Palace. It was the last place he was hoping to have to look, but if nothing came from the other courts, he might have to swallow that pill.

"Fine," he finally muttered. "I'm taking Amya with me."

Rion let out a chilling laugh so cold it seemed to crackle like fissures running over a frozen lake. "Yes, take your little sister, Nadir. I know you can't manage anything without her. Perhaps you should ask for her help next time you break into my study? The clumsy mess you made of my wards is going to take me weeks to fix."

Their gazes met, and now it was Nadir's turn to smirk. This was the one sore spot for the king, who seemed to care about nothing but himself. That Rion's precious daughter had rejected him and chosen to side with Nadir in this battle of family allegiances.

It wasn't much, but Nadir clung to her loyalty and this one advantage over his father with everything he had. He often wondered if Amya's hatred of their father was the single regret of Rion's long and miserable life.

Chapter Twenty-five

Lor

I choke on the dust coating the inside of my mouth as I roll over onto my back, sunlight stinging my eyes. The crowd is still cheering, celebrating the Tributes who've survived. I feel hands on me, someone gently tugging my leg, and I groan as fire shoots through my limbs. I can't feel anything but pain, my foot numb and my breathing cinched tight.

Two Fae healers hover over me, tending to the slice in my thigh. They work with efficiency, cleaning, then bandaging my wound. Atlas had said they could only heal us to prevent our death, so they're doing what they can to stem the loss of blood. My head spins and my vision blurs.

While they tend to me, I listen to the crowd celebrating, wishing I could muster up the same energy.

It takes me a few minutes to piece together everything that just happened. *Halo.* What was she thinking? I'm so furious with her that a hard knot of rage flares in my gut. She nearly dragged us both into that pit. Even if she could have leaped clear of the hole, why would she forfeit the contest? She was going to throw this all away. If she's eliminated from the Trials, she gets a cushy lifetime job as a handmaiden, but I can't drag up an ounce of sympathy, knowing that if it had been me who'd landed on the stadium floor, there would be no honored place in Aphelion for me.

One healer places a hand under my back and helps me sit, holding out two small pills. I take them and swallow them dry. They immediately take effect, dulling the searing ache in my leg. I'm surrounded by several people, including Halo, Tesni, Apricia, Gabriel, and Atlas, along with a trio of palace note-takers frantically writing.

The king drops in front of me, his large hand cupping the side of my face. "How are you feeling?" he asks, concern in his bright blue eyes. "That was quite a finish." He grins then, and while I'm exhausted and angry and hurt, there's so much evident pride in that smile that I can't help but return it.

Gabriel is now crouched down next to Atlas and rolls his eyes. "Let's get you back to the palace." He reaches out to help me stand, holding one arm while Atlas holds the other.

"Your Majesty," one warder says, "I can do that." Atlas waves him off.

"Lor," Halo moves in front of us. "I'm..." she trails off, not wanting to reveal her actions in front of the king. Throwing the contest would be an act tantamount to treason against Aphelion, and the consequences would be much worse than simply being cut from the Trials. But I have no desire to punish her to that extent, so I say nothing, pinning her with a glare that I hope conveys the scale of my displeasure.

"We'll talk about it later," I say pointedly, and she folds her lips together, nodding.

Atlas and Gabriel spin me around, one of my arms wrapped around each of their necks. They're both so tall they have to bend down considerably for me to reach. Atlas lets out a huff of frustration and scoops me into his arms. Startled, I look up at him, my eyes wide.

He grins. "Hello there."

"Hi," I say.

"Wrap your arms around my neck," he orders, and I nod, doing as he says. The movement sends a fresh wave of dizziness to my head, and I press my forehead to the curve of his neck, waiting for it to pass. He starts walking and I slowly peel open my eyes, looking over his shoulder. Apricia watches me in the king's hold. Blood streaks across her cheek, and her eyes are like daggers. It's then I remember someone shouting my name as I crossed the narrow balance beam.

I'd convinced myself it was Willow. In my stressed-out haze, my mind had been playing tricks. Realization dawns, and I throw her a searing glare. It was her. She made me slip and nearly fall into the pit. She smirks in response, her eyes glowing with her near moment of triumph. I'm going to kill her, too.

Gabriel files in behind Atlas, blocking my view, and I scowl. He returns it with an imperious arch of his brow.

"How many made it?" I finally ask, my thoughts settling slowly. I look up at Atlas, his expression growing dark.

"We lost one to the pit," he says in a low voice, and my stomach clenches. I see the flash of her red hair and hear the sounds of the thogrul as he smashed through her bones and chewed up her life. "Griane and Ostara were disqualified." I close my eyes.

"So there are four of us left." My voice is wooden, like its insides have been scraped out. There are two more challenges and only four of us left. I mourn the loss of Hesperia, though she was never kind to me. It's hard to not think about how I'm even closer to my goal. What if I survive to stand before the Sun Mirror? What will it do with me?

We've reached the palace gates, thanks to Atlas's brisk pace. He takes me through the halls as dozens of people offer to relieve me from his arms, but he brushes them all off. We reach my room to find Mag already waiting with her hands clasped together, bouncing on her toes.

She coos when she sees me, fluttering about me like a headless mother hen.

"Oh, you're a fright!" she declares. "Bring her into the bathroom. I have the tub waiting. We need to get her cleaned up." Mag bites her bottom lip in worry as Atlas brings me in and gently sets me on the upholstered bench where Mag directs him. She immediately drops to her knees and starts unbuckling my boots.

I lean against the wall, letting her take care of me. It feels nice to have someone worry about my well-being, even if she's paid to be here. When she's done with my boots, she reaches for the laces on my jerkin and then looks at the king, clearing her throat.

"Your Majesty, it wouldn't be proper for you to stay while I attend to the Tribute." She says this meaningfully, and I snort a tired laugh. Atlas has already seen plenty of me, but I guess we're pretending we've both been on our best behavior. Atlas tips his head to Mag and then to me. "Of course. I'll come back and see how you're doing later."

Before he leaves, he bends down and presses a gentle kiss to my temple before he takes a deep inhale. "You were amazing today," he says softly, and I smile up at him, a river of warmth trickling through my ribcage.

"Thank you."

He gives me a quick bow and then leaves, clapping Gabriel on the shoulder where he stands in the doorway, glowering.

Mag waves him in. "Help me get her out of these." She gestures to my blood-soaked pants, or what's left of them, after the healers tore away most of the fabric to get to my wound.

"Hey," I say. "Why can he be here? I don't want *him* seeing me naked."

Gabriel smirks and pulls out a dagger from his belt. "Nothing I haven't seen before, Tribute."

"That is hardly the point," I say through clenched teeth, pain flaring as Mag shifts me to remove my jerkin and the thin shirt underneath. I cross my arms over my chest, glaring at Gabriel, who eyes me with cool detachment.

"Trust me, I'm not interested in the unmentionable bits of mouthy human girls." He brings the dagger towards me, and I let out a small shriek, attempting to get away and then groaning as my leg gives a sharp throb. The pills the healers gave me helped, but they haven't taken away all the pain.

Gabriel digs his fingers into the waistband of my leggings and jerks me towards him with little concern for my injured state. "Sit still," he growls, and then deftly begins cutting away the leather.

"Mag," I hiss. "Could you get something to cover me?"

"Oh! Of course," she says, grabbing a towel and throwing it over me just as Gabriel peels away the last of my leggings, but not before he gets an eyeful of the unmentionable bits he *claims* he has no interest in. My cheeks flush and he smirks, clearly wallowing in my distress.

"Help me carry her to the tub," Mag says, standing up, and I can't believe how unbothered she is by Gabriel seeing me naked like this. "The healers gave her waterproof bandages so she can go straight in."

"Don't." I put out a hand when he reaches down to scoop me up. "I can walk."

He raises his hands in supplication and I prepare to stand, but my leg has gone stiff and as soon as I try to rise, I nearly collapse on the ground. Gabriel catches me, his large hands finding my bare skin. He wraps one arm around my shoulders and then sweeps another under my knees and rolls his eyes.

"Watch where you're touching," I snap, and he snorts. Mag keeps gesturing him over as though it's not completely obvious where the massive tub sits in the center of the room. Gabriel walks up the three steps, then stops at the top. He flashes me a wicked grin, and suddenly I'm worried.

"Enjoy your bath, Tribute."

Then he lets go, dropping me in an unceremonious heap into the tub. I scream as I land, my ass hitting the hard marble with a thud, pain flaring in my tailbone and up my spine. I flail in the water, the towel now wet and pasted to my breasts and stomach. Finding the edges of the tub, I hoist myself into a sitting position, my leg shrieking in protest.

Gabriel is laughing so hard he throws his head back, and I can see every one of his teeth. His wings flutter as though they're also in on the joke.

"You asshole!" I scream. He backs down the stairs, still laughing. "I hate you!" As he turns to leave, I shout at his back, but not before he gives me a mocking tip of his imaginary hat. I'm going to *kill* him.

When he's gone, Mag sets to work scrubbing my skin and dousing my hair in warm, soapy water. "Can I request a new warder?" I ask. "Is he this much of an ass to everyone?"

Mag flattens her lips. "He does seem to have taken a strong dislike to you," she muses. "He wasn't like that last time." At that, her eyes go wide and then she quickly looks away.

"Last time?" I ask. "What do you mean last time?"

She waves an absent hand. "What? Oh. I didn't say that."

"Yes, you did." Mag doesn't answer, wiping my arms with the soft sponge. I grab her wrist and hold it, forcing her to look at me. "What aren't you telling me?"

Worry trickles into the lines of her face. "It's forbidden," she whispers, looking around the room as though someone is here in the bathroom, eavesdropping.

"You might as well tell me now, because I won't stop asking until you do. Or I'll ask Atlas."

Mag shoots me an ominous look, but that's the right motivation because she says, "You didn't hear this from me."

"Fine," I agree. "A bird told me."

She glares. "I'm beginning to see why the captain dislikes you so much."

"Tell me," I say, ignoring her comment.

She dips the sponge in the water and then swipes it along my back, scrubbing my skin. "The last Sun Queen Trials weren't over five hundred years ago," she says. "They were two years ago."

Something drops in my chest. "What do you mean, two years ago? What happened?"

Mag stops scrubbing my back, leaning her forearms on the edge of the tub. "We're really not supposed to speak of it."

A snarl gathers in my throat. "But you're going to tell me."

Mag meets my gaze. "They all died."

That feeling in my stomach sinks even further. "What do you mean?"

She shakes her head. "It was during one of the challenges." She drops the sponge in the bath and squirts a dollop of purple shampoo into her hand. Standing behind me, she begins washing my hair as if she can't bear to face me. "I don't know what happened—they kept the details secret, but the Tributes went in and then no one came out. Just the king, the warders, and Madame Odell. The Trials were cancelled and then never spoken of again until a few weeks ago, when the king announced they'd be holding them again."

She's scrubbing my head vigorously now, her nervousness manifesting itself on my scalp. I let her continue, enjoying the feel of her digging into my skin. We both sit in silence, accompanied only by the squelch of the soap's lather.

A detail about what Mag just told me nags like a scratch I can't reach. If the last Trials were two years ago, then another Tribute from The Aurora must have been chosen. I rack my brain, trying to remember if another young woman from Nostraza left the prison. No one comes to mind. Most of Nostraza's inmates are men, and I would have noticed a woman around my age go missing. Unless the Aurora King chose her from somewhere else? I still don't understand why he let me go after everything that happened.

When Mag is done washing my hair, she flips on the hand-held shower and rinses it with a warm stream of water. I turn to look at her. "You have no idea how they all died?"

"I hear rumors. The servants talk."

"What rumors?"

"I'm sure they're not true." She squirts a dollop of conditioner on her hand, not meeting my eye.

"What rumors?" I repeat.

"That the king wasn't happy with the prospects and so he ended the Trials...prematurely."

I cut her a look, and her face has gone pale. "Is that true?" I think of the king. Of his kindness. Of the way he's been so good to me. There's no way that same Fae could do something like this. Is there?

"No," Mag says firmly, but it feels like she's convincing herself. "Of course it's not true. People will say all sorts of terrible things, won't they?" Her voice has taken on an edge, the pitch rising as she prattles on about how people love to tell lies and the king wouldn't do that sort of thing.

The more she denies it, the more skeptical I become.

If it's true, could it happen again? There are only four of us left and two more challenges. Will any of us make it to the end? How did those other Tributes fail to measure up? Atlas has hinted more than once he expects me to win, but have I just been hearing what I want to hear?

Mag must be mistaken. These are just cruel rumours spread by bored Fae who have nothing better to do than spin lies made of barbed wire.

She rinses the conditioner from my hair and then wraps my head in a towel to squeeze out the excess water.

"There," she says. "Much better. Are you okay to walk, or shall I summon the captain to help you out?" She makes to turn from the room and I call out, holding up a hand.

"No. Don't you dare get him. I can manage on my own." Gabriel would probably toss me off the balcony by "accident" this time. Mag holds on to my arms as I slowly ease up to stand, wincing at the ache in my leg. Sitting on my butt, I scoot out and drag myself down the steps before Mag wraps me in a fluffy robe.

Taking a deep breath, I haul myself up to stand, my arm wrapped around Mag's shoulders. She's about half a head shorter than me and the perfect height to use as a crutch while I limp heavily to the bed.

"You should get some rest," she coos and then helps me ease under the covers. Suddenly my eyelids are so heavy I can barely keep them open. I don't respond as I bury into the soft blankets and pillows and drift off to sleep.

I'm not sure how long I'm asleep, but when I awake, the sky is dark and the lights in my room are low. I stretch my arms overhead, wincing at the dull ache in my leg. Someone has left a glass of water and two more pain pills on my bedside table. I reach for them when I hear angry whispers from the bathroom.

The door is partially open, and I make out the hushed voices of Gabriel and the king.

"Who is she, Atlas? What is she doing here and why are you so interested in her? I don't trust this," Gabriel says, anger in his tone.

Atlas responds, but only the muffled sound of his voice reaches me. I hold perfectly still, not wanting them to know I'm awake. I have every right to hear what Gabriel is saying behind my back.

"You could have any one of these girls. They'd be a much better choice for you," Gabriel says. "Get rid of her."

At that, my eyes go wide as I lay perfectly still. *What?* Get rid of me?

"You're being ridiculous," Atlas says, louder this time. The exasperation in his voice loosens some of my tension. "There's nothing to worry about. Trust me. She's the right one. I'm sure of it."

"Atlas—" Gabriel says, a warning in his tone.

"I said enough," Atlas replies. "You are responsible for her safety and ensuring she passes the Trials. Zerra knows I've done my part."

"That's what I've been doing," Gabriel says, and I can practically hear him gritting his teeth.

I frown as several events piece themselves together. Atlas giving me the book in the library and the hint about the clothing. The mermaid monster chasing me and suddenly stopping in its tracks. Gabriel drilling me on the balance beam. That magical hand that seemed to have saved me from falling off the gauntlet.

"If one single hair on her head is harmed, you will answer for it. Do I make myself clear?" Atlas says next.

There's a long pause and I imagine them in a stand-off. Am I safe around Gabriel? If Atlas is truly worried, should he still be my warder? And why have they been helping me? What does Atlas want?

The *Aurora King* chose me for this, *not* Atlas. Right? Suddenly, that distinction seems very important. I think of the riot Gabriel claimed didn't happen that night he took me from Nostraza and wonder if everything I've been told here is the truth.

Finally, I hear Gabriel reply, "Yes, Your Majesty. Perfectly clear."

"Good," Atlas bites out. "And don't question my judgment again. Our friendship only extends so far. I am still your king, and you are still my servant."

I'm not sure if Gabriel replies or just nods, because a second later, the door swings open and I shut my eyes, feigning sleep.

I hear footsteps move towards the bed, and I try to regulate my breathing and relax my face. A moment later, I feel a soft hand touch my cheek and a thumb sweep across my bottom lip.

"I'll come and check on you again later," Atlas says in a soft voice. I then hear the sharp clip of his steps as he turns to leave the room.

"Come," Atlas barks, followed by the sound of Gabriel's footsteps. I wait for the door to close before I open my eyes and sit up, wondering what to make of what I just heard.

CHAPTER TWENTY-SIX

I spend the next few days recovering in bed, the healers tending to me twice a day with fresh bandages and a steady supply of painkillers. They say it was a clean cut and is healing nicely. I'm told Halo comes to my door more than once, but I decline to see her, not all that interested in hearing what she has to say. I'm still furious that she nearly got me thrown out of the competition. I thought she was my friend. I expect this behavior from Apricia, but not from her.

I also can't get over the conversation I overheard between Atlas and Gabriel. What is his problem with me? As far as he knows, I'm a mortal prisoner from Nostraza and couldn't hurt a flea if I tried. I also have to consider Atlas's true intentions, knowing he's been cheating for me. I wonder if he's been doing the same for any of the other Tributes.

I also can't stop thinking about the previous Sun Queen Trials.

Who can I ask for more information?

Mag ignores me completely every time I bring it up, changing the subject. The only other person who comes to my room is Atlas, but after Mag said speaking of the Trials is forbidden, that doesn't feel like the right move. Then there's Gabriel, who treats me like I'm something he's considering having lanced. I definitely can't ask him.

It occurs to me the other Tributes must know. They were all alive and living in Aphelion two years ago. Perhaps I will go find Halo, if only to ask her. She at least owes me that.

With that thought in mind, I decide to go for a walk, feeling stronger and stir-crazy from lying around. I slip out of bed and dig out some comfortable clothes. A yellow tunic and leggings made of buttery soft suede, along with a pair of soft golden slippers. I check the locket around my neck with a reaffirming tug, thinking of Willow and Tristan. What are they doing right now? I've been gone for weeks—do they know I'm alive? Surely no one has told them what really happened to me.

My hair has continued to grow, thanks to Callias's magic, and is well past my shoulders now. I comb it out with my fingers and shake my head, loving the way it feels swishing against the back of my neck.

Exiting my room, I choose a random direction and proceed through the halls. As usual, the palace is alive with activity, parties in full swing, stuffed with Fae and mortals drinking, eating, and carousing in various states of undress. I wonder if all the courts are this liberal in their carnal enjoyments or if this is a characteristic unique to Aphelion.

Though I understand the Fae are generally enthusiastic when it comes to matters of the bedroom, I can't imagine anyone in The Aurora having this much fun. It's far too dark and gloomy. The Aurora Keep seems more appropriate for funerals and raising the dead.

With a smile, I watch the people as I pass, infected by their joy. What a life this must be, to just exist for pleasure. Is that the reality that awaits if I become Aphelion's queen? Would that satisfy me? It's not the kind of queen I'd ever imagined myself to be.

As much as the parties seem happy and warm, I'm not in the mood for a crowd today, especially when I catch sight of Griane and Apricia sipping champagne. I wonder why Apricia isn't also subjected to endless lessons with Madame Odell, but I suppose I can already guess the answer to that.

As I pass, they both spot me. Griane offers me a tiny smile now that she's no longer in contention. Really, she owes me a thank-you for helping her survive the gauntlet, but I'm not holding my breath. Apricia's stony stare is the same as always. I shudder at the notion of becoming one of her handmaidens and wonder if going back to Nostraza might actually be the more pleasant option.

Not letting her ruin my mood, I continue past and find a wide set of glass doors. Pushing them open, I emerge into a tranquil garden. There are rows and rows of bushes bursting with sparkling golden roses. They bloom in every direction, the sun's reflection infusing them with life. The effect is mesmerizing.

Trailing my fingers along the soft petals, I make my leisurely way down the paths.

The roses are so soft they feel like pillows wrapped in velvet. I bend down to sniff one, the scent rich and luxurious. It transports me back to Nostraza and that tiny sliver of soap that smelled like a phantom shadow of these potent buds. That innocuous bar of soap that landed me in the Hollow and then led me here to this garden, tossing me into the unpredictability of fate's path.

Hoping no one minds, I pluck one of the blooms to carry with me, spinning the stem between my forefinger and thumb.

The sound of the ocean roars in the distance, and I make my way to a low stone wall on the far side of the garden that overlooks the sea. "Lor," a voice calls, interrupting my reverie. Halo stands with Marici, both of them watching me with wary expressions.

"Hi," I say in a clipped tone, still harboring the sting of her betrayal.

"How are you feeling?" Halo asks, coming closer, Marici keeping at her side.

"I'm...fine. I guess."

"I came to see you. Many times."

"I know," I say.

"I wanted to explain." Halo bunches her skirt in her hands and casts an uncertain glance at Marici. The other Fae steps closer, laying a pale hand on Halo's arm and nodding.

"Tell her," Marici whispers. "She deserves to know."

I frown, wondering what's happening. Is there anywhere I can escape secrets in this place?

"Marici and I," Halo says, and then stops. Marici squeezes Halo's arm again, and they share a look filled with so much tenderness and raw emotion that I let out a small gasp.

"You're in love," I say, and both their faces transform with surprise and relief.

"Yes," Halo says, but then her expression dissolves into panic, her eyes widening. "But you can't tell anyone."

I hold up my hands. "It's okay. I'm not going to say anything."

A shadow falls over her eyes. "It is treason to *be* with anyone but the king once you join the Trials."

I run a hand down my face as several things click into place.

"This is why you wanted to throw the challenge." Halo nods, her lips pressed together. "What's your plan? To live together as handmaidens and..." I trail off as that knowledge settles between us. Standing up from the wall, I shake my head. "This is dangerous. You could both be jailed or hanged or whatever it is they do to traitors in Aphelion."

Halo's eyes drop to her feet. "We could," she says softly before looking back up at me. "But we've been friends for a very long time..."

"Our families have no idea," Marici adds. "They were expecting one of us to bond with the king. We had no choice but to enter the Trials."

"I'm so sorry I nearly got you killed on the gauntlet. You have every right to be furious," Halo says.

She did, and I was, but my anger has already dissipated as I note the sadness and tentative hope in the slope of their postures. "You'll have to keep it a secret," I say.

"Unless the king decides we no longer belong to him in that way," Halo says, a blush creeping up her cheeks. "Tribute hand-maidens can never take a bonded partner, but some have gone on to have other relationships if the king wasn't interested in them. With his blessing."

I scowl at that. Aphelion really has some issues with how they treat their females. And they call *me* the uncivilized one.

Marici is leaning against Halo like a tiny flower seeking shel-ter against a tree. "If you win..." Halo says, not finishing the thought.

"I'm not going to win," I say, sure that despite what I heard between Atlas and Gabriel, the odds of me actually making it in front of the Sun Mirror are infinitesimal.

"But if you do," Marici says.

I cut a sharp look her way. "I'm not going to win," I repeat. Atlas might have forbidden Gabriel from harming me, but that doesn't mean I'm safe. It would be so easy to make anything look like an accident during a challenge.

Marici nods, her eyes downcast, and I feel guilty for snapping at her, but I don't want her getting her hopes up. Or mine, for that matter. I let out a sigh and run a hand down my face.

"*If* I win, I'll see what I can do. Trust me, *if* I win, I won't abide my partner welcoming anyone to his bed but me."

Both women perk up, smiles on their faces, but my words carry a bravado I have no claim to. If I win, then it's clear I'll still be second to the Fae who holds the real power in this realm. Could I stop him even if I wanted to? Does he answer to anyone?

"Thank you, Lor," Halo says, taking my hands. "Thank you."

"Don't thank me," I reply. "I haven't done anything yet."

"Of course," Marici says. "Thank you anyway."

I sigh again, the weight of the world pressing down on my shoulders like a ceiling of stone.

Tristan. Willow. Halo. Marici.

The list of people counting on me to win the Sun Queen Trials is getting longer and longer.

CHAPTER TWENTY-SEVEN

Apricia, Tesni, Halo, and I stand in a line facing Madame Odell, who's looking us over like an appraiser in a diamond shop. The way she wrinkles her nose at me suggests she's uncovered a stone with too many flaws to count.

"Congratulations on being the final four," Madame Odell says. "While I'm not surprised to see some of you here, I am utterly baffled by one of you."

If a miracle happens and I become the queen of Aphelion, Madame Odell is going on the list with the Aurora King of the people I will punish.

I roll my eyes, resisting the urge to stick out my tongue. That would be childish and I am...well, not a lady, exactly, but I'm done with allowing her to make me feel small. I've outlasted six other Tributes and made it this far, even if it wasn't entirely on my own steam. I look at Apricia and don't believe that I'm the only one Atlas is helping. He'd said he had his favorites. Plural.

Regardless, I'll never earn her respect—that much is clear—but she isn't better than I am.

I notice Halo open her mouth, about to defend me, but I lay a hand on her arm. It isn't worth it and won't make a difference. Madame Odell will think what she wants. Halo gives me a reluctant nod. I sense she feels like she owes me for keeping her and Marici's secret, but she doesn't. I would never tell or do anything to cause them trouble.

"The next challenge will happen at the Sun Queen Trials ball in three days' time," Madame Odell says. "This is a tradition of every trial and a premier event in Aphelion. The rulers of every court attend to get a look at the potential future Sun Queen." She smiles in Apricia's direction as though it's all been decided, and I huff out a derisive snort that she ignores.

But her words leave me reeling. All the rulers.

That means I'll see the Aurora King again. After all these years. A knot tightens in my stomach.

Is he here to check on his hostage? Does he even know or care that I'm still alive? What was his intention in sending me here? Is this a part of some greater plan? It's been so many years I was sure he'd forgotten about me after he tried his best to break me. It's been so long since I've seen the face of the Imperial Fae I vow to destroy someday.

I'm not sure if I'm ready.

"The ball is a masquerade," Madame Odell continues. "You will join the other guests anonymously, not as Tributes, but as regular partygoers. Your task will be to mingle, charm, and seduce. Several attendees will be selected to participate in the challenge, though they will not know they are part of the game until it's over. They'll each be wearing an object of great sentimental importance to them. A ring, or a brooch, for example. One hour after the start of the ball, your warder will be told the specific object you are to retrieve. Seek him out to find out who your mark will be.

"Your goal is to convince the owner of this item to turn it over to you. You may use whatever means necessary short of telling them who you are and what you're there to do. Whoever retrieves their trinket last fails the task and will be eliminated. The other three will move to the fourth and final challenge."

Madame Odell stops her slow pacing and turns, her hands clasped at her stomach. "Are my instructions clear?"

We all nod. This trial seems somewhat simple compared to the others, but I'm sure there must be a catch. At least it doesn't seem like death is a likely outcome this time, but that's what I thought about the trivia test.

"Excellent," Madame Odell says. "I look forward to seeing you make use of your wit and wiles." As usual, she looks at me with an expression that suggests each of those traits have taken a wide turn and passed me by. She's probably right. I don't know how to charm anyone. Hopefully, I'll get someone malleable as my target.

"You are dismissed," she says then. "Good luck, Tributes."

Callias bursts into my room, pushing his cart laden with combs and potions, and gives me a once-over. I'm drinking a glass of champagne and finishing the lunch Mag brought in for me earlier. It's the day of the Sun Queen ball, and apparently it's going to take hours to get ready.

"Oh, good!" Mag says, clapping her hands. "You're finally here."

Callias arches a sardonic eyebrow. "Yes, well, I had to fend off the maid of that insufferable Apricia." He curls his lip. "Zerra help the king if she wins. And all of Aphelion, for that matter. Do you know she screamed at me for twenty minutes because the highlights she asked for weren't *lustrous* enough?" He scoffs as he unpacks things from his cart, laying them on the dressing table. "As if I'm responsible for the lack of natural shine in her hair. I'm not her regular stylist. I don't know what swill she's been using to wash and condition, and I swear—"

"Callias," Mag snaps. "Focus, please. We haven't much time."

I'm about to protest that we actually have hours, but Mag silences me with a look.

Callias lets out a harried breath and plants a hand on his hip. "Yes, fine." He scrutinizes me, tilts his head, and then smiles. "I see my pills have been working." His shoulders do a smug little dance before he resumes unpacking his tools.

"They have been," I reply. My hair has grown midway down my back now, and thanks to the shampoo Mag insists I use, it's so soft and shiny it feels like silk. It's probably not as lustrous as Apricia's, with her thick sheet of hair, but compared to the hacked locks I arrived with, it's an astonishing improvement.

Callias walks over with a comb in his hand and circles me where I sit in the chair at my small dining table.

"What should we do tonight?" he muses. I don't think he's actually speaking to me, so I don't answer as I pour myself another glass of champagne. The bottle is now empty, and I hold it up as a signal to Mag.

"Can you get me another?"

She nods, heading off to do my bidding. I'm so nervous about tonight, and I need a little liquid courage. The thought of seeing the Aurora King is dredging up my carefully tucked away memories like waterlogged bodies surfacing through sludge.

Still circling me, Callias stops to pause and then circles in the other direction. He makes several noises, *hmms* and *hahs*, and I'm starting to feel like a horse at an auction.

"Are you quite finished?" I ask. "Am I so hopeless it takes an hour to figure out what to do with me?" He stops and winks, not at all fazed by my outburst. He takes the glass in my hand and I protest, but he waves me off.

"Come, come. You can get drunk over here."

He sets the glass on the dressing table and directs me to sit. "Fine," I say, sliding onto the seat. He considers me from a few more angles and then finally starts on my hair, brushing it as he meets my gaze in the mirror.

"Having fun?" he asks casually, and I snort.

"If you call getting injured and nearly dying more than once fun, then sure." Callias smiles to himself as he combs through my tresses and then picks up a heated blue roller. He blows on it for a moment and then wraps it with a lock of my hair, letting it rest against my scalp.

"Rumour has it the king is quite taken with you," Callias says, his expression sly. "I did say you'd make things interesting, didn't I? Can you imagine? The Final Tribute being one of the favored? I hear they're losing their minds in The Umbra. You're quite the little inspiration, Lor."

I don't respond as he continues working, wrapping more locks of hair around rollers of various sizes. The Umbra. It feels strange to be "from" a place I've never seen. Do they realize no one there knows who I am? Or is The Umbra so destitute they can't even recognize one of their own? I'm not one of theirs, though, I remind myself. I'm from Nostraza and when I lose, I'm going back there.

"You're awfully quiet," Callias says. "Drink some more. That'll pep up your step." He picks up my glass and refills it from the bottle Mag just retrieved.

I smirk as I accept it and drain it with a large swallow.

"Have you kissed him?" Callias asks, and I see Mag stiffen where she's been going about her business, making the bed and tidying up. "I won't tell."

I meet his gaze in the mirror and see only curiosity without judgment.

"Yes," I find myself admitting. "I have."

Callias makes a noise like he expected that. "Well, I, for one, would be thrilled to see the Final Tribute win. It's disgraceful how they drag up some poor Umbra rat, all thin and scraggly and pathetic, put her in a silk dress, and expect her to compete against the most accomplished young females across Aphelion."

My forehead furrows, and then he seems to remember himself. "Oh, not you, sweetheart. I didn't mean you. You've done very well, haven't you? You are proof anyone can change their lot in life, just like they say." He beams and continues applying curlers to my head.

When all my hair is wrapped up, he refills my glass again and I drink some more, hoping if I keep going, this snarl of tense ribbons in my stomach will loosen. I've faced monsters and heights and Apricia's hair flip, but the Aurora King is my personal rock bottom. No one has made me suffer like he has.

I go to refill my glass again when Callias puts a hand on my wrist. "Maybe you should slow down a touch? You're not going to make it through the night if you keep going at that rate."

"I'm fine," I say, shaking him off before I continue pouring. He shrugs his shoulders and starts to remove the curlers one by one, revealing a waterfall of shiny spirals.

"Do the rumours suggest the king has taken a liking to anyone else?" I ask, trying to sound casual, but sure I'm failing. Callias raises an eyebrow and bites his lip.

"They say he has also been seen in the company of a certain dark-haired viper."

"Whose golden highlights lack luster?" I take a sip of my wine, the bubbles dancing on my tongue.

"Hmm." Callias's response is noncommittal.

"It's fine," I say. "I don't care. He's supposed to spend time with the others."

Callias pins the top half of my hair to the back of my head while I watch his every move in the mirror. He nods.

"Of course you don't."

I narrow my eyes at his patronizing tone. "Do you think he's the kind of Fae who will call for the handmaidens when the queen is chosen?"

Callias barks out a derisive laugh. "Oh, all Fae are that kind, sweetheart. We aren't good at keeping anything in our pants. Clearly, you haven't spent enough time around us."

"All?" I ask, frowning.

"Not all," he says. "There are some who are faithful. The ones lucky enough to find their true mate and all that." He waves a hand as if to show he doesn't buy it. "But that's so rare, it's practically a legend, and regardless, Fae are fickle creatures in general."

I don't want to care. I tell myself I feel only a passing fondness for the king. He's been kind and generous and made me feel good about myself in a way no one ever has. But I have to keep sight of my mission. Of what I'm really here to do. Tristan and Willow. Their names ring through my head like a chorus of beating drums. I have to win and I have to get them out. Halo and Marici are counting on me, too. Atlas can fuck whomever he wants. It makes no difference to me. That's not what I'm here for.

I polish off another glass of champagne with an intentional flourish, tipping up my chin and following it with a hard swallow.

"That's right," Callias coos, patting my shoulder. "Drink away your feelings. That'll make everything better."

"Shut up," I say, and he laughs. "I'm drinking away my nerves, not my feelings."

"Well, either way...you're done."

Callias has rendered me into a masterpiece fit for the portrait over any fireplace. My hair shines like it's been kissed by the sun. A gentle sweep of curls is piled on top of my head, tendrils framing my face. He leans down so his cheek is next to mine and places his hands on my shoulders. "Dare I say, you rather look like a queen?"

As I smile, a soft belch escapes, and I cover my mouth. Callias curls his lip in disgust and stands. "You can take the girl out of The Umbra, but you can't take the..." he mutters to himself as he packs up his things. Still covering my mouth, I giggle at the look on his face.

He cracks a smile and shakes his head. "Try not to get yourself killed. Hmm?" He taps the end of my nose gently in a strangely paternal gesture.

"Time for the dress!" Mag declares, gesturing me over and shoving me behind a changing screen. She strips off my robe and then holds open the gown for me to step into. It's gold, of course, and covered in thousands of twinkling crystals. The fitted bodice goes over one shoulder, covering the brand from Nostraza and leaving the other bare. The skirt billows to the floor in gentle folds, the material so light and airy I feel like I'm wearing a cloud.

Mag sits me back down and proceeds to dust my eyelids and cheeks with gold. She also takes out a fine brush and a pot of gold paint and draws a long floral vine down the length of my bare arm. The shimmery lines stand out beautifully against my light brown skin.

When she's done, I gasp at my reflection. It seems impossible I could look like this when just six weeks ago I was wearing my worn grey tunic, lying at the bottom of a dirt hole, so wasted away my bones were nearly tearing through my paper-thin skin.

I *do* feel like a queen, even if I'm still a far cry from one.

The backs of my eyes burn with a tangle of unrequited emotions I don't have the freedom to examine right now, and I push them away. Now is definitely not the time to reflect on the future that might have been had things gone differently before I was ever born.

Mag finishes off my ensemble with a delicate golden mask, covered in silk and edged in gold beading, with a pale yellow feather attached to the corner. She places it over my eyes and ties the ribbon at the back of my head.

"Is she ready?" Gabriel calls from the other side of the screen, and I suppress a groan. I've been trying to keep my distance ever since I overheard his conversation with Atlas, but since he still makes me train every day, it hasn't been easy. I mostly just keep my mouth shut around him, not in the mood for his insults as he works me until I'm a quivering mess every day. Since he clearly wants me gone, I don't know why he even bothers.

"She is," Mag says in a singsong voice, dragging me out from behind the screen. For an uncomfortable moment, Gabriel and I stare at each other. I brace myself, waiting for the inevitable dig.

The reminder that they can truss me up in all the pretty dresses they want, but it will never erase who I am.

For his part, he looks glorious in a fitted golden jacket that falls just past his hips, the cut showing off his broad shoulders and muscled arms. Brown breeches skim the curves of his strong thighs where they meet the cuffs of tall brown boots, polished to a high gleam. His dark blond hair is swept back and left loose, hanging down his shoulders where it curls against the sun tattoo on his neck. He wears his sword, as usual, hanging from his hip, but there is something casual and luxurious about this version of Gabriel.

He scans me from head to toe, his shoulders tightening and his snowy wings flexing. Then he grunts an evasive sound that almost might be mistaken for approval.

"Come on." He spins on his heel and heads for the door, stopping at the exit and waiting for me to follow, his gaze doing another assessment as I pass. We walk side by side down the halls, which are quiet for a change. I suppose everyone is at the ball tonight.

"Where's your mask?" I ask, scurrying to keep up with his long strides. He offers me a condescending look. "Isn't this a masquerade?" I make my voice shrill because I know it annoys him. The deep breath and flare of his nostrils, along with the glare I receive, tells me I've succeeded. I smother my smile of triumph.

"The rulers of the other courts are here," he says, his voice low.

"Yes, Madame Odell told us...including the Aurora King." My tongue trips over those words.

"No, Rion sent his regrets. The prince is coming in his place."

The prince. Not the king. A knot loosens in my stomach, though it still sits tangled with a stream of conflicting thoughts.

"Does the prince know about me?"

Gabriel cuts me a sidelong glance full of venom. "No. *You* are a citizen of Aphelion. Keep it that way. Do you understand?"

I nod as we turn down a hall where a wide set of doors reveals the twirl and laughter of the ball already in full swing.

"Ready, Final Tribute?"

I smooth down the front of my dress and throw back my shoulders, preparing to conquer another challenge on the ladder to my destiny. "Don't call me that."

Gabriel gives me one more penetrating look and then steps aside, gesturing me in. "I'll see you in an hour, Lor. Try to stay out of trouble."

CHAPTER TWENTY-EIGHT

NADIR

Taking a sip of wine, Nadir leaned against one of the marble pillars and surveyed the party. He'd flown from The Aurora without a retinue and had no intentions of lingering in Aphelion if he could help it. Amya had declined to come in the end, leaving him to suffer this evening alone.

He glanced at the head table, where the other rulers of Ouranos sat conversing pleasantly like they didn't all hate each other's guts. Where was Atlas, and why couldn't his father have just come? Every other king and queen had managed. The answer, he supposed, was none of them had heirs to order around.

Nadir tried to pick out the Tributes from the guests, just for something to do. They wouldn't be revealed until the "game" was complete, apparently. No one had told the guests what would happen, only that the girls would appear as part of the crowd until the end of the event. Nadir shook his head, taking another sip from his glass, spying a young woman with ebony skin and bright silver hair walking through the throng alone, her hands wringing. She seemed nervous, her anxious eyes darting around.

Nadir snorted. These poor girls were so easy to pick out. Who else would be walking around solo? Nadir spied another girl with dark hair down to her waist, flipping it over her shoulder. She scanned the crowd until her gaze met one of the Sun King's guards. He gave her an imperceptible nod. Her warder, then, Nadir supposed.

A moment later, his gaze snagged on another female who walked into the room. Her glittering gold gown floated around her like wisps of honeyed smoke. She stood at the railing, her hands pressed against it, her knuckles white from the pressure.

Though her eyes were covered in a golden mask, he marked their curious and assessing spark as she watched the dancers. She seemed both overwhelmed by her surroundings and yet completely grounded. Determined, if the set of her jaw was anything to go by.

Nadir narrowed his eyes as he took another sip, only to find his glass was empty. He glanced at the scant contents and then looked up to see the female he'd been watching now talking to a tall male with wavy brown hair. Nadir rolled his eyes at Atlas's pathetic attempt to appear as one of the crowd. Did he really think he was fooling anyone? He was so arrogant he probably enjoyed everyone pretending they didn't know who he was.

He led the female down the stairs onto the dance floor, pulling her in close with a possessiveness that suggested he believed she already belonged to him, regardless of the Trials' outcome. Nadir curled his lip. How embarrassing to be paired off with someone who was only there for a crown. When he bonded to his queen, he would settle for nothing less than someone who set his blood on fire.

"Why are you hiding here in the shadows, *Your Highness*?" a voice said next to him, and Nadir found Gabriel, who stared straight ahead, his hands clasped behind his back.

"It's where I'm most comfortable," Nadir said as Gabriel's mouth pulled into a wry smile.

"Always the life of the party, aren't you, Nadir?"

Nadir smirked, turning his gaze back to the crowd. "I've heard no complaints."

Gabriel chuckled softly before the two Fae went silent for a moment.

"You think he'll pick one this time?" Nadir asked. "No more innocent blood on your hands?"

Gabriel's mouth went tight. "That was...unpleasant."

"Still Atlas's good faithful hound, I see."

Gabriel cut a sharp glance to Nadir. "It's not like that."

"It's none of my business." Nadir handed his glass off to a passing servant, taking a full one from the tray balanced in his hand. "Can I ask you something? And it stays between us?"

"What?"

"You haven't gotten wind of anyone showing up in Aphelion who doesn't belong here?"

Gabriel's eyebrow rose. "Doesn't belong here? Have you lost someone, Nadir?"

"You could say that. A girl from The Aurora."

He watched Gabriel go still, his eyes scanning the room. "No. I haven't," he replied a moment later. Nadir watched the other Fae, his eyes narrowing, sure Gabriel was lying.

"Do you plan to make your presence known?" Gabriel asked, changing the subject and gesturing to where Atlas still danced with the Tribute.

Nadir let out a deep sigh. "I suppose I'll have to, lest anyone think The Aurora doesn't take its commitments to duping and murdering young Fae females seriously."

"The Mirror—" Gabriel said as Nadir cut him off.

"The Mirror is bullshit."

"Keep your voice down," Gabriel said through clenched teeth, his back straight.

"Don't you tire of all this?" Nadir gestured to the head table where the other rulers sat.

"This is my duty," Gabriel said, his tone like someone who had memorized the words and said them over and over until they'd lost every ounce of passion or purpose.

"Yes. Duty." Nadir rolled his neck.

"You know I don't have a choice," Gabriel said, so softly that Nadir could pretend he hadn't heard it. He turned his attention to where Atlas was beaming at the Tribute in his arms. The Sun King looked over and caught Nadir's gaze, his smile dropping.

Nadir laughed to himself. He supposed he'd just made his presence known.

"I guess I should go be diplomatic," Nadir said with another sidelong glance at Gabriel. "If you see or hear anything unusual about a girl from The Aurora..."

Gabriel nodded. "Of course."

Nadir clapped the Captain of the Aphelion Guard on the shoulder, tugged on the hem of his dark jacket, and strode away.

Chapter Twenty-nine

Lor

Nothing could have prepared me for the splendor of the ballroom when I step inside. It's enormous, the ceiling soaring overhead and hanging with dozens of chandeliers dripping with crystals and golden pearls. The curved walls, covered in gold brocade silk, sweep around to encompass hundreds of well-dressed Fae like a goddess's embrace.

I'd thought my glittering gown was the height of extravagance, but it's just another in a sea of hundreds of ensembles that burst with gold and jewels and riches. Everyone is dressed in their best, hair lacquered, makeup perfect, and eyes sparkling. I realize then Callias has left my ears covered so as not to give away my lowly mortal status.

I glance around the room, wondering if any of the other Tributes have already arrived. My balance is a little off-kilter, and I cautiously place one foot in front of the other, approaching the golden railing that circles the edge of the room. Maybe I shouldn't have had that last glass of champagne.

Short, wide staircases spaced at even intervals lead down to the sunken dance floor. A small orchestra sits in the corner and couples spin to the notes of music like autumn leaves twirling in a gust of wind. The atmosphere is lively and energetic, the guests all brimming with smiles. I swallow down my apprehension. How did I end up here? How has this become my life?

"May I have this dance?" a deep male voice asks, and I turn to find a towering Fae looking down at me. He wears a fitted golden jacket embossed with flowers. A mask covers his face, much like mine, but without the feather or adornments. His copper-brown hair glows so bright it's like it's been highlighted with ribbons of fire.

"Atlas," I say, looking around and wondering if someone is playing a prank. He lifts a finger to his mouth and makes a *shh* sound.

"I am just an anonymous reveler at a masquerade, my lady." He bends at the waist, his mouth turning up into a half smile. I huff out a laugh. Even with a mask on, there can be no mistaking who this Fae is. His pull is undeniable. Eyes follow him everywhere he goes, trapping us under his spell.

He holds out his hand, and I arch an eyebrow and curtsy before I place my hand in his. I remember how scared I'd been to do this when I first met Gabriel all those weeks ago. Perhaps

Madame Odell's lectures were of *some* use. "Very well. I would be honored."

He grins and leads me down the steps to the dance floor covered in pale yellow marble veined with gold.

"I've never done this before outside of my lessons," I whisper, knowing his superior Fae ears can pick up on my words.

"Don't worry, I'll help you." His hand slides along the small of my back and he pulls me close so I'm pressed right up against him. No chaste distances between us here. He takes my other hand, holding it in his large palm, and begins to lead us into the dance.

"You look stunning," Atlas says, his voice low as he leans to speak directly in my ear. "Perhaps after the party, you'll come visit me?"

I press my lips together, looking up into his bright blue eyes. I should refuse. I think of what Callias told me regarding Apricia. Is Atlas playing us both against each other? Does any of it matter if the Sun Mirror has the final say? He'd said the Mirror considers his preference. I remind myself I'm here to win this contest. That I have everything riding on it. I can't rescue Tristan and Willow if I don't win, and I certainly can't get my revenge on the Aurora King without the resources of a queen. Apricia may want to win so she can live in a palace and hang off the arm of this beautiful Fae, but for me, this is a matter of life and death and so much more. Surely mine is the more noble cause.

I've used my body as a weapon and as currency for twelve long years with the worst types of men I've ever known. Why should I stop now, when the stakes have never been higher?

Besides, Atlas has only made me feel good and beautiful and wanted. There's no reason for me to resist. No reason for me to hold back, especially if it gives me an edge.

I've already decided I don't care if Atlas has been helping me. I don't need to win this "fairly." Nothing in my life has been fair.

He's watching me expectantly, as though he really thinks I might say no to his request. Finally, I nod. "I'd like that."

His smile is radiant as he spins me around the room. My interest wanders to the raised dais at the far end, where a long table draped in golden cloth sits in front of nine magnificent chairs. In the center is a large golden throne that I assume is meant for the Fae I'm dancing with.

To one side sits a slightly smaller black throne, the back upholstered in emerald velvet. Next to that are two wooden chairs covered in curling vines where two Fae with deep olive skin sit. The first is a male with long, flowing brown hair wearing an elegant green tunic. Next to him is a stunning female, also with long brown hair in an intricate dress of sage green. They both sport a pair of leathery brown wings tucked behind their backs.

"The King and Queen of The Woodlands," Atlas says, catching my stare. "Cedar and Elswyth. Cedar and I have been friends for centuries. He's a good Fae, despite the rest of his *family*." I wonder at the bitterness in his voice and watch as Cedar whispers something to his bonded partner before she smiles. Love beams in her eyes like heart-shaped rainbows when she looks at him, and something tugs in my chest.

"Was she chosen the same way? Through a trial?"

"Sort of," Atlas says, spinning me across the floor. "Every realm has their own version of the Imperial Fae ascension."

"Will you tell me about them?" I ask, looking back at the couple who seem to be so in love that everything around them has ceased to exist.

"Of course," Atlas says. "You'll need to know these things if you find yourself ruling Aphelion." I look up at him and he smiles.

"Who are the rest?"

Next to The Woodlands King and Queen is a translucent blue throne made of what looks like glass. A beautiful male lounges in his seat, his posture loose and casual as he sips his wine and surveys the room. His skin is so pale it's almost blue. It complements the fall of indigo hair that hangs so long it disappears behind the height of the table. Sharp cheekbones, a strong jaw, and deep blue eyes only add to his appeal.

"The Alluvion King," Atlas says. "Rulers of the ocean. Cyan is an arrogant bastard, but his heart is in the right place. He's yet to find his bonded, though he's been searching for a long time."

On the other side of the Sun King's seat is a pair of stone thrones with two more Fae. They're two of the most beautiful females I've ever seen, with olive-brown skin and long silver hair. They, too, have wings, these ones covered in shimmering grey feathers. "Those are the Queens of Tor. Bronte and Yael. While they aren't our allies, Aphelion and Tor have had their moments of cooperation."

Another throne is made of some kind of silvery material that almost looks like liquid. Upon it sits a female with skin as pale as alabaster, her hair a sheet of pure white. Black eyes look out over the crowd with cunning curiosity. "D'Arcy, the queen of

Celestria," Atlas says, his eyes going dark. "The coldest witch in all of Aphelion."

I watch the ethereal beings at the front of the room as they engage occasionally in polite conversation. Mostly they just looked bored, save for The Woodlands King and Queen, who can't stop touching each other.

"Shouldn't you be up there entertaining them?" I ask, and Atlas grins.

"They'll be fine for one dance."

Another song has started, but Atlas doesn't let go and it's then I get the courage to ask. "Where is the Aurora Prince?"

Atlas shakes his head. "Late, I suppose. Typical of The Aurora. They respect no one and nothing but their own authority. The prince is vicious and cruel."

"Just like his father," I whisper, unable to stop the words from slipping out.

Atlas's shoulders drop and concern reflects in his eyes. "Yes. Just like his father." He scans the room. "Maybe we'll get lucky and he won't even come. I only invited The Aurora out of diplomacy. I'd rather they kept as far away from my court as possible."

Words caught in my throat, I nod. The champagne I consumed earlier has made me light-headed. I probably should have listened to Callias.

"Who sits at the end?" I ask, looking at the final seat. It's a small black throne with a single red jewel embedded into the high back.

"It's the honorary space we keep for the Heart Queen."

My gaze whips to Atlas. "What? I thought the last Heart Queen died centuries ago?"

"And left no heir," he adds, an odd pitch in the tone of his voice, like they're words he doesn't really believe. "Yes. But Heart was once the most powerful realm in Ouranos. It only seems fitting to keep a place in their honor. Who knows, perhaps the Heart Crown will be found someday and a new queen will ascend."

Atlas fixes me with a piercing look, his arm cinching me tighter.

My head swims and I close my eyes, reaching for the locket around my neck before gripping it tight.

Through the holes in his mask, I notice his eyes drop to my mouth. Dipping his head, his lips brush against the shell of my ear. "I want you again, Lor. I can't stop thinking about you or our dinner on the beach."

My skin wrenches tight and heat drips from my stomach to the place between my thighs.

"I've thought about it too," I admit. "Quite a lot." He lets out a low chuckle that I feel in my bones.

"Try to find your trinket quickly," he says, chucking me under the chin. "For me?"

I nod. "Of course." I would agree to anything when he looks at me like that.

The song ends and much to my disappointment, he lets go and then offers me a quick bow. "As much as I'd love to dance with you all evening, I should, as you say, go entertain my guests." He kisses the back of my hand. "Until later."

With that, he spins on his heel and walks away as I'm left to contemplate everything he just explained. I scan the kings and queens again, watching each one in turn. I stare at the empty seat meant for the Aurora Prince, wishing I could have seen his face. If I can't have the king for my vengeance, perhaps I can have the prince.

Checking the large clock suspended at the end of the high room, I realize it's been almost an hour since the ball commenced. I need to find Gabriel. Circling through the guests, I catch sight of Halo, who waves at me from across the crowd. I spy Apricia hanging off the neck of a Fae male, flipping her hair, and I wonder how Atlas feels about that, or if he's noticed. Tesni doesn't seem to be anywhere, and I hope she's okay. While this challenge feels less perilous than the others, I know better than to let down my guard.

Some of the other warders loiter along the edge of the dance floor, all dressed in gold, like a battalion of angelic warriors. No Gabriel, though.

Getting annoyed now, I keep searching, wondering if sabotage is how he plans to get rid of me once and for all. Did he disappear with my clue? A row of high arches lines one wall of the ballroom, and I duck under one to enter a long hallway lined with smaller chambers.

People fill these too, seated on the plush couches as they drink and chat. I check each of them, trying to spot Gabriel's head of dark blond hair and snowy white wings, all while keeping an eye on the clock. The hour is almost up and if I don't find him in time, it will impede my chances of persuading my target before the others. I'm going to kill him.

At the end of the hall is another room, the door partially adjacent. I open it and duck my head inside. There are no lights, only a window where a beam of moonlight slices through the darkness. I hear a deep moan and feel my cheeks flush, realizing that I seem to have come upon a tryst. But a moment later, my eyes adjust to the dimness, and I see a winged man wearing a gold jacket kneeling in front of a settee, his dark blond hair hanging down, covering the side of his face.

Gabriel. That jackass. He's supposed to be *helping* me, not doing...this. Frozen to the spot, I watch. A male figure sits on the settee, his long legs stretched out and his head thrown back. I can't make out any other details with the moonlight illuminating only the back of Gabriel's head as it moves up and down. There is another deep masculine moan, and I can't tell who is its rather satisfied owner.

Mesmerized by the sound, I can't seem to tear myself away. I should make my presence known. Or I should leave. But I need my clue from Gabriel.

"What do you want, Lor?" Gabriel says in a bored voice, startling me so much I jump nearly a mile. My heart pounding, I press a hand to my chest.

"I was looking for you." My voice is breathless and high, and I'm not sure why I feel like I should be the one who's embarrassed.

Gabriel pelts me with an irritated glance. His body and wings are blocking most of his companion. The man in question lifts his head, but I can't make out his features, only the glint of his eyes in the darkness. He drops his head back as though he'll wait there patiently for Gabriel to finish him.

"And you found me. Well done."

Fuck this. He knows why I need him.

"I need my clue. It's time."

"I still have two more minutes. Get out." His grin turns feral. "I'll be done here in a moment."

My mouth opens and closes, unable to believe this.

"Get. Out," he snarls.

Absolutely mortified, I don't wait for him to tell me again. He doesn't seem to care at all that I've just caught him sucking on another male's cock in the middle of a party with hundreds of people milling about.

"Fine," I say and leave the room, slamming the door behind me. I'm about to storm away when I realize I can't. I still need him.

Furious, I lean right up against the door, sure to make a loud enough thud that he knows I'm there. Folding my arms in anger, I mutter under my breath about asshole Fae and their primitive needs.

Chapter Thirty

The hour ticks past, and Gabriel still doesn't appear. I see Tesni talking with her warder, their heads bent together before they pull apart and both scan the room, seeking her mark.

Halo and Apricia also confer with their warders and then begin moving through the crowd. I huff out a breath of frustration. Now I'm already behind. Gabriel is such an ass. He's busy fucking around while I stand here waiting like an idiot. The sound of deep laughter drifts through the door, and my teeth grind together.

Another minute passes and I watch as Tesni approaches a beautiful woman with straight black hair and dark angled eyes. She's wearing a large silver brooch pinned to her collar. In another corner, Apricia is talking to a tall Fae male with cropped chestnut hair. He has an ostentatiously sized diamond winking in one of his pointed ears.

Shit. I'm going to be the last one to get my trinket.

I spin and pound on the door, not caring what I'm interrupting anymore. "Gabriel! Get your asshole ass out here!" I keep pounding and calling his name until a few seconds later, the door finally pops open and I stumble forward, crashing into my warder. He does nothing to break my fall, just stares down where I'm crumpled at his feet like a pile of dirty laundry.

"My asshole ass?" He cocks his head and raises a brow. "Surely you can do better than that, Tribute?"

I snarl as I stand up, smoothing my skirt. "Shut up."

"So eloquent tonight." He circles my biceps with his large hand and shoves me out of the room, slamming the door behind him.

"Who was that in there with you?" I demand. "You're supposed to be helping me, not sucking random cocks! Is this what you get paid for?"

He doesn't answer me as he continues shoving me further from the door until we're on the other side of the ballroom. "You're hurting me." His grip is so tight, I feel like my arm might snap. Finally, we stop and he whirls me around so I'm facing away from him.

The room is spinning, the music playing, the dancers swirling like dandelion seeds across a golden meadow. I touch my forehead, really regretting those two bottles of champagne now. Gabriel leans down and whispers in my ear, "Your target is him."

I follow his gaze to the table at the front, where the kings and queens of Ouranos sit. Atlas is standing, facing a male with wavy dark hair that falls past his shoulders. Not all of them are kings and queens, then.

His black-as-midnight suit is a dark smudge against the gilded brilliance of the palace. He's an inch or two taller than Atlas, broad and muscled, though he's leaner than the Sun King. Nevertheless, he's every inch a warrior, draped in the elegant attire of a dark Fae prince.

"Who?" I ask, sure Gabriel can't mean who I think.

"The ring on his hand." I look to the prince, where a silver ring with a black stone flashes on his index finger. Not black. When he moves his hand ever so slightly, I see the striations that run through it. Crimson and emerald and teal and violet. Waves that undulate against a dark, star-strewn sky. The only source of beauty in my life for twelve long years.

"The Aurora Prince," I whisper, the air around me shifting as if to make room for the syllables of his name. It's not the king, but his son veers close enough to the object of my loathing that something sharp and familiar twists in my stomach. Everything The Aurora stands for has been distilled down into my bottled rage with a potency that has kept me going through every moment of misery that my siblings and I have suffered.

And now the Aurora Prince is here, standing in this room.

"His name is Nadir," Gabriel says, and there's an inexplicable sense that at that moment, everything has just changed forever. I shake off the strange feeling, the room spinning around me again. I *really* shouldn't have had that second bottle of wine.

"What if he recognizes me?" I look up at Gabriel, who stands so close I can feel the brush of his body against my back.

"Why would he recognize you? You were nothing more than a prison rat. Even if he had seen you, you look nothing like you did when I pulled you out of that hole."

I take a deep breath, conceding his point.

"But why him? The others have regular guests." I look around the room and see Halo sitting down next to an elderly Fae who wears a sparkling tiara nestled in her silver hair.

Gabriel's chuckle is low and definitely a little menacing. You'd think he'd be in a better mood after what I just caught him doing. "Afraid of a little challenge, Final Tribute?"

I look up at him, scowling. But he has a smug smile on his face that dares me to back down from this test. He wants me out of this contest, but I am determined to win and will never give him that satisfaction. I swallow the hard uncertainty in my throat and smooth down the front of my dress. I can do this. Stuffing down my acrimony for the Aurora King and everything he holds dear, I flick the hair off my shoulder and then take a tentative step forward before I glance back at my warder.

"Problem?" Gabriel asks with a tip of his head.

"Zerra, you are such an insufferable ass," I say, because he really is. First, he made me late, and now he's clearly fucking enjoying this. I turn back to face the front of the room and then blink. The Aurora Prince is no longer there.

Atlas is now sitting on his throne and speaking to The Woodlands King. Their angry gazes drift to the side of the room, where I catch the prince weaving through the crowd. Is he leaving? *Shit.*

Without thinking about it, I pick up the hem of my skirt and make my way quickly to the edge of the room, speeding up the short staircase to intercept him. A server passes with a tray of full glasses of champagne, and I snag one without missing a beat before I make a beeline for the prince.

Just as he's about to pass through a group of partygoers, I turn my head as if I'm looking away and casually sidestep in front of him. We crash and the world seems to tilt. The glass in my hand goes flying, spilling its contents as I trip and fall into his arms.

Chapter Thirty-one

Nadir

Instinct made Nadir reach for the girl. One arm banded around her waist and the other gripped her arm. He was covered in champagne, and his suit was probably ruined. He made a low sound in his throat as he pulled her back up and their gazes met through the holes in her mask.

Nadir blinked, noting the strange mixture of fury and fear in her eyes before they cleared and she exclaimed, "Zerra!" Her smooth brown cheeks turned red. "I'm *so* sorry!" She looked around and caught a passing server, snatching a napkin off his tray and using it to blot the front of his jacket. "I've gotten champagne all over you. I'm so sorry. Oh, I'm so clumsy."

She kept on talking, keeping up a stream of chatter that Nadir could have sworn sounded forced, like she was a second-rate actress in a play.

He narrowed his eyes. "It's fine," he replied, his voice gruff as he waved her off.

"No, it's not," she said, looking up at him with those big, dark eyes. They were endless. Like the deepest wells sunk into the earth. He'd never seen eyes like that. He shook his head, trying to dislodge that wayward thought. It was then he recognized her as the Tribute who'd been dancing with Atlas earlier.

"Please let me make it up to you," she said, having discarded the napkin, her voice imploring. "How about a dance?"

Nadir hesitated, looking her up and down. From what he could tell, she was beautiful with smooth brown skin, but for the tail end of a scar that ran from the middle of her cheek and disappeared underneath the mask. It was so unusual to see anyone in a Fae court with a scar. Vanity, wagging tongues, and judgmental sneers could bring even the strongest Fae to their knees. But she seemed to bear it proudly, even if, right now, she appeared on the verge of desperation.

"No thank you," Nadir said, finally coming back to his thoughts. "I was just leaving."

He brushed past her, but she grabbed his arm. "No. Please, don't go." Nadir stopped and turned slowly, wondering why her touch felt so energetic even through his clothing. "Please, Your Highness." She whispered the last two words as though she'd just realized she'd made a fatal error in grabbing a royal Fae. She dropped her hands and dipped into an artless curtsy before quickly glancing at the large gold clock above the ball-room. "Just one dance."

Nadir scanned the room, debating with himself. He should leave. As usual, he'd gotten into an argument with Atlas and had outstayed his welcome. Not that he'd ever really been welcome here in the first place.

The girl moved closer. Not a girl. A young female. A very appealing one. She stepped closer, looking up at him with those soulful eyes, and laid a gentle hand in the center of his chest. It was a strangely bold way to touch him, but his heartbeat kicked up. He frowned, staring at her hand and then back at her, not understanding his reaction.

"Please," she said again, and this time Nadir found himself nodding as if his body was operating outside of his brain's signals. The smile she gave him still felt forced, even though relief sagged in her shoulders. Nadir couldn't puzzle her out.

When he realized she was waiting for him to lead her to the dance floor, he admonished himself. *Get it together, Nadir.* He held out a hand, and she placed hers in his. Her fingers felt small, yet substantial, when he wrapped his own around them. A jolt shot through him at the touch and she stopped, looking at him with a curious expression. Had she felt it, too?

For a moment, neither of them moved.

"Shall we?" She tipped her head towards the dance floor and Nadir nodded.

They strode down the steps and took their place in the middle of the throng. Gently, he placed a hand on the small of her back, that same disorienting feeling threatening to tow him under.

She rested a hand on his shoulder and they began to dance slowly, their steps effortlessly falling in sync.

He couldn't tear his gaze from hers, the rest of the room melting away in a smear of noise and lights that blended into the background. She looked to where their hands were clasped, lines furrowing in her forehead.

"That's a lovely ring," she said, her gaze once again flicking to the giant clock above them.

"Are you late for something?" he asked, and her cheeks went pink.

"No." She gave a nervous laugh. "No, I'm not late."

They continued moving to the sway of the music, couples brushing past them, but he saw none of them, wholly fixated on her.

"A family heirloom?" she asked, gesturing to the ring again. Nadir frowned, perplexed by her interest in it.

"Just something I picked up in the Violet District in The Aurora."

Her lovely features twisted into confusion.

"It's not precious to you? Not a treasured heirloom?"

Nadir shook his head. "No. Why are you asking about my ring so much?"

She stopped moving, dropping her hands and stepping back as though he'd become contagious. She ripped off her mask and stared at him, her dark gaze so penetrating Nadir suddenly had the most uncomfortable sense that he was falling through a pit with no bottom. She was trembling. In anger, he realized, noting how her hands fisted and her teeth ground together.

"Did I do something?" he asked, taking a step towards her, wanting to fix whatever it was and choosing not to examine why he felt that way.

"Lor!" someone called, and the girl looked away. Atlas was storming towards them, fury burning in his expression. Gabriel suddenly appeared through the crowd, coming from the opposite direction. He lunged for the girl, who leaped back from his grasp.

"You tricked me! He's not my mark!" she hissed at Gabriel, who took two long strides and gripped the girl by her shoulders. "Let go of me, you *asshole*!" She tried to wrest herself from his grip, but her strength was no match for one of the king's warders. Gabriel spun her so her back was to him, one arm around her waist and the other hand still gripping her shoulder while she tried to kick herself free.

It all happened in an instant.

Just as Nadir was preparing to intervene on her behalf, the material on her shoulder slipped, exposing a smooth patch of her skin.

It was only a second before the fabric slipped back, covering her up, but Nadir had seen it.

The black tattoo of three wavy lines set against a circle.

The unmistakable brand burned onto any prisoner who had ever been thrown into Nostraza.

CHAPTER THIRTY-TWO

LOR

I strain against Gabriel's grip. "What the fuck are you doing?" I yell at him. "Why did you lie to me?"

It's then that several things happen at once. Atlas bursts through the crowd, fury in his blazing eyes. He grabs me by the arm and yanks me towards him.

"Get him out of here," Atlas says, gesturing to the Aurora Prince, and several guards materialize around him. "Now."

"Why?" the prince demands.

Atlas's voice is cold. "You are not welcome in Aphelion, Nadir. If I see you within my kingdom again, you will be shot through the heart with an iron bolt on sight. Do I make myself clear?"

"You can't do that, you pompous asshole."

"You are in my territory. I absolutely can."

The two Fae square off against each other, hostility radiating off them. I don't know who would win in this fight, but right now I'm pinned between them and am hoping it doesn't come to that. The prince's eyes flick to me, his expression unreadable before he steps back and casually smooths down the sleeves of his jacket, as if suggesting a fight with Atlas isn't worth his time.

Nadir snarls at the guards hemmed in on every side. "Call off your dogs, Atlas. I'll see myself out." With that, the prince sticks me with a look that implies he's not done with me, spins on his heel, and walks away. My heart is beating so hard it feels like it's trying to explode from my chest.

As soon as the prince clears the room, Atlas lets go and turns me around. "What did you do? Why were you dancing with him?" He's shaking with rage, his eyes blazing. He's gripping my arms so tight he's pinching my skin.

"Atlas, you're hurting me."

"Why were you dancing with him?" he roars, and I flinch.

"Gabriel said he was my mark," I say, my voice trembling. The entire room has gone quiet, and everyone is staring at us. "He said I had to get his ring."

Atlas's expression darkens as he finally lets go and whirls on Gabriel. "What did you do?"

Gabriel's posture straightens, his hand going to his sword. "I was trying to protect you, as is my sworn duty."

"You had no right!" the Sun King roars so loud that it shakes the entire room, a chorus of gasps emanating from the crowd. He's breathing so heavily his chest is heaving, his eyes wild as his gaze finds me. I step back, sensing everyone gathered behind me doing the same.

"This challenge is over," Atlas declares. "Everyone will compete in the final round." Another ripple goes through the guests, this one confused, and I look around the room, wondering where Tesni, Halo, and Apricia ended up. Did they trick their marks? It doesn't matter anymore.

Atlas addresses his guards. "Make sure Nadir is gone and set up extra security to ensure no one else from The Aurora enters Aphelion. Every guard is on duty until the Trials are complete. Do I make myself clear?"

Gabriel takes a step, preparing to follow through on Atlas's orders.

"Not you," Atlas says to him and then gestures to the warder that once guarded Solana before she fell to her death in the first trial. "Rhyle, you've been promoted to the Captain of the Guard. See to it this traitor is thrown in the dungeons until I can deal with him."

Atlas points a finger at Gabriel. The other warders exchange wary glances, clearly hesitant to touch him.

"Do it!" Atlas roars, and Rhyle finally leaps into action, signaling for another warder to join him. Gabriel doesn't resist as they each take an arm and escort him to the edge of the dancefloor. Before they ascend the steps, Gabriel turns and says to Atlas, "I was doing this for you. You're making a mistake."

"Get out," Atlas snarls. Rhyle and the second warder guide Gabriel from the room. "The party is over!" Atlas shouts to the shocked crowd. Then his gaze finds me again, fury mixing with something desperate and full of hunger.

Despite everything, I feel that look flare through my skin and plummet right to my toes.

He takes my hand. "Lor. You're coming with me."

Chapter Thirty-three

Atlas pulls me through the gaping ring of party guests as they jump out of the way to let us pass. He doesn't slow when we reach the doorway, dragging me up next to him before he circles my waist with his arm.

I say nothing while we wind through the endless hallways, and I try to keep up with his long, furious strides. I replay the events of this evening over and over in my head. The prince wasn't my mark and yet Gabriel sent me to him, anyway. Why? Gabriel said the prince didn't know who I was, and that I was to keep it that way, but was he trying to find some way to reveal it? And to what end? Maybe *this* was Gabriel's plan to get rid of me? But then why tell me to stay quiet about where I came from?

My thoughts rush in a loop as our steps echo through the silent hallways. Finally, we approach the massive set of doors emblazoned with the Sun King insignia. Two guards stand outside, their backs straight and their eyes forward, as Atlas throws the door open and ushers me inside. He's not hurting me, but he's not being gentle, either.

"Atlas, I'm sorry," I say, not sure who he's angry with. He seemed furious that I'd been dancing with the Aurora Prince, but it's hardly my fault that Gabriel lied. "I didn't know."

He finally lets go and starts pacing the room, his eyes on his feet and his hand rubbing his jaw before running it through his hair. "What did you talk about?" he asks, finally whirling on me. "What did you say to him?"

I open my mouth and shake my head. "Nothing. I was asking about his ring."

"His ring?"

"I thought I was supposed to convince him to give it to me, but then he said it was just a trinket he'd purchased and it meant nothing to him and..." I trail off as Atlas stares at me, blue flame burning in his eyes.

"That's it?"

I nod mutely. "He hardly said a word. It was mostly me trying to convince him to dance so I could ask about the ring. I swear." I don't know what I'm swearing on or why he's so concerned about what I said. "I didn't tell him I was from Nostraza. Gabriel said I was to continue pretending I was from Aphelion."

A line forms between Atlas's brows. "He did?"

"Yes." I whisper it, my voice soft. Finally, the ire in his expression starts to drain away as his shoulders drop.

"You're telling me the truth? You didn't reveal to him where you came from?"

"I didn't...but what is this all about?"

Atlas's demeanor shifts then, anger replaced by concern. The transformation is so abrupt, I blink and take a step back. But he's approaching me now, his large hands circling around my shoulders as he peers into my face. "When I saw you dancing with him...I'm so sorry...I just lost my mind."

He pulls me to him, pressing me against his chest and wrapping his arms around me in a tight embrace as he presses his lips to the top of my head. "You're mine," he murmurs. "You're going to be mine, and together, we're going to be unstoppable." His voice is distant, as if this is a story he's recited to himself many times.

I pull back and look up at him. "We are? Why are you so sure about this?"

His nod is earnest, his hands reaching up to cup my face, a thumb tracing the scar along my cheek. "Because I feel it, Lor. Surely you must feel this pull when we're together?"

I nod slowly because I do feel something. I'm drawn to this Fae whenever he's in the room. He's a flower and I'm a bee searching for nectar. I've wondered before if it was *him* or just an effect of being Imperial Fae.

I think of when I danced with the prince. When our gazes met, there was a different kind of pull there. Not the same thing I feel around Atlas, but something wider and deeper. Like being tossed around in a hurricane versus thrashing against a single wave. But that's ludicrous. We danced for less than two minutes and most of the time he just stared at me. He barely said anything. He's not Imperial Fae yet, so maybe it's a Fae thing, but I've been around dozens and dozens of those in the past few weeks and have never felt anything similar.

"I feel it," I say, because it's not a lie, but I'm also not sure what it really means. Atlas smiles then, and that warmth I've become so used to resurfaces. He blows out a breath of relief. "I'm sorry if I frightened you. I just...I can't lose you."

His voice is impassioned, and I cover his hands with mine and nod. "Two more weeks until the final round, and the Mirror will decide," I say, more sure than ever that I have to win this.

"Right." His brow furrows. "Two more weeks." His gaze slides inward as he seems to draw into himself.

"Atlas?"

"Nothing. Yes. Soon, nothing can stand between us, Lor. Nothing," he repeats, as though to convince himself, and then draws me in close, his mouth brushing mine. Immediately, I feel the heat of his touch melt through my limbs. I've missed the way he's held me, and the way being around him makes me feel like I'm floating. Like I'm in another life and another world where fairy tales are real.

His hand cups the back of my head and he tips it back, deepening the kiss with a moan. As his tongue sweeps into my mouth, gooseflesh breaks out over my body.

"I need you," he says. "I need to taste you and touch you." He kisses me again, this one so deep and frantic it leaves me gasping for air. His hands cup my ass as he drives his hips against mine. "I want to fuck you until you can't walk straight," he growls into the curve of my throat before he bites my skin gently. My gasp is an unintelligible response when he presses the hard length of his cock into my stomach.

I'm not sure if this is a good idea, but I'm finding it hard to care as he scoops me into his arms like a knight rescuing me from the evil witch's clutches. I haven't read many books in my life, but my favorites were always the romances with happy endings and handsome heroes, and it feels impossible that this is my reality now. He drops his forehead to mine and whispers my name.

Then we're moving through his grand apartment, down a wide hallway to a set of doors at the end. He shoulders one open and we enter a palatial bedroom. It's massive, at least twice the size of the mess hall in Nostraza. One wall is set with wide windows that overlook the moonlit sea. The biggest bed I've ever seen sits against another wall covered in golden sheets and pillows, as well as a canopy of layers and layers of more gold and yellow silk. At the other end is a massive marble fireplace smoldering with embers.

That's the entirety of my assessment before Atlas slams the door and places me on my feet, spinning me around and pressing my back to the wall, his mouth and his tongue already devouring me. It's obvious this time he's not going to stop me from touching him, and so I take the opportunity to enjoy it as I tear at the buttons on his golden jacket, wanting to feel those miles of rippling, golden flesh under my hands.

With a low sound in his throat, he helps me tug it off and then pulls his shirt over his head. I take in a deep breath as he's bared before me; the lines and dips and curves of his glorious body are wondrous to behold. I run my hands over the swell of his shoulders and down the curve of his chest and stomach as he lets out a groan.

Atlas captures my wrists and then my mouth with his, pressing me back to the wall, where he grinds his hips into mine.

His hands slip up my back, where he starts to pull at the laces of my dress. Making short work of the ties, he tugs them loose and then pushes the bodice down to my hips. For a moment, I hesitate, wondering if I should go through with this. I think I want this, but despite Atlas's claims about wanting to be with me, a part of me still wonders if he's just been telling me what I want to hear. He could be spinning the same words for any of the other Tributes. He could be trying to use me. Maybe that doesn't matter. After all, I'm using him too, because I *need* to stand before the Sun Mirror.

His words feel real, and the way he kisses me now feels real, too. I've never been in love, so I don't know what it feels like. I don't think this is love, but there is infatuation and lust and passion. Right now, maybe that's all I need.

"Lor," he says, his voice rough. "Don't stop. Please. I need you." He pushes my dress down, leaving me only in my underwear. His gaze sweeping over me, he eyes me like a predator and my blood heats, warmth pooling between my thighs.

His eyes grow wild and his breathing more labored as he leans in to kiss me again, his large hands sliding up the backs of my legs before lifting me and wrapping them around his waist. With a moan, he grinds his thick, hard length into my aching center.

"Atlas," I say, barely able to get the strangled words out. "Maybe we should stop. You said we should wait until after the Trials." His mouth is dragging over my skin, down my throat, and across my collarbone, and part of me is wondering why I'm trying to stop him.

Atlas lets out a frustrated breath, collapsing against me.

"You're right," he says, cupping my face in his hands. "I'm sorry. I was getting carried away."

"Are you sure?" I ask with hesitation, understanding all too well the consequences of saying "no" to a male who doesn't know how to deal with rejection.

"Yes, of course it's okay." His eyes soften. "I'm sorry about my behavior tonight. This isn't who I am. It's just so close to the end, and I want to claim you as mine. I don't want anyone or anything getting in our way."

I let out the nervous breath I'm holding, sliding my arms around him and peering up. "Thank you. And I'm yours...if the Sun Mirror chooses me."

"It will," he says, tightening his grip as though I might dissolve into a puff of ashes. "It will."

His gaze meets mine, his eyes full of blue flame. His face is flushed, his hair wild, and he's never looked more beautiful. If the mirror chooses me, then I might just become the luckiest female in all of Ouranos.

"Will you stay the night, though? Just sleep next to me."

I nod eagerly. "I'd like that."

He takes my hand and leads me to the bed, pulling back the covers before I slide in. He shucks off the rest of his clothing, leaving only his underwear before he gets in next to me, curling his warm body around mine.

His hands slide over my hip and up my back, pulling a delicious shiver up my spine.

"Lor," he says, softly. "Lor, you're incredible." He drops his mouth to the curve of my throat, sucking on the skin before he moves to my mouth and then kisses me deeply. His forehead touching mine, he says, "I feel so many things when I'm around you."

"Oh, Atlas," I reply, feeling shy and unsure of myself in this moment. I've never had anyone speak to me this way. It feels big and overwhelming and I want all of this to be mine forever, so badly I can taste it.

Tonight, Atlas makes me believe I can win the Trials. He makes me think maybe I'm worth loving. That I can become the Sun Queen, get Tristan and Willow out of Nostraza, and find some version of a happily ever after the three of us were never destined for.

I want it all.

I want love and passion.

I want my revenge.

I want the magic and the power I was denied.

I still don't know what the Sun Mirror will do when I face it, but I have to win so I can find out.

Atlas is still kissing me, pressing random nips to my shoulder and my cheek and my collarbone, his hands sliding up my sides and down my hips. "You're so beautiful," he says over and over until we both fall asleep in an exhausted tangle of limbs.

CHAPTER THIRTY-FOUR

NADIR

Nadir's feet slammed onto the balcony outside his study, luminescent wings of light drawing into him as he pulled up his stance. Flinging the door open, he stormed inside, heading straight for the bar cart on the far side of the room.

He wrenched open a decanter, filling a glass with triple the usual amount, and then picked it up, tossing the entire contents down his throat. Once it was empty, he slammed the glass down so hard it shattered, razor-sharp bits flying in every direction.

"Fuck," he growled.

He barely glanced at the mess as he grabbed another glass and filled this one even higher.

His ice hounds had both risen from where they were lying, their thick white tails swaying at the sight of their master. They padded over and sat before him, their pink tongues lolling.

"Things went well, I take it," Mael drawled from the sofa where he was sitting, an ankle crossed over a knee. Amya was next to him, her legs curled up under her.

"Don't you both have your own rooms somewhere?" Nadir asked, as he bent down to lavish a moment of attention on Morana and then Khione. "Why are you always in here?"

Mael tipped his head and adopted an expression of mock hurt. "You wound me, my prince. What would you do without us?"

"She's there." Nadir stood and whirled around. Mael and Amya now sat perfectly still, their eyes wide.

"She is? You saw her?" Amya asked, uncurling herself and leaning forward. Nadir took another big gulp, his nostrils flaring and his mouth pressing together.

"I saw her. I saw the mark from Nostraza. Atlas has her competing in his fucking Trials."

Amya blinked. "What? Why would he have a prisoner from Nostraza competing in the Trials?"

Nadir stormed to the center of the room, his magic flaring in agitation, refusing to be contained as it formed an iridescent aura that surrounded him. He paced along the dark carpet, his mind whirling.

He detailed his encounter with the girl to Amya and Mael. How she'd asked him to dance. No, pleaded, until he'd finally relented. He kept the information about how she'd made him feel a little unhinged to himself, not entirely sure what it meant.

"She kept asking about my ring," he said.

"Your ring? Why?"

"I don't know." He took another deep draught of his drink, the effects of it finally working as it warmed his blood and cleared his head.

"And then Atlas lost his shit when he saw me with her. Ripped her away and then ordered me out of Aphelion and barred me or anyone else from The Aurora from ever returning."

Mael let out a derisive laugh. "To be a fly on the wall when you tell Rion you got him banned from the Sun King's court. I imagine Cyan and Cedar will do the same."

Nadir shot his friend a cold look. "Very helpful, Mael."

Mael shrugged and put his hands behind his head. "I'm not the one who couldn't attend one fucking party without causing a continental incident."

Nadir started pacing again. "I was dancing with her. Nothing more."

"Why did he get so angry, then?" Amya asked.

"I don't know, but clearly there's a reason he stole her. There's a reason he wants to *ascend* her to Imperial Fae and then bond to her."

Nadir's memory went back to the Hollow all those weeks ago, when he'd gone to investigate and realized now that who he'd smelled, at least in part, was Gabriel. How had he not realized it right away? It had been years since he'd seen him, and the memory had been buried too deep.

But Nadir was sure the way Gabriel had grabbed her had been intentional. He'd slipped the material of her dress so the tattoo would show right after he'd told him he hadn't heard of any girls from Nostraza being in Aphelion. Which could only mean Atlas had forbidden Gabriel from speaking to anyone about her origins. The ties that bound Gabriel made it impossible for him to disobey a direct order from his king, but there were ways around that tether.

"Nadir," Mael said, standing up as he watched Nadir pace. "Your father seemed only mildly concerned about her disappearance. Why are you making such a big deal about this?"

Nadir scowled. "I'm sure he never meant for me to know about her, and is acting that way to make it seem like nothing. Or maybe he's arrogant enough to believe she's no threat. Maybe she *is* no threat, and Atlas believes something that isn't true. *Or* Atlas knows something no one else does." Nadir's gaze drifted to the single red rose that sat on his mantle, now darkened and dried with age.

"Nadir," Amya said, pulling his attention with a warning in her voice. The one she used to remind her brother he was getting obsessed and was losing himself.

"No." Nadir whirled on her. "I don't want your lectures. There was something—" He stopped, looked at them both and then resumed his pacing, back and forth, back and forth. He took another sip from his glass, only to find it empty. He growled at the glass, and Mael snatched it from him before he had the chance to hurl it at the wall in frustration.

"Let me get you another one," Mael said carefully.

Nadir took in a deep breath, ignoring Mael as he stalked to the fireplace and braced his hands on the mantle, the rose snagging on his thoughts once more.

He felt Amya's presence as she came up behind him and placed a gentle hand on his shoulder. He didn't shrug her off.

"There was something, what, Nadir? What happened?"

He turned his head, his dark eyes flashing with violet and crimson. "I don't know. I just felt...something."

Amya's brow furrowed in concern as she tentatively reached for a lock of hair that had fallen, brushing it away from his face. "Are you sure you're not just looking for...something?"

Nadir grumbled low in his throat. "I know what I felt."

"What did you feel?"

He didn't want to talk about it. He wanted to get to the bottom of this. He wanted to know what his father, and now Atlas, was hiding.

"Nothing." Nadir straightened and turned, taking the glass Mael held out to him.

"So, what do you want to do?" Mael asked, perhaps sensing there would be no talking Nadir out of this.

"We're going to get her out of there." He took a sip, noticing Amya and Mael exchange worried glances.

"And then what?" Mael asked.

"Bring her here and find out what she's hiding," Nadir said.

"What if it's nothing?" Amya asked, moving to stand next to Mael.

"Then it's nothing. We get rid of her and move on with our lives."

"And you'll let this go?" Amya asked.

Nadir pinned her with a look. "I'll let this go."

Amya waited, but whatever was on his face made her nod and reply, "Okay. Then we'll help you."

She looked up at Mael, who wore a skeptical expression as she elbowed him in the ribs. "Right?"

Mael raised his brows, looking between the siblings. "Right. Sure."

"We can't let him bond to her," Nadir said. "We have two weeks before the final round to get her out of there."

"Why can't he bond to her?" Mael asked.

"Because whatever he's planning must hinge on her winning the Trials. Why else would he have taken her to compete in them?"

Amya pursed her lips, looking thoughtful. "What could a mortal prisoner from Nostraza possibly offer that a Fae couldn't?"

Nadir looked at his sister, weighing the impossible thoughts in his head.

"You have a hunch," she whispered, as all the air was sucked out of the room.

"Maybe." Nadir stared at the fire as he took another drink. "And if I'm right, this could change everything."

Chapter Thirty-five

Lor

I'm so cold. My eyes are closed, and I shiver as a gust of wind blows right through my clothing. With a groan, I curl into a ball, wrapping my arms around me. The ground is hard, something sharp digging into my hip and my arm and my shoulder, making it feel like I'm being assaulted by a barrage of pellets. There's a howl of wind and I shiver against its icy blast.

The last thing I remember is falling asleep in Atlas's bed with his warm body around me. This is a terrible dream. It's awfully realistic, though. Another attack of arctic wind has my teeth chattering, and I shift, the rough sting of gravel biting through my thin tunic and leggings. Something definitely doesn't feel right. Slowly, I peel open my eyes, my lids weighed down by anchors.

A blank canvas materializes before me, stained only with shades of white and grey. My cheeks are raw, the cold wind stinging like nettles as I attempt to move, rolling over and swinging my leg so I can push myself up. I'm expecting solid ground, but it meets nothing but air, and I scream, gripping the rock beneath me when it becomes clear I'm about to roll off the edge of a sheer cliff. I scream again and scramble back on my hands before I bump into something hard and warm. Another body.

Clambering over it, I scream again, terror squeezing my heart in its fist as the sloped surface keeps dragging me back towards the edge. My vision fills with nothing but a blur of white until finally my back hits a cold wall.

Halo, Tesni, and Apricia are stirring from sleep, each waking to the same monstrous sight. We're in a small cave hewn into what seems to be the side of a mountain. Only about ten feet deep, the far end opens to an endless drop. In front of us loom more mountains, grey and impossibly tall, covered in snow and frost.

Halo gasps and also backs up, crawling across the cold stone floor to sit next to where I'm huddled, my hands wedged into my armpits to keep them warm. It's freezing up here and we're all wearing nothing but our thin brown tunics and leggings with soft brown boots. They're comfortable but offer no protection against this biting cold.

"Where are we?" Halo asks, her teeth chattering.

I shake my head, too frozen to speak. Tesni crawls along the floor and plants herself on my other side, also shivering from head to toe. "Is this the next trial?" she asks, blowing on her hands and rubbing them together.

Halo shakes her head, her dark curls bouncing. "It's not for another two weeks. The ball was last night...wasn't it?"

We exchange a wary glance. "Were you wearing that when you went to sleep last night?" Tesni asks us, and I feel my cheeks heat when I think about where and how I fell asleep. I touch my mouth, my lips still swollen from Atlas's feverish kisses, confirming what happened wasn't a dream. And couldn't possibly have been two weeks ago. I reach up, finding the icy metal locket where it rests against my skin, and clutch it like a lifeline.

"No," Halo answers. "I was in my nightgown."

Apricia is watching the three of us with her usual disdain, huddling against the side of the cave.

"Why don't you come over here?" I ask. "We can try to keep each other warm." She scoffs and flips her stupid hair over her stupid shoulder and peers out into the blank white-and-grey scene, serving as our only view. "Suit yourself." I roll my eyes.

"So last night, the king ended the third trial," Halo says, as if trying to remind herself. She cuts a glance to me. "What happened? Why did he get so upset about you dancing with the Aurora Prince?"

I hesitate, not entirely sure how to answer that. "I don't know." And then, to prevent them from asking where he took me after we left the ballroom, I keep talking. "And we all fell asleep and woke up here? In different clothes?"

"It *must* be the fourth challenge," Tesni says, getting up on her hands and knees slowly. She approaches the edge of our tiny cave and lies flat on her stomach to look over the edge.

Wanting to see for myself, I follow, being sure to make careful movements. The cold air has formed a crust of ice at the edge, rendering it even more treacherous.

Sliding on my stomach, I inch over, the dizzying effect of the floor's incline pitching me forward like a demon sucking its teeth. Standing up here would be impossible. Tesni is still peering down when I join her. There is nothing but stone and snow and an endless drop so far down I can't see where it ends. We are positively fucked.

I look over at Tesni, and her dark eyes are full of worry.

"What are we supposed to do?" she asks, and I shake my head. It's colder out here than at the back of the cave, so I inch away, returning to my place next to Halo. Linking my arm with hers, we press our bodies together, trying to coax out a sliver of warmth.

"I don't like heights," she says, her voice wooden and her brown skin ashen.

"Stay away from the edge." It's an unnecessary warning, but I give it voice anyway, needing to say something. Tesni has slid back on my other side and links her arm through my second one.

"There's no food or water," Apricia finally comments. "They must mean us to get out of here quickly." She says it with such confidence, I nearly believe her.

"Why? Because they've been so careful about our safety before this?" I snap. Somehow, she's managed to get through every challenge with barely a scratch. I can't help but wonder if Atlas had a hand in that.

Apricia arches a black brow like she's already the fucking queen, and I've never wanted to slap someone so much in my entire life. Doing my best to ignore her, I study the walls of the cave, searching for some variation in the rock that hints at what we're here to do. "Should we explore the walls? Maybe there's a latch or something hidden."

Tesni and Halo follow my gaze, questions written on their faces.

"Sure," Tesni says, letting go of my arm and moving into a crouch before she presses her hands along the wall behind us. Slowly, she touches the wall higher and higher, stretching her arms as far as they'll go, but she can't feel much more without standing. She hesitates, and I understand her predicament.

"Wait," I say, scooting over and sitting behind her legs to help her balance on the uneven floor. She nods and then extends to her full height, reaching overhead. The cave isn't high and Tesni is several inches taller than me, meaning she can reach the top.

Her slender brown hands slowly explore every bit of space as we work our way through the cavern, Halo and I continuing to act as barriers so she doesn't fall.

"You could help, you know," I say to Apricia, who's sitting against the opposite wall, watching us like we're here for her amusement. She just shrugs as both Tesni and Halo glare at her, too. I let out an exasperated breath before we continue searching. While Tesni tests the walls, I do the same with the floor, hoping it will reveal something. A staircase? A trap door, perhaps? I shiver as I continue tapping the stone.

I'm not sure how long it takes to explore the cave, but the sky is dark by the time we're done. It seems we're going to be spending the night here.

"We should huddle for warmth," I say. "We can take turns with who sleeps on the outside."

I pin Apricia with a glare as she opens her mouth to protest. "Don't be an idiot," I say. "If you don't, you're going to die of the cold. Never fear. No one will forget how superior you are for even a moment."

She narrows her eyes, but then reluctantly crawls over, somehow keeping her pointy nose thrust in the air. Her skin is pale, and her hands are red and raw. She slides into the space between me and Tesni, lying on her side, and we all squish together as closely as we can. The ground is hard and rough and it's so cold I can feel every knifing gust of wind through my clothing. This is miserable.

The night passes slowly as I doze off for brief spurts, unable to actually sleep. I must eventually drift for a moment because the sky begins to lighten, welcoming another day. I swallow, my throat dry and my stomach aching as it grumbles. Hunger used to be a feeling as familiar to me as breathing, but the weeks of rich, decadent food have softened the sharpest corners of those memories. Now they come screaming back at me with razored clarity, reminding me, yet again, of everything I stand to lose.

"I'm starving," Apricia whines. "Couldn't they have given us *something*?"

Blinking, I sit up, peering out of the cave's opening. The air feels a little warmer, which is a blessing, and I notice then it's gently raining. Crawling on my hands and knees, I inch forward and reach my hand out, letting the water fill a tiny well in the middle of my hand. Bringing it in, I lick my palm, savoring the water's sweet, fresh taste. Just like those nights I spent in the Hollow, the rain becomes my dubious savior once again. I'm not sure which option is the worse one right now.

The other three Fae are mimicking my movements, absorbing as much water as they can.

While they drink, I look out over the desolate space, wondering what the four of us are going to do. We must be missing some vital clue to our escape.

Something catches the corner of my eye—a glimmer of light, so small it would be easy to miss, but the longer I stare, the more apparent it becomes against the blank backdrop of snow and rock. It flickers in and out, glowing brighter and then dimming like a star waving a signal flag.

"Do you see that?" I ask, pointing into the distance.

"What?" Tesni asks, squinting.

I scan the space again, searching for the light, but it's gone. After a few more seconds of waiting, I shake my head. "Never mind. I thought I saw something."

We continue sipping on drips of rain until it stops falling, abandoning us for now. The wind picks up again, sending us back into a huddled mass at the rear of the shallow cave. Even Apricia joins us, the tips of her hair turning white with frost.

"What do we do?" Halo asks, her eyes closed and her cheeks wet, her breath fogging in filmy puffs of air. "What do they want from us?"

There is some trick, some puzzle, we're not seeing. They can't have just left us here to die...but then my stomach drops to my feet with a thud that vibrates straight to my frozen fingertips. I think of Mag's slip and how the previous Sun Queen Trials were cut short last time. I never did get answers about what happened then. I decide now is not the time to bring it up.

Could Atlas have done the same thing a second time? Did he leave us out here to die? But he seemed so sure I'd win and that I'd be his queen. I'm still not sure I can trust any of it, though.

For another day and night, we shiver on the ledge, searching the cavern over and over again, hoping something useful materializes. But it's nothing but impermeable blank stone staunchly withholding whatever secrets it's keeping.

It's daylight again, the air a hazy grey so thick it feels like I could scoop it up like cotton stuffing. I stare ahead, willing the scene to change. If I never see the colors white and grey again, it'll be too soon.

My nerves are brittle and frozen, liable to snap under any more pressure, and I will myself not to cry. If I start, I may never stop. I was so close to winning. So close to finally getting everything I've ever wanted, and now it's slipping away through my fingers like curls of frost off a frozen lake.

Halo is lying in a ball on the floor completely still, only her lips moving in a whispered prayer. I reach out to run a reassuring hand down her back, but she doesn't acknowledge it. Tesni and Apricia are doing no better, both of them speaking little and barely able to open their eyes.

For the first time since I came to Aphelion, I pity them. These poor Fae have never experienced this kind of suffering. They aren't built for this. Maybe I should be grateful Nostraza left me as hard and unscratchable as nails, but all it means is that I'll probably be the last one alive, left to suffer out here alone.

Something snags the corner of my vision and I see that same flash of light I noticed yesterday. It shimmers, brighter this time. More clearly and more defined.

It's then I remember the night Atlas showed me his magic during our first dinner together. The faux ocean he'd created had been speckled with similar points of brilliance. I blink, everything snapping into place.

"It's an illusion," I say, and Apricia and Tesni raise their weary heads, looking at me with confusion. "It's not real. This is Atlas's magic."

Pushing myself to stand, I take careful steps to the edge, the wind buffeting me and threatening to throw me off balance. Looking down, I quickly back away as my head sways from the plummet of the dizzying drop.

I'm sure I'm right, but this still all feels very real.

"An illusion?" Apricia scoffs, some of her verve returning thanks to her need to disagree with me. "That makes no sense."

"Can you see it?" I point to the shimmer, noting where more spots are visible now. They're brighter today, thanks to whatever false vision Atlas has created. Maybe he did it on purpose because we weren't figuring it out on our own. "There. Look. This isn't real."

"How can you possibly know that?" Apricia asks, folding her arms. I describe what Atlas showed me. At first, I can tell they don't believe me, and I don't miss the fact that Apricia doesn't say anything about Atlas giving her a similar demonstration.

Though I'm growing increasingly desperate, this is still a competition, and we've just been handed a lifeline.

"So, what do we do?" Tesni asks, her arms wrapped around her knees. I look over at her and press my lips together, knowing no one is going to like my answer.

"We jump."

"What?" Apricia exclaims, definitely more herself now. "Don't be absurd. We'll die."

"We won't. This is the test. This is what we're supposed to do." I infuse a confidence into my voice I don't entirely feel.

"What if you're wrong?"

With a shrug, I tell Apricia, "Then I guess we die. Either way, we won't survive out here much longer."

As if agreeing with me, the wind gusts so fiercely it shoves me back like a hand slamming into the center of my chest. Halo has uncurled from her position on the floor and is watching me warily. I reach for her.

"Come with me."

"Lor," she whispers. "I don't know."

"Trust me."

Our gazes meet. She didn't want to be here. She wanted to be out of these Trials and I stopped her without understanding why. If I'd just let her fall, then she'd be warm and secure with Marici, where she wanted to be.

No, I remind myself. She wouldn't have cleared that jump. She would be nothing but bones and shredded meat for that monster in the pit. She's stuck here, and while she doesn't want to win, I need her to survive.

"What do we have to lose?" I ask, imploring them all now.

Another howl of wind sings to us with its taunting melody, daring us to remain out here, but still she hesitates.

"Come on," I say again, taking her hand and pulling her up to stand. "We can't stay here any longer or we'll die for sure." I scan everyone's anxious faces.

"You coming?" I ask Apricia.

She flips her hair, and I resist the overwhelming urge to march over and hang her with it. "You have got to be kidding me. I am not jumping off that cliff." Tesni's uncertain gaze is darting between me and Apricia, clearly not sure which one of us she agrees with.

"Fine. I'll go first."

Halo yanks her hand from mine, clutching it to her chest, her eyes wild with fear. "I don't want to do this."

"Okay, I'll jump. You'll see. I'm going to pass through the illusion. When you see it's safe, you can follow."

She nods, though I can tell she still doesn't believe me.

Fuck, I hope I'm right.

But there is nothing else out here, and this is our only option. If they have left us here to die, then I might as well get it over with. At least this will hurt less in the end.

I keep that last thought to myself.

I *have* to be right, and if I'm not...well, let's just hope I am.

Taking a deep, steadying breath that doesn't work at all, I stand at the back of the cave, my back pressed to the wall. Clutching my locket, I gather my courage and toss a prayer to Zerra, hoping that for once in my life, she's listening.

Maybe I've always been too reckless for my own good. Maybe I should think about this further. This might be the proverbial nail in my *act-now-think-later* coffin. But there are no other choices before us now.

"Here goes nothing," I say, three sets of eyes watching me with a mixture of hope and fear.

And then, I don't allow myself the luxury of deliberating any longer before I sprint for the edge and leap into nothing.

CHAPTER THIRTY-SIX

I'm falling. My stomach lodges in my throat, and I'm falling so fast I see only a smear of stone and snow and white and grey whipping past. My hair tangles in my eyes and my mouth and my ears as I continue plummeting.

I was wrong.

I should have passed through the illusion, but this drop is very, *very* real. I've just sealed my own death. A scream tears from my throat as I continue falling faster and faster, the wind ripping at my clothes and my eyes watering, tears streaming across my cheeks. I'm a stone sinking to the bottom of a lake. A bird whose wings have been clipped. A defiant angel banished from the heavens.

But then the air shifts, warmth billowing up and enveloping me before I crash into a hard but pliant surface, rolling end over end until I come to a stop.

Lying on my back, I blink up at a clear blue sky, waiting for the world to stop spinning. My chest flutters with my tight breaths, abject terror still pumping adrenaline through my veins.

Holding still, I allow the new sounds and sensations of my environment to sink in. It's warm and humid. There are birds chirping and the unmistakable rush of a breeze rustling through leaves. With my arms stretched out on either side of me, I feel blades of soft grass tickle my palms. And the sun, oh the glorious sun, shines down in welcoming beams of molten pleasure. My fingers and my toes burn as they thaw, the buzz both agony and bliss. For the first time in days, I wiggle my joints without the biting restraint of frost.

This is it. I'm never leaving or moving from this spot. Have I finally died? This feels so much like the day I woke up in the Sun Palace after Gabriel took me from the Hollow.

My stomach growls with a painful twist, suggesting I must still be alive, and this is the next leg of the challenge.

Reluctantly, I force myself up and take in my surroundings. I'm in a grassy clearing bordered by high, neatly clipped hedges, all of them lush with emerald green leaves and covered in small yellow flowers. Large trees dot the clearing, erupting with apple blossoms, their trunks wide and their roots thick with age. Still blinking at the onslaught of sunlight, I search for the telltale sparkles that confirm this is yet another false reality created by Atlas.

But a honeysuckle scent wafts on the breeze, catching my attention. It's sweet and delicious and tickles a long-buried memory of a warm, cozy kitchen in a small house in the woods where I stood on a stool, helping knead dough for sweet buns, preparing them for the oven.

Spinning around, I take in the incomprehensible sight before me.

A long, massive table sits surrounded on three sides by the tall hedges, covered in food. There are towering tiers of desserts, covered in dainties as bright and colorful as gemstones. Tureens of chicken in creamy sauces. Vivid pink juice in crystal pitchers and thick slices of dewy fruit piled on golden plates.

Immediately, I'm on my feet running for the feast, my stomach protesting painfully after days of consuming nothing but stolen raindrops.

I skid to a halt in front of the feast, not sure where to start first. It looks like perfection. I know I should distrust this. We're in the middle of a trial and this has to be a test, but I'm so hungry, and surely they wouldn't poison us?

I scoff at my own continued naivety. Of course they would.

A moment later, I hear a cry and spin around to find Apricia vaulting for the table like her pants are on fire. Tesni and Halo are close behind, their eyes wide with disbelief. Apricia whizzes past me and moves in on a giant turkey leg dripping with fat and juices. She holds it up and bares her teeth while I shout, "Wait! You don't know if it's safe."

But, unsurprisingly, she pays me no mind and is already tearing out her second bite, her other hand digging straight into the center of a tall chocolate cake. She scoops out a chunk and stuffs it into her face.

Keeping watch for signs that anything is amiss, I study her like a specimen under a magnifying glass. How fast does poison work? Will she froth at the mouth immediately or will it be a slow sort of death, like being stretched by a noose?

Tesni is at the table now too, devouring hunks of white cheese and a lobster tail dripping in butter. Halo and I exchange a glance and then, deciding it seems okay, we both approach the offering.

Throwing caution away, I bite into a fluffy loaf of bread, the crust crumbling all over the front of my soiled tunic. Then I down a giant glass of lemonade filled with clinking chunks of ice. My parched throat practically cracks in relief before I reach for a second. Stuffing a piece of roast beef in my mouth, I chew thoughtfully, one ear trained on our surroundings. Maybe this is a reward for solving the illusion. Still, this seems too easy.

I venture a few more bites. A peanut butter square. A slice of vanilla cake. A piece of poached chicken. And water. All the water I can drink. It's so good I moan in ecstasy. I'm so distracted by the food, I haven't even had time to truly appreciate how warm I am. The air is so thick my tunic clings to my body, my hair sticking to my forehead.

I stuff a crispy pastry in my mouth, the raspberry center bursting on my tongue, when the ground rumbles like we're stranded on top of a hungry whale. Of course, this was too good to be true. It's then I notice the breaks in the hedges, forming tunnels that lead away from where we're standing. I stop eating, trying to understand what's causing the shaking and what direction it's coming from.

The others have noticed it too, their eyes darting from one corner of the clearing to the other, but nothing materializes.

"What is that?" Halo asks, her voice wobbling. Something terrible is coming for us. I can feel it in the very marrow of my bones.

Movement in the periphery of my vision snags my eye and I whirl, catching the back of a figure darting between the hedges. Compelled to investigate, I head to the entrance of the maze and stop, peering into the darkened, leafy corridor. The figure is no longer visible, and before me is an empty stretch of nothing. When I look back at the other Tributes, they're all watching me with careful expressions.

"Don't go in there," Halo says, her voice soft.

I shake my head, understanding there is no option.

"We have to. This is the challenge." I take another step, the shadows of the tall hedges falling over me, the air growing cooler. Another movement grabs my awareness. Someone is now standing at the far end of the tunnel, their features obscured by the distance. I walk further inside, the panicked shouts of Halo following me and imploring me to come back.

But I can't.

This is the final challenge, and I'm so close to getting everything I want. So close to getting my crown and my magic after all these years. So close to getting Tristan and Willow back. *So close* to exacting my revenge on the Aurora King.

Picking up my pace, I break into a slow jog, sweat already breaking out on my forehead. The dry cold wind has been replaced by a heat so cloying it's sticking to the roof of my mouth. When I breathe, it's like trying to draw breath from a brick wall, but I press on, knowing this is the path I must navigate on the tightrope of my future.

The leafy corridor seems to grow longer as I run, but I'm catching up to the figure waiting at the end. From this distance, it appears to be male. Tall and lean with a shock of dark hair. He wears a tunic of some undetermined color. Grey or brown, perhaps. I squint, wondering if my eyes are deceiving me. It can't be. My mind is playing tricks.

The figure breaks around a corner and disappears through the leaves. Not willing to lose him, I pick up my pace and sprint for the spot where I think he vanished. I catch another fleeting glimpse of his back, and then I'm running again.

We chase around corners and down narrow pathways until I'm so turned around I have no sense of the direction I've gone. All I can see is a stretch of green walls in every direction and a strip of blue sky overhead. Taking a moment to catch my breath, I listen, wondering where the other Tributes have gone. I couldn't find my way back to them now if I tried.

A rustle in the leaves catches my attention and I take off again, turning a corner into a small courtyard with a stone fountain in the center. On the opposite side of the fountain stands the man I've been chasing.

My heart stops and my breath breaks in my lungs, my knees melting out from under me.

Tristan.

"Tris?" I whisper, hope filtering into the chinks of my voice. Our gazes meet and the world spins out on its axis. What is he doing here? Tears pool in my eyes. I've never been so happy to see anyone or anything in my life. But why is he just standing there staring at me? Something feels off. His eyes don't look right. They're distant and fractured, and it feels like he's not even seeing me. "Tristan?" I take a step forward, reaching for him. "Are you okay?"

Not answering me, he pivots on his heel and sprints out of the clearing, once again dissolving into the darkness of the maze. "Tristan!" I run to the spot where he just disappeared, finding no trace of him. "Come back, Tristan!" I scream so loud my voice cracks, despair bleeding out in corrosive drips. "Please! Come back!"

I run. I don't know what direction he went, but I run. Screaming his name again and again, I peer down every opening and path, hoping for a trace. Sweat puddles down my back and my temples, the humidity encasing me in a viscous bubble. Using my sleeve to wipe my forehead is useless and does nothing to cool the blood boiling under my skin. Still hunting for my brother, I scramble blindly, desperate for another glimpse.

A moment later, I go flying, landing on the soft grass, my knees and hands skidding against the rough grain. Too winded to move, I suck in several deep breaths before I roll over with a groan and sit up. My knees and my palms are stained with green. It's then I notice what tripped me.

A sword.

A gleaming silver sword lies in the path. It's simple but elegant, with a golden hilt and a single crystal-clear jewel at the end. I look around, wondering who left it here, but I seem to be alone. The only sound is the gentle rustle of a breeze moving through the leaves. I pick up the sword, testing its solid weight in my hand. Part of me is happy to have an extra layer of protection, but another part is wondering why the maze has gifted me this. It can only mean I'm going to need it.

A scream demands my attention and I take off running again, trying to follow its source. It doesn't sound like Tristan, though. It's higher pitched, and my heart does a hopeful leap in my chest. Maybe it's Willow. But she's screaming, so maybe I should be careful what I wish for. I rub a hand down my sweat-slicked face, confused by this conflicting tangle of thoughts threatening to split my head open.

"Willow?" I yell. "Is that you?" The screams have transformed into pained whimpers, and they seem to be coming from just beyond the hedge. "Willow," I chant over and over again, trying to will her into existence.

It's not Willow on the other side, though, it's Halo. She's kneeling on the ground, her face buried into the chest of a body. Her anguished sobs fill the air as I realize the body she's clinging to is Marici. Blood stains the front of her pale yellow gown, her skin ghostly white.

Dropping the sword in my hand, I fall to my knees and wrap my arms around Halo.

"She's gone," Halo moans, her voice low and keening, her hands clutched to her stomach. "What did they do to her?" She looks at me as though I hold the answer, and I shake my head.

"I don't know, I'm so sorry, Halo." Marici's dead blue eyes stare at the sky and I reach over and gently close her eyelids, her skin clammy to the touch.

"I don't want to do this anymore," Halo says. "I never wanted this. I want out."

She lifts her head up and screams. "Do you hear me? I don't want to be a queen! I never wanted it! This contest is barbaric! You're all animals!" She stands up, her fists balled at her sides, blood streaking her tunic and cheek. With her chin tipped to the sky, she shouts, "Get me out of here!"

"Halo!" I jump up, wrapping my arms around her. "Calm down."

She struggles against my hold, tears streaming down her cheeks, her fists beating at my chest. "No! I want out! Kill me! Lock me up! I don't care! I won't serve the Sun King for another moment! He's a monster!"

She shrieks, her hands clasped on either side of her head, and then suddenly goes silent, her chest heaving in and out in ragged gasps. Again, I wrap my arms around her, trying to give her something to cling to. She drops her face against my neck, her warm tears mingling with the drops of sweat sliding down my throat.

"Why won't they let me leave?" She grasps my tunic like she's drowning, and I decide that's exactly how she must feel.

"I don't know," I whisper, smoothing her hair. "I don't know."

They brought me here to compete for an honor in this beautiful place of brightness and golden light. It seemed so different from Nostraza, but as Halo clings to me and Marici's mutilated body lies at my feet, I realize that this, too, has all been an illusion. They pretended I was from the slums of Aphelion. Paraded me around as an example of what one could achieve if they believed. If they worked hard enough. But why did The Umbra ever have to exist when a few nights ago I slept in a bed made of gold? Aphelion is no different from Nostraza. The surroundings might be gilded with rivers of gold, but this is a prison, just the same.

But *I* can't give up. I don't have that luxury, and I still need to win. My chance at this kind of freedom is so close I can taste it.

If I'm a queen, everything will be different.

There's a rustle from the leaves as Halo sobs quietly against me, and I wonder if it's Tristan, my blood chilling to a sluggish pace. What if whatever they did to Marici happens to him? Are they trying to destroy us completely?

I have to find him. Why did he run from me? But I hesitate. I can't leave Halo alone, either.

The leaves on the far side of the clearing rustle again, and a figure steps out.

My vision catches fire and my chest fills with stones.

Willow.

Chapter Thirty-seven

Willow's brown eyes are wide with uncertainty, fear reflected in their depths. I know that look like I know my own heartbeat. That lovely face I've seen during every restless night I've spent in Aphelion. Frozen to the spot, I'm too afraid to move, worried she'll also run away.

"Willow," I whisper, her name hanging in the air like a white flag of surrender. Halo peels her head from my shoulder, our gazes clashing as we both finally understand. They've corralled the most important people in our lives together with the intention of putting them all in harm's way. Marici has already succumbed, and I wonder what Tesni and Apricia are up against inside the maze.

Willow looks right through me, as though I'm not even here. I remember the same strange look in Tristan's eyes, too. Are these also illusions? Could an apparition manage to capture her very essence that way? But if Atlas really intends to hurt them, I can't take that chance.

"Willow," I say louder, but she doesn't react as she looks around, her eyes growing wider. Suddenly, she takes off at a full clip across the clearing and plunges back into the hedges. "Willow!"

I have to go after her. I have to protect her. That has always been my job. I look at the sword I've left on the ground.

"Go," Halo says. "Go after her."

"I can't leave you here."

Halo drops to her knees, covering Marici's body with hers. "I'm done here. I'm not moving until they come find me." She looks up. "Save your loved ones and then win this thing, so Aphelion isn't left with Apricia as its queen. You must do this, Lor. I know you're the Final Tribute, but you've made it this far, and it's time for you to change history and change this entire kingdom."

"Are you sure?" My eyes search the place Willow fled, knowing she's getting farther and farther away. Halo leans over Marici, grabbing the sword by its hilt and handing it to me.

"Go. Now. Please. Don't let her death have been in vain."

With a firm nod, I sprint away, following Willow's trail. Of course, I've lost her, so I keep running, ignoring the shaking in my limbs and shoving down a nauseating wave of light-headedness. I've barely eaten in days, and the brief feast at the maze's entrance feels like hours ago. I'm sure the only reason I'm standing is due to all the training Gabriel forced upon me these past weeks. Though I'm still not sure why he ever bothered.

"Tristan!" I call, hoping it will force him to materialize. "Willow!" This isn't working, but I keep trying anyway, losing count of the minutes as I track every rustle and echoing hint of footsteps dragging me deeper and deeper into the maze. At the same time, I try to puzzle out the rules of this challenge. Save our loved ones? Why weren't we told what to do this time? And why did they move up the date?

Still running, I slow at the unmistakable sounds of whimpers followed by a snarl. Knowing I'm about to face yet another test, I alter my course, heading towards the sounds. I find myself at the mouth of what appears to be a dead end, greenery surrounding me on all sides, so overgrown it's created a canopy of vines and leaves overhead.

Tesni is shielding the body of a young girl with dark skin, her long silver hair in braids. She's crying hysterically, fat tears sliding down her round cheeks. A quick assessment tells me this must be Tesni's younger sister, or at least a cherished loved one.

They're facing off against a creature covered in dark fur that towers at least twice their height. It looks like a cross between a wolf and a bear, with a humped back and a snout full of needle-sharp teeth. Standing on its hind legs, it has arms as thick as tree trunks, and the growl that pulls from its mouth rumbles so low the ground beneath my feet trembles.

"Get away from them!" I shout, holding up my shaking sword, the hilt slippery in my sweaty grip. My clothes are pasted to me now, making it harder to move, every step weighed down as though I've been encased in cement.

"Lor, no!" Tesni says, not taking her eyes from the beast that now turns its giant head towards me. With eyes so dark they're like bottomless wells, it focuses on me with the confident gleam of a predator that knows its prey doesn't present any threat. This is no rabid beast. There is an intelligence and cunning in its expression. It lights up with delight at my approach, like I'm the gravy about to be poured over a thick slice of roasted beef.

"Run!" I shout at Tesni and her sister. "Get out of here."

My command is futile, though, because we stand blocked by a dead end and there's nowhere for them to go. Their only hope is for me to lead this monster away.

"Come get me!" I yell, dancing on the balls of my feet. "You big, ugly monster. You're just nothing but hair and muscles, aren't you? Who let you out of your cage? Shouldn't you be on all fours like the dog you are?"

The beast narrows its gaze as though it's trying to decide if it's just been insulted.

"Come and get me," I snarl, spinning and bolting in the opposite direction. Racing at top speed, I crash through the hedges, casting a glance over my shoulder. It's taken my bait and lumbers down the narrow tunnel, moving with more speed than anything that large should have a right to. Fear makes my steps erratic, my ankles and knees stiff, and I hope I can hang on long enough to outrun him. I pray Tesni and her sister are taking this opportunity to get as far away from here as possible.

My arms and legs pumping, I check behind me to ensure the beast is still following, when it surprises me and breaks away, heading down another path. *Shit.* I skid to a halt, wondering what's drawn its attention. Is it Willow or Tristan? That thought spurs me on, terrified of what I'll find.

Around corners, I chase the monster. But it's faster than me, and it's drawing away as my chest grows tighter and my legs become heavier, like I have anvils strapped to my ankles. Eventually, I lose sight of it, but it's large and its body doesn't quite fit through the tight tunnels, so I follow the rustling of the leaves, attempting to track it through the maze.

And then come more screams.

My eyes burn with unshed tears, the pressure building in my forehead. This is the worst challenge yet. *What do they want from us?*

I take another turn and then another before I stumble into yet another courtyard filled with low flower boxes, blooming with color, and lined with a low stone fence. It's Tesni and her sister again, and my frustration pulls into a rock-hard pellet that sinks through my stomach. A sob heaves from my throat as the beast licks its chops where it corners the two Fae, who tremble and clutch at each other.

"Leave them alone!" I try again. "Come on, you overgrown mutt. Come here and get a bone." It peers over its massive shoulder and this time I swear it smirks, telling me it's not falling for my shit again. It's staying here for the easier prey.

Before I can react, it swipes out a massive arm and snags Tesni's sister around the waist, trapping her in an enormous claw. "Kyri!" Tesni screams, grabbing Kyri's arm, attempting to pull her back. But the beast is a hundred times stronger and easily yanks the girl out of Tesni's grip, plucking her with the same ease as a petal off a rose. Kyri is shrieking so loud my ears throb. Her short legs flail and kick as the monster steps back, hauling her over its shoulder.

"No!" I scream, lunging at the monster and swinging my sword, slicing a deep gash into the back of its leg. Blood blooms bright and red, soaking its fur, and the beast roars, turning on me with spittle dripping down its fangs. It swipes out its other hand, catching me in the stomach, and sends me flying across the clearing.

Pain shoots through my arm and my head when I crash into one of the stone fences before collapsing to the ground in a heap. Blood stains my vision as I groan and roll over. Peering through a crimson curtain, I see Tesni still trying to reach for her sister as the beast toys with her, darting in and out, a rumbling sort of snicker dragging from its snout.

Slowly, I push myself up, my wrenched shoulder screaming in protest. Getting on to my hands and knees, a knifing jab of pain rips through my center. I gag on the force of it, bile climbing up my throat. Looking down, I see my tunic is slick with blood where four long slashes have sliced through the fabric and my skin. It pumps out of me in a scarlet haze, and I sway in my crouched position, willing myself not to faint.

The beast roars, drawing my attention to where Tesni is still trying to free her sister.

"Put her down," I shout weakly, but it's no use. The beast tips its head, piercing me with one last look. Then it turns and bounds away, melting into the hedges to the sound of Tesni screaming at the top of her lungs. She follows the beast, leaving me where I've crumpled on the ground, breathing heavily and trying to gather my strength. I'm not done here. I have to find Willow and Tristan if they're not already dead.

Time slips away as I blink, willing clarity into my consciousness. Then I feel gentle hands touching me and hear the rip of fabric. Tesni is wrapping a piece of her tunic around my midsection, her face dripping with snot and tears.

"Your sister," I whisper.

"She's gone," Tesni replies, her voice wooden as she wipes her nose with her remaining sleeve. "The beast was too fast. She's gone. I've lost her." Her voice splits apart on the last two words as I practically hear the rip of her heart shattering in her chest. She tears off one of my sleeves and continues wrapping me with makeshift bandages.

"The cuts don't appear deep," she says. "I think you might have hit your head, though." She gingerly touches my temple, and I wince. Is that why I can't seem to form a coherent thought?

"Lor!" someone screams in the distance, and that's what I need to bring me back from the brink. "Lor!"

"Willow?" I sit up slowly, the world tilting and pain clattering through my torso.

"Lor!" the voice shouts again, and this time, there's no doubt in my mind.

I clasp Tesni's arm.

"I have to find her."

Tesni nods and helps me to stand. "Perhaps it's not too late for you."

She hands me the sword that went flying when the beast tossed me and squeezes my hand. "Find them, Lor. Protect them. I think that's the game."

"Lor!"

I shake my head, grim resolve coalescing in my blood. This is the only thing that matters. Forget the contest. Forget my revenge. The only thing that has *ever* mattered are Tristan and Willow. If anything happens to them, there was no point to any of this.

I take a step, pain lancing through my midsection, but I breathe through it, drawing on the grit that flows in my veins. I can ignore this. I've spent half my life living on the edge of agony. Mired in a torment so bone-deep it nearly crushed me. Pain defined the rigid corners of my existence for so many years, and those kinds of memories will never fade, no matter how many times I try to scrub them clean.

Pain is a language I know. A script I've written a thousand times.

Focusing only on my need to find Tristan and Willow, I keep walking, picking up my pace when Willow calls my name again. "I'm coming," I scream. "I'm coming!" I can't let anything happen to her. Loping as fast as my wounds allow, I circle towards her voice, greenery whipping past my vision.

Surrounded by verdant tunnels, I scatter around corners, trying to keep up with my sister, praying to Zerra that I won't lose her. When I turn into yet another long corridor, the end stretches into darkness, where a figure moves in the distance.

Dark hair and a slight frame, wearing a grey tunic so tattered it's only a memory of the color it used to be. I run faster, the slashes in my side throbbing, my bandages turning red. She's running so fast it's like something is chasing her. At the same time, I try to keep an eye on my surroundings, anticipating an attack at any moment. I trust nothing.

"Willow!" I scream, knowing she won't listen.

But then she slows down and looks over her shoulder, as if searching for the sound of my voice. "Willow!" I lob her name into the space between us like a bomb, hoping I can break through whatever barrier is keeping us apart.

She doesn't stop, though, turning forward and speeding up again.

"Willow." It's then I finally crack, my soul breaking open and cleaving apart. Tears, ones long since buried, wet my cheeks as I chase desperately after her. Nothing will matter if she dies. None of this will have mattered if I cannot save her. We're both running, the distance between us never changing. Why won't she stop?

"Willow! Please stop." I'm getting weaker, my bandages leaking blood, my temple throbbing, my throat dry, and my stomach cramping. "Willow. Come back to me."

We run and run as I slowly gain on her. The distance between us closes and I scream her name, but she still doesn't turn. Ahead of her looms an arched wooden door that stands in the middle of nothing. There are no walls and no building, just more green hedges tunneling in every direction.

Willow keeps running like the Lord of the Underworld is chasing her. Stumbling, I try to keep up. Then she reaches the mysterious door, flings it open, and disappears through it before slamming it shut.

"Willow!" I've lost her. Momentum propels me into the solid surface, my shoulder crashing into it before I turn the handle. Locked. I pound at it, screaming at it to open. Using my sword, I hack at the wood, trying to break through. "Let me in! Willow! Let me in!"

I circle around it, tasting my salty river of tears. It looks the same on either side—just a doorway to nothing.

Using my entire body, I heave against it, gagging at the pain that splinters through my shoulder and my stomach. I'm barely coherent as I slam into the door over and over again.

Suddenly, it gives underneath me and bursts open. I plunge through, tripping and landing on my face, skidding against a smooth surface as agony shreds me to ribbons.

Panting with my eyes squeezed shut, I wait for the pain to subside, willing myself not to faint when suddenly thunderous applause breaks out, synchronized to the sound of hundreds of voices cheering, whoops and hollers arcing into the air and skewering me like hail.

Confusion, complete and utter confusion, forces my eyes open. My eyelids stick together, congealed with blood and sweat and tears. Through the fog, I'm greeted by the sight of golden marble and a soaring glass ceiling open to a clear blue sky. I lift my head. I'm lying in the throne room, and Atlas stands over me with a beaming smile on his beautiful face.

CHAPTER THIRTY-EIGHT

He drops into a crouch and lays a gentle hand against my head, smoothing back a strand of what is now my disgusting hair. "You did it," he says, still smiling. "I'm so proud of you."

"Where's Willow?" I ask, my throat dry and cracked. "And Tristan? Where are they? Are they okay?"

Atlas's expression gathers into a concerned grimace as someone's hands help gently roll me onto my back. Healers swarm around me, laying soothing touches on my head and midsection. A bright light bursts in my vision, and I gasp as wounds knit together. "Why are they healing me?"

The applause dwindles, the crowd now watching, whispering to each other in low voices.

"Atlas? What's going on?" He bestows me with a benevolent smile, but the edges are blurred, like he's a wet painting someone smeared with their hand.

"You made it through the last challenge," he says, touching my cheek softly and helping me sit up, his fingers stopping under my chin before he tips my face to him. "You're going to stand before the Sun Mirror."

"What?" I'm so disoriented, I can't make sense of anything. "Where are Tristan and Willow?"

Atlas presses his mouth together. "I'm sorry, Lor, but they're not here."

"What? No, I saw them! Where are they? If you hurt them—"

Atlas drops a heavy hand on my shoulder. "They were an illusion. They weren't really here." Something putrid and rotten churns in my stomach as the sick realization washes over me. "Your challenge was to protect your loved ones until they could make it through the door. Only one other Tribute succeeded." He gestures across the room to where Apricia sits, looking as worn out and bloody as I feel. That smug smile I'm used to is absent as she sits on the steps of the dais with her head in her hands.

"So Marici and Tesni's sister?" I ask.

"They're perfectly fine," Atlas says in a kind voice, as though that's supposed to make everything okay.

"But Halo and Tesni. They were terrified." Anger bubbles in my chest like a cauldron stewing over an evil witch's fire. "I was terrified Tristan and Willow were going to die!"

"I'm sorry, Lor. But that was the final challenge."

I shake off his hand, scooting away. The healers have finished their work sealing up my wounds, leaving behind only a dull ache.

"They thought they were dead!" I say, my voice getting louder. "What is wrong with you? I thought Willow was in danger!"

"Lor," Atlas says, standing up from his crouched position and coming closer, his hand outstretched. "Calm down."

"I won't calm down! You're a monster! Where are Tesni and Halo? Where are they!"

Atlas holds his palms up in a placating gesture. "They're fine. Lor, they're with the other fallen Tributes."

"Only the ones you didn't kill, you mean!"

The tether on my control has gone slack. I'm shaking. I'm so angry the layers of my rage pull apart, threatening to unglue me, turning me into paper-thin sheaves.

Finally, I stand on wobbling legs and absorb the faces of everyone in the throne room. It's filled with well-dressed Fae, all open-mouthed and gaping.

"You're all monsters, too!" I scream, and there's a collective flinch, like I've just slapped them all with the back of my hand. I wish I could. My chest is heaving, struggling to draw enough air to keep pace with my mounting fury. Even after I've been healed, the strain of the days trapped on that cliff and the hours I spent running through the maze bend me in half. I clutch my heart, coughing so hard the just-healed wounds in my midsection pull.

"Lor," Atlas says softly, placing a hand on my back, running it up and down my spine. "I understand that was unpleasant, but those are the rules of the Trials."

Still bent over, I watch as a tear lands on my boot, leaving a defined track through the dust as it rolls off my toe. I'm still crying and I hate that so many people are here to witness this moment that I finally split in two. "I thought Tristan and Willow were here," I sob. "I thought they were in danger."

Atlas moves closer, bending over and placing his mouth near my ear. "They're still in Nostraza," he whispers so low only I can hear. "And soon you can get them out. The Sun Mirror is waiting for you."

My eyes close and I inhale a deep breath, teeth gritted. "If you think I still want to bond to you after all this, you're delusional."

"Lor," he says, lines of tension forming around his eyes.

"Bond to Apricia. She makes far more sense. Send me home, Atlas. I don't want any part of this court. I want to go back."

"What are you saying? You'd go back to that shithole over being bonded to me?"

Standing up straight so everyone can hear me, I pin him with the most hostile look I can drag up from my exhausted spirit. "Yes."

His expression shifts, a façade cracking, revealing slivers of darkness underneath the light. That kind patience in his eyes drops away to be replaced by cold blue fire. *Ah, so this is it then.* Something has always felt off about his words and his affection. I could never quite settle into it. Dazzled by his beauty. Charmed by this entire existence, so at odds with my life in Nostraza, I was blind to everything.

I wanted to believe he wanted me for *me* and not what I could do for him. But I should have known better all along. I was so stupid not to see it.

"Well, that's too fucking bad, Lor," Atlas whispers, a deadly threat in his voice. "I stole you from the Aurora King, and you are *mine*."

Before I have time to process those words, he straightens his shoulders, tugging on the hem of his golden jacket. "It's time for the Mirror to choose," he announces to the room.

"I'm not doing it," I say, drawing myself up. I want to collapse in a heap of exhaustion, but I stand my ground, staring up at Atlas, who towers over me like a golden star about to implode in a blinding flash.

"You don't have a choice."

In response, I spit. He blinks as the spray hits him across one of his perfectly high cheekbones and the entire room gasps in horror. "I won't do it," I hiss.

"Your Majesty," a guard says, glowering at me. "I'll take her down to the dungeons." Two guards appear at my sides.

"No," Atlas says, holding up a hand, not taking his eyes off me. "She's going to stand before the Mirror. Gabriel, bring her."

Gabriel materializes before me, and I growl as he sticks me with his usual disapproving glare. I guess Atlas let him out of the dungeon. "Don't make this harder than it needs to be, Lor."

"What do you care?" I shout. "You wanted me dead!"

He blinks—the only sign I've surprised him.

"Gabriel!" Atlas says. "Bring her now."

Gabriel reaches for me, and I start screaming and kicking. "No! Leave me alone! I want to go home!"

Gabriel and several other guards surround me, grabbing my limbs. He's now behind me, pinning my arms at my back, his grip around my wrists like a vise. I jerk my hands to get out and he pulls on my arms so hard my shoulders groan.

"Hold still," he says, seething.

"No!" I scream.

"Are you sure about this, Your Majesty?" Gabriel asks Atlas, his tone tight. "I can do as she asks."

"Absolutely not," Atlas replies. "She's going to the Mirror."

"But why? What could she possibly have to offer you, Atlas?" Gabriel's voice is on the edge of desperate, his normally cool demeanor cracking.

Atlas stands in front of us both, his gaze matched with Gabriel's. I reach out to kick Atlas, but Gabriel tugs me back with a snarl. "I am your king and I order you to bring her to the Mirror. Don't make me regret letting you out of the dungeon, Gabriel—you're still on a very fine edge."

There is a pause, the crowd in the room so silent you could hear a pin drop. I feel Gabriel nod.

"Yes, Your Majesty," he says in a dispassionate voice. He shoves me then, guards surrounding me on all sides, Gabriel still clutching my wrists as I fight and kick with every bit of purpose I have. Dragged along, I'm forced to stand next to Apricia, who glances over at me, her expression wary. Blood smears her forehead, and her normally perfect hair is a mess.

Our gazes meet, and it's clear neither of us is going to win today. Atlas has made it apparent he wants me here, despite Apricia's willingness to bond to him instead. But he doesn't want her, and now I'm the only one in this room who really knows why.

What I don't understand is how Atlas could possibly have discovered this secret.

Still holding my wrists, Gabriel shoves me forward with a grunt.

The Mirror is huge, standing three times my height. The thick oval frame is made of gold, molded with curls and flowers. It sits against a wall covered in gold silk, the surface so shiny and smooth it looks like a still lake.

I confront my reflection. The blood on my face. The wild look in my eyes.

"I'm going to let go," Gabriel whispers in my ear. "And you're going to stand here and do as you're told. If you put a toe out of place, I don't care what Atlas says or what happens to me, I'll kill you instantly. Is that understood?" Slowly, I look over my shoulder and up at him. What I see in his eyes tells me he absolutely means it. I nod.

"Thank you," I say.

He furrows his brow. "I just threatened to kill you, Lor. You're a strange little creature."

"I know you didn't want me here, but you helped me anyway. Made me stronger. I don't think I would've gotten this far without your help. I would have died along the way for sure."

"I was just doing my job," he replies, his voice cold.

"Still. You did it well."

"I told you, if you look good, so do I." I'm not sure if I imagine the glimmer of softness I catch in his eyes before he says, "And you would've made it here with or without me, Lor."

I frown up at him, surprised by his words, the tears in my eyes building again. Now that I've finally let them go, I can't seem to get them to stop.

"It's time," Atlas interrupts. With his arms folded over his chest, he's just as beautiful as always, but his shine has tarnished to a dull luster.

Gabriel finally lets go of my wrists, and I shake out my arms, still looking at Atlas. Slowly, I direct my gaze to my feet, preparing myself for the next step in a journey I never imagined I'd set out on. For weeks, I've wondered what would happen when I stood here. What the Mirror would see.

With the deepest breath of my life, I take a step forward, and then another, my soft footsteps echoing in the room before I look up and stare into the Mirror.

Chapter Thirty-nine

The smooth shiny surface ripples like a stone dropped into a pond and then melts away, revealing another place and another time.

A memory stowed away, but never, ever forgotten.

A cottage in the woods and the sound of thundering hoofbeats in the distance. My mother standing at the counter kneading bread with a streak of flour on her face.

My father enters the room with a sword in his hand. They exchange a look loaded with fear and then they're ushering me and my sister out the back of the house.

A trap door and a necklace with a single red stone on the end. My mother's tears and my father's grim resignation. In the dark, I huddle with Willow, hearing the frantic sound of our parents' screams as they died to protect us. But it wasn't enough. A flash of light and a man's leering face and then the screams become mine.

Weeks, days of traveling, trussed up like a pig in the back of a cart with my brother and sister. They found Tristan hiding in the woods where he killed three of the Aurora King's soldiers before they subdued him. We huddle together, mourning the loss of our mother and father. Mourning the loss of everything we've ever known. Of the legacy that was now really gone forever.

The dark stone walls of Nostraza loom where we stand in the courtyard, snow falling in soft flakes around us.

The Aurora King stands before me, his hands behind his back as he studies us. He's almost twice my height. My father wasn't small, but this Imperial Fae is the biggest man I've ever seen. Sharp lines define a flawless face bred for cruelty and malice. Ribbons of color swirl in his endless black eyes.

His words echo in my ears. Words I'll remember for the rest of my days.

I'm to be placed behind those walls and forget who I am. Forget who I might have become. To never tell another living soul. To understand he's chosen to allow us to live—me, my brother, and my sister, the only people I have left in this world—because we're children and he believes us to be harmless. And there's still an off-chance I may someday prove useful. Either way, if I succumb to the harsh realities of Nostraza, he's not to be bothered either way.

Children or not, our innocence was stripped away that day forever.

Twelve long years pass.

My lungs compress as I relive these events in flashes. I've relived them so many times they're written under my skin in blood and ash. They're as much a part of me as the soul barely clinging to my body.

Then a voice floats through my head like a lilting waltz, spinning out in harmonious notes. It's the Mirror, and it's speaking to me.

Ah, what do we have here?

The rumors were true then.

We've all been waiting a very, very long time, Your Majesty.

What are you doing in front of me?

How did you end up so far from home?

Perhaps you don't even know.

What you are? Who you are?

It's been so very long, maybe that knowledge has been lost to memory.

But there are those who still remember.

I suppose he wanted you for your power?

These Fae are such fools.

They never learn from their mistakes.

I'm sorry, Your Majesty, but this isn't where you belong.

This is forbidden.

This can never happen again.

Ouranos would not survive it, nor would you.

I don't know where the Crown ended up after

she tried to break the world.

It, too, has been lost to time.

Succumbed to destruction, perhaps.

I'm not sure if it still exists.

That knowledge extends beyond my power, but I do

know it is the only way for you.

If you find it, please return and bow before me again.

When that day comes, I'll have a gift for you, Your Majesty.

Seek out the Crown and find me again.

The Mirror turns black and then blazes with pure white light as I lurch back, gasping as though I've just emerged from underwater. The room is completely silent until I hear the slow click of footsteps.

Atlas approaches me, his eyes searching me all over. "What happened?"

I shake my head, willing my voice to sound meek and broken. "It rejected me."

"What?" Atlas says, coming closer, his hand grabbing the front of my tunic as he pulls me into him. "What did it say to you?"

"Nothing. Just that I was not the true queen of Aphelion. That it was her." I point an unsteady finger at Apricia, the lie tripping off my tongue and falling with a thud between us. Atlas snarls, gripping my tunic tighter.

"That can't be," he says, bringing his face to mine. "Are you telling me the truth?"

"Of-of course," I stammer out.

He glares at me and then lets go, pushing me away.

"I'm ready for the Mirror, Your Majesty," Apricia says, flipping her messy nest of hair over her shoulder. The effect isn't quite the same, but I have to admire her spirit even now.

"No," Atlas snaps. "This contest is over."

He spins around and glares at everyone, his shoulders hunched and his fists balled at his sides.

A Fae in a long robe steps forward. "Your Majesty, you must finish the Trials. The fourth challenge was completed this time and each Tribute must stand before the Mirror. If you do not do so, the consequences will be dire."

Atlas grinds his teeth and another Fae steps forward. "He's right, Your Majesty. You must complete this now or risk losing your crown and all of your magic. You know the rules."

A muscle in Atlas's jaw ticks, his eyes blazing. He looks like he wants to destroy every single person in this room. "Fine," he growls at Apricia. "Do it."

She leaps to do his bidding, stepping in front of the Mirror while Atlas looks on with white-hot fire. Gabriel is at my side again, but he doesn't restrain me.

Apricia squares her shoulders and steps before the Mirror. The room hangs in silence as she faces it. I wonder if it's speaking to her, too. If she too is being forced to revisit some of her most painful memories.

The silence stretches on for what feels like hours, the air so tense you could cut it with scissors and hang it up over the windows. Atlas paces behind Apricia, his hand cupping his chin, periodically watching her and then throwing a look to me that makes my knees weak with fear. What was his plan for me? What is he going to do now?

Suddenly, the Mirror explodes in a flash of golden light that fills the room with brilliance. Apricia lights up, her skin glowing as if the sun has just been captured inside her chest, her dark hair rising around her in ribbons of ebony like she's floating underwater.

Brighter and brighter, she glows until we're forced to shield our eyes, arms and hands covering our faces. There's a vibration, a low hum, that sings through the room, the tenor rattling into the backs of my teeth.

A few seconds later, the light dims, leaving only a faint out-line of gold shimmering on her skin. Slowly, Apricia turns to face us, and it's clear she's no longer the same. She's still beau-tiful, but now possesses that same unearthly quality as Atlas. Something not of this world. Her smile is so wide she could light a thousand candles with a single breath.

It's then everyone in the room drops to a knee and bows their heads.

"The Sun Queen," ripples through the whispers in the crowd.

Gabriel, Atlas, and I remain standing as we survey the room of bent bodies, paying homage. Apricia smiles, clasping her hands together and looking at the king with such an expression of adoration I almost feel bad for her. Atlas, on the other hand, looks angry enough to tear down the sky, ball it up, and launch it into the heavens.

Unable to stop myself, I blurt out, "Can I go home now?" I want to get as far away from this place as possible. I look at Gabriel. "You said if I lost, you'd send me back. I want to go home."

"No," Atlas roars, sending a mutual flinch around the room. "This isn't over! You aren't going anywhere."

He addresses Gabriel. "Lock her up."

"What! You can't do that! I haven't done anything wrong."

He storms over to me, lowering his voice to a deadly whisper. "You aren't leaving, Lor. I told you that you're mine, and I meant it."

"Why? What do you want from me?"

He narrows his gaze, sizing me up, maybe finally seeing me for the very first time. "Do you know, Lor? Have you been playing the innocent, doe-eyed liar all this time?"

"I don't know what you're talking about," I say, and anger sloughs from him in visceral waves that threaten to peel off my skin.

"Take her away," he hisses. "Make sure she's secure and put a twenty-four-hour guard on her."

With that, I'm hauled away and dragged through the palace, down, down, down into its depths until the gold walls and shiny floors vanish, giving way to bleak stone and a lonely, cavernous echo.

After I'm shoved into a cell, the door slams behind me with a resonant clang that feels both foreign and familiar. I spin around and grip the bars, shaking them. Gabriel stands on the other side, studying me curiously, his head canted.

"What is Atlas not telling anyone? What did he just mean up there? *Who* are you, Lor?" He asked the same thing a few weeks ago, and I lied to him then, just like I'll keep lying to him now.

"I'm no one! I'm a prisoner from Nostraza! A lowly mortal with nothing! I want to go home!"

Gabriel shakes his head, regret painting the liminal space between us. "I can't do that, Lor."

"Who are *you*, Gabriel?" I shout. "One minute you're trying to kill me, and the next you're acting like you might actually care about someone other than yourself."

He steps towards my cell, his face so close to mine I feel the kiss of his breath. "I'm a loyal servant to my king, Lor. I was worried he was doing something reckless. That you were a danger to him." He stops and his nostrils flare. "But maybe a tiny—an infinitesimally tiny—part of me kind of liked you and admired your spirit. But it doesn't matter. Atlas is my duty now and forever. *You* are now a loose end."

"Atlas is a piece of shit," I snap, and Gabriel's eyes darken. "He doesn't deserve you."

Gabriel's shoulders drop, and I regret the way my words land, delivering a stronger blow than I meant. "Maybe not, but I have no choice, Lor. This is the life I am bound to."

He turns to leave, but I call out to him. "Wait!" He stops and looks over his shoulder. "That night you took me from Nostraza, I heard a riot. Did you lie to me when you said I imagined it?"

He shakes his head. "I needed to create a distraction so I could get you out. I had people working on the inside for months."

"Did you see if anyone died?"

His expression softens. "I don't know what happened to your friends. I'm sorry."

"Okay," I reply in a whisper. I knew there was a slim chance he'd know anything, but still, I hoped. They *have* to be alive. I'm sure I'd have felt it if they were gone.

Reluctantly, he turns, leaving those ominous words between us, and orders two guards to monitor me. With that, he disappears and I listen to his receding footsteps until they fade away.

When he's gone, I look at the two guards. They stare straight ahead, not acknowledging me. I walk further into my dark cell, sheltering myself in the shadows. Sliding down the wall, I drop to the floor and fish out the pendant I wear around my neck, cracking open the locket.

I pull out the stone, holding it in the palm of my hand, where it pulses with life like a drop of blood. The day the Aurora King's army came for my family, my mother placed the jewel in my hand, telling me I had to keep it safe. And without fully understanding the implications, I have done so every day since he took her from me.

One side is sheer, like it's been sliced with a blade or, maybe, a lash of errant magic. The others faceted so they catch the faint light, sparkling with the multitudes of history and destiny contained in this tiny shard of stone.

The Mirror's words replay themselves again and again in my head.

Your Majesty...this isn't where you belong.

The crown...has been lost to time...it is the only way for you...I'll have a gift for you...Your Majesty...Your Majesty...Your Majesty...

Atlas miscalculated everything.

He thought the Mirror would bind me to him, but now I know my path leads in another direction. One I'm sure he isn't meant to follow.

What if the Mirror had chosen differently? What had it meant when it said *this* was forbidden? *What* was forbidden? What would Ouranos not survive?

Regardless, the Mirror saved me from whatever the Sun King's plans are, for now.

And I will carry my secret, as I promised Tristan and Willow, as I have for the past twelve years. They've kept my memories as whole as they could, filling me in on the stories my parents never got the chance to share.

Tristan was seventeen when the Aurora King found us, nearly a man grown. He's always been the keeper of our past, waiting until I was old enough to understand.

No matter what Atlas threatens, he will never have these secrets from me. I will hold them with every dying breath until I honor the legacy my parents gave their lives for.

Until I'm ready. Until I understand what I must do.

Still clutching the crimson jewel in my palm, I look up from my position in the corner, seeing the path to a future that was clouded and murky, but has now been wiped clean.

Once again, I am a prisoner, but I am no longer caged.

As I peer into the gloom of my cell, the corner of my mouth tips up and I smile.

EPILOGUE

I'm roused from sleep by the sounds of muffled thuds and grunts. A body falling. Someone crashing against my bars and then the telltale slump of them dropping to the ground. I sit up, trying to discern what's happening through the webs of darkness coating my sight. It's been several days since Atlas threw me in here, and I've seen neither him nor Gabriel since.

But now a figure looms beyond the bars of my cell and some instinct tells me no one invited him here.

A Fae male, tall and broad, stands with his hands planted on his hips. I think he's wearing armor, though it's hard to be sure. When he moves into the light produced by a single torch outside my cell, he smiles, a mischievous glint in his eye.

"You're quite the pain in my ass lately, you know that?"

I blink. "Me?"

He gestures to someone who also moves into my vision, her hands circling the bars of my cell. Another Fae. Slim and petite, she wears a full black skirt that hangs to her knees and a black leather corset. Fingerless gloves cover her hands and she glows with a colorful aura that surrounds her like a halo. She flicks her wrist, and I hear the click of the lock.

"You're coming with us, darling," the male says, his stance casual despite the fact that it's becoming obvious he's here to steal me from the Sun Palace.

"Who are you?" I ask, standing up and pressing myself to the wall.

"Call us interested bystanders."

The female rolls her eyes and backhands his thick biceps. "Stop scaring her," she says, and then gives me a kind smile. "We mean you no harm. We're here to get you out of Aphelion."

I frown. "Why should I believe that? Of course, you're going to say you mean me no harm."

She lets out a puff of air and plants her hands on her hips, mimicking the male's stance. "Well, that's true."

"You can come willingly, or we'll make you," the male says, still smiling, while he folds his arms across his wide chest. There is no menace in his words, but I understand them for the threat they are. The female sighs again and tosses him a dirty look.

"Look, you're not doing so well in this place. I hear Atlas isn't...happy." She gestures to the cell walls. "So, what have you got to lose?"

She has a point there. The female moves, and I catch the flash in her black eyes. Ribbons of color. Emerald, crimson, and violet. Suddenly I'm seized by a strange bone deep melancholy for a place I've hated for so long, but is also the only home I can remember. I long so much for Tristan and Willow. Though our lives weren't enviable, at least we had each other. Even if they were only an illusion, seeing them in the maze sliced deep into that chamber of my heart that I keep reserved specifically for them.

I take a tentative step forward, understanding she isn't really giving me a choice. I already know Atlas won't let me go willingly. He's probably scheming right now for a way to break Apricia's claim to the Sun Queen crown. One way or another, Atlas is going to try to get what he wants. The way he threatened me in the throne room told me I won't be safe here ever again.

"Okay," I say, emerging into the light.

The woman dips her chin. "Excellent choice."

Before I have a chance to protest, I'm whisked away by the male, his powerful arms lifting me and tossing me over his shoulder. I don't bother objecting or fighting him off. I agreed to this, and my options are rather limited right now.

I feel the cadence of his steps as we steal down several darkened corridors and eventually emerge outside, the crash of the ocean sounding in the distance. I'm deposited into the back of a carriage with plush velvet seats. The male grabs my wrists and lashes them together with a thick leather cord.

"Hey!" I complain, but he ignores me, his movements quick and efficient.

A bag is placed over my head, my muffled protests also going unheeded. Next, he ties my ankles together, and I'm starting to wonder if I should have taken my chances with Atlas, after all.

I feel the carriage dip as someone else enters. "Is that really necessary?" I hear the female Fae ask.

"Yes," the male replies. "Sorry about this, sweetheart."

There is a sharp pain in the side of my head, and then there is nothing but blackness.

When I come to, I'm being carried again. The world is dark and quiet. I'm set down on the ground, my heart thudding in my chest. I've made a terrible mistake.

Finally, someone pulls the bag off and I shake my head. Slowly, my eyes adjust to the gloom. We're in a stone room with a small window providing the only light from the moon outside.

Someone is standing in here with me, his posture casual and his hands tucked into his pockets. A male Fae with long black hair and dark eyes steps into the light as the air is swept from my lungs.

The Aurora Prince tips his head, cunning crafted into the exquisite lines of his expression, his gaze sweeping over me from head to toe. His black eyes flicker with those jewel-tone hues that are the reminder of so many things I've lost.

But in that moment, a thread, one made of fate, made of fortune, made of an ostensible sense of possibility, spirals its way through the room. It stitches a new story into the crumbled remains of a legacy that was shattered but never forgotten.

I am a prisoner, but I am no longer caged.

"Hello, prisoner 3452," the prince says, a smirk tipping up the side of his mouth. "Welcome back to The Aurora."

ACKNOWLEDGMENTS

This whole writing thing has been such an adventure and I can't even begin to express how fortunate I feel to be on it.

Melissa, my writing spouse, I don't know what I'd do without your enthusiasm and your humor and just your wild and lovely spirit.

Bria, you've become one of the first people I go to when I've got another book done.

Shaylin, I feel like I found a writing soulmate in you. You're so talented and brilliant, and I can't thank you enough for putting your mark on this manuscript and all the rest.

Ashyle, thank you for your insight and wisdom—you have such a keen eye for everything.

To Priscilla and Elayna—thanks for being my last eyes on this book and for joining me on this journey. I look forward to publishing so many books next to you in the years to come.

Thank you to the slew of beta readers that helped me make this book everything it could be: Raidah, Elyssa, Nefer, Suzy, Ashley, Alexis, Catina, Emma, Rachel, Chelsea, Stacy, Holly, Elaine, Rebecca, and Kelsie.

To the reading community on BookTok and Bookstagram, thank you for being so enthusiastic and supportive of a brand new author who still had to prove herself. You're honestly the ones who made this all possible.

To my mom, who was the one who always read books and looked at me and said "couldn't you write this?" Yah, I guess I finally did.

To my kids, Alice and Nicky, you are a never ending source of joy in my life, even when you're driving me crazy. It's a good thing you're cute. Thanks for being patient with me when I get distracted writing stories in my head when you talk to me sometimes.

And of course, to my husband, Matthew, whose support and belief in me has never wavered a single day since we met all those years ago. Thank you for giving me the space and the freedom to pursue this and for allowing me to be the dramatic one. I'm not exaggerating when I say I couldn't do this if I didn't have a partner who gets it.

ALSO BY NISHA J. TULI

Artefacts of Ouranos

Trial of the Sun Queen

Rule of the Aurora King

Nightfire

Heart of Night and Fire

Cursed Captors

Wicked Is the Reaper

Standalone

To Wake a Kingdom

About the Author

Nisha is a Canadian fantasy romance author, whose books feature kick-ass heroines, swoony love interests, and slow burns with plenty of heat. She loves to draw upon her Indian heritage and her love of fantasy to bring her stories to life, weaving together vibrant and compelling characters, settings, and plotlines. When she's not writing or exploring, Nisha can be found enjoying travel, food, and camping with her partner, two kids, and their fluffy Samoyed.

Follow Along for More

Website and newsletter: https://nishajtuli.com

TikTok: https://www.tiktok.com/@nishajtwrites

Instagram: https://www.instagram.com/nishajtwrites

Twitter: https://twitter.com/NishaJT

Pinterest: https://www.pinterest.ca/nishajtwrites